Life Guards
IN THE
HAMPTONS

A Willow Tate Novel

CELIA JEROME

DAW BOOKS, INC.
DONALD A. WOLLHEIM, FOUNDER
375 Hudson Street, New York, NY 10014

ELIZABETH R. WOLLHEIM
SHEILA E. GILBERT
PUBLISHERS
www.dawbooks.com

DAW TRADEMARK REGISTERED
U.S. PAT. AND TM. OFF. AND FOREIGN COUNTRIES
—MARCA REGISTRADA
HECHO EN U.S.A.

PRINTED IN THE U.S.A.

To old friends and new readers.
Thank you for believing in me.

Acknowledgments

Thanks to:

Carole Pruzan, as always
Richie Etzel for nautical assistance
Jeri Seiden for Taz and Tino
Brett Bausk for the pictures
Anne Bohner for being a great agent
Russell Pulick for technical support
Donna Etzel for Axcl
Jane Liebell for the music
Dawn Berkowski for cheering
Sheila Gilbert, Debra Euler, Josh Starr, and Marsha Jones at DAW for taking such good care of my books
Robin Strong at the Montauk Library for help with the maps
And the Friends of the Montauk Library for bcing friends

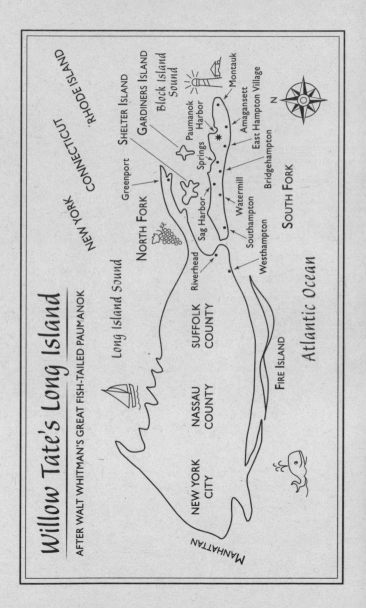

Celia Jerome lives in Paumanok Harbor toward the east end of Long Island. She believes in magic, True Love, small dogs, and yard sales.

You can visit Celia at www.celiajerome.com

CHAPTER I

CRAZY THINGS KEPT HAPPENING in the Hamptons. I had nothing whatsoever to do with any of them. I swear.

The new nutso stuff wasn't my kind of crazy, like ten-foot trolls and telepathic horses and pyrotechnic lightning bugs from a secret parallel universe.* The latest events weren't the usual East End insanity either, with billionaires claiming they owned the beach so no one could walk along the ocean, or some do-gooder causing a riot by throwing surfcasters' striped bass back in the water, or the government allowing people to rebuild houses on land destroyed by hurricanes and storms, when they'd only fall in the ocean at the next big blow. Those were irrational, but not unusual.

Nope, what they now had on the South Fork of Long Island was a surprising off-season crime spree: a bank robbery in Southampton, another in Wainscott; jewelry store heists in Sag Harbor and East Hampton; stickups at the American Legion Hall in Amagansett during a fund-raising dance and at a pub quiz in Springs. No one could remember so much crime in the area in so short a time, especially in mid-September. Even the dumbest thief had to know how effective roadblocks could be, with only two roads, Montauk Highway and the Sunrise

* Trolls in the Hamptons, November, 2010; Night Mares in the Hamptons, May, 2011; Fire Works in the Hamptons, November, 2011.

Highway, leading across the Shinnecock Canal and a clean escape off the Island. What made it odder was how no witnesses saw getaway cars. No one recognized the robbers' voices or accents, or could identify their clothes, only the black ski masks they wore. The people whose watches and wallets were taken couldn't say how many thieves, how tall, what sex.

Mass amnesia? I loved it, especially since no one in Paumanok Harbor could blame me the way they usually did. I sat cozily in my New York City apartment, minding my own business of writing and illustrating graphic novels for young adults, getting updates from family and friends.

They'd made the six o'clock news tonight, though, after the latest natural disasters. This time a million dollars went missing from the bank account of East Hampton Township, in which the Harbor was the smallest village. Cyber-embezzlement, they said, and called in the FBI. When my book characters—totally products of my imagination, I used to believe— suddenly sprang from my computer to life here on Earth, I had to call in the guys from DUE, the Department of Unexplained Events. Their agents created more chaos in my life and my head and my heart than any five trolls or felons.

Not this time.

My hero stayed on the page, hot and honor-bound, while men in suits and shades chased up and down Route 27 looking for bandits. Spenser Matthews was too busy hiding his real, otherworld identity and fighting evil to care about a crime spree on Long Island. Hell, if he were real, no beaches would be coated with oil.

The pod of dolphins that swam near East Hampton last week herding the late summer swimmers back to shore had nothing to do with him. Or with me. So what if my super-powered Spenser's alter ego was the sea god M'ma, protector of oceans and nurturer of his symbiotic minions? M'ma's buddies were magical lantern beetles, not ordinary bottlenose dolphins. Okay, not so ordinary when they swam east and wrecked the fall surfing contest in Montauk yesterday by upending every board until the surfers gave up and got out of the water.

Odd, but not my problem. Neither were the first-ever tornado in Watermill, the purple pumpkins in Bridge-hampton, or the new tick disease found only on the East End, to say nothing of the earthquakes and volcanic eruptions across the globe. Finding a companion for Spenser Matthews, in the tradition of Batman's Robin or Superman's Lois Lane, was my problem. I refused to think about who the real Matt Spenser—the veterinar-ian who'd won naming rights by being the highest bidder at a benefit auction after Labor Day—was spending his time with. I'd given up men again. Or still.

I had my own sidekick, a six-pound, three-legged, at-titudinal Pomeranian named Little Red. He didn't like being in the city, on a leash, smuggled in and out of my rent-controlled, no-pets apartment like a take-out meal in a tote bag.

Too bad. I lived in Manhattan, not Paumanok Harbor. I only went to the country when my mother needed someone to take care of her elderly rescue dogs. With the summer season over, my cousin Susan cooked fewer hours at her uncle's restaurant, so she could watch them. Of course I missed the clean salt air, the bay beaches a couple of blocks away, the quiet nights with no sirens or horns blowing. And Matt.

"We'll go back when I finish the first draft," I told the dog, who was licking his toes. "The weather will still be nice enough for long walks—" Little Red got carried, mostly, "—and there'll be less traffic, too." And maybe by then Matt Spenser wouldn't look at me as if I had two heads or spoke in tongues. I couldn't blame him, not after the night he saw the real M'ma, a being from the hidden world called Unity, not my imagination. M'ma broke a million sacred rules to trespass here, and broke a million of our physical laws to metamorphose from a lump of decaying whale-like blubber into a fiery winged god that threw me a kiss good-bye before diving into the bay.

Neither Matt nor I, nor anyone else who happened to

be out in the salt marshes that night, could ever forget the scene. Only a handful of spectators could actually understand it. No one would let me tell Matt about forbidden contact with the otherworld, not when he was no kind of esper, and an outsider in Paumanok Harbor besides. The agents from DUE wanted to wipe his memory clean, or worse.

He was our veterinarian, I shouted at them. And he swore not to tell anyone what he'd seen. I trusted him. They should, too. Who'd believe his absurd account anyway? No one.

They weren't convinced. Protecting Paumanok Harbor and its secrets had priority over one untalented, unpsychic, unimportant individual. Surprising them and myself with my emotional reaction, I started screaming.

"He is important! He saved my dog. He helped me protect M'ma when the rest of you were too busy putting out fires. He believed me!"

I threatened to tell the world about the Royce-Harmon Institute for Psionic Research myself if they stole Matt's memory or harmed him in any way. They let him go, but it was too late. I knew Matt worried about his sanity. Or maybe he just believed I was the crazy one. I worried about that, too.

So I left.

Leaving Paumanok Harbor with its small-town gossip, its oddball inhabitants, and my guilt about Matt took a weight off my shoulders. Unfortunately, most of the weight settled around my butt and belly. Yeck. That was another reason I stayed away from the Harbor: my cousin's four-star cooking and the leftovers she brought home from the restaurant, plus the jams and fresh bread from my grandmother's farm stand. Not that Manhattan didn't offer every kind of takeout and food truck, but I could be more disciplined here.

So I ate another Oreo and went back to work looking for a sidekick.

The real Matt Spenser was an animal doctor. My Spenser Matthews owned a pet shop, maybe in Massachusetts or New Jersey, somewhere on the ocean, of course, so he'd be close to his alternative environment. He'd carry birds and fish and little furry creatures and a couple of slimy ones, too, but only adoptable dogs and cats from the local shelters. If he had puppy mill dogs for sale, my animal-rights crusading mother would kill me.

I sketched Matt—that is, Spenser—with a parrot on his shoulder. Too piratical. A ferret? Adorable but smelly, and where would it go when he transformed into the sea god? A fish? He couldn't very well carry a bowl around with him, and no hunky guy talked to goldfish. A lizard? People would think he sold insurance.

Frustrated, I put on the ten o'clock news. The Hamptons made the headlines again. This time two restaurants in Noyac got hit, the tills emptied along with the patrons' pockets. No one saw anything but ski masks. The dolphins were back in the news, too. This time with video. They'd left the surfing beach at Ditch Plains and headed east to the Montauk Lighthouse. They knocked surf casters there off the rocks and pushed them to shore, then they went after the spearfishing scuba divers, in teams. One grabbed the spears, another disconnected the air hoses, while two more grabbed the guys by the flippers and towed them in backward.

"I guess the dolphins are tired of sharing their suppers and their territory," the newscaster said with a nervous laugh. "But people are being warned to stay out of the ocean. These animals are big, and getting more aggressive, although they have not harmed anyone yet. Furthermore, the oceanographers remind us that they are a protected species. Injuring or harassing one of the sea mammals is a federal crime and the laws will be enforced. Scientists from NOAA, the Riverhead Foundation for Marine Research and Preservation, and the Woods Hole Oceanographic Institution in Cape Cod are all monitoring the pod and its unusual behavior."

He flipped a page on his desk. "Speaking of unusual, there's still a reason to go out to the Hamptons, despite the no-swimming ban and the crime wave. An extremely rare, endangered shore bird has been spotted in tiny Paumanok Harbor, on the north side of the South Fork of

Long Island. The pink-toed Patagonian oiaca is so rare and reclusive we don't have a clear picture to show you, but several experts have identified the species."

I turned off the TV. "We're not going back there any time soon," I told Little Red, "so you better get used to your wee-wee pads. Traffic will be at a standstill and the whole town will be filled with telescope-toting bird-watchers. At least the restaurants and delis will do good business."

Red didn't care about rare birds, traffic, or tourists. He wanted to go o-u-t. Like on a leash, downstairs, in the dark, with plastic poop bags, where people yelled at you if your dog pissed on the straggly petunias around the pollution-stunted trees in their tiny squares of dirt.

Maybe Paumanok Harbor had its good points, like Mom's fenced-in yard and floodlights, with my relatives living across the street and down the block. Except one of my relatives was a witch, and I wasn't altogether sure about the rest of them.

"All right, all right, I'll take you out. Stop barking before we get reported to the tenants' association."

By the time I'd put on shoes and combed my hair, taken the Pomeranian in his tote down the three flights of stairs, around the corner where none of the neighbors could see him, then waited for him to find the perfect spot so I could clean up the filthy gutter, then do the whole trip in reverse, it was too late to get back to work.

"Come on, we're going to bed. I'll get more done tomorrow after a good night's sleep."

Except I didn't get a good night's sleep. Something kept nagging at me. Not the pink-toed Patagonian oiaca that I couldn't find on the Internet or in my bird books, not the search for a likable cartoon companion, not even Little Red's snoring. I rolled over again.

The dolphins and the robberies were someone else's responsibility, I reminded my weary self, not mine. Susan assured me the old dogs at my mother's house were doing well. Why not, on Susan's leftovers? I untwisted my nightshirt.

I had time on my deadline and money in the bank. I threw off the covers.

Dad in Florida had a new girlfriend, and Mom said she'd found homes for most of her retired greyhounds. Little Red snarled when I shoved my extra pillow away and threw myself facedown on the mattress.

What the hell was bugging me?

Frigging chiggers, that's what.

CHAPTER 2

I NOW HARBORED THE MOST OBNOXIOUS, disgusting blood-sucking parasites—and I am not talking about my former boyfriend Arlen. City people might have bedbugs, but eastern Long Islanders had chiggers. The repulsive, maddening monsters hung out in tall grass and weeds, in places only an idiot would go, or someone trying to save a lost sea soul. I'd spent days sitting in bramble trying to comfort what I thought was a dying creature. Now I felt like I'd been on the wrong end of the autopsy.

You couldn't see the little bastards, only feel them. They burrowed under your skin, causing the worst burning itch of your life. They usually started at your ankles, filled up on your blood and moved on, anywhere warm, like in your socks, beneath the elastic bands of your underwear, or your crotch, the perverted pestilences. Hot showers raised up more burning, tormenting welts, and if you scratched them, ichor dripped out. I wanted to rip my skin off and send it to the dry cleaner. Or the fumigator.

I needed help.

My cousin Susan worked late and partied later. She'd still be sleeping.

I called her mother instead. Aunt Jasmine had lived her whole life in Paumanok Harbor. Her husband helped Grandma Eve run the farm. Surely Aunt Jas would know what to do. Besides, she dealt with hysterical people in crisis all the time. She taught school.

"Your grandmother makes up a lotion that gets rid of them," she told me.

"I'm never coming back to that godforsaken, infested place," I told her. Nor was I about to use any of Grandma Eve's grimoire formulas. Not after a gang of cabbage-smashing kids all ended up with genital warts last year. "What can I do, here in the civilized world?"

She laughed. "You call dodging messenger bikes and breathing bus exhaust civilized?"

"I need help here, Aunt Jas, not a country mouse/city mouse spiel. I'm scratching myself bloody."

"Okay, first you have to wash your sheets and towels and pajamas in hot water. As hot as you can make it. Otherwise you'll keep breeding the nasty little devils and getting reinfested. Then get some anti-itch ointment. Any drugstore will have it."

So I took my laundry and everything I'd brought back on the bus from Paumanok Harbor downstairs to the basement laundry room. I filled every washing machine, which didn't earn me any points with the first-floor pregnant tenant who had to wait. As soon as I shoveled the sodden stuff into the driers, I raced up the three flights, fetched Little Red and my credit card, and hustled to the nearest drugstore. The dog didn't get much walking, sniffing, or marking done, but I bought three different kinds of ointments for bites, burns, and scrapes. By now I had them all.

The creams worked for about half an hour. Then the itching started again, worse, in new places where my sneakers had rubbed or the top of my jeans. Susan had to be up by now. My younger cousin had been born in the desolate east-of-everything and never missed a beach party, private picnic in the dunes, or a good-looking surfer dude. It was a miracle she didn't have STDs, much less parasites. She had cancer last year, though, so I should stop complaining. But, hell, I itched.

"Yeah, chiggers are a bitch, but they don't carry diseases like ticks."

"So what can I do about them? I'm going crazy."

"Grandma—"

"No."

"A doctor? They have prescription meds that kill the bugs."

I had a dentist and a gynecologist and a walk-in clinic that took my insurance for flu shots. I never saw the same doctor twice. No way was I showing my pox-covered ass to a stranger. "What else?"

"I heard you could try putting clear nail polish on the bites. Suffocate the bastards."

I only had red polish, but so what? So now I looked like a leper.

And I still itched, except where I'd drawn blood. I guess the blood flushed the venom out. I scratched harder.

I blamed my mother, of course. I wouldn't have gone to Paumanok Harbor in the first place if not for her and her dogs and her well-rehearsed guilt sermon. I wouldn't have encountered M'ma, or the troll, or Grant whom I almost married. I wouldn't have gotten involved with the paranormal or the parasites.

I called her cell. Heaven knew where she was.

"I'll be home soon," she said. "We've shut down another dog fighting operation, and have one more breeder to investigate."

"I need help now, Mom! I'll be a bloody mess by the time you get here, with permanent scars."

She sniffed in disapproval. "You always enjoyed melodrama, Willy. The bites'll go away in a day or two. Maybe a week. Or two."

She must have heard me gasp. "You could always try flea powder. That kills almost anything. Of course I never use those horrible chemicals on any of my dogs when I can avoid it."

"But it's okay for your only daughter?"

Snort. "There you go, finding fault and acting like an abused child. You're thirty-five, Willy, so stop whining."

"I'm not whining." Or sniffing in deviated septum scorn. I wasn't surprised either. My mother always put her animals ahead of her family, which made sense for one of the world's best dog whisperers.

She never claimed to be the world's best parent. "Just like your father, taking yourself so seriously and never listening to what I say. You asked me, I told you."

She was right. So I called Dad in Florida.

"That's what I always hated about the summer place," he said when I explained my problem. "Poison this, stinging that. Undertow here, sharks there. And your mother—"

"Dad! I called about chiggers, not about your divorce." Which occurred almost two decades ago. Neither one ever got over it. Mom had gone to Florida, where I am certain they have fire ants and snakes and alligators, to help Dad after his bypass surgery in the spring. He survived the surgery better than he survived the visit. Mom discovered the plight of racing greyhounds and hadn't come home to Paumanok Harbor since.

My father didn't have any advice about the bites. "The old bat will have the solution," he said, referring to my grandmother. "But don't let her read your tea leaves. She makes up that fortune-telling crap anyway."

Considering that my father was a precog himself, I never knew who or what to believe. "Any danger in sight?"

"I don't think anyone's ever died from chiggers. Blood poisoning, maybe. But now that I think of it, I did have a glimpse of something foreboding last night."

"What, one of your lady friends trying to pin you down to a long-term commitment?" My father'd had a long string of widows and divorcees since he moved to Florida after the divorce. Maybe before, according to my mother.

"Stu."

"What, she's a lousy cook?"

"Not cooked stew, I sense, but S-t-u."

"Oh, she has a jealous husband. Find another ch—" My mother called Dad's women chippies. "Charmer. You don't want to break up a marriage."

Oops. That's what caused the divorce, I guess. "I mean there's a lot of women in Florida."

"We're talking about you, not me, baby girl. You know

I only get bad feelings if someone I love is in danger. All I know about the threat is its name is Stu. Be careful. Watch out. You know how I worry."

"Sure, Dad." That may have been another reason for the divorce: my father's constant fretting and half-assed presentiments. What they lacked in sense, they made up for in sincerity. "I'll avoid any man named Stu, and stewed prunes and stewardesses, just to be safe. Love you."

By now I'd peeled the nail polish off, slathered on all three anti-itch creams again, and took an allergy pill for good measure. But every time I sat down I felt a new bite. Chances were I'd already contaminated my clean laundry, too, and I'd forgotten to buy clear nail polish at the drugstore. Tough. I used the red again. I was tired and cranky and I hated this day. It wasn't even lunchtime yet. I'd never make it for a week.

So I knocked on Mrs. Abbottini's door. She and I shared the third floor of the old brownstone. I had the front unit, my parents' old apartment where I'd lived most of my life. My front windows overlooked the street. Mrs. Abbottini's apartment faced the sooty back of the building behind us. She resented that. Still, she and my mother were good friends. The old lady visited Mom at Paumanok Harbor every summer after my parents split. Maybe she knew about chiggers.

"They gave your father a heart attack, your mother says."

"Chiggers," I shouted, "not chippies."

"Chicago? Never been there."

I turned down the TV so she could hear me yell "chiggers." Now the whole building knew I had bugs.

Her false teeth clacked. "What were you doing, rolling around in the grass with one of your lovers? Your mother told me all about you and your carrying on this summer."

Okay, I'd spent time with a couple of different guys recently. I was thirty-five and unattached. My personal affairs—not that I'd call them affairs, of course— were no one's business but mine. Besides, I dared any female, pushing Mrs. Abbottini's eighty or not, to resist Agent Grant from DUE and the British peerage, or Ty Farraday, the famous equestrian rodeo star, or Piet Doorn, the intrepid firefighter. All three were secret superheroes, with supernatural talents, and super sexy. And nice. I don't regret being close to any of them or loving each of them in his own way. What I do regret is how we all lived such different lives that nothing could come from the relationships but a summer romance.

"Bug bites, Mrs. A. Not my love life."

More clacking and cackling. "Too bad. If you married that Englishman and moved to his castle, I could have had the front rooms."

"Maybe I'll die of cooties." I headed for the door. "You can always hope."

"Oh, sit down. I'll go get my razor."

Holy shit. "It's not that bad! Sorry I bothered you."

"Maybe you ought to do it yourself anyway. My eyesight isn't what it used to be."

Neither was my heart rate. I was halfway across the hall before she shouted directions. "You shave the bites really close to open the hard crust."

I was nauseous already.

"Then you pour in peroxide to kill the buggers. Or is it alcohol? Maybe vinegar. I'd go with scotch." She licked her thin lips. "Hmm. I think I will."

I went home and tried to work, but nothing came to me except a fierce itch where I'd been sitting. I took a long walk down Third Avenue so I'd be tired enough to sleep, but couldn't. I started to read a book, but got bored and put on the Yankees. They lost. That's how things were going.

I didn't sleep all night. The bastards liked the dark. Now I had welts up and down my legs, my thighs, my stomach.

Little Red didn't even ask to sleep on my bed. He curled up on the sofa and licked his toes.

I gave up, conceded defeat, and called my grandmother. I loved her. I knew she loved me. We just couldn't get along. She knew what was best for everyone and told them so, often and loudly. She thought every child born in the bloody, bewitched Harbor should be tested for psychic ability by the people at the Royce Institute. Then they should marry according to some genetic pattern, like breeding horses for stamina or cows for better milk. I wasn't a freaking labradoodle. I wasn't a freak.

Half of Paumanok Harbor was terrified of her after that incident with the cabbages. The other half relished her fresh vegetables and tea readings. I didn't want to know the future she had in mind for me.

I guess she had a point about studying with the espers at Royce, though. I'd had to learn in a hurry about Royce, DUE, Unity and the rest, and still had no idea what a Visualizer like me was supposed to do half the time. Not that any of the so-called experts did either. But this was chiggers, nothing arcane or out of the ordinary.

"Of course I know how to get rid of chiggers."

"It doesn't involve a razor, does it?"

"No. They're bad this year. I have to make up a new batch of ointment, but I am too busy right now. You have heard about the Patagonian oiaca, haven't you?"

"Yeah. It's got pink toes."

"It's wrecking my fields."

Grandma Eve had experimental gardens tucked all over the working farm, growing exotics, illegals, and heaven knew what. Some had government approval; Eve Garland was such a renowned herbalist. Most witches were.

"I thought it was a small bird. How much could it eat?"

"It's not the bird. It's the jackasses come to gawk at the poor thing."

I almost asked if any of them were named Stu, but she was on a rant. "They're trampling everything in sight, showing no respect for private property or ripening crops. I've had to hire extra workers just to guard the perimeters and put up more fences. The bird can't survive here, anyway, not with winter coming. It has no mate, either."

Either? People could survive without a mate. People like me. Grandma Eve never missed a cheap shot to remind me of my unmarried state, or my lack of propagating the species of paranormals. We'd ridden this merry-go-round enough times that I ignored the dig. "Why don't they catch it and take it home to South America?"

"The ornithologists think it escaped from some private contraband collection. They can't bring it back to its original habitat in case it picked up a disease that could wipe out the last of the species found in some obscure bit of forest. Now the high muckety-mucks in charge are trying to decide where to take it. If they can find it. The dratted thing keeps flitting around, hiding in the shrubs. One faction fears they'll hurt it worse by capturing the bird. Another says let nature take its course. I say they're already traumatizing the creature with all the hubbub."

"Is anyone worried about a hawk or an owl or a feral cat carrying it off?"

"They're not sure that hasn't already happened. No one has seen the oiaca in two days. You should be here."

"Why, to look for pink toes something spit out?"

"No, Willow, you should be here to stand by your family in time of need. That's what we do."

No, what we did was more complicated than that. Grandma Eve brewed herbs and incantations. My mother talked to dogs, my father predicted doom. Susan's cooking could change moods, her father read dirt, and her mother wrangled schoolkids. Before she died, my other grandmother talked to invisible people who answered her back. Some family, huh?

As for me, sometimes I imagined magical beings that actually appeared, but mostly I wrote books. I tried, anyway, after hanging up the phone to cut off my grandmother's usual disappointment in me.

My hero still had no sidekick and I had a wastepaper basket filled with wasted paper. After that I spent another night wrestling with the sheets and the scratching before I took a Tylenol PM. Little Red woke me up before dawn with a loud, constant slurping at his toes.

"Damn it, Red, go back to sleep."

He didn't.

I put on the light so I could yell louder. Then I looked at him. He had wet, raw wounds on both his front feet where he kept frantically licking, pulling the hair out. He didn't stop to look at me, and snarled when I tried to nudge his mouth away from the ugly sores.

Oh, shit. My dog had chiggers, too.

CHAPTER 3

MIDWEEK, MIDMORNING, MID-SEPTEMBER, the Hampton Jitney was middling filled. Little Red got a seat of his own, out of his carrying case, without my having to pay for an extra ticket or hold him on my lap for over two hours. He got the window seat so he could look out, which kept the Pom too excited to gnaw at his toes. I'd put some of the anti-itch cream on his feet, then wrapped them in gauze and taped them so he wouldn't lick off the salve. That was the best I could do until we got to the only vet I'd trust with the snarky, snappy little dog I'd come to love. Abused and abandoned, he couldn't be blamed for being insecure and unsociable. We were working on it. Right now, for better or worse, we were going home to Paumanok Harbor, to Matt.

Whose life I may have ruined.

I wasn't quite as excited as Little Red to be headed east.

Before the bus had reached us at its last pickup spot on East 40th Street, between Third and Lex, some of the passengers—the ones whose thumbs or ears or mouths were not connected to one electronic device or another—chatted about the latest news from the Hamptons.

More robberies had occurred last night, this time at the new 7-Eleven in Montauk, then the East Hampton Cinema's box office. Ski masks, no arrests, no IDs. The bus passengers credited the thieves with great skills and savvy. They blamed the local police for great stupidity and sloth. I had my doubts about both, an uncomfortable feeling that something was not right about the crime scenes. Not that I'd ever written detective stories or researched police investigations.

I made a mental note to pass on my father's vague warning about someone named Stu to Uncle Henry in case there was a connection to the break-ins. Uncle Henry Haversmith was Paumanok Harbor's police chief and not really my uncle, just an old friend of the family. He knew about my father's forecasts and might take them seriously.

Sure, and traffic might go the speed limit on the Long Island Expressway. No one gave credence to Dad's premonitions except me, when I could figure them out.

One woman on the waiting line said she'd left all her jewelry home as a precaution. Another said she had her cash and credit cards stuffed in her bra. A tourist couple visiting their daughter in Hampton Bays worried about going out to dinner. The gang had already targeted a couple of the more expensive restaurants. A man in a last-summer's fashion fedora thought they'd be safe eating in small, cheaper places where the cash register didn't hold so much and the patrons' wallets weren't as fat.

Two older men toting huge telescopes in well-padded cases thought the crime spree, which would be business as usual anywhere else in the country, was being hyped as part of a conspiracy to keep people out of the Hamptons, to keep the Patagonian prize avian for themselves.

According to a blond young man with a ponytail, who heard from the girl he was going to visit in Montauk, the belligerent dolphins had turned the corner around the lighthouse. Last seen, they'd hassled a handful of paddleboarders readying for a race to Block Island. I couldn't imagine how anyone could stand up on a surfboard, much less paddle it all the miles across open waters. Or why they'd want to. Block Island was in a whole nother state.

Now they couldn't hold the race, due to the dolphins who stole the paddles and pushed the boards back to Gin Beach, the paddlers on top, willing or not. No one got hurt, but, boy, did the race organizers get pissed when they had to return the entry fees. Half the paddlers got mad, too, but the rest of them were thrilled with the chance to meet another sentient species face-to-face. If not for the Coast Guard and marine mammal stranding officials keeping boats away from the pod, and the beach patrol keeping more boardsmen out of the water, every dude with a board and a paddle might have jumped in to play.

The ponytailed guy said he didn't bother bringing his wet suit with him. The beaches were closed along the whole coast.

He shrugged. "Guess I'll have to spend more time with my girl."

Experts thought the pod intended to head around Plum Gut and down to Long Island Sound along the North Fork. They frequently chased schools of baitfish there, occasionally getting trapped in tiny harbors when the tide went out. Worse, dolphins sometimes tried to navigate the clogged East River past Manhattan. The Coast Guard stood by, ready to try herding them to safety.

Other experts believed the dolphins might turn back toward Montauk and head for the open ocean. No one knew their goals, or the reason for their sudden antipathy to anyone in the water.

Another conspiracy theory claimed they'd secretly been trained and sent by the Jersey shore, the major competitor for big surfing events in the east. A lady in a lavender jogging suit suggested the dolphins were getting even with us for polluting the ocean.

The marine science people had plans to dart one of the animals with a tracking device. Another boatload of specialists were on their way with underwater sound equipment. They hoped to record the dolphins' vocalizations for comparisons and interpretations. Meanwhile, swimming, surfing, and kayaking were prohibited in the area. Which, I was sure, did not stop kids from sneaking out to get a look and maybe a ride back to the beach.

On another front, a worried-looking man in a rum-

pled suit told us that the personal data of every employee of the town of East Hampton—as opposed to
East Hampton village—had been hacked. Someone
posted social security numbers, salaries, and home ad-
dresses on line for every cop, clerk, and town board
member. Judges, secretaries, department heads, all had
their bank accounts locked down to prevent cyber-piracy.
Now over three hundred people couldn't pay their bills
or buy groceries. The man was bringing a new ATM card
for his wife. And cash, I guessed, from the way he kept
checking his wallet and his inside jacket pocket. The
town budget director feared the tax rolls were next.

I feared a lot of things. Okay, I was a complete
chicken-shit coward, and not just about the usual cul-
prits. Thunder and heights and tunnels and bridges and
guns and little boats and big boats and snakes and
spiders—I shook at them all. Add in taxi drivers with eye
patches, choking on chicken bones, going crazy or getting
Alzheimer's, dying alone and unloved, and I was a basket case. The last shrink I'd been to, years ago, blamed
my anxieties on my parents' divorce, like Little Red's
foibles. He said it didn't matter, though, because I didn't
let my fears rule my life. I coped.

If I'd ever told him that my father made doom-filled
prophecies, my uncle recognized if someone told a lie,
and my grandmother was a witch, to say nothing of the
family friend who controlled the weather or the librarian
who always knew what book I wanted to read, the shrink
would have me locked up in a second. Instead, he wanted
to prescribe drugs, which made me worry I'd lose my
creative instincts. I stopped going.

But right now I didn't have a single qualm about anything except Little Red and Matt. And the chiggers, of
course. I tried not to scratch where anyone could see.

Maybe I had to close my eyes when the bus went
through the seemingly endless Midtown Tunnel, which
was far underground, with dark, cold water on every
side. But the goings-on in the Hamptons didn't faze me
a bit. After what I'd seen and been through recently,
simple robberies were child's play. I didn't have enough

cash to worry about, or an account in Paumanok Harbor in case the bank there got hit. My name wasn't entered in any database with the local government. Identity theft? That could happen any time. I took as many precautions as I could and left the rest to fate. Pushy dolphins? They should meet my mother. Like everyone else, I wondered about their odd behavior, and I suppose I'd like to touch a dolphin once—maybe at Sea World in Florida—but I never, ever swam in the ocean's strong currents. Besides, it was September. I'd put my bathing suits away with my white capris. I was safe.

I did have one piece of treasured jewelry, though, that I never took off. My mother gave me the pendant she'd had made from her wedding band, with the diamond from her engagement ring set into the gold strip. According to people who should know, the inscription on the back is in an ancient language from an ancient world, when true love lasted forever. It gave me hope. It gave me courage. I tucked it under my shirt.

The trip went quickly, with no long traffic snarls. The hostess passed out juice boxes or water bottles and the *New York Times*. I did the puzzle, in ink. Little Red got tired of standing up on his one rear leg to look out the window, so he curled in my lap like a little fox, his plumy tail tucked around him. I forgave him for peeing on my shoe after I bandaged his feet.

When people got off at the various stops, the driver called, "Good luck, stay safe," instead of the usual "Have a nice trip," or "Thank you for coming." By the time we got to Amagansett, the last stop before Montauk, only a handful of passengers were left.

The bus didn't run to Paumanok Harbor, so I got off in Amagansett, across from the railroad station. The birdwatchers got off after me, then a dark-haired man who'd been sitting toward the rear of the bus. We all had to wait for the driver to come around to open the cargo bay beneath the bus, for the rest of our luggage.

"Are you nervous about the robberies?" I asked, just to make conversation.

The birdwatchers clutched their telescopes closer, but

the other man patted his pocket. "Bring them on," he said. "I'll take care of the hoodlums."

So now the populace went around with concealed weapons. I wondered if they'd be shooting the dolphins next, or if I should warn Grandma Eve.

He got in a car and headed west, thank goodness, not toward Paumanok Harbor. The birdwatchers left in a taxi. Little Red and I waited for Susan on a nearby wooden bench. She showed up almost on time, before Red pulled the tape and gauze away from his feet.

I hadn't seen my cousin in a week, and I swear she had another hoop in her eyebrow and new magenta streaks in her sandy blonde hair. Her nipples showed through the skimpy T-shirt; her stomach showed above her jeans. She cooed over Little Red, though, so I guess it didn't matter that she looked like a hooker. I didn't comment on her looks and she, for once, didn't give me the what-have-you-done-now stink eye. My twenty-six-year-old baby cousin always knew when I was in trouble. She used to squeal to our parents, too.

"Poor puppy, stuck in the big city with no one but a bookworm. What, did she forget your flea and tick drops?"

"No, I did not. I think he got chiggers, too. That's why I came back."

She smiled when she carried the Pomeranian back to her car—my mother's old Outback—across the street. "I thought you came home to see Matt."

"I did. Red needs a vet."

Her smile turned into a grin. "Uh-huh. And they don't have any vets in the big, bad city."

"So how's the restaurant doing?" I asked, changing the subject to her favorite topic, after men. "Are people still eating out with all the robberies around?"

"We'd be in deep shit except for the naturalists. Sitting on your ass behind a shrub all day works up an appetite, I guess. Would you believe they order the chicken and the game hen instead of going vegetarian? Go figure."

Susan made a U-turn right across Amagansett's main street and barreled east to pick up Cranberry Hole Road and the Paumanok Harbor turnoff from Montauk Highway. I hung on to Little Red so he didn't go flying at the corners.

"You think you could go a little slower? I thought you didn't have to be at work until late today."

"Yeah, but Grandma needs me at the farm until the high school kids get home to direct traffic."

"There are that many people here to see a bird?"

"They say it's a life bird. A once in a lifetime chance to put it on your list. Some of these people travel the world to spot a rare bird."

"Do they actually get to see it?"

"A few of them might. But they can hear it sometimes, and they say that counts."

"Have you seen it?"

"No, but the damn thing tweets all night near your house." Where she was staying, to take care of the two old dogs my mother adopted, and to be away from her mother's disapproval. "And no, it doesn't use a Blackberry to tweet. The oiaca chirps, 'Twee, twee.' No one answers, of course, so it's kind of sad. And annoying. It's got a really loud, scratchy call. Distinctive, though, they say."

"It's near my house now?"

"Sometimes, but the naturalists don't know that. Grandma makes the bird peepers leave at night."

Now I felt sorry for the poor pink-toed castaway. "Maybe it'll leave soon when no mate answers its call."

"That's what Grandma's hoping. She's really upset. For the bird and for the farm."

Eve Garland got scarier when she got upset. Maybe the oiaca heard about her, and that's why it hung out at my house, rather than get changed into a toad.

I could see what had my grandmother so aggravated. Cars littered the dirt road and all the way to the farm, parked in front of my house and on Susan's mother's lawn, blocking the farm stand. Who knew where the occupants were.

"Can't the police help?"

"It's a private road. If Grandma closes it to all traffic,

there's no business for the farm stand, only rotten vegetables, wasted food, and out-of-work pickers and cashiers. Mrs. Donohue won't get her egg money, and the Berkmans can't sell their breads. No one wants that."

"I thought she hired more help."

"Kids, mostly, and posthole diggers for more fences. She's afraid to string electric wires because of all the children who come to pick pumpkins. And the bird. My father's tearing his hair out trying to figure out a solution that keeps everyone happy."

"I'll think about it. After I get Little Red fixed up."

"You still think he got chiggers from you?"

I pulled up my pants leg to show her the red spots. Some were new bites, some nail polish. "Nothing's working. Now Red's itching himself hairless."

"Talk to Grandma."

I'd talk to Matt first.

CHAPTER 4

"PAUMANOK HARBOR ANIMAL HOSPITAL."
"Hello. This is—"
"Please hold."
"Okay."
Click.
"Okay." So I listened to the veterinarian's office hours and the phone number for the emergency clinic in Riverhead that was open twenty-four hours a day. Fine, except in a life-or-death emergency. Riverhead was almost an hour away. Then again, if you had a heart attack in Paumanok Harbor, the ambulance ride to the nearest hospital could be that long or longer, depending on the season. This wasn't a great place to be sick.

I wrote down the number for the emergency clinic while I waited, and checked to see it was in my mother's address book. It was, with directions to find the place. I felt like I could be halfway there by the time the receptionist came back on the line.

"Paumanok Harbor Animal Hospital. How may I help you?"

Eck. The voice belonged to Matt's snooty young niece. She hated me.

"This is Willow Tate and I need to make an appointment." I once came to the vet's without an appointment and the girl—I don't remember her name—acted like I was Michael Vick.

"Dr. Spenser is all booked for today and tomorrow. He can see you on Friday. What is the dog's name?"

"It's Little Red, but I cannot wait for two days. He's licking his fur and biting his skin away in a frenzy."

"I can give you the number for the emergency veterinary clinic in—"

"I already have it. Are you sure I cannot come in today?"

"We can fit you in as an emergency, for a hundred dollar fee."

"What? That's ridiculous."

"Not when the staff might have to stay later, at overtime rates, and the doctor has to cancel his own plans. The policy is to discourage frivolous calls that destroy the office schedule and cause great inconvenience for the employees and for those patients with legitimate appointments."

"Having your dog hit by a car is pretty inconvenient, too."

"Was your dog run over?"

"No, I think he has chiggers."

"And how long has he had them?"

"A few days, I think."

"And you waited for now to call? It couldn't have been much of an emergency, could it?"

If I trusted Little Red to any other vet I'd hang up now. I didn't. "Damn it, I'll pay the hundred dollars, just tell me when I can come."

"That's a hundred dollars plus the regular fee, of course."

"I understand already. When?"

"Oh, we put emergencies in as soon as they get here. But the hospital closes at six."

"Yeah, I heard that five times. I'll be there in fifteen minutes."

I made it in ten. The waiting room was empty. The bitch pretended she didn't know me.

"Yes, can I help you?"

Little Red was shaking so hard in fear I had him wrapped in a towel. That was more to protect my fingers than to keep him warm. He tended to turn his terror into aggression. I felt like snapping at someone, too: Melissa Kovick, according to the small sign on the front desk. I knew she'd graduated from junior college last May with a diploma in computer science. I guess they don't teach people skills to technology students. Just read any online manual.

Melissa had straight, swishable, satiny black hair, unlike my short, streaky curls that already frizzed from the ever-present damp sea humidity. Janie at the beauty salon thought I needed the yellow streaks to make me look young and hip. Melissa's raised lip said I'd need botox and a boob job. At least I didn't look like an anorexic Afghan hound that hated the smell of its own shit.

"I called about my dog's sores."

"Right, the emergency."

Someone should tell her that her lip might stay curled if she kept sneering. Someone should tell her to go back to school so she had more right to be so arrogant. Or maybe someone should just tell her to go to hell.

I almost drew blood biting my tongue. The little snit was Matt's niece, after all. "That's us, the emergency. Red's records should be here."

She tapped a folder, to prove her efficiency. And that she did know who I was. "Take a seat. The doctor will see you soon."

Only if she told him we were here, it seemed. After ten minutes of me trying to convince Little Red he wasn't going to lose another body part, like he had lost his bad leg and his balls, Matt came into the waiting room. His light brown hair needed a trim, but he looked good in khakis and a navy polo shirt with PHVH embroidered on the chest. The broad, well-muscled chest.

He started to say, "We're all done, Sissy. You might as well go—" Then he saw me. "Oh."

First he smiled. A really nice smile, as if he was glad to see me. Lots of even white teeth and crinkly lines around warm brown eyes. Then he remembered me, the weirdo who ruined his life, and the smile slipped away.

"I, um, that is, Little Red has chiggers, I think. And sores from licking at the bites."

He led me back to an examining room. I unwrapped Red and set him on the high metal table, keeping hold of his harness to stop him from leaping down. "You might want to muzzle him."

Matt already had a length of black tubing with a noose clip in his hand. "I remember."

I petted Little Red so I didn't have to look at Matt to see what else he remembered. Or what he'd been forced to forget.

"So what makes you think he has chiggers?" Matt asked while he carefully unwrapped the gauze I'd put on Red's front legs.

"Because I have them and he was with me out in the salt marsh a couple of times. And he's itching frantically, the same way I do, when I can."

Matt started to put his hand on Red to keep him where he was, but our hands met and he jerked his back. He hated me.

Still, he stepped around the table so I could see his leg when he raised his pants hem. "You mean like these?"

He had the same small red welts I did, only his didn't look as angry.

Crap, I'd given him parasites, too. At least mine were worse. I pulled my jeans up and my sock down.

"Jeez, that's horrible!" He cringed and went back to his side of the exam table and stroked Little Red.

"No, some of it's red nail polish. I forgot to buy clear. It doesn't work anyway. But yours look almost healed. Did you use the dog flea and tick killer?"

"No, I bought kids' lice shampoo, like Walter at the pharmacy recommended. Put some on a cloth, wiped my legs, waited ten minutes and showered it all off. Changed the sheets, washed the towels, and done. No more itching."

"Damn, I wish someone had told me. I've got bites up and down my body."

Matt started wiping Red's feet with a damp cloth to get rid of the cream I'd put on them. Without looking at me, he said, "I guess that means I should forget about getting in your pants for a couple of days."

My cheeks felt as hot and red as a stewed tomato. For sure my brain was as mushy as one. "I, uh, um." And I thought I could write books.

"Come on, Willow. You knew there was something between us. I know you did. I'd hoped—"

I shook my head, hoping an ounce of sense broke loose. "No, the circumstances made us— That is, made you think there was more than us working together. Unseen dangers, uncertain events. You know, the closeness of comrades in a foxhole. That's all."

"You know it was more than that. You got rid of the fireman."

Piet was staying at my house, not in my bed, no matter what everyone thought and the matchmakers at the Royce Institute wished. And I told Piet to go without a minute's doubt. Regret, yes, because he happened to be close to a knight in shining—or smoky firefighter's— armor. Just not this maiden's knight. "He wasn't helping. He had to leave."

"You didn't have to leave, though. I kept calling. I thought we had something special."

"I know. I saw the messages when I got here this afternoon."

"I didn't have your cell or phone number in New York. I didn't want to ask anyone here for them and start up a frenzy of speculation. I sent you an email. Why didn't you reply, or call me?"

Because I felt guilty. "Listen, I messed up. You weren't supposed to see M'ma." I remembered Melissa in the other room, most likely listening. "What we saw that night."

"You mean the fireworks on the beach?"

That was safe, except the dazzling display wasn't pyrotechnics, it was pyro-beetles lighting up the almost dead whalelike creature that helped hatch them, after he turned into a god. That didn't make sense even to me, who was right there and ought to be used to such impossible occurrences when the otherworld got involved.

How could Matt understand what he'd seen, or how much trouble he was in for witnessing it? I put him in jeopardy. Coward that I am, I couldn't face that, or his rejection.

"Did they hurt you? Threaten you? The, uh, town officials."

"They came to visit me and we had a talk. The mayor, the chief of police, Rick from the boatyard, the barber, your grandmother, some others. We chatted, your grandmother passed out muffins, they left."

"Oh, God. What was in the muffins?"

"Blueberries. She said Susan baked them."

That was all right, then. Susan's cooking could spread cheer or calm or patience when she chose. "But you shouldn't have seen it. Maybe a firecracker or two, or when the harbor police set fire to the oil slick in the water. Everyone with a view saw that blaze. As for the rest, you must have thought we were all crazy. Me, especially."

He brought a lighted magnifying glass over to Red's foot and stared at the sores, dabbing with the cloth. "Listen, I saw what I saw because you granted my wish to see."

"Not me. M'ma. That is, my neighbors."

"Half of them right there couldn't see it. I asked. A lot of the others forgot everything but the fireworks."

That's the mayor's effect, when he remembers his duties to protect the village.

Matt shook his head. "I saw what had been a maggot-covered creature rise up and fly—"

I looked back toward the reception area. "Don't say anything else, please. You must not."

"I know. I promised the town elders. And I know how much trouble you got into for letting me stay and watch. But you have to understand, that was the most amazing, earth-shaking experience I'd ever had. I might never understand what occurred, but I'll cherish it for the rest of my life. Privately, I swear. Not that anyone would believe me if I did tell. I swore to the council to keep it quiet and they accepted my promise."

Of course they did. The police chief must have lined up every truth-seer in the village. And Grandma Eve might have threatened him some, too, or doctored Susan's muffins. Paumanok Harbor did not take chances with exposure. "But they didn't wipe your memory?"

"No, although they led me to believe they could."

"They could. And they haven't been mean to you? Ostracized you?"

"Like the locals used to do to the newcomers to town, meaning anyone not born here or related to a native? No, if anything they've been friendlier than ever. My practice is so busy I'm thinking of taking on a partner."

I didn't believe him. I knew this town and its attitude to outsiders, especially ones who threatened the old secrets. "There's no one in the waiting room."

"I take Wednesday afternoons off usually, unless there's surgery or an emergency."

"Oh. I'm sorry to bother you, then. But I was worried about Red. He's so small, and he's suffered so much already."

"It's all right. I understand how these guys get to you. And they can't tell you where it hurts."

Well, they could tell my mother, but I wasn't pushing the issue. How much weirdness could one man absorb?

He sprayed something on Red's right leg. "He'll need antibiotics for the sores, but it's not chiggers. Dogs rarely get them, especially not ones on Frontline."

"At least you didn't accuse me of neglecting my dog. I appreciate that. He gets the puppy size one every month. I've never seen a tick on him."

"I've seen you cry over a dying creature and I've seen you try to rescue injured fireflies. I'd never believe you could neglect an animal. I think that's what made me lo— Anyway, a flea might have bitten Red before it died. Dogs can get allergic reactions. Or something else could have caused what's commonly called hot spots. They're a bacterial infection or moist dermatitis and drive dogs crazy. Sometimes stress can do it, too. Maybe he didn't like being carted off to the city and apartment life."

Was that a hint that Matt didn't like me leaving Paumanok Harbor? I told the dog how good he was behaving, only growling between his closed jaws.

I told Matt, "He did fine in the city." I lied.

"I'll give you some of this spray for the sores."

He sprayed Red's other foot, but did not wrap the legs.

"Won't he lick it off?"

"It's made to taste bad. Dogs leave it alone. If not, we can put one of those plastic cones around his neck. I try to avoid them. Dogs hate them at first, and bump into things. The air is better for healing than bandages, anyway. I'll also give you some drops to help him relax."

"A tranquilizer?"

"Nothing heavy-duty, just a calmative so he doesn't worry at the sores."

"My grandmother used to make up something like that for my mother, for the dogs she rescues."

"Where do you think I got it? If that doesn't work to keep him from gnawing on himself, we'll have to switch to prednisone."

"But he'll be okay?"

"Sure. Bring him back in a couple of days if he's not. That is, if you're here that long."

Was he fishing for information? Hinting he cared? Or snidely assuming I'd scarper off as soon as I could. "I don't want to put him back on the bus or in a carry case so soon. And my grandmother needs help."

"Yeah, I heard it's a circus out by the farm. Good. And get something for those bites of yours. No, I have half the bottle of shampoo left. If you wait till I make one more round of the kennels, I'll go across to my house to fetch it."

"That's okay. I need some things in town. I'll stop by the drugstore and talk to Walter myself."

"Uh, I have a better idea. Why don't I go with you? That way you'll see that the townsfolk don't mistrust me. We can do your errands and pick up my dry cleaning while we're there. Then maybe we can have an early dinner? Nothing fancy."

"I'm not staying here long."

He held up his hand. "Just dinner and dry cleaning. That's all I'm asking."

I thought about it. And putting off Grandma Eve for a couple of hours. "Okay, but I have to get back in time to talk to my family, see what they think I can do to help with the traffic."

We decided I'd go home, get Red settled in, and feed the other dogs. By then Matt'd be finished at the kennel, while the stores in town were still open. We'd meet at the library, because it closed earliest. I wanted to see if Mrs. Terwilliger had any books mentioning the oiaca. And I wanted my own car, so this didn't count as a date.

"Great," Matt said. "I don't like eating alone all the time."

"What about Melissa?"

"She drives back to Hampton Bays. That's why I told her to leave early, to miss the traffic."

But she hadn't left. She waited at the desk, her purse packed and waiting, tapping a pencil, the possessive little bitch. I bet she had a crush on her handsome uncle, or hero-worship or something. She sure as hell didn't want to share him.

Or let me go without paying for anything but the antibiotics and the ointment. She scowled when he told her to write off the office visit as a courtesy call.

I wasn't sure about that either. "But you spent time with us, on your afternoon off."

Matt waved that away. "You can buy me dessert."

Miss Priss was fuming by now. "What about the emergency fee?"

Matt smiled at me. "Oh, we always waive the extra fee if it's a true emergency. I'm not out to rip people off, especially when they care so much about their pets."

"Do hot spots qualify?"

"Sure. They could lead to infection or loss of appetite, which can be dangerous in small dogs."

I almost stuck my tongue out at Melissa. Instead I asked her, "Could you hold Red please, while I write the check for the pills and the spray? I don't want to put him down in case any sick dogs came in earlier."

She had no choice when I thrust the Pomeranian into her arms. Little Red peed on her. I have to admit I thought he might. He did sometimes when he got mad enough at being manhandled. And when I squeezed him on the handover.

CHAPTER 5

I HAD NO TIME FOR A SHOWER, but this wasn't a date, right? I spritzed some perfume, walked the dogs in a baseball cap to flatten the curls, looked in the fridge to make a list, and left messages for my mother and father so they'd know where I was.

I called my grandmother on my cell from the car. I know I shouldn't drive while distracted. I was afraid of getting a ticket or getting in an accident. I was terrified of hitting a deer.

I was more afraid of my grandmother. If she found out I'd arrived two doors down without calling until the next day, there'd be hell to pay. Susan undoubtedly told her as soon as she left my doorstep.

With luck, Grandma Eve would be busy browbeating the birdwatchers and I could leave a message. Yeah, and with luck I could win the lottery and move to the south of France. Not that I spoke French or knew anyone there, but that wasn't the point.

Not only was my grandmother home, she had caller ID and knew my cell number.

No "Hello, who is this?" Just, "Well, it's about time, but I suppose dogs come first, like they always do for your mother. Perhaps if she paid more attention to her own—"

"Little Red will be fine, thank you."

After a few such pleasantries, I said I'd be by later. No, I didn't need to come to her house for dinner. Yes, I ate healthy meals in the city. I'd fetch something while I did errands in town. We were low on dog treats, I'd forgotten to pack deodorant, and Susan told me the porch light burned out yesterday but that there were no replacements in the utility closet. Grandma Eve wouldn't want me coming home to darkness, would she? I doubted she'd care, except Susan stayed here, and my cousin got off work at the restaurant in the middle of the night.

"Susan said the dog was sick?"

"He'll be all right. I thought it was chiggers, but Dr. Spenser says not." Dr. Spenser, not Matt. I couldn't afford to give her an opening.

"What about you? Jasmine said you called her about the parasites."

"I have it under control now."

"Why didn't you call me? I could have told you what to do. Lord knows I treat everyone else in this town who's foolish enough to go rambling in the weeds without long pants when it's cool and damp."

"I, ah, didn't know I was coming out to the Harbor until the dog got sick, so I couldn't fetch whatever you thought I needed."

"It's at every drugstore. Lice shampoo."

Damn. "I know that now. I'll see you later."

I think she muttered, "It's about time" again, then she told me to get off the phone and put both hands on the wheel.

"It's okay. I've got Bluetooth."

"I don't care if you've got a gold tooth. It's dangerous and stupid and rude. Besides, the sooner you finish your errands the sooner you can get here and do something about those dreadful ornithologists."

I don't know what she imagined I could do when no one else seemed to have an idea. At least she wasn't blaming me for the onslaught of ecotourists. She did say she was glad I came.

She must be desperate.

Maybe I'd ask Matt what he thought could be done about the rare bird.

Or maybe Mrs. Terwilliger at the library had a book

on exotic South American species, what they ate, how long they lived, how far they traveled. Or a law book concerning private roads and trespassers.

We agreed to meet at the library steps. I saw him waiting at the top, so I drove past to find a parking spot where I could pull in. No way did I want to try parallel parking with him watching. Not that I lacked confidence, of course, or that it mattered what he thought. This still wasn't a date.

He had a Giants sweatshirt on over his polo shirt, which made me wonder if he ever played football in high school or college. He was tall enough, at least six-two, I guessed, and broad. I knew he was strong from seeing him pick up Mom's fat old retriever without effort. And his agility had shown when he rescued Red. Fit best described his physique, even in a baggy sweatshirt.

Fit and casual and unconcerned that I was late. Good, he didn't treat this as a date, either.

So I could swallow my last breath mint, stop worrying I had hat hair instead of dandelion head, and hurry back to the library before he worried I wasn't coming. I'd earned his doubts.

He smiled—in relief?—when I climbed the steps to where he waited, looking over the village green and the stores on either side. The church faced the library, actually the old school building, across the treed and grassy area in the middle.

"Looking good," he said.

"The town square always looks nice in the fall, before the trees lose their leaves and the garden clubs' flowers have all died."

"I didn't mean the village." He didn't wait to see if I blushed—I did, the plaguesome curse of fair skin—simply turned and held open the door to the library.

A couple of people sat at the computer desks, someone I didn't recognize browsed the fiction stacks, and one of the high school girls earning public service credit wheeled around a cart full of books to be reshelved. Mrs. Terwilliger sat behind the front desk like the Queen of England surveying her kingdom. Lord knew Mrs. T was

nearly old enough to be Her Majesty's mother. She'd
been here forever, and always had a pile of books waiting for me. Sometimes they were books I'd requested;
sometimes they were what Mrs. Terwilliger thought I
needed to read. She was usually right. Uncanny, but not
unusual for Paumanok Harbor.

"I'm looking for a book about the rare South American bird that's—"

"Oh, no, dear, you want this one."

The book she handed me had to do with mythical
beasts.

"I'm sorry, but I'm not doing research for one of my
books, just for what's at Garland Farms."

She took another off the stack clearly marked Willow
Tate. This one had tropical fish on the cover.

"But I don't—"

"You will."

Oh, boy. No one argued with Mrs. Terwilliger, ever.
Not unless they wanted their library card permanently
lost. Besides, I didn't want to make an issue of it in front
of Matt, or draw attention to one of our town's minor
eccentricities. I took the books. The bestiary looked in-
teresting, at least. The next one, by James Herriot, had
always been a favorite of mine.

"I'm sure I read this years ago."

"Yes, but this time you'll have different eyes."

Cryptic but pointed, definitely embarrassing, except
that Matt was looking at the poster board to check up-
coming events, talks, and movies.

The last book in my pile had a couple on the cover, in
historical garb. Mrs. Terwilliger loved Regency romances
and passed on her favorites to everyone. I enjoyed them
when I had the time for pleasure reading. Not everyone
gave them credit for being intelligent, well written, and
entertaining, so I slipped it under the others before Matt
could read the title, *The Bargain Bride*.

"It's about compromising," the white-haired librarian
told me.

"A compromising situation?" That was a popular
theme in historicals, when the couple was found in fla-

grante delicto or merely kissing, and had to wed to save the woman's reputation. As far from modern mores as it could get. Honor meant more then.

"No, just compromising. You might learn something." Another jab.

I stepped aside and Matt took my place. Clearly I was dismissed now that I had the books Mrs. T had selected for me. No matter that I really wanted one on Patagonia. I wandered toward the travel section. "Those are all out," she called after me.

So I waited while she lifted an encyclopedia-sized tome for Matt, a technical book on heart disease in dogs.

"I got it through inter-library loan," Mrs. Terwilliger told him. "I thought you'd like to see this before you spent a hundred and forty-five dollars on it."

While he flipped the pages, she told me how her cousin's dogs in Georgia had both died of congestive heart failure. "That's not going to happen in Paumanok Harbor, not if I can help it."

"Or I," Matt said.

I looked at the other books the ruler of the library dispensed to Matt, curious as to his taste and the librarian's opinions. The new Reacher mystery, two of my books, and *Men are from Mars, Women are from Venus*.

Now I was curious about Matt's reaction. He laughed, said thank you, and we left. No comment that the librarian picked books for us. Not recommended, but selected, checked out to our names, and kept right by the desk as if she knew we'd be arriving. Both of us, which was far less likely since I'd had no plans to be in Paumanok Harbor until this morning.

"You don't have to read my books, you know," I told him when we went to put both sets of books into Matt's car so we didn't have to tote them around. "Mrs. T is always urging people to read local authors."

"I asked her to save these two for me. They've been checked out for weeks. I've read all the rest."

The writer in me couldn't help wanting to know what he thought. The sniveling coward in me was afraid to ask.

I didn't have to.

"I wouldn't keep reading them if they weren't fun and clever," he offered. "I keep being amazed at your creativity and talent."

Wow. And he liked dogs, too.

We headed for the hardware store.

I bought the yellow bug light for the front porch. Matt bought batteries. On our way out, Bill, the store's owner, set the blanks at the key-making machine to playing "Getting to Know You," from *The King and I*. Usually, no one but the locals—the talented locals—could make out the tune. Everyone else supposed the floor had shaken the keys to jangling, or the wind. When I visited as a kid from the big city, I thought a subway must run beneath the village main street. Funny how the mind rationalizes what it can't explain. I guess I never recognized the songs.

Matt smiled as if he knew all the words.

At the drugstore, I got the medicated shampoo, after making certain Walter knew I had chiggers, not lice. At least chiggers weren't contagious.

Matt bought Band-Aids. Occupational hazard, he told Walter. Trying not to be obvious about it, both of us peeked inside our bags as soon as we were out of the store, checking for condoms. I used to take it for granted that Walter simply believed in safe sex and gave them out to everyone. Nope. He put little tinfoil presents in the bags only when they'd be needed soon.

I was glad my bag had deodorant and lice shampoo, nothing else. I'd given up on men, or casual sex at least. I had scruples. And no rubbers in case I changed my mind.

Matt looked in his bag and stopped smiling.

We passed Big Eddie checking parking meters along Main Street. He was short for a police officer, but his nose made up for the lack of inches. He sniffed, then said, "Nice perfume, Willow. It almost covers up the smell of the bus exhaust and scared dog."

He flared his nostrils at the air around Matt. "Lots of scared dogs, antiseptic, disinfectant, dog food, and cologne. Good effort, both of you. Want to know what kind of perfume and cologne? I need the practice."

"No, thanks." I shook my head, confused that Big Eddie talked about his knack in public. He always let outside people think his German Shepherd, Ranger, had the nose to sniff out drugs, lost hikers, bombs, and dead bodies. I glanced at Matt.

"You missed the rabbit that came in this morning."

"Oh, I figured that was the one living under the box-woods around the library."

How could Matt not think that peculiar? On top of the keys and the condoms and the library books? If I didn't know better, I'd guess he knew something.

Joanne handed us to-go cups, without our placing an order. An iced tea for me, sweetened. Coffee, black, for Matt. Then we decided we might as well get sandwiches to eat on the park benches since the day stayed so pleasant.

Joanne asked if I wanted my veggie burger on a bun or a roll. Considering I'd only recently decided to be a vegetarian, Joanne had no way of predicting my choice. I'd never, ever ordered a veggie burger from the deli that made the best roast beef sandwiches anywhere.

"A roll is fine."

Matt read the menu board. "I think I'll have a—"

"Ham and Swiss on rye with mustard, no mayo."

"Yup."

No raised eyebrow, no questions about how she had one waiting for him.

He knew?

We had to walk past the barber shop on our way to the village green. Vincent, the barber, was out closing his awning. He smiled at me, pointed to Matt and gave a thumbs-up sign. "But . . . but that means . . ."

I couldn't finish.

Matt did. "That I have an aura."

How could he know? "Everyone has an aura. That's what the television psychics say, anyway."

"Yes, but Vincent only sees the auras of talent."

"You are a good veterinarian."

"Not that kind of talent. I'm trying to show you that I've changed. The town has changed. Thanks to you."

"No way." I dragged him around the corner to Kelvin's garage. Kelvin's son, K-2, had a bag of potato chips and his schoolbooks open in the little office. I pulled Matt right up to the kid's chair. "He has talent."

K-2 didn't sneeze, didn't wipe his nose, the way he would if someone told a lie. He crammed another five potato chips in his mouth and swallowed. "So? Can he do algebra?"

Kelvin came out of the mechanic's bay, wiping his hands.

"Matt has talent."

Kelvin didn't flinch, and didn't try to rub one foot against the other, the way he itched at falsehoods.

"Seems so. He got you to come back, didn't he?"

"I came back for his veterinary skill." I looked around, saw no one but Matt and K-2, Matt wearing a grin, K-2 wearing a chocolate milk mustache. I lowered my voice anyway. "But I mean the other kind of talent. You know, Royce Institute stuff. Department of Unexplained Events talent."

"Yup. Their agent Lou says some expert is coming next week to figure it out. They want to test you, too."

"No way."

"You did it."

"No way."

"That's what we all think. Matt's not a native, not related to one, never showed esper ability before. How else can you explain it?"

Matt told him. "She wished it."

Kelvin smiled at me. "Well, you can wish me luck for the poker game tomorrow night. You coming, Matt?"

"Wouldn't miss it."

I led him outside. "They cheat."

He knew.

Chapter 6

"S O HOW MUCH DO YOU KNOW?"
"Know or understand? There's a world of difference."

We were sitting on a bench, enjoying the lowering sun. His ham and Swiss looked and smelled a lot more inviting than my veggie burger. I'd lost my appetite, anyway. "No one I know understands much, including me. Just talk."

"About the town or about us?"

"There is no us. What do you know about Paumanok Harbor?"

"Whatever I know is because of us. You. Before, I found some of the people odd, standoffish, cliquish. You know, like an old boys club or a secret society. And they were damned eccentric, too. Every time I went to a concert or a barbeque, I felt they were telling insider jokes the rest of us could never understand. I supposed it to be locals versus tourists, natives versus newcomers, even well-off versus those less fortunate. No one theory fit the facts, though, so I gave up wondering. Give them time, I figured. I had friends, my practice had patients, people were generally polite."

I nodded. That sounded like Paumanok Harbor. When I summered here as a kid, I always felt like an interloper, too. I attributed the residents' peculiarities to the Harbor's isolation from the rest of the world, like Shangri-La or some unstudied tribe in the outback. "You didn't notice the weird stuff that happens here all the time?"

"I forgot."

"You forgot how it never rains on the Fourth of July or how the judge knows if someone is guilty or innocent before he opens his mouth?"

"I forgot. Everyone did, it seemed. Like when half the people in town had nightmares at the same time. Or that horse show you helped put on. No one I talked to could remember the finale."

"So what changed?"

"I didn't forget our time in the salt marsh with the creature you called Mama at first."

"I thought that's what the fireflies were saying."

He laughed. "I didn't forget that Mrs. Tate's pretty daughter talked to beetles either. I fully expected to lose the memory any minute."

"The mayor knew you were helping me. He didn't dare wipe away your recollection."

"Then I expected to be fitted for a strait jacket when I started to believe you knew what you were doing. That you really could talk to bugs and half-dead blubbery things."

"I begged you to trust me, and you did."

"Because there is an Us."

"No, you went along with me because you were curious and you felt sorry for the creature and wanted to help."

"I wanted to help you, too, because you believed with all your heart that the beast could live."

"I had to believe enough for the whole town. No one else could see M'ma for what he was, either."

"Or talk to him the way you did. I know you tried to hide it, but I figured there had to be some kind of telepathy going on."

"That's how they communicate mostly. The troll, the night mares, the lightning bugs. I can't speak their language, but they can use our words. That's what M'ma did, in my head."

"Right, the necrotic whale that turned into a flaming

manlike figure in the night sky. Well, that sure as hell didn't fit anything in my medical books or my mental almanac of the ordinary world."

I took a bite of my veggie burger. At least the tomato came from a farm, not a refrigerator truck. "Not even close. The transformation, I mean."

"I asked, later. All the people permitted to come out to help saw something different. Shooting stars, the aurora borealis, firecrackers. They heard different sounds, too. Some of the chosen—the talented ones, I know now—said they heard a symphony, the music of the spheres. I heard an impossible heartbeat. Colors? You saw rainbows; I saw dull skin, getting shinier, but still dark. Few of your special neighbors saw the colors or heard the music. They forgot about it afterward."

He tossed a bit of crust to some sparrows near our feet. Six more arrived for the handouts. I crumbled my roll for them. At least someone could enjoy the meal. "Go on."

"Something happened. M'ma's final transformation, I supposed. I know it was magical, stupendous, amazing, and I wanted to see what you saw, to feel what you felt, more than I ever wanted anything in my life. And you wished I could experience it, too. Suddenly I could."

"But M'ma granted the wish, not me, because you deserved to share the glory, when you worked hard for something you only half trusted."

"Then you begged the mayor to leave me alone. So I remembered. More importantly, maybe, I suddenly understood what had been out of my reach. Like Mrs. Terwilliger said, I saw with different eyes. I can't read minds or speak to dead relatives. I can't tell anyone if their bitch will have more male or female pups. My only weather forecasting comes from a bad knee from a ski trip. I have no idea if what anyone says is a truth or a lie, or any of the other astounding abilities of some of the Harbor residents. But now I know my neighbors for what they are."

"Wizards and witches."

"No, extraordinary people who have to be protective

of their gifts. And protected. I can understand why they've kept the truth hidden for generations."

"So what is your talent? What gives you an aura of power?"

"No one is sure. Maybe that I changed simply by being there, in the shadow of true magic. Like getting dusted with stray pixie dust or something out of a fairy tale."

"They wouldn't let you remember so much, if that were all. Half the espers in town don't fully recall what happened at the horse show or the night you say you changed. I think it's built into their talents, to shield them."

He studied the sparrows, squabbling over the crumbs. "You may be right. But I think your friends left me alone because of you. You told them not to mess with my head and they didn't."

"They never listened to me before."

"Of course they did. They listened, but they couldn't relate to what you told them."

"So what changed for them?"

"I think, and don't take this the wrong way, they're a little afraid of you."

I went "pfft." The sparrows flew off.

"It's true. The other stuff, the knowing the lottery numbers, the telekinetic keys, the telling time without a watch, those are everyday extrasensory traits, like well-practiced parlor tricks. But you?" He reached over and took a piece of my bun and held it out in his hand for the birds. "You can move worlds."

"Not on purpose, I swear."

He shrugged, still holding his hand, palm up, away from his body. "Things happen around you. That's what everyone says. And now they think I can see what you do. That we're tied together somehow. Like getting hit by lightning at the same time."

"I don't see how."

"I know. I didn't think so at first either. And no one wants to test the theory, because when you see things,

things no one else sees, then mayhem follows in your wake."

"It's not my fault!"

"No one says it is, precisely. Half the people want you here, to see if you can expand our knowledge, broaden the base. The other half wishes you'd never step foot in Paumanok Harbor again."

"Yeah, I got that from a couple of them. Did you see how fast the gallery owner locked up his shop when he saw us coming? He paints in his sleep, you know."

"No, I didn't know that, but I never liked his artwork. Anyway, that man Lou from the Department of Unexplained Events explained a little to me about a parallel universe where your, ah, friends are supposed to stay."

"I can't believe he told you. That's the most dangerous secret of all. Only a handful of the psychics in town know about Unity."

"I had to know, to help you. Lou thinks you need a watchdog."

"That's supposed to be your talent, helping me?"

"He and the others think it might be. Helping and protecting. They also think you have way more power than you believe, that you can bend events to your will. And share your talent. Imagine if you could tap anyone, and give them your insights."

"I can't! I did not do anything at all to help you, if help is the right term. The Others are very good at paying debts, is all. They give something back when we come to their aid. The lost colt's sire let people see him, and left gifts of magic, too. The stallion made promises, some for the present, some for the future." He'd promised my children would never be sick or hurt. I didn't know if I wanted kids, ever. "There's no way of knowing if they'll come true. Like M'ma's gift to you. It was a reward. And maybe it was only a one-time thing." Except Vincent's aura-sensing said no. "I had nothing to do with it."

"It's you, Willow. The Others come to you; they talk to you. They trust you. And you convince them to grant wishes. That's a lot of power."

"I never asked for it."

"I bet your mother never asked to hold conversations with dogs."

"You know about that?"

He looked up, at a chickadee bobbing around in the nearby evergreen the village used as a Christmas tree in December. "I've always known that. Just not how or why."

"So you don't think we're all freaks?"

"I might be one of you now. Time will tell."

"You can just accept all this?" I waved my hand around, toward the shops and offices. The chickadee flew off. Matt did not lower his hand, but he did frown at me.

"Accept what? That some people are better at certain skills than others? That you have a police markswoman who never misses, another whose nose is better than a bloodhound's?"

"What about Piet the fireman whose presence put out fires, the plumber who can locate a person by looking in the toilet bowl water? It goes on and on."

"If they did not think I could accept it, the town and the people, then my memory would be wiped clean, according to Lou, and I'd most likely be relocated far away."

"Damn him."

The chickadee came back, made a pass at the crumbs, but kept flying. "They'll come for sunflower seeds. I guess this guy isn't hungry enough." Matt tossed the crumbs out for the sparrows, who were always hungry, it seemed, and brushed his hands off. "He's right. People have already tried to expose Paumanok Harbor, make a Roswell out of it. That must never happen or we'll lose a lot of the magic."

I crumpled my napkin and waxed paper from the sandwich back into the deli bag and got up. "So what now?"

"Now we hope that you don't conjure up any more disasters. And we hope that I can help if you do."

"They're trying to marry me off, you know," I said on my way to the small grocery store at the other side of the village. I still needed dog biscuits. "That's fair warning, and maybe why they let you slide."

"It's been mentioned, but it's not on my calendar. I've been married and divorced, you know. I'm not exactly eager to jump into those waters anytime soon."

"Shark-infested, huh?"

"Great whites. Man-eaters. She took the dog."

"I'm sorry."

"Oh, I'm well over it. We're friends now. I still miss the dog, though."

"You can borrow mine any time."

We laughed. No one in his right mind would take Little Red.

Matt helped me pick out the best dog treats from the narrow selection in the pet food area. The sedentary old guys got a different kind from Little Red with his bad teeth and tiny throat, so he wouldn't choke. He told me to buy a bag of those baby carrots, too. "Dogs love them and they're non-fattening and healthy."

Matt bought a box of cereal and a carton of orange juice.

We paid and left. We walked to his car to pick up my books, then he walked me to Mom's Outback around the corner.

"You know," he said when he put my books on the back seat, giving the James Herriot dog stories a fond pat, "no one will push us to blend your genes with mine. I'm not—what do they call you?—a Visualizer. I couldn't call up anything. Not even you when I left messages."

I apologized. Again.

"Yeah, I'll get over it. What I'm trying to say is don't worry about that Royce Institute I heard so much about, or that M word. You changed my head around, but not my ancestry. They won't encourage a match between one of their most unique talents and a mostly ordinary man. That's like breeding a Westminster champion poodle to a five-generation mongrel from the pound."

The genealogists at Royce mightn't like the match, but my mother? My grandmother? Matt was a healthy male with a steady job. That was enough for them. I got in the car and opened the window so we could still talk.

"Well, you don't need to worry about the M word either. Or the Other stuff. I'm not visualizing anything these days. I'm writing about the past, what we saw, embellishing, not inventing. I haven't drawn a single stressed-out dolphin, rare bird, or bank robber, so the town can relax, too. I'm here to help my grandmother, then I'm gone. Back to the city and my deadlines and my normal friends and neighbors."

"Fair enough. If you need me, call. I have to earn my place at the poker table."

"Thanks. I'll be fine, now that you've fixed up my dog. That's enough."

He leaned against my door. "You will let me help, won't you?"

I didn't know.

CHAPTER 7

WHAT I DIDN'T KNOW COULD FILL AN ocean. What I didn't like about what I *did* know was the *Titanic*, headed smack for the iceberg.

I didn't know if anything the council theorized was true. Paumanok Harbor had a regular mayor and a town clerk, board members and department heads, all elected and salaried by the taxpayers. It also had an underground council that met privately, loosely, usually for emergencies. That unpaid, unelected, illegal, and un-American committee consisted of anyone who heard the call, land line, cell, in the street, or in their heads. A bunch of members served on both village boards, like the mayor and the police chief, so while one administration selected the date for the annual tree lighting on the village green, the other made sure there'd be a light dusting of pretty snow.

The esper council rarely interfered with the legitimate government, but their pronouncements held sway with the psychics. I think my grandmother ran it.

Now they'd concluded that I was contagious, a Typhoid Mary of the mentalists. Could it be true? I didn't think so, but I'm sure they had a handful of truth-knowers on the committee. They guessed I'd somehow transferred a touch of power to Matt, contaminating him. I know they all thought of those talents as gifts. To me, they were a plague. Who wanted such responsibility, such paralyzing danger, as much tension as I'd known this summer? All I wanted was to be left alone in my comfortable, safe apartment writing my books.

Now I had a watchdog, besides a lapdog. I didn't like the word Lou used. For that matter, I didn't like Lou much. He always scared me, even before I knew he was an agent from DUE. They told me Lou had guarded me in Manhattan from mad kidnappers, but I never believed it. My grandmother liked him. Susan thought they'd had an affair. I didn't want to believe that, either. The silver-haired psychic psychiatrist from Shelter Island I could understand, but Lou the Lout?

And he thought I needed a guardian. Was Matt supposed to watch me, or watch out for me? Two whole different things. I didn't need a babysitter, and I didn't like the ominous feeling that word "watchdog" sent down my spine. Pit bulls and Rottweilers, fangs and snarls.

I also didn't like knowing I'd endangered Matt more. Not from any of the otherworld beings, but from ruthless agents like Lou. Lou's job consisted of keeping the paranormal private. Which meant protecting Paumanok Harbor and its citizens, and following orders from the Royce-Harmon Institute for Psionic Research in England, which few people knew existed apart from the reputable Royce University. Lou would do anything to keep it that way. Anything. Fangs and snarls. Guns and grenades.

And I'd put Matt in the ring with the pit bull? Damn. I liked him too much to feel good about that.

He was a nice guy, really nice. And sweet and smart and kind. Good-looking without being drop-dead gorgeous, sexy without being a tomcat. I mean, a woman wouldn't have to worry about him chasing every skirt in the state. No one ever gossiped about his affairs or dates that I knew of, and his divorce happened before he moved here. He reminded me of a rock, a steady, calm, solid rock you could lean on, not altogether smooth, but not affected by every passing breeze either. Maybe a rock near a thermal spring, because there was nothing cold about the warm-hearted vet.

Except he wasn't for me. Not Matt, not this suffocatingly small, ingrown town, not my mother's neighbors, not this breeding ground for sorcerers. Maybe Matt's talent was being intelligent enough to figure out that the whole of frigging Paumanok Harbor had gone bonkers and he'd leave. If Lou let him.

Either way, I could always find a decent vet in Manhattan. I was *not* staying here.

I called my grandmother on the cell phone from the car again. She lectured me about that, again.

"I just wanted to let you know I'm on my way home. I'll walk the dogs, hop in the shower, and be there soon."

"Did you eat?"

The sparrows ate more. "I didn't have dessert." No lie, and the best part of meals at my grandmother's. The worst part was worrying what she put in the food to get her way.

I took the extra ten minutes to do the lice shampoo on a washcloth thing. The fierce itching was back, now that I wasn't concentrating on Matt and his story. I put my clothes in the washing machine, fed the big dogs a treat and a carrot, thought about leaving Red home with one to gnaw on. There he sat, though, right next to the front door, looking mournful, as if he'd been abandoned, again. I swear he raised his sore front paw, as if threatening to gnaw on that if I didn't take him.

"Okay, but if you pee on Grandma Eve's antique rugs, she'll turn you into a rabbit and make stew out of you."

We walked. I carried Little Red, a flashlight, and a sack of fresh shelled pistachio nuts I'd bought for my grandmother before leaving the city. They might be one of the few things she didn't manage to grow on the farm.

The fields were dark and the farm stand was closed, but nearly every light in the big house glowed in the twilight. Grandma Eve had the door open, the tea kettle whistling on the stove, and half a peach pie made from the last of the local fruit. Oh, boy.

"Jasmine and Roger"—Susan's parents—"just left. They wanted to welcome you home"—Paumanok Harbor was *not* my home—"but they looked half asleep over dessert, so I sent them off to their own house. You can see them tomorrow."

That last was an order. But I liked my aunt and uncle. They didn't try to manage my life too much. Having their precious daughter turn into sleep-around Sue had to shatter their child-rearing confidence. I appreciated that they'd left me half the pie, too. "I'll walk over before Aunt Jas goes to school in the morning."

"And you can tell her about your date with Matt Spenser."

"It wasn't a date."

"Who paid for your roast beef sandwich?"

"Hah! You don't know everything, after all. I had a veggie burger."

"You should have gotten the roast beef as usual. Joanne never could make a decent vegetable burger. Too much soy, not enough vegetables. Who paid?"

I sighed over the slice of pie she put in front of me. "Joanne must have told you already."

"No, she told Janie at the beauty salon, who told Martha at the real estate, who came by for an eggplant. The vet paid. That's a date."

"He didn't drive me, didn't take me home. I was going to treat for the ice cream, but it got late while we talked, and I knew you were waiting for me. So, no, it wasn't a date."

She sniffed, just like my mother.

I turned down Grandma Eve's tea—she kept trying to read the leaves—in favor of lemonade, settled Little Red on the kitchen floor with a carrot, and watched my grandmother try to hide her yawns while I scarfed down the peach pie like I hadn't eaten in days.

"I won't stay long. I can tell you're ready for bed yourself. Keeping late nights, are you?" I looked around, half expecting Lou or Doc Lassiter to pop out of the living room.

"I'm not keeping company, if that's what you are hinting at. It's that damn bird, keeping all of us up at night. Tweet, tweet, for hours. Here, at Jasmine's, at your place, Susan says."

"She said it had a loud squawk, but loud enough to keep everyone awake?"

"Tweet, tweet," she screeched. Little Red jumped into my lap, soggy, half-shredded carrot and all.

"Damn, that bad? Somehow I thought it was a little bird without enough lung power for such a shriek. Have you seen it?"

"I thought I caught a glimpse a couple of times, not enough to guess its size. It hides if anyone gets too close. In the corn stalks, in the pumpkin patch, among the cabbages and broccoli plants. A month later, with the fields plowed for cover crops, it would be easy to spot. At night it keeps away from any light. Just tweets, so we know it's still there. It starts tweeting after midnight, and keeps it up for hours. Never in the same place, in case I wanted to go out with a net. I'm thinking of a shotgun."

I knew she didn't mean that. "If it keeps moving, that means it's a good flier. That's a good sign that it might keep going."

Grandma Eve ate some pistachios. "We can hope."

"What about during the day? Does it tweet then?"

"Not a peep, damn it, or we'd have it caught. There have only been a couple of sightings after the first few days when someone spotted it, just enough to keep the jackasses with the binoculars out in force."

"I saw the cars this afternoon. Practically on my lawn. And no one got a photograph of the bird?"

"No, but they identified it from a reliable description, they say, verified by the top birder in Suffolk County. And now they are everywhere, making ruts, raising dust, taking up the farm stand parking, setting their tripods smack on a cabbage. Come six o'clock when we close up the stand, I threaten to have all of their cars towed, government endangered species people included. And I have Kelvin at the garage on speed dial, too. Word got out how much he charges to reclaim the vehicles, so they leave. The environmental people threaten to get a court order allowing them to stay, but they know they'll never see it at night, anyway. The birds are supposed to be diurnal, fast asleep in a burrow or something at night. No one wants to be the one to step on a rare bird in the dark."

"But it doesn't sleep at night if it's calling."

"We don't mention that, or they'd be here in tents and sleeping bags, in the pumpkins."

I had another bite or three. "So they bother you during the day and the bird keeps you up at night?"

She nodded and sipped at her tea. She looked older than she did last month, the lines on her face deeper, her hands bonier. And she'd only eaten three or four of the pistachios.

I wiped peach juice off my chin and fed Little Red a tiny crumb from the pie crust. "Okay, the oiaca and the traffic are both nuisances. What do you think I can do about it?"

"You can talk."

"To the birdwatchers? If they don't listen to a witch—"

"Don't be snippy. I'm too tired for that. Talk to the bird, of course."

"You must be thinking of my mother. She's the one who chats with dogs."

"I am not thinking of your mother. I know very well my own daughter's capabilities. It's you I need. You inherited enough from her to be able to do it. You talked to the troll, didn't you? And the lost colt and the fireflies."

"But they were telepathic creatures. They talked to me. I could only try to communicate with pictures and hope they understood. What kind of drawing could I do for an off-course avian? One that no one sees, either."

"I didn't say draw for it, I said talk to it."

"There's no way I could chat up a Patagonian peahen. What language do they speak in Patagonia, anyway?"

"It doesn't matter. You need to calm it down, figure out what it eats, how to get it home."

I swallowed a mouthful of lemonade wrong and sputtered. "Me?"

"Who else? The so-called experts who are ready to put tranquilizers in bowls of water? The fools with their butterfly nets? Or the self-righteous twits prepared to let nature take its course and let the bird die?"

None of those plans appealed to me. The rest of the pie did, so I slid some more onto my plate. "I wouldn't have the least idea what to talk to it about."

"You'll make it up, like one of your stories."

"But it's a bird!"

"A bird that is going to die out there, tweeting its heart out in loneliness. The nights will get cold, the fields will be stripped. What will it eat? And what about the rest of its species? Who knows if they need this one's genes to stay viable? What if it's a female, already pregnant?"

"But . . . but . . ."

"Don't tell me you don't know how or you won't try. As much as I hate to admit it, you inherited genes from your father, too. You care."

"Of course I care. I don't like to see any creature suffer. But my father?" Grandma Eve never had a good word to say about the man since he moved to Florida, except good riddance.

"Yes, him. Him and his cockamamie clairvoyance. Do you know why he dreams of disasters? Because, for all his faults, he cares deeply about you and your mother and his best friends. Even me. Did I tell you how he once warned me about an Indian chief?"

"Good grief, no." Grandma Eve would have skinned him alive.

She poured me another glass of lemonade. "I belittled him. In front of your mother and the others."

"You should not have done that. He never, ever meant harm to anyone."

"I know that, and I apologized the next day, right after I got rear-ended by a Pontiac. Do you know what they look like?"

"I don't pay attention to that kind of thing. I don't think they make them any more."

"They used to be big and flashy, with a silver statue on the hood, like the Jaguars have. This one was Chief Pontiac himself. I found it in the road when they towed my car away."

"But could you have prevented the accident if you knew Dad meant a car? You couldn't stay home forever, or pull over every time you saw that make."

"No, but the point is your father tried because he has a good heart. That's all I am asking of you. Try. Oh, and if you come upon a doddering Brit, call Lou. Royce University in London has misplaced a beloved retired professor."

CHAPTER 8

I WALKED HOME FROM MY GRANDMOTHER'S house, full of pie and resolution to be a better grand-daughter. She believed in me, whatever I was. The least I could do was try to deserve that trust.

No tweeting came across the fields or from the trees that bordered the private dirt drive. No missing profes-sor either. As I stepped around the ruts from the rain and the extra traffic, I heard crickets and a bullfrog in the pond behind Aunt Jas's house. Sometimes the pond dried up in the summer. Where did the frogs go then? But this year we'd had plenty of rain, floods, in fact.

I didn't like walking in the dark this way, with nothing but Little Red and a flashlight for protection. My grand-mother would have sneered if I'd taken the car for such a short distance, though, and I needed the exercise, espe-cially after the pie. Besides, I could see the many lights I'd left on at my house.

And, I told myself, none of the Hamptons' new rob-bers would be stupid enough to come down a narrow dirt road, not that I'd heard of them housebreaking or waylaying pedestrians. No masked man was about to ride out of the trees shouting, "Stand and deliver," like they did in Mrs. Terwilliger's romance novels. Still, I'd locked the house up tight, so it took me three tries with two keys to get the front door open.

All shut up that way, the house felt hot. Summer lin-gered and the breezes didn't blow tonight. Off came the sweatshirt, up went the windows. The front door stayed locked.

I decided to work a little, since the day hadn't been productive beyond a couple of notes and sketches on the bus ride out. That deadline loomed.

I checked my email, checked Facebook in case I got fan mail, played solitaire till I won, then got to it. Blank screen, blank sketch pad, blank mind. Blech.

So I played solitaire some more. Got a Diet Coke from the fridge. Did a mental smack in the head, kick in the butt, poke in the ribs. And sat and thought about my plot, my character, my readers. And, hot damn, I finally figured out the perfect companion for my hero. Not a young boy, a butler, or best friend, but a creature that was both fanciful and fun. I did a bunch of sketches, added colors that would look good on the cover, adjusted the size, fixed the highlights in the eyes to look more intelligent. Lost in the creative cloud, I tried out names, abilities, character traits. Maybe I'd give it a limp. No, a lisp. It had to talk, to fit the story, but a speech impediment made it unique, like my three-legged dog.

Before I knew it, hours had passed. My back ached from sitting. My eyelids felt scratchy. I let the big dogs out in the fenced front yard, then put a leash on Little Red so I didn't lose him in the dark. He hated being in the dog run with the old guys, most likely thinking they were going to gang up on him, which they never would. He yipped every time they got close, and yipped when they didn't move. Aunt Jas deserved a quiet night, especially if she was too exhausted to eat peach pie. I led the Pomeranian around to the side of the house, in the new light from the wrap-around porch.

He stopped, tail up, ears perked, straining forward. A skittering in the brush?

"Red, heel up."

He didn't, of course. I pulled him closer on his leash and got a better grip on the nylon loop in my hand in case it was a fox or a feral cat, not the usual rabbit.

Now we both heard rustling in the trees. Red gave a low growl.

I scooped him up. It might be a sleepy squirrel or a bird, but no night-hunting owl was going to get my little dog. Red growled again, at me, not the owl.

I admit I was spooked, imagining threats without seeing any. "Hush up."

The big dogs didn't bark. I took that for a good sign, except one couldn't hear, the other barely saw. Watchdogs, they weren't. So why hadn't I brought the flashlight out with me, instead of relying on the light from the porch and the windows? It was one of those big suckers with rechargeable batteries that weighed a ton, if one were thinking of swinging it at someone's head.

Of course I was back up on the porch by this time, my cell phone in my hand ready to dial 911. My other hand, with Little Red in it, could still reach for the front doorknob.

I waited.

Nothing stirred but the hairs on the back of my neck. And I had to get Buddy and Shad back in the house.

Then I heard it. Not the bullfrog. Not the high rustling. Not the low skittering, but a tweet. A definitely scratchy, loud, unfamiliar tweet, the way Susan had described it. Only more of a *twee*, without the final t. I put my hand over Red's nose so he didn't start yipping and there it was again, *Twee, twee*. Kind of plaintive, although maybe I read more into the squawks.

I called back. "Twee." I didn't have that abrasive rasp in my call, but a "Twee" answered back.

"Twee?"

"Twee!"

Buddy barked, his woof loud and deep. The night instantly turned silent. "Damn, you scared it away. It must think you're some kind of bird dog, Buddy, instead of a couch dog." I whistled the dogs inside, and shut Little Red in, too, just in case the bird turned violent. I could run faster without the Pom.

I retrieved the flashlight from beside the door and went out again, feeling brave. I left the lights on, not feeling brave enough to face an unknown entity in the dark. I did step down off the porch to the edge of the glow cast by the windows. We had floodlights for the backyard, but the noise had come from the front, maybe across the dirt road nearer to Aunt Jas's house.

I stayed where I was but called, "Twee? Twee?" This time my voice had a hoarse tone, from trying to make less noise. I didn't want to wake my aunt and uncle, but I did want to catch a glimpse of this life-list bird. Not that I had a life-list, or ever intended to, but hey, if I started with the rarest avis I was ever apt to see, I was ahead of the game.

I raised my voice a little, not to the raucous screak I'd heard, but almost a caw. And it answered back.

"Twee?"

Okay, I talked to Little Red all the time, and he didn't understand much beyond cookie, out, and bad dog. Trying to hold a conversation with a wild bird—from a foreign country, no less—was dumber. Talk to it, Grandma Eve had said.

"Okay, oiaca, tell me how to get you back to your friends."

"Twee."

Oh, boy.

"Then come on out in the open and maybe I can—" I didn't know what. If it had escaped from a zoo or a private collector, maybe it would land on my hand like the chickadees Matt tried to entice. I reached into my pants pocket and pulled out a couple of dog treats. One never went anywhere with Little Red without bribes. These were soft liver chews that couldn't do much for my pockets or my ambient aroma, if Big Eddie were here now. They might appeal to a bird.

I never did find out if pink-toed Patagonian oiacas ate meat or flies or fruit. Liver treats were all I had. I held my hand out without looking toward where I thought the last *twee* had come from. Matt said wild creatures didn't like to make eye contact. My mother said the same thing about unfamiliar dogs, which took a stare for a sign of aggression. As if I'd take my eyes off a dog ready to go for my throat. A lost oiaca, maybe. Except, again, no one said if it was a hawklike raptor. The thing could be as big as an eagle, from the volume of its call.

Thinking of calling, I realized I'd left my cell phone inside when I switched to the flashlight. Which meant no 911, and no camera to take a picture.

Someone would have said if the bird was picking off rabbits or squirrels — or dogs and cats — so I figured I was safe.

"Twee. Twee, come on, twee. I have goodies."

I could swear I heard what sounded like a disgruntled "awgh" before a louder "twee."

"Okay, no liver treats." Maybe I read too much into its screeches, anthropomorphizing big time, but I put my arm down, happy to do so. I regretted my lack of time on the rowing machine, and the muscles that went with it. No matter, I rationalized. Maybe the bird saw my raised arm as a threat. Maybe it remembered an outstretched arm holding a net.

Who was I kidding? I hadn't a glimmer of an idea of the thoughts of a thing with a head full of feathers. How much gray matter could it have in a tiny skull, anyway? I think I once heard that owls' heads were filled with eyes and optic equipment, not brains. They relied on sight and instinct and habit. Like with everything else, no one seemed to know the oiaca's habits or instincts. This one's wits seemed to be leading it to certain doom. Birdbrained, for sure.

"Come on, pretty boy. Or girl." Everyone liked flattery, I figured. "I won't hurt you. I have carrots inside. And crackers. Polly want a cracker?" Thank God no one was nearby to hear me.

The next "twee" came softer.

Maybe Oey, for want of a better name, was farther away, maybe listening, maybe trying to figure out if I could be trusted. So I kept talking. I wished I could remember more of "Ode to a Nightingale" than "Adieu! Adieu!"

"Rockin' Robin?" I couldn't remember much of that ancient classic either.

"Papa's gonna buy you . . . ?" Wrong image.

"Bye-bye Blackbird?" Good hint, but all I got was another "twee."

Damn, Willy, think.

"Birds fly over—No, don't fly away. Unless you know where your home is."

No response, and I was out of bird songs. I never could whistle, and the "twees" weren't getting us anywhere. "Um, okay. Once upon a time there was a mama duck and she had a nest full of eggs. Only one of them was bigger than the rest. She sat on it anyway. And then the eggs hatched and there were six little fuzzy yellow balls of ducklings, and one gawky, long-necked, grayish—"

"Awgh!"

I jumped. "All right, no bedtime stories." But I did have the "awgh" sound down now, kind of like a pirate's parrot's "arrgh," or a bird with a bad taste stuck in his throat. "Awgh, yourself. So what do you want?"

Silence. Frustrated, I wondered what everyone wanted from me. Hell, it had to be more than I had to give. It always was.

When ten more minutes went by without a sound, I got up to go inside. "If you won't meet me halfway, I'm not wasting my time. Like I told Matt, I don't belong here. Grandma asked me to try. I tried. Now I am going to bed. Try not to disturb the neighbors, okay? Tomorrow I'll bring some carrots and crackers, maybe lettuce, okay? Or you could leave me a grocery list."

I almost reached the door when I heard a sad little "twee."

I turned around and there it was, at the very edge of the porch light's reach. The pink-toed Patagonian oiaca bird.

It had pink toes, all right, Barbie-shoe hot pink. After that, things got dicey. I sincerely doubted this animal came from Patagonia. And I wasn't entirely sure about the bird part, either. The darkness made the feather colors hard to distinguish, but the wings glittered in rainbow shades. The head appeared parrotlike, with a big curved beak, round eyes, and more bright feathers. It was huge, bigger than the scarlet macaw at the dry cleaners around the corner from my apartment.

The problem—one of the problems—was that instead of plumes at the back end, this creature had shiny scales, translucent fins, and a forked tail. Like a fish.

Holy shit, it was a parrotfish. Not the multicolored tropical variety—oh, no. This . . . this apparition was my freaking sea god's freaking companion, the one I'd finally drawn an hour ago. The one that could sit on the hero's shoulder at Spenser's pet store, then transform itself into a fish to accompany M'ma in the water. The one that could blink in and out of shape. In and out of sight. In and out of this freaking world. I'd drawn it disappearing as a starburst, a "pock" in the frame.

Damn it, Grandma Eve must have known from the way the thing vanished. "Go talk to it," she said.

Mrs. Terwilliger at the library must have guessed. Books on mythical beasts and tropical fish, my ass.

Double damn.

"You're no oíaca, are you?"

It shimmered, and then the head of a fish, gills, and dorsal fin appeared, only with a long feathered tail and wings. Except the fish kept gasping. It turned back to the bird, wheezing some, catching its breath.

"Stupid creature. Fish can't breathe air." I watched it change, then change back, until I was dizzy. "Pick one or the other, for crying out loud."

It picked the fish, gasping, floundering, falling on its side in the grass.

"Crap, not that one."

It didn't change back. The wings tried to flap, but they hit the ground. The mouth opened and closed, silently crying while the gills made a valiant effort to draw in oxygen. Shit, shit, shit. I killed it!

I ran into the fenced-in dog pen, dragged out the kiddie wading pool my mother kept for hot days, so the big dogs could sit in it and cool off. The damned thing was full of leaves and twigs and old tennis balls. I tipped it upside down and dragged it toward the gasping fish-parrot. "Wait, wait. I'll fill it."

I ran back around and turned on the outdoor faucet full force, unreeled the garden hose and pulled it over to the pool, trailing a solid stream of water the whole way. By now I was gasping, too. And soaked.

As soon as the bottom of the kiddie pool was covered, I tipped it to make a deeper corner until the rest filled up. The fish dove in. All I could see was a pink and blue and yellow tail, a feathered tail, sticking over the lip of the pool. I kept the hose running until it overflowed, then set the whole thing level.

I wasn't sure if it lived. I didn't want to put my hand in the water, either. The thing was as long as a striped bass, legal keeper-size, with a wide mouth and big teeth I'd seen while it panted for air. What the hell was I supposed to do now?

It splashed. I saw the scales glisten under the water. I let out the breath I didn't know I'd been holding. "I guess we're both breathing okay again, huh?"

I figured the critter must have been hanging out near the pond. Or in the farm fields with the irrigation system. I'd give it some time to recover, then try again to have a conversation. I wish I had my sketches with me. No, I wish I'd burned them.

I sat on the grass, not caring that my pants got colder and damper. "Now I can't leave Paumanok Harbor. You know that, don't you, Oey? I bet you planned it that way."

Another splash.

"All right, you've had your swim. Now get out and talk to me. If you're like every other creature from Unity, you can do it. I'm no Verbalizer, no Translator, but I'm all you've got, one piss-poor Visualizer."

The bird head rose from the water, even bigger, it seemed. Beady eyes stared right at me—so much for no eye contact—until I felt like the one being examined and threatened. Then it hopped out of the pool and kept hopping, flapping wings, waving the fish tail, bouncing into the air, swimming across the pool, screeing, "Twee! Twee!"

"Shush. You don't want any birdwatchers sneaking

back to see you." Lord, that was the last thing we needed. "Now calm down so we can talk."

The non-oiaca stopped hopping, but kept the fish tail wagging like a dog's. It was happy to see me? I wasn't happy. "Go home. Go back to your own universe. Go on, get. You don't belong here. It's against the rules. You'll get me in trouble. Shoo."

I swear it chuckled. "Haw haw."

Then a car raced down the dirt road.

Oey disappeared. It didn't fly away, didn't swim away. It frigging flicked out of this world the same way the troll, the night mares, and the fireflies had all done. Pock.

Yeah, Willy, in case you didn't know, the shit just hit the fan. Again. Awgh.

Chapter 9

IT WASN'T A CAR MAKING ALL THE NOISE. A beat-up black pickup rattled to a stop right at my front gate. I could smell the exhaust from the rusted-out muffler way around the corner, and choked on the dust it had kicked up. Cousin Bernie kept the old junker at the restaurant to haul garbage and fetch fresh produce from Grandma Eve's farm. I smelled those, too.

Susan got out. Usually she came home in a taxi from wherever she'd gone after the Breakaway's kitchen closed, so she must not have spent a lot of time in the local bars. She left the keys in the clunker and the headlights on, so I might be wrong. At least she hadn't dragged another strange man home, or spent the night in some motel in Montauk.

"Hey, Susan. I'm over here."

She started toward me, walking a line that could never pass a sobriety test. Then she tripped over the hose strung across the yard. She screamed louder than the bird ever had. I waited to see if lights came on at her mother's house across the road. Aunt Jas must have taken sleeping pills tonight if those vaunted maternal instincts hadn't woken her.

Susan got up from the wet grass, then tripped again over the pile of muck I'd dumped out of the wading pool. This time I gave her a hand up.

She squinted, shook her head, and looked me right in

the eye. Definitely hostile aggression. "What the hell have you done now, Willy?"

"I—" I started to deny everything, but she'd know. She always did. I wasn't ready to talk about Oey yet, either. Chances were she couldn't see it or she would have called out the cavalry. The people from DUE anyway. I didn't want them swarming around yet, not until I tried to get rid of the birdfish on my own. The agents might decide the interloper was too much of a threat to Paumanok Harbor and the rest of the world as we know it. So they might expedite its departure. In a hostile, aggressive, and permanent manner.

I went on the offensive. "Why is it always my mistake? My sin? My fault? You're no one to speak, driving drunk like that."

"I am not drunk. Just a little high."

"High? That's worse! It's a hanging offense. Or jail time, anyway."

"Come on, there's never anybody on the roads so late this time of year."

"You were on the road, and the deer are there, too."

"The deer can hear that old bomb coming a mile away and get out of the road."

"The police are on patrol, especially with all the robberies."

"So what if one of Uncle Henry's cops pulls me over? You think they'll arrest me? Not if they want to eat at the Breakaway again. Not if they don't want their wives to know where they hang out after work. Not if they know Grandma Eve. They'll give me a lecture, that's all. So you can save yours."

She headed back around toward the front of the house. "Let's do this again soon, huh?" This time she tripped on one of the dogs' old tennis balls. "Fuck."

I didn't help her up. I was wet and filthy enough on my own, and I was so mad at her, being reckless, taking chances, scaring away the oiaca that wasn't an oiaca, I might have rubbed her nose in the mud. "You're too stoned to drive, and too stupid to take a cab."

She wiped her hands on the denim shirt she wore, not the one she'd left the house in. Then she wiped her nose on the sleeve. Yeck.

"When the hell are you going to grow up?"

"When are you going to stop playing big sister? You don't understand anything, Saint Willow, including yourself, so how can you possibly understand me? You don't know what it's like to almost die, to wonder if the chemo and the radiation will work. To lose your hair and not be able to work at your job. To have to depend on other people driving you back and forth from one doctor to another. And then wait to see if the cancer has shrunk. Then wait for the three-month CAT scan to see if it's come back, and go through that every fucking three to six months for years. With everyone watching, waiting for the bad news. And you're sure every time someone is going to hand it to you. Then what? You start all over again, only this time is worse? No, you'll never understand where I'm at."

A lot of people survived worse, and didn't make a mess of their lives. "No, I'll never understand why you are living your life like it's not worth anything, shacking up with every man you meet, driving under the influence of booze and who knows what else. You fought so damned hard to keep living. Why are you trying to kill yourself now?"

She put her hands on her hips and stuck her chin out. She had a smear of dirt on it, making her look like a bratty kid, not a college graduate and a professional chef.

"I am not trying to kill myself, only have a good time. I deserve that."

I pointed to the mud up and down her, the smelly old truck with its lights on. "This is fun?"

"It's all there is."

"It's all there is here in this backwater bog." Not even I believed that, but I said it anyway, to make my point. "This place is a horrible influence if you can't find anything to do but go to bars or beach parties. You are a fantastic cook. You can get a job anywhere, own your own restaurant. Meet people with your same interests in cooking and feeding people. Write a book, write a cooking column, take more courses. Go abroad to study with the masters."

"Hah! You had your chance to go to Royce University in England and you turned it down. You had your chance to go to London to visit a wonderful man, an English lord, no less. You didn't do that either!"

"We're not talking about me, and I like my life. Enough that I don't try to escape it every way I can. And I am fulfilling my goals, not wasting my talent. Why, you could get your own show on television."

"Why should I? That's not one of *my* goals. None of your bullshit is. I'm not you. I don't have your ambition, your burning need to be someone else, someone who wouldn't deign to live among us common folk."

"I resent that! Just because I want to have more of the world than this tiny corner. And no one here is common! You are all as rare as . . . as that bird no one can find."

"Well, just so you know, my cooking isn't as good out of Paumanok Harbor. I've tried. I got through cooking school, got a job. I wouldn't have advanced much further, anywhere, except here. You of all people ought to understand the power of this place. My cooking is magic in the Harbor. Combined with Grandma's ingredients, it's almost irresistible. My meals show people how to relish life and savor all its tastes. They are as happy to eat what I cook as I am happy to feed them. That's my goal, my ambition. So, no, I will not leave the Harbor, where my friends and family live, where people stood by me when I was having treatments, where they ran pancake breakfasts to help pay for my doctors, and Uncle Bernie kept up my health insurance when I didn't work for six months. I am a little more loyal than that." She picked up the sodden tennis ball and tossed it into the woods. "Unlike some I could name."

"Yeah, well I am sure you're making everyone proud and happy, playing the whore."

"You're not my mother."

"Thank God."

"And you're not so perfect yourself."

"I never said I was. But you're not my mother, either. So stop accusing me of heaven only knows what every chance you get. Or running to Grandma Eve with your snitchy stories. I haven't done anything!"

"Sure." She headed toward the house, this time over-concentrating on where she put her feet. She turned back when she got to the porch. "You haven't done anything but fill the wading pool in the middle of night. You think we're weird? Well, you can go to hell. You cause more damage and danger than any fifteen of us, and it takes fifty of us to mop up after you. No one ever got hurt by a weather magi or a clairvoyant or a telekinetic. But you? You're havoc on wheels."

"Wheels? I don't drive drunk like you do."

"Hah. You operate really heavy machinations, Willow Tate, playing in your own head, drunk on your creative high. So go back to your precious big city where no one gives a damn about you and your stupid plots that come true."

The front door slammed.

Then it opened. Susan stuck her head around the corner. "And you look guilty as hell." Then she slammed the door again.

I waited, but the door stayed closed.

I stayed outside for another hour, in case the un-oiaca came back. I also stayed out so Susan wouldn't hear me crying. I hated confrontations of any kind, but especially with my cousin, the relative I was closest to. Now I knew what she thought of me, and that made me cry more.

I hated being a nag. Mostly I hated to think I was turning into my mother, who specialized in it.

Susan hated me. According to her, the rest of the town did, too. Maybe I should be afraid to let Janie at the beauty salon touch up my hair color again. Or let Kelvin put air in the Outback's tires. Maybe I should simply camp out in the back of my house going "twee, twee" until someone came to lock me up.

The flashlight batteries gave out. Camping mightn't be such a great idea, not when I couldn't see past the side yard, and I never did find out what the aberrant parrot-fish ate.

The dogs were glad to see me, at least. They hadn't received their good-night cookies. See? Everyone wanted something. Little Red wanted to be carried and cuddled, after being left alone for a whole two hours.

I needed the affection, too.

The answering machine light flashed for a new message I missed while I was outside feeling sorry for myself. Such a late phone call had to mean more trouble. I thought about leaving it till morning, but what if it had been a real emergency? Not Aunt Jas checking to see if Susan got home safely.

"Sorry to call so late, baby girl." My father's voice sounded shaky and I started to panic. "But I woke up in a sweat, gasping for breath."

"And you called me instead of nine-one-one?" I shouted at the telephone. "You are—"

"I am worried about you. I dreamed someone tried to hit you on the nose. I love your nose, Willy. It's just like your mother's, not mine, thank goodness. So you be careful, okay, sweetheart? I'm going back to sleep. We have an early tee-off tomorrow, so don't try to call when you get in. I don't know any more about it, anyway. Just that someone is going to try to hit you on the nose. Love you." There was a pause. "Oh, this is your father."

As if I didn't know. Who else had me running to the mirror to make sure I didn't have Mom's nose? Nope, it was my own, and I liked it just the way it was. Not perfect, but better than crooked, or black and blue, or heaven forbid, needing surgery. Damn. And I couldn't call my father until his golf game ended.

I gave the two big dogs their cookies and belly rubs and carried Little Red up to bed. The door to the guest room where Susan slept when she stayed here, which was most of the time because her mother didn't approve any more than I did, was shut tight. Locked too, I bet.

"It's a good thing I have you," I told Little Red, and kissed him on the nose. No one better try to hit *him* on the nose, not if they liked their fingers.

Sleep didn't come. The whole argument with Susan replayed itself over and over, along with my dad's warning and the fish/bird encounter. I left my window open to listen for its call, but if the creature returned, I didn't hear it.

Until I eventually fell asleep. Then I heard the "twee." Only I couldn't, because I stayed asleep.

Twee, twee, echoed plaintively in my dreams, like the nightingale's "Adieu! Adieu!"

Twee? begged in my head. I turned over to find a more comfortable spot. Red growled to remind me not to roll on him. Half awake now, I listened for real noises, not carryover dreams. Nothing. I went back to sleep.

This time I dreamed pictures instead of sounds. Not of the hero I'd been drawing, not of Matt, its model, not of the faceless man who wanted to hit me on the nose. No, I pictured a flounder in feathered drag.

Twee?

A cockatoo with scales.

T-wee? T-wee?

The bird was not in my room, yet I could sense its presence in my dream, even smell the wet feathers and the oily fish scent. I dreamed in the vivid colors I'd seen outside, too.

Then a new image crept into my sleeping unconscious, only not new to me. The familiar drawing of a tree, a weeping willow tree, was one I'd drawn to show the previous trespassers from Unity my name. I couldn't mindspeak the way they did, so I did my best trick, I visualized. Willow, that's me.

Twee! Twee! Now Oey perched in the tree, hopping up and down, wagging its fish tail furiously enough that I felt a breeze on my cheek.

Bloody hell. In the depths of sleep I remembered how I'd fiddled with my hero's companion. Make it unique and sympathetic, I'd thought. Make it a little silly.

Give it a lisp, a speech impediment.

Argh.

Awgh?

Chapter 10

"NAH, WILLY, NOT EVERYBODY IN TOWN hates you." Uncle Henry Haversmith, Paumanok Harbor's Chief of Police, shoved some papers aside, leaned back in his swivel chair, and patted his bulging gut.

I watched in case he reached for the antacids, a sure sign that he lied. He didn't seem to be in distress, so I guess what he said was true. A few of the locals hardly knew me enough to have an opinion.

"Some people even like you. Of course, the mayor helped them forget the chaos your night mares caused, and the fires from your lightning bugs."

"They weren't my—"

"And there are those in town who think you've brought more excitement to the Harbor than we've seen in decades. Some are grateful to catch a hint of the ancient True Magic, thanks to you."

We were sitting in the chief's cramped office in the police department wing of the village hall. I'd passed Mrs. Ralston at the central office and she'd waved, with all five fingers. Baitfish Barry gave me a wide berth, but he always did, to save everyone's sensibilities from the fish smell he never lost. He never went fishing without catching something, either. He always shared, so no one minded the odor except Big Eddie, the master sniffer who stayed outdoors. They both gave me smiles.

So did Joanne at the deli when she handed me a but-

tered roll, just the way I liked it, warm but not toasted.
Two customers at the counter nodded politely, too.

No stink eyes. Maybe Uncle Henry was right and
Susan was wrong about the whole village blaming me for
all its troubles.

She slept late as usual, with the door closed, not as
usual. I left a note near the front door, apologizing. The
note had a quick caricature of her, eyebrow rings and all.
I like you just the way you are, I'd written across the top.

I doubted if anyone was going to like me when they
heard about the bird, if the whole thing wasn't a dream,
which I felt likely, by the light of the crisp September
day. Still, I had to give the chief fair warning. I started
slowly. "Well, I think we might have a small problem
now."

Uncle Henry reached for the Tums.

I held up one hand. "No, it's just one of my father's
premonitions."

His hand went back to rubbing his stomach. He did
that a lot, now that he'd given up the horrid cigars he
used to smoke and chew on all day. Every employee of
Town Hall had signed the petition protesting the second-
hand smoke and stench. Mrs. Ralston threatened to quit,
which would have shut down the local government,
courts, and tax office.

"I know all about your father's knack. Played cards
with him every summer for years, didn't I?"

"He could predict the deals?"

"No, but everyone thought he could tell what card
he'd get next, so it changed the game."

"He only sees dangers, and then only to people he
loves."

"Yeah, but he didn't live here, only came out weekends in the summer when you and your mom stayed
here. All people knew was he had precog talent. That
was enough to discourage betting against him."

"Well, right now he's predicting that someone wants
to hit me on the nose."

"Hell, Willy, I could have told you that and I've never
had an inkling of the future yet. Sometimes I wish I

wasn't an officer of the law, sworn to protect and defend. You were bad enough as a standoffish kid— "

"I was shy."

"Who wouldn't let anyone check you for talent."

"I was a good artist, for a child."

"Not that kind of talent. You could have gone to high school in England, where the experts could have figured you out."

"I didn't believe in all that crap then. No one bothered to explain it to me."

"You didn't want to hear it. Or see what was right under your eyes. You went your own way—not that we're not proud of your books and all—but now you're our headache."

I chose to ignore him. "The man's name might be Stu."

"The man who wants to hit you on the nose? What did you do to him? Leave this one at the altar?"

"I don't even know anyone by that name. And Grant and I never set a wedding date, as you know very well. We were almost engaged, that's all, and not for very long."

"When you broke the cowboy's heart by not going out west with him."

"Ty's heart belonged to his horses, not me. And Piet the fire-damper? He had no intention of settling down in one place with one woman, so our relationship never— Hey, this is not about my private life, although you and everyone else in Paumanok Harbor feels they have a right to comment on it, as if you've all friended me on Facebook. Wrong."

"Still standoffish. What's wrong with being friendly?"

I'd spent too much time with Little Red; I almost growled. "I didn't come here to discuss our different definitions of friendliness, or my personal business. What I want to do is to pass on my father's warning to me before I left the city to watch out for Stu. He was pretty certain the Stu he glimpsed wasn't like beef stew, or a stewardess. I can't call him until later to find out if Stu and my would-be attacker are one and the same."

The chief pulled a pad closer to him, then searched his desk for a pencil. "Okay, I'll put out the word. Between them, my guys know almost everyone in town. They'll ask strangers for ID. Although we can't arrest every moke named Stu. On what grounds? A precog's intuition?"

"I understand that. Thanks for checking around, though." I let him lean back in his chair, then said, "There's more."

"I figured. No one drops by here without a better reason than Tate's iffy talent, not even some ancient professor the big shots in London think might have wandered our way."

"We might have a bigger problem than Stu and a missing scholar."

"You already said that, and we already have enough problems to last a year. The robbery gang hit a Lion's Club dinner at a restaurant last night in Quogue, where the Suffolk County squad didn't have cars patrolling."

"I had nothing to do with that!"

"I never said you did. Or the fact that they traced the embezzlement of East Hampton town money right back to here."

"Paumanok Harbor has a cyber thief?"

"Not Paumanok Harbor, but right here, in Town Hall. That's where the order to transfer the money came from. Where it went is anyone's guess. Offshore secret accounts, the Feds suppose."

"But here?" I thought of Mrs. Ralston who knew the sex of pregnant women's babies. The cops, the judge who made his verdicts without hearing evidence, only the accused's plea. "Everyone who works here is . . ."

"One of us, and honest, right? There's not a one who'd use his or her power for that kind of villainy. We might bend the rules here and there for the good of all, but break them for personal gain? I don't know anyone here who'd do such a thing. Problem is, people come and go all the time. They need to get parking permits and clamming licenses, hand in a lost wallet, pay their taxes, and plead their traffic violations. It's wide open to the public."

"That doesn't give anyone the opportunity to hack into the system."

"They don't need to work so hard. The mayor keeps all the passwords taped under his chair so he doesn't forget them. Mrs. Ralston has to remind him where they are whenever he needs to communicate with East Hampton Township. The Feds think his computer was used. They took it away."

"Oh, dear."

"Oh, crap, more like it. So unless you have useful information I don't have, I don't need another problem."

He moved some papers around on the desk, waiting for me to leave. Then he stopped pawing through his correspondence. "You don't have anything to do with the crazy dolphins, do you?"

"No, and before you ask, they are not in my new book. There's a massive, majestic water god, yes, but he's fighting an evil, sapient sea serpent."

He nodded. "Sounds good." Which meant no indigestion. Which meant I hadn't lied. "And the computer thefts are far beyond your skills. Mine, too. The robberies? You have alibis."

"You checked?"

"Shit, Willy, you're the number one troublemaker around here. Where else would we start? You're all clear."

Thanks for nothing, Chief. Now I didn't feel like telling him about Oey.

He bent over a stack of folders in front of him. "So are we done?"

Someone in charge had to be told, to prepare for whatever else could happen. Like they prepared for hurricanes. Sometimes they hit close to home; sometimes they passed on by. I took a deep breath. "It's the rare bird. Only it's not a bird."

"Tell me its name is Stu and I swear I'll hit you in the nose myself."

"I have no idea of its name. We didn't really converse and the whole thing might be a dream anyway. I figured you should know."

I think he groaned, so I hurried on: "I'm calling it Oey, for the oiaca everyone supposes it to be. It's not."

"You're saying it's not a bird, not Stu, not an endangered species, maybe not real?"

"Uh-huh."

"And what do you want me to do about it? I could have sworn you'd come to ask for more traffic cops near your grandmother's place."

"That, too, until we get it to go home."

" 'We'? There is no 'we.' I'm going to find the burglars. *You* are going to get rid of it, whatever the devil it is, before its friends come. Or its enemies."

I sighed. "I thought you might say that."

"So what's your plan?"

Did I have a plan? "So far I'm thinking about asking Matt to come over tonight."

"Your plan about the bird, Willy, not about your piss-poor love life. Of course he is a nice guy. You could do worse."

Teeth gnashing gave me headaches. I did it anyway. "I thought I'd invite Matt to my yard to look for Oey. To see if he really can see things no one else but me can."

"You can't."

"Why? He knows enough about the otherworld to understand. And he doesn't think I'm crazy."

"Well, maybe he's not so bright after all. Either way, you can't invite him. It's poker night."

"The quasi bird is more important. Disinvite him."

"I can't. We're playing at his house. He called early this morning to say he's got emergency surgery this afternoon, the Camerons' beagle jumped the fence and got hit by a car. Doc will operate as soon as the pup is stable enough."

"That's terrible. The beagle was one of my mother's rescue dogs, wasn't it?"

"Right, and the Camerons are real attached to it. We've got people saying prayers, and healers ready to put hands on the animal if Matt needs us. Or if the poor woman who hit the dog does."

"But he's still going to play poker?"

"He said he'll be up all night anyway, checking the dog every half hour, despite having a kennel man on duty. So he asked us to his place."

"But I need him."

"Yeah, well, I'm sure Susan can fix you up with some-one."

"I need him to see the bird, not for sex!"

"There's nothing wrong with sex. That's how you get little espers. You two might make psychic history with your kids."

"Jeez, we are not even dating and you are talking about our children?"

"I heard you went out last night. Those veggie burgers taste like sawdust, don't they? It's a start. You know how everyone's anxious to preserve your genes."

"All I know is that no one here minds their own god-damn business. I might not ever have children. I haven't decided."

"You're thirty-five. Don't take too long thinking about it. But adopting might be the ticket, Willy. If you can pass along your gift without sharing genes, like you did with Matt, you could raise up a regular basketball team of talents."

"I didn't pass on my talent. M'ma gave it to Matt as a gift."

"Because you were there, right? That's close enough. Anyway, I know Matt likes children."

"I don't care for infants and toddlers."

"Come on, kiddo, you were great with Janie's grand-niece."

"I stank at babysitting Elladaire. The fireman from DUE kept her from setting the town ablaze, not me. I couldn't stand the responsibility."

He shook his head. "The whole world is your respon-sibility now. One baby can't be more effort. Or three."

"No babies! A bird. Matt. Tonight."

"I don't see why it's so important for Matt to see your

new friend. Others have spotted it. That's why your grandmother is having catfits about the cabbages."

"Others see what they expect to see. Pink toes? Odd shape? Never seen hereabouts? It must be an oiaca. No one has a photo, do they? And it disappears, right? And it's calling *twee, twee*."

"I heard it went *tweet, tweet*."

"No, it's definitely a twee. The thing lisps. It means tree, as in Willow. It came to see me."

He waited for the burn in his stomach, one hand on his belly, one reaching for the bottle of pills on his desk. "Crap, it's true."

That's about how I felt, too.

CHAPTER II

JOANNE HANDED ME THE HAM and Swiss on rye as soon as I walked into the deli.

"That's real thoughtful of you, Willy. He'll be too busy to eat otherwise. I hear the dog is in bad shape."

The thing was, I hadn't called ahead. Hadn't thought about getting Matt a sandwich until I drove past the deli. I was thinking about him, the poor beagle, and if I had enough bread in the house. Scary.

Worse had to be Joanne's sudden anguish, as if someone had punched her in the gut. Her face crumbled, a stack of napkins fell from her hands, and tear watered her eyes.

"What's wrong?" I looked around to see if the burglars had shown up, to steal my last twenty bucks before I stopped at the bank.

"I . . . I can't tell what you want," she said on a snivel. "That almost never happens. And they say you can bring someone talent. Can you take it away, too? Please don't, Willy. I love giving people what they want."

"I can't give or take away anything! I swear. And I wouldn't if I could. Take away, that is. You run the best deli anywhere. It's just that—"

"I know you didn't like the veggie burger. And you're going vegetarian, right? How about chicken salad? Will you eat that?"

I thought about Oey, cawing my name. I shook my head.

"How about tuna?" Joanne sounded almost desperate now.

Oey the fish, gasping for air. I'd gag on tuna, too.

Joanne almost cried. "A bagel with cream cheese? Grilled cheese? Peanut butter and jelly?"

"Hey, I'm not hungry, that's all. I had a big breakfast. But how about . . ."

"A salad for later! That's what you want. Whew. You had me scared for a minute there."

Yup, scary.

I appreciated Joanne's knack. Incomprehensible talent or not, she worked hard to please her customers.

Melissa at the vet didn't. She had no talent that I knew of, and no personality either, unless you counted a constant sneer.

Today Miss Snark went for the Goth look. Or maybe the recently embalmed look. She had enough pale makeup for a Kabuki dancer, and enough black clothes for a ninja . . . or a cat burglar. Hmm. No, she couldn't be one of the local bandits. Put a ski mask on her and you'd have . . . a hissy fit. The girl was too vain to put on a mask.

The enviably shiny and sleek black hair of yesterday was dull and crimped today, with long white hairpieces woven in, or bleached in, a la Cruella. Melissa's long-sleeved black T-shirt had the neck cut so low you could see the dragon tattoo breathing fire down her ample décolletage almost to her navel. Any infant of hers'd get nightmares from breast-feeding. The idea of this vampire wannabe being a mother made my palms sweat. And wait till Melissa tried to explain that tattoo to the nurses at the rest home when she was ninety and the dragon lay flat against her rib cage. How could this . . . this person be related to Matt?

Then again, I was related to Grandma Eve, the village witch.

"He's busy." Her lip curled. Good grief, had she had her teeth filed into fangs? No, they had to be false caps. I got it now; Melissa was practicing for Halloween next month. So I smiled instead of writing her into my next book as the evil sorceress who sucked joy away from the world.

"I know." How could I not, with the whole waiting room full, trying to cram a full day's appointments into the morning before surgery? "That's why I brought him a sandwich."

"You won't get to him that way. Better looking old maids than you have tried. Better cooks, too, with casseroles and cakes. All you brought is a lousy sandwich? You're wasting your time."

Maybe she should tattoo a chip on her shoulder in case anyone missed it. "Just give him the sandwich between patients. And tell him I hope the beagle is all right."

I wasn't sure about the sandwich, but I knew he'd never get the message.

Then Elise called out from where she sat with a cat carrier on her lap: "Ginger and I are next, Willy. We'll make sure he takes time to eat. I should have thought of that, too."

Elise always had a cat in distress. She picked up the feral or abandoned cats in need and paid for their medical care out of her own pocket. Rumor had it she grew fifty-dollar bills in her greenhouse. I suspected pot. She offered to help pay for the sandwich.

Phil, the music teacher at the school, offered to bring Matt dinner. He was coming tonight for the poker game anyway. Phil had perfect pitch, like a lot of people. Like no one else I ever heard of, he could tune all the school band's instruments at once just by humming a C-note. He made big money as a piano tuner, but he loved the kids better.

Margo Minskoff nodded. So did her Scottie. They both wore red bows in their hair.

The whole waiting room approved. They mightn't like me, but they liked Melissa less.

Melissa uncurled her lip enough to say, "I was going to call out for pizza."

None of us believed her. Mrs. Minskoff's face turned red. She was one of the truth people.

"Don't worry, Willow, dear. We'll be sure Dr. Matt gets your message. Both of them."

I thought I only left one.

After visits to the community center, the school, and the fire department, I stopped by the bank to use the ATM. Mr. Whitside assured me he'd hired extra guards to protect his customers and their money. Since his mind knew to a penny how much his bank had on hand, he'd notice anyone messing with the computers, too.

Finally I went back to my mother's, to address the traffic situation.

First I posted "No Parking" signs along the dirt road, except for three spaces reserved for government officials. Next I put a "Private Road" sign at the entrance to our street: "No Trespassing except for Garland Farms customers."

Then I made another sign to mark the empty field right before the turnoff to Garland Drive. "Birdwatchers Park Here. $5/hour."

I had senior citizens watching the new parking lot this morning, collecting the money to buy a pool table for the recreation center. The volunteer firemen were coming in the afternoon. They wanted a new pumper truck. School kids had the late shift, Boy and Girl Scouts, the nature club, the eighth grade to finance their trip to Washington DC. I had the Lions, the Kiwanis, and the VFW all lined up for a turn.

A policeman stood by, in case the birdwatchers got ugly, or tried to drive down our street. The farm stand might lose some business, but it made up for the loss with birders thinking to get closer to the oiaca if they bought a carload of veggies.

My grandmother seemed more comfortable, now that the crush of vehicles eased. She and Uncle Roger had put flags out, showing the binocular crowd the paths to the back fields, where the farm workers had strung orange plastic snow fences to keep them from trampling the fall crops. No one had spotted the rare bird so far that day.

I wondered if it was back at the kiddie pool in my side yard, where no one could see it from the roadway. Or maybe it had left altogether, having made my acquaintance.

I could only hope.

So did my grandmother. First she managed to thank me for the signs and organizing the volunteers. "That was a fine idea, Willow, raising money for good causes out of this chaos. Luckily, it will all end soon." She gave me a hard stare. "Won't it, Willow?"

I could only hope harder.

Joanne made a great salad, with oranges and walnuts and cranberries and chunks of butternut squash. Now I was fortified enough to call my mother.

"I heard you bought Matt a sandwich."

"Already? What, you have a direct line to some Willow Watch?"

"Don't be foolish. It's a Paumanok Harbor Facebook list. People thought I should know about the Camerons' beagle."

"He's not good, I hear, but Matt's going to try this afternoon. You ought to come home, talk to him."

"To Matt?"

"No, to the dog. Find out if he's hurting too bad. No one wants him to suffer."

"Matt will know. But he's not right."

"He's a good vet."

"I mean he's not right for you."

"I know, he's not one of the Paumanok Harbor insiders. But he's changed somehow. They think he has talent now, just not why or what yet."

"I heard that. I might even believe it. Lord knows stranger things happen there, especially around you. But it's still not right. He's got nothing in his DNA to pass on."

I started to say that Uncle Henry was all for the match, right down to the number of kids we ought to beget or adopt. Then I wondered how come I was defending Matt as a prospective mate. "Don't worry. I'm not setting my sights on your hunky vet. He's planted here, like an oak tree. More firmly now, after . . . after whatever changed him. He's not going to move. I am not staying."

"Still?"

"What do you mean, still? No one knows about the bird yet, no one who would have mentioned it to you. They only suppose. I'll leave after."

"After the bird leaves? You mean you have something to do with that lost creature that's on the national news? Don't tell me. Just handle it."

"I've got the traffic under control. I'm working on the rest." I looked out the window to where I'd put a tray full of salad greens, fruit, sunflower seeds, and a slice of bread with peanut butter on it next to the kiddie pool. No Oey. "What did you mean, 'still'?"

"I meant that you still insist on living in Manhattan. I was hoping you'd come to your senses and appreciate the Harbor the way I do. I've always wanted you to make it your home."

Live with my mother? I spread peanut butter on another slice. This one for me.

"Mom, I have a life in the city. You have yours in Paumanok Harbor."

"And I am not getting any younger. Neither is your grandmother. You belong here." She snorted for emphasis.

What did she do, have a kid as insurance against old age and rest homes? Maybe my father's heart attack had given her those intimations of mortality. "I can't be your caregiver. I stink at it. Besides, both you and Grandma Eve are fine. If you are worried about her, maybe you should come home already and help at the farm stand."

By the silence at the end of the line I deduced that helping at the farm in the busy months was partly why my mother stayed away. "You've been gone all summer. Surely there are dogs on the Island that need saving."

She sniffed this time. "Of course there are. And I have a backlog of wealthy private clients that goes on for pages. The dogs will be so set in their ways and spoiled

by the time I get there to straighten out the owners, it'll
be a regular battle. I could use the money, too, after this
trip."

"So why don't you come home? One more month or
so and Grandma Eve shuts down the stand."

"I didn't say I wouldn't help out, between my own clients. For your information, I stayed away so long because
I hoped that if you spent enough time in Paumanok Harbor, you'd come to see that you belong there. They need
you. You need them."

The peanut butter stuck in my throat. "I don't want to
be needed that badly. I don't want the responsibility for
you and Grandma Eve in your dotage, much less the
whole village. So you're wasting your time. Grandma
needs you, not me. She's worn out by the strangers and
their interference."

"I'll be home by Halloween, of course. I haven't
missed Halloween in the Harbor in decades."

I'd never been, not that I remembered. What did they
do to make it so special? Hold a witches' coven and
dance naked around the flagpole on All Hallow's Eve?
Most towns simply held a ragamuffin parade for all the
children to walk through the main street in costume and
grab candy from the storekeepers. Others had fancy parties to keep the kids off the streets and out of mischief
altogether. Chances were Paumanok Harbor had its own
kind of celebration. They could hold it without me.

Mom pressed, as always. "You'll be there, won't you?"

"Six weeks away? I'll be long gone. I do have deadlines, you know."

Sniff. "You can spare us three days."

They took three days to carve pumpkins? I can see
three days to eat all the candy, but I sure as hell wasn't
going to spend three days waiting for ghosts and goblins
to come out. In this place, they might be real. "I'll see." I
lied.

"And leave Matt Spenser alone."

"Okay." I lied again. Mom had no truth-detecting
ability, thank goodness. I was counting on Matt to help
with the oiaca pretender.

*   *   *

My father returned my call after his golf game, lunch, and a nap.

"How'd you do?" I asked.

"I met a nice woman at the clubhouse bar. We're having dinner."

More than I needed to know. "Dad, when you mentioned someone hitting me on the nose, could it be that Stu person?"

"No idea, baby girl. They were two separate visions, so I doubt they're connected. Might be, though."

"Okay. Do you get any vibes from a fish or a bird?"

"I thought I'd have the steak."

"I meant danger coming. From a parrot, maybe, or a shark?"

"Hmm. Now that you mention animals, I've been thinking about skunks. They can be rabid, you know, so stay away if you see one."

A skunk? They didn't live around here. Unless he meant Melissa with her black-and-white hair streaks. The more I thought about it, I could see her holding up banks and restaurants after all. She was mean enough. Then another thought occurred to me, after my mother's worries. "Do you have any premonitions about Grandma Eve?"

"Old bats can be rabid, too."

"But threats? Her health might be a problem, or her age. Can you sense anything? She told me about the Pontiac. Do you still have enough affection for her to feel she's in peril?"

"To be honest, sweetheart, I think of that woman as rarely as possible. So I guess she's not in any danger. Either that or she dislikes me too much to make the whole impending doom thing work."

"What about Mom?"

"She stopped taking my calls, so it wouldn't matter if I saw an earthquake in her future."

"She took you seriously enough when you said not to eat anything on the plane and the woman next to her found a cockroach in her pretzels or something."

"Yeah, but the dryer thing got to her. I convinced her to stop using the blow dryer while she traveled, so she let her hair go all curly, like yours, the way I like it. Then the clothes dryer at some motel blew up, burned all the clothes she'd brought to Florida with her, and half the motel. The managers blamed her for the damage, for overloading the damned thing. She blamed me. Like always. Now we don't talk and I try not to think about her. So do you think I should stay away from the steak?"

And the bars and the women, unless he wanted another heart attack.

At least he didn't ask me to take care of him.

CHAPTER 12

SUSAN AND THE OLD TRUCK WERE GONE, but she'd left her clothes and her usual mess in the upstairs bathroom. She also left me some brownies, fresh-baked, so we were okay, I guess.

I walked the dogs down to the beach. How many more days would be warm enough to enjoy outdoors? How long would I be here, with the whole bay beach a block and a half away? I wondered if I'd have to buy Little Red a coat. The Pomeranian had thick fur, but not much heft to him. Every little dog I saw in the city wore sweaters. One of my neighbor's Yorkies had a wardrobe bigger than mine, and boots, which I had absolutely no intention of buying. If Red's feet got cold, I'd carry him. Or let him use the papers in the apartment.

He didn't need a coat this afternoon, even though clouds were covering the sun and the breeze picked up. Little Red kept warm chasing gulls and sea foam from the whitecaps, and the two big dogs who ambled along, ignoring him.

I wondered if dogs worried about growing old. If they worried about making it up the stairs, or getting outside in time to avoid accidents. Were they ever concerned that no one would be around to fetch their kibble and clean their water bowls? According to my mother, Little Red feared he'd been abandoned again every time we left him alone, which kept him anxious and aggressive. She felt he acted hostile because he was afraid of being abused again, or afraid of bonding to another person who might break his heart.

I thought he had a mean streak. And a stupid streak that forgot who bought the dog food. Like now, when he was tired and wanted to be picked up. Other dogs might sit down in front of their owners, or simply stop walking. Not Little Red. He lifted his leg on my shoe to get my attention. Luckily, the well was dry by then, and also luckily I wasn't wearing sandals. I didn't know if I had that much tolerance in me. I picked him up anyway, tucked him inside my unzipped sweatshirt and promised to buy him a boy dog's coat, no sissy plaid with ruffles and bows. And nothing that matched my winter jackets.

Funny how you could love something so annoying.

Which reminded me of my mother. When would she get the idea I didn't belong in Paumanok Harbor, didn't want a vanload of kids, didn't feel responsible for perpetuating her genes or protecting her whole damn town?

Feeling guilty—what else were daughters and granddaughters for?—I stopped by the big house to ask if Eve wanted to go out to dinner with me, my treat.

She had a casserole in the oven. Vegetarian lasagna. Oh, boy. I locked the dogs inside my mother's house and brought the brownies back with me.

The table was already set for two, with flowers and candles and the hand-thrown blue pottery dishes. For me? I was touched.

She handed me the garlic bread to put on the table while she carried out the lasagna. Trying not to drool, I asked, "So have there been any spottings of the oiaca today?"

"Someone thought they saw pink toes under a shrub near Jas and Roger's house. Someone else said they heard a tweet from the field nearest the bay. I keep it for summer flowers, because the wind is too strong for tender vegetables and there's a low spot that gets poor drainage."

Where the parrotfish could wet its gills.

"It'll likely flood tomorrow with the rain that's coming." A cold front, according to the weather station. A squall off the water late tonight, according to Bud at the gas station and Elgin, the harbormaster.

I'd trust Bud and Elgin any time. I wouldn't be sitting outside too long, waiting for Oey to show up.

The lasagna was too hot to cut yet. I would have scooped it up with a spoon, but Grandma Eve insisted it set and firm up. I ate a piece of garlic bread. "Did anyone go check that field?"

She chuckled. "I got the Boy Scouts to lead the observers out, the long way around. For a fee. And they sold enough cans of mixed nuts to pay for a camping trip next spring. The Girl Scouts get their turn as tour guides tomorrow, if the storm passes."

"Any problems with the cars? Anyone else giving you grief?" Her food, my concern. Fair trade.

"Only the idiots who thought they'd carry in supplies to build a platform in the middle of my corn maze. And the group that wanted to charter a plane for a flyover. They'd likely scare the poor bird to bits."

Some bits with feathers, some with scales. The lasagna contained neither, and was as delicious as it smelled, when she finally put a serving on my plate.

"But people behaved?" I asked around a mouthful.

"Mostly, especially after I made tea for the EPA folks and the Audubon Society photographers."

Heaven knew what was in Eve Garland's tea. I never drank the stuff.

She smiled. "The Wildlife Federation and National Geographic people come tomorrow. I hope they're thirsty."

I never trusted her smiles, either. They reminded me of the witch in Hansel and Gretel inviting the children into her parlor. "Come here, my pretties."

This time the smile seemed genuine. It made her look younger, too, more rested. I could give my mother a good report. No need to call out the reserves.

"Not much noise last night, right?"

She took another bite and nodded. "I heard some commotion from your house. Then it got blessedly quiet, thank goodness. Whatever you did seems to have brought some calm to the street. I don't suppose you want to discuss it with me, do you?"

"You already know your visitor is not going to appear in any rare bird sighting magazine. No cell phone photo will show up on the Internet. After that, I don't know why it's come, or what it wants. I'll try again tonight when it's more vocal and may be easier to track."

"Do you need to borrow my galoshes and rain gear? Or a heavier jacket? Bud says it might turn cold, too."

"That's really thoughtful of you, but I've got all of Mom's stuff in the closet."

"Here, I'll pack up the rest of the lasagna for you so you don't have to cook tomorrow. And don't forget the brownies. I know how you love something sweet."

I felt all warm and cozy. Until she said she made the lasagna for Lou—and set the pretty table for him, I supposed—but he couldn't get out from the city. DUE had news of some psychic disturbance in the lines of power, maybe connected to that missing professor, some kind of hero in his heyday.

"None of their precogs have more specific information, so every agent is on alert."

Lou was on a diet, too, so she didn't want my brownies around.

I wasn't complaining. "Maybe it's just the coming storm throwing off the charts or the meters or the mentalists."

"Maybe. I wouldn't be surprised if whatever it is leads them back here, not with all the peculiar occurrences. And you're here now."

Which meant I'd have the whole Department of Unexplained Events on my doorstop, checking my moves? Or else they thought I caused the irregularity on whatever woo-woo counter they used. Grandma Eve obviously did.

She ranted on while she packed the lasagna, how the renovation of the old Rosehill estate into a Royce Institute outreach center was taking too long. The grand old house couldn't pass inspection for a meeting hall without more extensive remodeling than originally thought.

Part of the delay, she griped, slapping the lasagna into

three different plastic containers—"So you can freeze some for later"—was that East Hampton Township didn't like taking Rosehill off the tax rolls as a nonprofit, or the Bayview Ranch, either, destined to become an equine rescue and training facility, also sponsored in part by the Royce people.

"They ought to be here now, not leaving us with no one but you to figure things out. That's why the whole university got established in England, to look after the descendants with psychic abilities. Well, we're descendants, too."

And I was chopped liver? No one from Royce saw the troll. No one from DUE found the night mares' missing colt or figured out the lantern beetles' symbiosis with the blubber-shedding leviathan in the salt marshes. I did. And I'd take care of the fishbird, too. On my own. Without calling on their high and mighty experts. They couldn't even find their missing professor.

I *twee*-ed all the way home, with a week's worth of meals and a day's worth of desserts. And determination.

They couldn't blame me and they couldn't make me fight their battles. But I'd show them what Willow Tate was made of. I'd wade into trouble, just like one of my superheroes, and save the day.

Right after the thunderstorm. I saw the first bolt of lightning and ran the rest of the way home, where I pulled Little Red into my lap and a blanket over my head.

So there.

A half an hour later the storm seemed to pass. So the weather mavens could be wrong, too.

I went out and refilled the tray of tidbits to tempt all tastes, including the squirrels I had to chase away. The wading pool held enough water, but I filled a bowl from the kitchen tap in case Oey was too fastidious to drink where he bathed.

I circled the house, tweeting, whistling, okay, begging. Come back, little shebass?

It wasn't working. I got no spark, no rush, no answers, only the wet wind in my face. And Bud was right, the evening turned much cooler than last night. And darker, earlier, with the rain-heavy clouds scudding along like a video clip.

So I went inside, got my sketch pad and a warmer jacket and the brownies. Then I dragged one of the porch chairs closer to the pool and sat, drawing what I had seen last night and thinking about it. Thinking hard, trying to make contact, knowing full well I had no clairvoyance or telepathy, only what and when the Others chose to share. I thought hard anyway, and drew fast.

Bird. Fish. Fish. Bird. Oey. Pretty, strong, smart. Oey. Lost, alone, needful. Oey. Oey in a willow tree, Ocy swimming in a stream alongside one, Oey cold and hungry, shivering. Oey going back where it came from.

I drew until my hand got tired, thought until my brain went numb. I sat out there until it grew too dark to see a damn thing, even with the porch light on. The wind kept trying to grab my pages, and spatterings of rain blown from the trees blotted the marker ink. And I needed a glass of milk to go with the brownies.

I decided to wait inside for the blasted thing to call me. If Oey wanted my help, my company, it had to meet me halfway. So there.

When I opened the fridge to take out the milk, a chill hit me. Not the usual refrigerator cold, but like a shadow across the landscape, or what they used to call a goose walking on your grave, whatever that meant. Maybe I was coming down with the flu. Or—heaven help me—receiving a premonition. Was this how my father felt? Shivers in his blood, a ticking clock in his chest, a big fist squeezing his head?

I didn't know what, but I knew something was desperately wrong. I raced around, checking the dogs, checking the furnace, checking the phones for messages.

Oey! It must be in trouble, trying to reach me via mental telepathy. No, I'd see pictures. That's how most of the Others communicated.

Grandma Eve? Maybe my mother had a premonition, too, when I spoke to her. Maybe she caught the power from my father, the way they say Matt caught his new perceptions from me. The last thing I needed was a foggy new "gift."

I called my grandmother and woke her up. Not a good thing.

"You're okay?"

"I was before you scared the life out of me with the phone call. And no, Lou is not here, if you were calling to check up on me."

"I, ah, just had a feeling."

"You've been listening to that jackass father of yours again, haven't you? Either find the bird, or go to sleep and let the rest of us get some rest."

I couldn't disturb my father on his date. Mom would have called if there'd been an emergency, which I couldn't do anything about from here anyway.

Maybe the coming storm? A lightning bolt I hadn't heard, the change in atmospheric pressure? But the dogs were all sleeping, relaxed. I heard they could tell changes like earthquakes and people's seizures.

It had to be Oey. I went to the door. "Oey, come on, boy, girl, whatever. We need to talk. Show me you are all right."

The feeling of dread stayed with me. "Twee! Twee!" I yelled, pouring my heart and my fear into the call.

"Twee?"

"You came! Are you all right? Hurt? Hungry? Lonely? Come in out of the storm."

But it wasn't Oey calling from the woods. It was Matt, standing on the porch, his head cocked, listening to me call a bird no one could see.

"What are you—?" But I knew. One look at his face told me the beagle had died. "Oh, I am so sorry."

I held my arms out and he came to me and we just held each other for a long time there, inside my front door. It felt right.

He'd come to me, not his poker buddies. Not his obnoxious niece. But me. And my heart went out to him. I could hardly bear the weight of the village's expectations on my shoulders; I couldn't imagine having a beloved pet's life in my hands. People depended on Matt to perform miracles all the time.

"I don't know how you do it." I made him come sit on the sofa before he fell down, he looked so tired and empty. I rushed to put on the coffeemaker.

"You never get used to it," he said when I got back, "but you have to go on, to save what you can." He laid his head back and sighed.

I waited.

"That wasn't the hard part. Homer didn't have much of a chance going in. We all knew it. The hard part was your mother."

"I'm sorry. I know she can be overpowering. I shouldn't have told her you needed her."

"I did need her, but she didn't call. Not on the phone anyway. I felt her talking to me, as if she stood next to me in the operating room. I thought I was delusional, not fit to take out a splinter, much less put poor Homer back together."

I kept quiet. What could I say?

"She told me Homer didn't want to live if he couldn't ever run again. That he'd be mortified if he couldn't control his bowels, couldn't play with his people. He knew he'd never recover and the pain would be too much."

"He was a good dog."

"Not really. He escaped every chance he got. The Camerons were his third adoption. They named him Homer, hoping he'd stick. He didn't. But do you know what? I believed her, your mother in Florida or wherever she is this week, that she knew what Homer wanted, that she'd somehow found a way to tell me."

Yeah, I'd have a tough time with that, too. Or I would have, a few months ago. "The mind is a wondrous thing." Lame, I knew, but all I could offer.

He took my hand. For comfort, I supposed.

"So I talked to the Camerons. That was harder still. I brought them in to say good-bye, for their sake. Homer couldn't know, I had him so sedated for the surgery. Except I felt your mother standing over my shoulder. 'He knows,' she told me. 'He's glad. He loves them. He thanks you.'"

We both cried.

Damn, I never let the dog die. In all my books, I'll kill off the hero. He can always come back in the next volume. His girlfriend? So what? But never, ever, would I let the dog die. It's a rule. It's not fair to the kids who read your books. I'll never forgive Fred Gipson for Old Yeller. And now . . . instead of comforting Matt, I was sobbing on his chest. He stroked my shoulder and I think he kissed the top of my head.

I fled to the kitchen so he couldn't see me all splotchy-faced and red-eyed. Men hated crying women, I knew. It makes them feel helpless, and Matt had enough failure today.

Chattering helped overcome the grief. "I bet you never had dinner tonight. It'll just take a few minutes in the microwave. I have some of Grandma Eve's vegetable lasagna. It's delicious."

He was beside me, handing me a tissue. "That'll be great. Thank you. But, Willow, I didn't really hear your mother, did I?"

"I don't know. It's possible. Anything is in this place. Or maybe you knew what she'd say."

"Do the right thing. For the animal."

"You did."

I pushed my drawing pads and notebooks and pens to one side so he had a place to eat at the dining room table, then served him right out of the plastic container, with a paper plate under it, and a bottle of water. Just like my grandmother. Hah.

The lack of ambiance did not affect his appetite. And the lasagna didn't suffer too much from the indignity of being nuked. The food revived him enough that he apologized for bothering me so late, without calling.

"It's no bother, I promise. I wanted you— That is, I was going to ask you to stop by tonight, but Chief Haversmith said you'd be playing poker."

"I couldn't. Not tonight. They moved the game to the

firehouse. The volunteers are on alert anyway. No one was saying why, but it's better they are at the station."

"I heard there's a bad storm coming. Maybe something else in the wind."

Something that let my mother's thoughts travel up the eastern seaboard? Something that had me attuned to Matt's sorrow? Something worse that had DUE sending out warnings? I didn't feel that bone-deep chill anymore—his arms had been great heating elements— yet a sense of impending doom stayed with me. I felt sorry for my father if this is what he lived with.

"I know what we need, brownies with ice cream on top."

"Gee, the chief suggested a stiff drink, and the guys left me a six-pack. But you're right. That's why they call it comfort food."

"With a dash of Kahlua, then, if the chief said so. And afterward we'll go looking for the oiaca bird."

"Oh, is that what you were doing? I thought you were feeding the racoons. I some saw run off when I drove up. I couldn't believe you'd invite them inside, though."

"Damn, did they eat all my offerings?"

"I'll go check while you scoop the ice cream."

"No, we'll go check together, after we eat dessert." I let him scoop, while I poured the coffee.

"You think it's here, in your yard?"

"I think it was last night."

"You saw the bird?"

"I saw something out of the ordinary. That's why I wanted you to come, to give me your opinion."

"I'm not much of an expert on ornithology, any more than I could answer your questions on entomology when the lightning bugs came by."

"How are you at ichthyology?"

"Huh?"

"Yeah, that's what I said."

CHAPTER 13

THE WIND HOWLED SO FIERCELY we couldn't hear each other speak. Thank goodness I hadn't brought Little Red out. He'd have been blown to Connecticut. He'd have to use his papers tonight. Or keep me up all night, whining.

Matt pulled me closer and shouted in my ear. "No bird would be out in this. It couldn't fly against the wind, and it'd get blown into the houses or trees."

But a fish could hunker down in the pond near Susan's parents' house, or that low spot in the fields. A creature from the otherworld could vanish whenever it wanted.

The porch chair I'd left out had been blown into the backyard, and the wading pool got overturned. Leaves were down, weeks early, and branches and twigs covered the grass.

"What a freaky storm. They never mentioned it in the forecast I heard on my way over."

I guess that depended on what station you listened to.

We turned to go back inside, where we couldn't be hit by falling tree limbs. But I heard a noise, different from the storm. "Pewil! Twee, pewil!"

"Is that the bird? It's calling for a pearl?"

"No, I think it means peril."

He looked at me as if I'd grown another head. Hey, he was the one who heard my mother.

"Oey? Where are you? Come out where we can see

you, or on the porch where there's less peril." I pointed toward the house.

Nothing. I ran inside and grabbed my pad and a marker.

"Twee? Twee?"

I drew two trees, and pictured two in my head. "That's right, two twees, er, trees."

I flipped the pages and made Matt's tree an oak, tall and proud and sturdy, shielding the willow from the wind. "Yes," I thought, and spoke aloud. "This is Matt, a friend."

Matt looked over my shoulder. "You see me as a tree?"

"Hush. You want me to draw a door mat? You think it'll understand a welcome sign? Besides, it's not exactly welcome. Everyone wishes it would go home."

I heard a loud, plaintive, "Pewil! Pewil" coming, I thought, from the roof of the house. I tried to hold up my pendant, so it could see. "Not now. Now all I want is to keep you safe. Friend, care, share, love."

"Fwiend? O-ey"—and a lot more syllables and pictures flashing in my head—"new fwiend?"

If not for Matt I'd be blown over, craning my neck up. "Yes, he loves all creatures. Now come to the porch where we can talk."

"Tweeth."

Matt got into the spirit of the thing. "Tweeth. Two trees. Friends." He wrapped an arm around me, to hold me steady, and to show trust and closeness. "And no peril."

I thought he muttered "I can't believe I'm doing this," but the wind carried his words away.

"Wuve?"

For crying out loud, had Oey been talking to my mother, too? "Friends."

But Matt was saying yes. Was he crazy, too? He held up our joined hands, then we made a dash to the back side of the covered porch, sheltered by the house from the brunt of the hurricane-force winds, which dropped off the second we reached shelter.

Oey must have been convinced because it popped up on the railing. The bird head turned this way and that, studying us. "Thecth?"

"None of your business. Oh, that. Yes, he is a male. I am female. What about you?"

"Bowff." I got a picture in my head of the bird laying eggs in the water, the fish coming to fertilize them. Good grief.

Matt hadn't moved an inch, except to drop his jaw. I guess the first sight of Oey could be a little unnerving, to say the least.

"You do see it, don't you?"

"I see something like a patchwork quilt, only it's talking."

"Can you see the pictures in your mind?"

"No pictures. My mind got blown away when your . . . friend showed up on the porch."

"Yup, that's Oey. Except its name is something huge and long and filled with pictures and emotions and clicks and glubs and past history and the future of its kind. Oh, and the parrot part is female, the fish is male."

I thought he might turn tail and run. Matt, not Oey.

"I'll explain later."

"If you can explain this, you'll have a TV show of your own, like Dr. Phil."

"For now it's enough that you can see what's not a pink-toed Patagonian pigeon. The mind thing is optional." I took a step closer to the railing while Matt shook his head, as if that would clear it.

"Okay, Oey, introductions over. Get serious now. We're friends, we want to help. But here's the thing, you don't belong here. You are disturbing the weft of the worlds. Maybe causing this freak storm. You have to go back."

"Pewil."

"Yes, but if you leave, the peril might end."

Oey jumped up and down on the railing, screeching, "Pewil, pewil!"

"Okay, got that. You're not making the storm. It's almost passed now anyway. But there's some other danger? And you've come to warn us?"

The parrot head bobbed. "Thinking."

"I am thinking. Matt is, too, aren't you?"

"Oh, yeah. I'm thinking we're both crazy, and this is some kind of science experiment gone haywire. Or someone put a little something extra in those brownies. I mean, a talking bird is one thing, but this . . . ?"

Oey changed to a fish, with the long feathered tail.

"Holy cow."

The fish flopped on its side on the porch near my feet, going *glub, glub*.

"Stop that, you'll hyperventilate or dry out or something. Get up and tell us what we are supposed to be thinking about."

The bird appeared again, with the fish tail flapping in agitation. Matt jumped back out of the way and almost broke my fingers, clutching my hand so hard.

"Pewil! Pewil!"

"Got it, for Pete's sake."

"Piet? Fiwa?"

"No, not Pict the fireman." If, as I suspected, Oey was a minion of M'ma's, he knew all about Piet and the fireflies. "What kind of peril?"

"Thinking!" And the fish fell on its side again, *glub glub*.

"Stop that! I cannot understand you when he can't talk."

"Thip thinking."

"I can't understand, damn it!"

Oey cocked her head and shut her eyes. I saw an image in my head, realized what it was and collapsed against Matt, shaking. "Oh, my God. It's a ship, sinking. People drowning. Glub."

"How do you know?"

"She shows me pictures, in my mind. I can visualize. You can't."

He accepted that, for now. "And she—it—they have come to warn us?"

"Pewil! Pewil!"

"Where, Oey? Where is it?"

"Thee."

I was learning. "Right, in the sea. Which sea? When?"
I thought I'd get a brain cramp from trying to read another picture that never came. I shrugged helplessly.

"Damn, it could be anywhere. How can we call the
Coast Guard and warn them that a bisexual birdfish that
does not exist on this world shows mental images of a
boat in danger? How can we rescue anyone when we
don't know when—"

Now.

We heard sirens over the storm, the emergency klaxon
to get all the volunteers, what used to be air raid warnings or tornado alerts. Every phone rang inside, and
Matt's cell in his pocket. Oey disappeared, now that he'd
done his job. I ran into the house. The emergency scan-
ner in the kitchen kept repeating code this and code that.
I had no idea what they all meant except the call for
volunteers to respond.

Matt was checking his cell for text messages.

"You're a volunteer fireman or EMT?"

"No, I can't be away from the practice for that long.
But they call me when an animal might be involved in
the emergency, like a house fire or a traffic accident. The
message said to stand by."

"I don't think this is any house fire or accident." The
sirens are coming from every direction now. I called my
grandmother, who knew every time someone sneezed in
Paumanok Harbor.

"All I know so far is that a cruise ship headed to Nova
Scotia with hundreds on board was off course because of
the storm, then got hit by a rogue wave and capsized.
Survivors are being brought to Montauk as the nearest
port. Only a couple of commercial fishing boats are
nearby, and they're slow and can't possibly take on
enough passengers. So all the big party boats from Montauk and the Block Island ferries are setting out. And the
Coast Guard cutters, of course. Private sea planes from
Montauk and East Hampton airports are already in the

air to shine lights and drop off more supplies. And the Air National Guard Sea Rescue helicopters from West hampton are on the way with divers. They're mobilizing everyone from Block Island to Shinnecock."

But they couldn't get there fast enough. The water was cold. The night was dark. Did they get to deploy the ship's rafts, put on life jackets? How many people were injured? Many, we had to assume.

How many sharks in the water?

Many. Oh, my God.

Susan rushed in. "We're making soup and coffee. Tons of coffee for the volunteers, too. Got extra blankets? Towels? Clothes?"

Matt helped us fill garbage bags to drop off at the police station. They wanted no one but emergency crews to drive to Montauk, clogging the only way in. They wanted Montauk Highway kept open for helicopters to land, for transport to Southampton and Stony Brook and any other hospital that could handle some of the estimated hundreds of victims suffering from hypothermia, injuries, shock. And sharks.

Matt put the TV on.

Every station had breaking news banners and dramatic music. On one, the commentator looked as if he'd just rolled out of a bar, his suit wrinkled, his tie askew. Another reporter got through makeup so fast his hairpiece kept falling over one ear. At a third, it was the weatherman who tried to juggle all the notes and memos as they got handed to him. He looked ready to cry. Streaming messages ribboned across the bottom of every screen.

The newsman Matt settled on read directly from a statement released by the Coast Guard. We knew most of it already. Then the reporter switched to first-person accounts as they came in from cell phones from the life rafts, with pictures and videos.

"Modern technology," Matt grumbled. "People taking pictures while their fellow passengers are drowning."

According to these new reports, the ship had over five hundred passengers. They first moved off course because a pod of dolphins refused to yield the usual shipping lanes. Then they got buffeted by a sudden storm. The passengers were told to don their life vests, but by the time they remembered where the things were stored—or ran to get their cameras—half of them were too seasick to follow the crew's orders. Without warning, a huge wave rose out of the water to starboard, three, maybe four times the height of the tall cruise ship. Opinions varied. There were no pictures of the wave, naturally, as everyone got tossed around as the ship heeled over under the weight of the wall of water. Half the people got washed overboard instantly. Others fell or jumped into the water as the boat tilted, one panicked woman cried into her phone. Some clung to the railings still above water. Many more, it was assumed, were trapped on board. We saw pictures of rafts floating here and there, some empty, but hard to count in the limited camera range.

The screen next flashed the cruise ship, looking like a turtle on its side. Susan started crying. Matt held us both.

"But here's the amazing thing, folks," the excited announcer said, while the screen changed. "Those dolphins stayed! And they are helping people into the rafts!"

Someone already in a lifeboat was talking, trying to hold his camera steady while the boat bobbed up and down in the waves. "There's one," he shouted, panning around to a dolphin shoving a woman toward a raft, then rising up so she fell in. Another swam with a man on its back, heading toward eager hands reaching down from a half-filled raft. All over, everywhere the camera aimed, dolphins kept people afloat and headed toward safety.

The reporter sounded as amazed as we were, watching. "We have reports of some of the filled rafts being towed toward shore! Can you believe that, folks?"

"Frankly, no," Susan whispered. "Could this be some kind of hoax?"

If so, every single station had fallen for the prank. They all showed amateur films, still shots sent from iPads and Blackberries. The pictures weren't of the best quality, but the tragedy was definitely unfolding, along with the astounding rescues.

Except some of the people being pushed to a raft had no visible dolphin under them. And one raft moving away from the half-sunk ship had no friendly sea mammal pulling it.

The commentator peered at the pictures along with the rest of us. "Those valiant dolphins must be under water."

No, they must be from another universe, where cameras don't work.

The local news on Channel 12 had pictures of the rescue operation: Montauk's motels getting ready to house hundreds, four-wheel-drive trucks nose to tail along the beach, with men in waders, wet suits, and dories ready to pull in rafts and, hopefully, survivors. We saw a view of Montauk Harbor, of boats loading up with blankets and life vests, then streaming out past the jetties. Another shot showed ambulances and fire trucks lined up facing west, ready to roll away as soon as the first rescues came in. We heard sirens in the background as Amagansett, Springs, and Paumanok Harbor emergency vehicles raced to join Montauk's crews already in position along the rows of docks in Montauk's harbor. The big parking lot near Gosman's Restaurant stayed empty, awaiting helicopter landings. More ambulances and volunteers, we learned, were being directed to the East Lake side of the harbor's inlet, near the small airport. Montauk's school, library, both churches, and the community center had their doors open for volunteers to prepare for the onslaught, hopefully, of cold and wet but uninjured passengers, the ones who didn't need ambulances and hospitals. After the medical teams were done, the volunteers would feed the people, hand out dry clothes, then ship them to the motels. There'd be room, thank goodness, in this off-season.

We also saw National Guard jeeps moving in a convoy across the Nappeague strip, hazmat units and school buses and all the Jitneys they could round up for transport, all headed east. There'd be enough help.

Uncle Roger came by to pick up our filled bags. He

was a volunteer with the fire police, heading toward Montauk in his pickup after stopping to gather more donated supplies at Town Hall. He'd drop Susan off at the firehouse to help prepare food for the rescuers and, with luck, the survivors.

After they left, Matt and I stayed on the sofa in front of the TV, changing stations to see the latest pictures. We'd be there all night, I knew, holding hands, sitting near each other, the way people did in a disaster.

The new pictures and videos came from the first private planes on the scene, small seaplanes that couldn't do much but shine their lights. The reporter had sense enough to keep quiet and let us absorb the images.

They showed helicopters arriving, dropping more inflatable rafts, then divers to help load people onto them. We saw a few brave divers in wet suits climbing aboard a vessel that could go belly-up at any moment, but coming out with injured people in their arms. They formed a chain with what we took to be crew members, getting survivors into helicopters, onto rafts, onto the first boats courageous enough to get close to the capsized ship.

More boats showed up in the distance, horns blasting, going full throttle toward the disaster. I worried they'd collide, or mow down people in the water, but Coast Guard and Marine Patrol boats circled the scene, giving directions, making order out of chaos, sweeping floodlights across the area.

And we saw the dolphins pulling rafts away, with smaller boats assigned to clear their path and take over if the dolphins showed signs of tiring. We saw other dolphins in a circle around some people floating in the water in life vests, protecting them from sharks until help arrived.

The reporter came back on. "We have a report that the manifest lists five hundred and twelve passengers aboard the *Nova Pride*, plus a staff of eighty-five. We do not know how many made it off the ship."

The station flashed clips from *The Perfect Storm*, to explain rogue waves, citing a recent rash of mid-ocean seismic activity as possible cause. That and a flurry of volcano eruptions across the globe. Maybe sunspots. We flipped to a different station that showed videos of people in the streets of Manhattan, pouring into churches, gathering in Central Park. Up and down the East River, all along the FDR, people held hands and held candles, a sign of hope in the dark night. Tragedy brought even hard-case New Yorkers together.

Matt's cell phone chimed. He listened. He swore. He said, "I understand." He swore some more. "I'm on my way."

"What—?"

"There were dogs on board."

Chapter 14

"THEY HAD FIVE DOGS LISTED: two toy breeds, a Maltese and a Yorkie, both already in rafts with their owners. And three Newfie pups, going to buyers in Nova Scotia, location unknown. The breeder has a broken arm, but she's near hysteria, refusing to leave the scene until her dogs are found. She threatened to jump back in the water if they tried to take her to shore. She'd just crated them for the night in the lower deck kennel facility. The others must have smuggled their dogs into their cabins somehow. The Coast Guard says they can't do anything until they have the people secured. No one knows if the dogs were released from their crates, or left in the lower level to drown."

I hugged Little Red so hard he tried to nip my fingers. "That poor woman. I'd be frantic, too."

"They put her on one of the Coast Guard boats for now, with a temporary splint on her arm. There's a vet in Montauk, but they want me on standby here. I am going there. I'll fetch more supplies and head out until someone tells me where to wait. I am not going to lose another dog tonight."

"Can I help?"

"I thought you don't know anything about veterinary medicine."

"No, but I can comfort a terrified dog while you work. If there are only two doctors for five dogs, you'll need an

assistant. And even if the little dogs never touched the
water, they'll be cold and frightened. If they did...." Neither of us wanted to think of a tiny dog, wet and freezing.
The Newfoundlands were built for cold weather and
water, except these were young dogs, and maybe caged,
without a chance. If they never got to shore, Matt still
needed someone at his side. "I want to help."

He had his jacket on and his keys in his hand. "Maybe
you can, if you can ask them where it hurts, like your
mother. After the bird thing, why not? Or you could get
your mother to tune in and help."

He wanted me to connect with my mother in my
head? I had enough trouble with her on the phone. I
grabbed more towels and blankets—Susan and I could
share what was left—and raced to his car. With the
brownies.

He started to back out of the driveway.

"Wait!" I unbuckled my seat belt and scrambled out
the door. "We need a bucket for fresh water."

"I'm sure they'll have bottled water at the scene."

"Not for us." I jerked my thumb to the back seat. "For
Oey."

Matt turned his head so fast I heard his neck bones
creak. "Holy shit!"

"Thit?"

"Not in my car!"

I got the pail, filled it from the garden hose and set it
on the floor of the back seat, where it wouldn't tip. Oey
changed, put his fish head in the pail and gave a few
glubs, then changed back and purred like a . . . catfish.

I had a terrible thought, among a lot of worst case
scenarios. "Oey, can you talk to the dolphins in the
water?"

"Fith?"

"No, that is, that aren't fish, but yes, the swimming
guys who are helping the people. The special ones, from
your world, I think."

"Fwiends."

Everyone—everything—from Unity was telepathic,
according to DUE. "Thank goodness. You have to tell

them not to eat the dogs if they see them. They might look like food, but they are not!"

I flashed an image of Little Red at Oey, me holding the Pomeranian.

"Fwiends?"

"Good friends. Pets. Love. I love my pet. Someone else loves the ones on the boat."

Matt kept driving, leaning forward as if that made the drive shorter. Grim-faced, he said, "I never thought the dolphins might eat the dogs, only that the sharks might."

"Oey, tell them to watch out for sharks. For the dogs, too, if they can."

"Yeth, Twee."

I got her long tail in my face while he dipped his face in the water, maybe communing with other denizens of the deep. Maybe getting a drink.

Matt's knuckles were white on the steering wheel, his jaw clenched. "Tell me that a ... a ..." He jerked one thumb toward the back seat.

"Oey."

"Isn't in charge of this rescue operation."

"Oey?" I asked the bird.

"M'ma. Fwiend."

That's what I thought. I remembered what he said about an old evil rising, for why he'd come to us. "He sent you to warn us? Or protect us?"

"Pewil."

"Yes, because it's his foe who's causing the trouble?"

"Foe?" Oey held up a bright pink toe.

Matt made a choking sound.

"His enemy?"

"N'fwend."

"No friend?"

The parrot head dipped. "Baad. Vewy baad."

And very big.

N'fwend had to be the sea serpent from my story. The one that could make itself out of water, sucking up acres of ocean to rise to the sky, swamping ships, swallowing land. The one M'ma came here to avoid, maybe, while he went through his vulnerable metamorphosis. The one I wrote as wanting to take over M'ma's realm in the otherworld. I flashed a picture in my head, from my latest book sketches: a huge column of revolving water, like a water spout, only with whirlpool eyes and huge breaking waves for scales and a mouth that roared with the wind of a tornado. Like we'd had an hour or so ago.

"He's here?"

Oey dove into my lap, wet tail and all. "Pewil!"

I tried to hug the bird part, not the fish. "No, he's not here right now. But he sank the ship, didn't he?"

"Thinking," she moaned against my shoulder. "Thip thinking. Baad."

"You tried, Oey. Your buddies in the ocean tried. And I don't know what we could have done about it if we got the warning sooner."

If I'd been in Paumanok Harbor sooner.

"Fwiends?"

I rubbed behind her neck until she cooed. "Luve."

Matt shook his head. "You mean you know what caused the rogue wave?"

No, I knew who *was* the rogue wave. This wasn't the time to explain the horrific connection between my supposed imagination and the forbidden otherworld, not when wc were on our way to see its dire handiwork. Not when any sane person would throw me out of thc car, then run me over five times. Me and Oey both.

I had a lot to think about while Matt gathered supplies from the vet clinic and his house. Had I brought this trouble here? Were all those lives lost or shattered my fault for writing fantasy novels?

No. I did not bring M'ma here. I did help him leave, so maybe N'Fwend came out of revenge, or simply thinking M'ma hadn't gone. Or maybe M'ma hadn't left and they'd moved their war here. Crap. The sea serpent I'd drawn was pure evil. I did not know how to combat such a foe.

As usual, I was in way over my head. Glub.

Instead of thinking about an enemy with no mercy, or the people in the water or maybe trapped beneath the ship, I concentrated on the dogs. I sent mental pictures to Oey of the three breeds, and encouraging murmurs to Matt. *You never kill off dogs in your stories,* I told myself. That was the rule. I kept repeating it.

We got to the outskirts of Montauk and went through several checkpoints before we were directed to the firehouse, command central for land operations. Matt and I agreed the efficiency and the cooperation of all the different organizations was impressive, especially on such short notice.

Oey disappeared when Matt parked the car. Matt sighed in resignation at the impossibility.

We were told to wait at the firehouse, since no one had any idea if the Newfoundlands were accounted for, or which landing site might receive the small dogs and their owners.

Another vet was already there, pacing. When we got introduced, it turned out Jenny was a stand-in for Montauk's local veterinarian, who was on vacation. She was short, young, and cute, a little plump, and very talkative, gesturing with her hands as they discussed hypothermia in dogs and how and where to treat it. Or else the gestures were to show off her ringless finger so Matt could see she wasn't married. Hmm.

They discussed the dogs' possible conditions, running through warm stomach lavages and hot water enemas to bring the body temperatures up to normal, and where best to treat them, on site or back at the Montauk veterinary hospital, which was no more than a well equipped trailer. I didn't get a sense of competition or one-upmanship, more like a confident but anxious study team getting ready for the test of a lifetime.

They had a lot in common, Matt and Jenny. They loved animals and the South Fork, had shared acquaintances and educations and experiences. They were a perfect match, in fact: two normal people who could share the expanding veterinary practice, settle down, and have a litter of their own. They were already smiling like old friends.

I hated her.

Rather than watch them get better acquainted, I sought more information from the command center, in the same big meeting room where I'd been to a pancake breakfast last year.

Not one survivor had reached shore yet, I learned. Not one dead body had been spotted or picked up yet, either. The feeling was that the mortality count would go up when they got into the ship, if they could before it sank. There'd be air pockets, but some passengers or crewmen had to be trapped underwater. The retrievals had to wait. First came the living.

"And the dogs," I put in.

I got a dirty look from the men waiting by the phones for information as it came in, so I moved over to the technicians setting up rows of computers.

Russ, the computer geek from Paumanok Harbor's town hall, tried to comfort me with news that the Navy had a salvage vessel on the way, and submarines coming from New London. They might try to keep the cruise ship afloat with air bags, or right it with booms. They'd find the dogs.

But in time?

He shrugged and went back to making computer connections no one else in all of Suffolk County could have made, or made so fast.

The communications specialist sent by the phone company stood over Russ' shoulder, watching in awe. "Dude, you are some effing kind of wizard."

Of course he was. He was from Paumanok Harbor.

I envied Russ his gift that helped people, that had a valuable use in the world. Unlike me. There had to be something I could do ...

I watched Russ' fingers fly over three different keyboards and remembered there was something I could do. My fingers still worked.

I tried to find a quiet place. The ladies' room was my best bet, so I pretended to wash my hands while I tried to contact Oey. I didn't get a response, but I pulled the pad I always carried out of my pocketbook and quickly sketched an idea I had. Maybe Oey could get M'ma to right the ship. Even a pod of magic dolphins couldn't do it, but a sea god who could swim and fly and start fires and grant Matt powers—he could do anything. That's how I'd write it in my book, anyway.

I stared at the pictures, willing someone to see what I saw.

Someone did, a stocky woman in full firefighting gear. "Do you really think this is the time for silly cartoons?" she snapped at me. "If you can't help, get the hell out."

I got out of the ladies' room and went looking for Matt, the silly cartoons tucked in my sweatshirt, next to my heart.

CHAPTER 15

I FOUND MATT WATCHING THE PICTURES
flickering along a blank wall of the huge room. Thanks
to Russ, all the information that came in could be ac-
cessed instantly, copied to the appropriate agency or location, and projected onto the white walls. They'd
dimmed the lights to make the various images show up
better.

One pseudo-screen held the passenger and crew lists,
alphabetized. I knew the computers could click on any
name and get the information from the cruise line's
ticket questionnaires: age, sex, next of kin, health issues,
other members of the tour group or family or friends
they traveled with, who they roomed with in what cabin,
and if they required kosher meals. Passport photos were
in the files, too, so identifying any unconscious victims
could be facilitated.

Another screen showed the local news station, with
its reporter on the Coast Guard cutter, one of the first
responders at the scene and lead agency in the rescue.

A third section of the blank wall switched from one
triage area to another, checking on progress.

As the first reports and pictures came in, we could all
see how efficiently this operation intended to proceed.

Every survivor got an identification bracelet as soon
as they reached one of the three triage stations: East
Lake Drive, West Lake Drive, and at Second House, the
big museum grounds close to the beach on Montauk

Highway, to handle anyone the dory fishermen and the surfers got into their four-wheel drives.

Thanks to Russ and the latest telecom technology, the names and bracelet numbers, conditions on arrival, means of transport and destination, were all immediately sent to the firehouse for data entry and posting on the PowerPoint screen. The names on the passenger list projection screen changed color from red to black when they got their bracelets and numbers. The crew changed from blue to green. The information also got embedded into bar codes on the bracelets that anyone with a smart phone could read. Russ had enough 'puters, printers, and trusted techs at each spot to get it right.

Paumanok Harbor had also sent a bunch of the truth-seers who kept checking the facts, lest people be too disoriented to remember their names. Which led to one embarrassing scene, right on camera, where a guy had to admit to his wife that he had a false identity, and another wife in New Jersey.

"How'd you know?" the guy demanded of Judge Chemlecki, wanting to pop the silver-haired jurist on the jaw.

The judge shrugged. "I must have seen you before. Have you ever been in court?"

The bigamist didn't answer, just hurried after his furious wife.

"That's going to throw off the records," one of the techs commented. "I bet they don't stay in the same motel room we've assigned them."

But they were all right, which was what mattered for now, stamped, sealed, and sent on their way for dry clothes and hot food before boarding the buses.

Others weren't as lucky. We saw stretchers carried to the waiting ambulances, and one helicopter didn't stop at the landing area, just kept going to the next hospital in line. The copilot radioed in what identification he had, and someone at the communications center read back ID numbers to be handwritten on each victim's arm in permanent marker. Those names and numbers got entered into all the computer bases.

The easternmost towns on Long Island were not going to misplace a survivor, not going to look as inept as other rescues we'd all seen. Un-uh.

They weren't going to keep loved ones or the world waiting for news, either. Every scrap of information we had got sent to news stations and the cruise company's hot lines and a website established minutes ago. A direct feed to the high school in East Hampton got set up for newscasters, so we did not have a thousand TV crews and trucks to contend with in the crowded Montauk facilities. One crew got assigned to each location, by lot, to share with the others. A special phone to the cruise line stayed open, waiting ominously for reports of fatalities, so the mother company could notify the families before the names got changed to another color for all to see. One name got highlighted in yellow. Royce's cherished emeritus, someone whispered to me.

I manned a different telephone for an hour or so, reassuring families that yes, survivors were coming in, no, no fatalities reported yet, and telling them how to access the computer information and twitter feeds as they got posted. No, they would not be permitted to enter Montauk.

Someone had me make a recording, so the ladies' fire auxiliary could be freed for other tasks than answering frantic calls.

The scores of official phones kept ringing, with reports from the field, from the scene, from the air. Everything got recorded, transmitted, sent over speakerphones.

I refused to be interviewed by the one reporter and cameraman assigned to the firehouse. "I'm with him." I pointed toward Matt. "He's waiting to tend to some dogs on the ship."

The reporter rushed to get a new story angle, since she couldn't speak with the survivors or the rescuers. All the techies and big shots were too busy for her, and too boring. Nothing like a handsome hero vet to pique a newswoman's interest. Except Matt had no heartwarming story to tell. "We're waiting," was all he said, before going back to watching the screens. The reporter went to talk to the next best looking guy in the place, Walter, the pharmacist from Paumanok Harbor. His job was to check medical histories when survivors got to the triage area, to warn the EMTs and doctors on site of drug interactions. He told her that almost every private doctor or nurse—retired or active—on the South Fork had shown up in Montauk or at the hospital, or the two emergency clinics where minor cuts, bruises, and sprains could be attended. Then he told her she'd be more help bringing water or coffee to the people at the computers who hadn't stopped working for ten minutes. She went off in a huff. Matt and I carried cases of water to hand out.

The statistics came faster now, as bigger boats came in with larger numbers of passengers. Montauk's Harbor Police waited at the mouth of the inlet to direct them to alternate drop-off sites to ease congestion. EMTs, ambulances, and the computer guys they were partnered with raced from dock to dock.

Now that more boats and divers were in the water near the *Nova Pride*, the helicopters concentrated on getting the worst injured to emergency rooms. No one was brought to the temporary morgue set up on the soccer field near the center of town.

A constant stream of rescues got reported from the beach, along with dolphin sightings, as kayakers and surfers joined the dorymen to bring the dolphin-towed rafts up to the beach, then load the people into the waiting trucks. As soon as one pickup or SUV left to transport, another moved over to take its place, up and down the beach. Huge flatbeds from the lumber companies stood nearby to carry the rafts back to the harbor, to go back out with the next empty boats.

Some of the volunteers showed up for coffee and sandwiches before returning to their posts. I handed out sodas and listened to the news. It was all good, all working like clockwork, making headway on the manifests of passengers and crew. More than half the names on the big screen were in black now, safe on land. A lot of the crew was accounted for, but the uninjured ship's officers stayed on the scene to help since they knew the ship better than the rescuers.

Matt's cell phone rang. We both jumped, edgy from the waiting. It was one of Montauk's fire captains, at the communications center, on a three-way call with the other vet.

The Yorkie and its people were landing. Since Jenny was the local vet—or her stand-in, anyway—and first on the scene, she got to take the first run.

She called back in an hour. She'd caught the Maltese, too, at the same location. She had both dogs warm, dry, and sedated at her facilities for the night, to make sure neither contracted pneumonia. The owners were at a bed and breakfast within walking distance. "I'll stay here. You wait for the Newfies."

Who might not be found, ever. Matt would be devastated; I could see it on his face. I hated her more for having two relatively unscathed dogs to tend.

No more calls came in. Matt and I found bunks in the big empty concrete space where the fire trucks were usually parked. Cots had been set up for the volunteers to take shifts. We chose two cots next to each other and pulled them closer still so we could whisper and hold hands, trying to reassure each other that there was still hope.

Matt fell asleep in minutes after the long day and tense night. I couldn't. My body was exhausted; my mind wouldn't shut down. Besides, there was too much light, too much snoring, too much coming and going as men and women came in for an hour's rest, and too much noise from the TVs on the upper level. I kept hearing the announcements, then cheers when another boatload arrived on the screen, when twelve more names changed to black, then eight when another raft came through the surf.

A dragger captain came in with his mate to get a quick nap before another run. They were still laughing about the last rescue they'd made when they had to argue with a guy in the water, with no life jacket. He didn't want to leave the dolphin that had kept him afloat for hours. It was the best experience of the guy's life, he swore, on top of the worst experience of his life.

"But the ship ain't gone down yet?" a sleepy voice from nearby asked.

"Nope. No idea why, neither. No one can figure it, but it's giving the divers and the captain of the ship time to search what they can. Unmanned subs and experts'll be here in the morning to give us a hundred reasons. I say it's the power of prayer."

I prayed it was M'ma.

Later someone whispered that the president had been on TV, praising Montauk and its neighbors for the fine job they were doing. We should all stand tall, he said, tall and proud. I curled up in a ball on my cot, mortified I might have had a hand in the catastrophe.

At least there were still no fatalities.

But no black dogs, either.

Chapter 16

"WE'RE GETTING YOUR DOGS."

The com-tech asked the caller to hold, then repeat when he was on speakerphone.

"Right. This is Cap'n Gino on the *Dorothy Mac*. They're bringing me three black dogs on a Zodiac, about ten minutes off, but the call said they lost the parrot."

"What parrot?" I recognized Russ's voice, sounding dismayed. "We have no parrot in our manifest data."

"I don't give a rat's ass about your manifest destiny. You want the dogs or not?"

Tempers got short, after a night without rest.

"Yes!" Matt and I shouted.

"Then you should thank the fucking parrot. They said the damn thing was yelling about pastry at the top of its lungs down in the cargo area, what was half full of water. The scuba guys would never have spotted the black pups on top of some crates in the corner, but for the screeching. Not much light except some weird emergency flares or something down there to help them see survivors. No sound from the dogs."

"Pastries?"

"They couldn't make it out so good. Sounded like pethtry to them. Figured the bird didn't have a big vocabulary, maybe didn't speak English, maybe he was hungry. Who knows? Then more lights came on so they could follow the sound. They figure the parrot could open the cages. You ever seen the beak on those things?

Take your finger right off. But how the pups got on top of the crates, out of the water, is anyone's guess. Anyway, they got the dogs out—took three of the guys to carry 'em—but the bird took off. Then they saw it fall into the ocean. Still yammering about pastries. Or pests."

Pets, Tree. Tree's pets. *You did good, Oey. Real good.* I don't know if he heard me. But I sent hugs and kisses across the mental void, with a picture of the birdfish nestled in willow branches. I added fireflies to the mind picture in thanks to the lantern beetles that must have lit the dark ship so the missing passengers could be found and brought to safety. Maybe they kept the dogs warm, too. Uh-oh.

"There were no fires, were there?"

"Hell, no, or we'd all have to back off and the divers'd have to evacuate."

"Do you know the dogs' conditions, Captain? This is Dr. Matt, from Paumanok Harbor."

"Sorry, Doc, word is not good. Not moving, cold to touch. They must have been in the water five or six hours. The guys in the raft think they're breathing, but barely. I've got some survival blankets still left to wrap them in. A couple of hand heaters. Not much else."

"Any hot water? Even a warm thermos to tuck under them? Can you lay them over the engine hatch or something?"

"I can try, Doc, but I've got half my quota of survivors on board in the cabin. More coming. They'll need all the hot coffee my galley can churn out."

"Do the best you can. What's your ETA?"

We could hear the captain shout to someone onboard. Then he came back. "Sorry. Dumbass female thought she'd climb up to the wheelhouse. In high heels. Not on my boat. 'Specially not tonight. Bad luck altogether. Not that we ain't had enough."

"Your ETA, Gino, please. The dogs need help fast if they've stopped shivering, stopped moving."

"Sorry, Doc. I've got two different rafts headed my way, and no one else near except a useless hotshot in a cigarette boat. Most of the others are still trolling for survivors or towing rafts. I can't leave until my latest batch are all loaded and secured. It goes slow with the inflatables, you gotta understand. Can't chance dropping one of the drifters back in the drink." He cursed. "Or convince some dipshit female to take her high heels off before she puts one through the rubber."

"What about the cigarette boat? Could he bring in the dogs?"

"Good idea. Rich asshole's not doing much of anything else but shining his light around. I'll get him on the horn."

Two minutes later Gino came back on the phone. "It's a go, Doc. We're rendezvousing with the rafts in three minutes. Tourist named Francis Costain says he'll get those dogs back quicker'n I ever could, passengers or not. Fifteen minutes, tops, once he clears this area in case we missed anyone in the water. He says to get clearance for him to dock at the Coast Guard station on Star Island. He's got to head that way anyway, toward the yacht club, 'cause he'll be out of gas by then."

"I'm on it," Russ said.

"Hey, do you think I can give him the woman, too?"

"Is she injured? Will she need an ambulance waiting?"

"Hell, no, not unless she makes another heel mark on my deck. The broad never got a fingernail chipped. She's just a pain in the ass. Tina, the lounge singer. Grabbed a life jacket and hopped right into the first raft. Now she's pissed she had to wait so long to be picked up while they went after people in the water first or the injured. She's ready to sue everyone in sight. I figure the hotdog who owns a half-million-dollar cigarette boat can afford her better'n I can."

Russ laughed. "I've got a Martina D'Angelo on my crew list as an entertainer. Get me confirmation and some details so I can track her on the computer, and I'll get her off your hands."

"You're doing good for a lubber, kid."

"And you're doing great for a bub, Gino," Russ said, using the local term for a native or near native, old-time seaman. "Thanks."

*   *   *

Susan had sent clean clothes for me with her father's last trip to drop off donated supplies and more soup. Bless her heart, she'd included a toothbrush, too. Uncle Roger reported the dogs at home were fine, except Little Red peed on my bed for being left alone so long. And we'd given away all our extra blankets.

I'd deal with it later. I changed and washed up as best I could while Matt was on the phone with the Coast Guard. They weren't accepting survivors, not with almost all hands out on the water. They only had a skeleton crew and two senior citizens from the Coast Guard auxiliary on base, but they'd take the dogs, gladly. And the lounge singer. Especially the lounge singer.

They promised to get pots of water heating, the thermostat turned up, and a bed turned down for Miss D'Angelo. And they were cooking bacon and eggs, okay?

That sounded like heaven to me, the vegetarian. The brownies were a long-ago memory.

"Good luck, Doc," all the dog lovers in the firehouse called after us.

"Don't let them be our first fatalities," someone else shouted.

One of Russ' crew handed us a slip of paper with the breeder's name and info before we left. Peg Winters, forty-two, divorced, professional dog breeder and trainer from the Bronx, traveling with three pedigreed Newfoundland dogs, age six months, had gone into shock. That time she couldn't refuse to be airlifted to Southampton Hospital. The telecom operator said he'd get word to her as soon as possible, with the doc's cell number. "Okay?"

"Fine. And tell her she can call and one of the returning ambulances can fetch her back to Paumanok Harbor if she's released tonight. This morning," he corrected, seeing the first hint of color in the sky. "Or I'll have my receptionist go pick her up later. She can stay at my place as long as she and the dogs need."

"Damn nice of you, Doc."

Yeah, I thought so, too. There he was, dead tired, in yesterday's clothes with yesterday's beard, ready to face another long, hard fight to save three drowned puppies, and he still cared about their owner. Damn nice.

He said, "Anyone who cares that much about her animals deserves to be near them. They'll all recover better that way."

"Got it. Oh, yeah, the dogs' names are Maggie, Molly, and Moses. They've got paragraph-long pedigree names, but that's what Mrs. Winters calls them. Moses was her grandfather's name, from what she told the crew on the cutter between crying jags."

"Good to know. They'll respond better to their names, too."

We left. The fire captain got us an escort, with sirens, even, now that the number of rescues had slowed down to a trickle. So we got through the checkpoints with no trouble, sped across the causeway to Star Island and pulled up at the big white building with time enough to spare for breakfast.

Matt ate standing up. We all did, because the three young guardsmen, Sean, Luther, and Ramon, had laid a blue tarp across the large dining room tables shoved together, then made mounds of blankets on them.

"They're warm from the clothes dryer," Ramon, who looked like he'd just graduated from high school said. "With more waiting."

"Great thinking," Matt said, taking off his sweatshirt. I did, too, already sweating in the heat they'd turned up.

Another of the young men in uniform, Luther, had his foot in a cast, and the third, Sean, said he was on sick leave due to Lyme disease, but he'd come in anyway to help man the station. The senior citizen couple introduced themselves as the Dwyers. They had a yellow lab themselves, so they were eager to help.

In minutes, it seemed, the sleek black-hulled speedboat tore through the harbor, its air horn blaring. The captain had no concern about making a wake; he had the harbor patrol boat right beside him, bullhorn blaring orders to other boats to get out of the way, rescue in progress.

The guardsmen had the boat tied to the dock in seconds. The healthy one, Ramon, jumped down and started

helping the captain, who told us to call him Frankie, un-
buckle the dogs from the leather bench seats.

"Heated, don't you know," Frankie said, handing the
first dog up to Sean, who looked too weak from the
Lyme disease to carry anything heavier than a cell phone,
but he managed. "And didn't want them bouncing
around on the deck."

A redhead next to him snapped out: "But it was okay
that I had nothing to hang on to."

"You hung on to me real good, sugar," said Frankie,
grinning at her. He handed the second dog to Matt, since
Luther had to lean on one crutch.

Ramon handed me the last dog. I almost staggered
under the weight—I refused to call it dead weight—of
the limp, sodden bundle in my arms. The dog must weigh
fifty or sixty pounds, and these were puppies! I couldn't
feel any sign of life before the first seaman, Ramon,
jumped out of the low boat and took the animal from me.

"What about me?" the redhead in her black spandex
dress complained.

"I've got you, sugar," the middle-aged boat owner
purred as he handed her up to the dock, then her high-
heeled slingbacks, then an enormous leather purse.
Frankie had a gold chain around his neck that could
have doubled as an anchor cable, a pinky ring that glittered like the last star in the morning sky, and coal-black
hair from Grecian Formula.

The elderly volunteer and Luther both stepped forward to take Tina's hand, but Mrs. Dwyer got there first.
She told her husband to take the purse while Tina put on
her shoes.

Mrs. Dwyer had Tina's ID bracelet all printed out.
"You need to wear this, miss. So they know where you
are and your condition. I'm to call your arrival in to the
firehouse."

I could see she felt important, as if fixing a paper
bracelet on a prima donna was worth giving up a night's
sleep.

Tina looked at Matt, who ignored her entirely, hurrying after the two Coasties with their dogs. She noted the

age of the young men and the weathered Mr. Dwyer. Then she looked back at the cigarette boat and its owner. She flashed him a million-dollar smile, or maybe a half million, if that's what the boat cost. "Do you think I can stay with you tonight, Frankie?" She gave a helpless hand wave at her high heels and the boards under them. "I'll only get in the way here."

"Wouldn't have it any other way, doll."

The auxiliary oldster got to help Tina back down to the low boat. I was afraid he'd have a heart attack. Luther hobbled around getting the lines untied and Frankie waved good-bye, a wide smile on his bronzed face.

Another match made in heaven.

The young men and Matt had the dogs on the tables, wrapped in warm blankets while Matt listened to their heartbeats, checked their pulses, looked in their mouths, felt their stomachs, and pulled their eyelids open. He didn't say anything. I was afraid to ask.

He took thermometers out of his tote bag, and a small jar. "We need to take their temperatures before we go any further."

He handed me a thermometer.

"Um . . ."

"No, you don't put it under its tongue, Willy. Shove it up its ass, but gently."

Oh, my. Luckily, Mrs. Dwyer took over. "I had four children, dear. I know what to do. You hold the tail up."

We got it done and Matt looked relieved. "They're not beyond help. No telling if they warmed up in the boats, or if there will be permanent damage from lack of circulation to their brains. But we have something to work with."

He took out lengths of rubber tubing.

Lord, were we going to have to do hot water enemas like he and Jenny discussed? I wasn't any hothouse flower like the Tinas of the world, but I didn't know if my stomach could take that.

Thank goodness I didn't have to find out. Matt slipped nooses of the tubing over each muzzle.

"But they're not moving!"

"I know, but they'll be in pain when the blood flows back into their limbs, like when you get pins and needles. We're strangers and they won't understand we're trying to help. Even the gentlest dog can react badly." He gave each a shot of antibiotic. "As a precaution. You never know what was in the water with them."

He held out three plastic pouches for Sean to run under hot water at the kitchen sink while he started IV lines. "It's only saline, but it'll help. Anyone got a shaver so I can get down to bare skin to find a vein?"

Ramon ran to get his. He brought back a blow dryer, too. Mr. Dwyer took that and started working on whichever dog Matt wasn't handling.

Matt had me hold the paw while he taped the needle in place on the first dog's front leg. I read the tag on the leather collar while he worked and Luther, on one crutch, held the dog steady, just in case it woke up. Mr. Dwyer kept the blow dryer going and Mrs. Dwyer kept rubbing the other two with heated towels.

"This one is Mollie," I told them. "She looks the smallest."

"And weakest and coldest. That's why I started on her first."

Next came Maggie. I thought I heard a whimper when the needle went in. "Good girl. We're making you better. You'll see. Dr. Matt won't let you get pneumonia like that fou-fou Yorkie."

"That's it, Willy. Keep talking. Channel your mother for me."

I gave him a sour look, while the Dwyers and the guardsmen appeared curious. "My mother has a way with dogs, that's all. She's written books about it."

And she was in Florida. Not in my head.

Everyone went back to work. Rubbing, talking, starting the IVs, holding the saline pouches elevated until Ramon dragged in two floor lamps and a clothes tree. We put baggies of hot—not boiling water—on bare skin where we could find it on the shaggy animals. They looked like bearskin rugs for all the life in them. But we had hope.

The biggest pup was Moses, and he opened one eye when I talked to him. "He's going to make it!"

"They all are."

Except Mollie didn't seem to be warming up like the others. Matt had packed for the emergency and had a longer length of thicker tubing. "I'm going to have to fill her stomach with warm water. She's going to bring it back up."

The seamen in their uniforms stepped back. I had to step forward, with my clean clothes and buckets and towels, to hold her up. I felt bad. Poor Mollie almost drowned, and might have swallowed half an ocean for all we knew. Now she had a tube down her throat filling her up with more water.

She brought it up, all right, and peed, too. That I was used to, from Little Red, but not the gallons.

"It's a good sign. The kidneys are working."

"Here, miss, I'll take over."

I was astounded to see Frankie back, coming to help. We all looked around for Tina, who'd be as out of place here as an angora cat.

Frankie laughed. "I've got her all right and tight at my rooms at the Yacht Club. She'll be in the Jacuzzi for another hour, I'd guess. That'll warm her up enough to call down to the boutique. They're ready to bring her some clothes to choose from, on my tab."

"That's really generous of you, Mr., er, Frankie."

"Oh, I put a limit on the credit card, but the girl could have died in that wild storm. She deserves some pretty things, doesn't she? 'Sides, I'm betting she'll be real grateful."

He winked. I couldn't help laughing, despite myself. Here was this middle-aged Lothario, not making the least effort to conceal his true persona, unlike me, the Visualizer. I was even afraid to mention Paumanok Harbor.

I didn't have to. Frankie only wanted to know about the dogs. "These guys valuable, Doc?"

"Very, I'd guess. They're good-looking pups from what I can see, excellent conformation. If someone is paying to have them delivered from New York to Nova

Scotia by luxury liner, rather than ship them in the cargo
hold of an airplane, you can bet they're paying plenty."

"Like how much?" Frankie persisted.

"Dogs like this? It depends on the parents and the
show quality and the temperament of course. I'm no
judge, but I'd guess four, five thousand. Maybe more for
the male, for stud purposes."

He kept stroking poor Mollie, who was having her
temperature taken again. Matt seemed pleased. He left
her with Frankie and rechecked Moses and Maggie. Now
that they were almost dried, I could see how big the boy
dog was, far larger than his sisters. I was happy I hadn't
had to carry him. By the time he reached a year, no one
could. Matt said he wouldn't reach his full growth until
he was two, at least.

He moved some, then tried to lick Matt. "There's the
boy. What a good dog. I'll bet you don't need this anymore." He took the muzzle noose away. Moses shook his
head, sending drool and sandy salt water flying. He tried
to crawl to the edge of the table, closer to Matt.

"I'm right here, big guy, but you need to warm up a
little more, then we can take you to my house. I'll build
you a fire, and you guys can share a mattress on the
floor."

He looked over at me. "The kennels have cold cement
floors and I've got a couple of sick dogs there. I'll need
to watch them for hours anyway. Then Mrs. Winters can
take over if she's up to it."

I offered to help, too, and the Dwyers gave their
phone number. Frankie said he'd be over in a flash, or
he'd hire a dog sitter.

Now Maggie started to stir and we all cheered. Moses
whimpered when Matt left, but I tried to console him.
"You'll have a good home of your own soon, with people
who wanted you badly enough to pay more than a used
car for you." Not that money meant a good home, but it
beat eating the cheapest brand of dog food and sleeping
outside. "I bet you're hungry, too. Big guys like you must
eat three times a day."

"We'll wait till we get them back to the house, to

make sure their stomachs can handle it. You can give these two a sip of water, to see."

Frankie wouldn't leave little—relatively little—Mollie. "Come on, sugar. You can make it. Then Uncle Frankie can take you home. You'll like Westchester way better than Nova Scotia, won't you? And riding in the boat, with the wind in your hair? It's black, so you'll match. We'll be hot stuff, you'll see. And I can trade in the Porsche for a Land Rover, so you'll have more room."

I didn't have the heart to tell him a lot of dogs got seasick. Hell, I got seasick. Or that a Newfoundland loved the snow and cold, and did poorly in the heat. I felt I did have to remind him that the dogs were all sold.

He laughed. "Not if I offer double. I saved this little girl. I get a chance to keep her."

Kind of like Tina.

Matt said, "I'll talk to Mrs. Winters when she's well enough. I'll give her your number and you can talk. But you know the dog might be damaged, her brain affected."

"Yeah, well she still needs a good home, doesn't she? And I can afford vet bills and doggie day care if she needs it. 'Sides, maybe the buyers won't want her now."

"Maybe. Especially if they were counting on showing her."

Mrs. Dwyer asked, "What about Miss D'Angelo?"

"Who? Oh, Tina? They come and go. But a dog . . ." He sighed. "I had a Newfie when I was a kid. Bigger'n I was in all the pictures. I gotta have this dog."

I figured Frankie usually got whatever he wanted, but he did seem to love the dog, so maybe it wouldn't be a bad idea.

Then he tried to pay Matt, who got kind of offended and said there'd be no charge to anyone.

"What about your time and efforts, Doc? They would have died without you."

"Everyone gave their all tonight. No one expects to be paid."

"Yeah, I saw that. But I can afford more than most. How about a donation?"

"Fine, and much appreciated. The volunteer fire departments always need money. The boatman's association, to help pay for all the gas those guys used. There must be some fund in Montauk to help pay for all the food and stuff the survivors and the volunteers ate. Closer to us, they're trying to establish a horse ranch in Paumanok Harbor. Jobs for the local kids, homes for wild ponies from overpopulated Federal lands."

"And a camp for handicapped children," I put in.

Frankie nodded, one hand rubbing Mollie's ear. "Sounds good. I went to the horse show they held to make money for that ranch. Hey, weren't you the woman the cowboy dedicated his show to?"

"Uh . . . not quite."

"Sure you are. I never forget a pretty woman, even when she's dressed like something the cat dragged in."

I tried to finger comb my hair, uselessly.

"That was some night, wasn't it? Except the end. We got herded out of the VIP tent faster than those border collies herded the sheep."

"There was a storm coming. They had to get everyone out of the open."

"It's a weird place, Paumanok Harbor, but I'm happy to contribute, if you put in a good word with the Winters woman for me."

I promised to add my recommendation to Matt's, who declared us ready to roll once he started the SUV and turned the heater on high. He wanted all the dogs, especially Mollie, back near the clinic in case they needed X-rays for broken bones or internal injuries, now that they were stable.

Everyone helped carry the dogs, the blankets—maybe I could borrow one—and their good wishes out to the parking lot. I hugged the Dwyers and Frankie and each of the young men, and Matt for good measure and because I wanted to.

Chapter 17

WE WENT HOME, UNDER ESCORT AGAIN.
This time I drove while Matt sat in the back with
all three of the dogs, keeping them from sliding or loos-
ening their blankets. I tried to drive carefully, avoiding
bumps, but the Paumanok Harbor cop car ahead of us
went faster than I was used to, and I drove a car bigger
than I was used to.

Mollie stayed lethargic, which I knew worried Matt,
but the others showed signs of improvement. Moses put
one leg on top of Matt's, to maintain contact with his
new hero. If love and caring could make them all better,
they'd be running alongside the car.

Or flying beside it, like Oey. I opened the window. "No,
get in, get down. Don't let anyone see you. Maybe they'll
forget about the mystery bird." Sure, when the report of
a parrot had gone out over the speakerphone in hearing
of the whole command center. At least they thought she'd
drowned.

I shut the window quickly to keep the heat in the car
for the dogs. Then I wondered if I'd needed to bother
opening it. Who knew if Oey could teleport through
glass?

She perched on the back of the front passenger seat
looking at the dogs, rotating her head from side to side,
then almost upside down, peering between the front
seats. I shoved her over when I got a whiff of the fish tail
near my face.

"Dwowned fwends good, Twee?"

"Drowned friends very good, Oey. Getting better. Thank you."

"Peth?"

"Not mine, but someone's, thanks to you."

I wanted to know how she did it, if the lantern beetles really had shown up, and if we were still in danger from N'fwend. Did she have any healing power like others of her kind? Could she see ahead if the puppies had long-lasting damage?

I guess all the questions floating in my brain confused her. Oey disappeared. Through the closed window, which answered one question anyway.

"I didn't see that," Matt said from the backseat.

"Good. Tell the dogs they didn't either, in case the CIA wants to interrogate them."

"I think they saw it before."

So did I. Funny, I no longer had palpitations every time I saw the marvel that was Oey. She—I had trouble relating to the masculine, fishy side of the creature—was an extraordinary, beautiful, astounding creature. I was honored to share the wonder of her, for that's what she was, a marvel from another world. Now I wished she would go away and take all the rest of that world with her: the dolphins, the beetles, the sea monster that ate ships. I'd been proud of the honors I got from my writing, like my prized GRABYA award, the best of Graphic Arts Books for Young Adults. I didn't need to be singled out for more, especially when this blessing carried the weight of two separate worlds.

They should stay separate. I silently bid Oey farewell. I'd miss her, but she could live on here in my books. Maybe we'd win another award.

When we got to Matt's house and the veterinary hospital, the police officer—one I did not know, but he drove like a maniac—got out of his car to help carry the dogs. We brought them into Matt's living room, a pleasant, masculine place where the furniture looked more comfortable than elegant. It was like him, good quality, without a lot of flash and fanfare. I saw stacks of magazines near the recliner and three pairs of shoes near the front door, but no bachelor-type litter, no empty beer cans or dirty dishes. His house looked cleaner than mine. He must have a housekeeper.

Matt raised the hall thermostat, then put down newspapers and extra blankets in one corner of the room, explaining that he had no crate big enough for the super-sized pups and he didn't want to separate them, which would stress them further. Their almost normal body heat would help them, too, if they slept close to each other. He and the policeman went out to the clinic to fetch bowls, baby gates to make a rough enclosure, more towels and blankets, and a forty-pound bag of special puppy food. I'd hate to think how much they'd eat when they were healthy.

The dogs lay quietly where we put them, only Moses lifting his big head to follow Matt's movement out the door. He sighed, then put his head down on his paws.

"He'll be back," I promised. I sat on the floor with them, stroking Mollie, because she seemed the neediest. Maggie tried to crawl into my lap, so I petted her, too. Moses wasn't interested.

After the cop left, I meant to stay a minute or two until Matt got everyone settled. The girl dogs seemed too bewildered and exhausted to do more than curl up on the blankets, piled together like a Turkish rug bazaar or a stuffed animal display in a sloppy toy store. Even Moses seemed to understand where he was supposed to stay, not follow Matt around. Fluffed up by the hair dryer, they looked even bigger, and a whole lot more adorable. I could see why people loved the huge, goofy, drooly breed.

Matt listened to their chests again, nodded his approval. No rales, no rattles, no signs of fluid in their lungs, he told me. They weren't out of danger yet, though. He'd keep checking for fevers, coughs, discharge from nose or eyes. Tomorrow, if they stayed lethargic or had no appetite, he'd do more thorough exams at the clinic. He made a fire in the stone hearth, not because the house had a chill—it didn't—but because he'd promised.

When he had the pups and the gates arranged to his satisfaction, he came to sit beside me on the couch where I sat watching. He pulled a slipcover tighter as if I hadn't noticed the worn spots on the sofa's arms.

"Coffee?"

"The last thing I need is more caffeine, unless you want me to stay while you take a nap."

"No, I had a good sleep on that cot at the firehouse. I'm used to being up nights for emergencies, anyway."

I knew I should go, but I felt too comfortable, relaxed for the first time in days, it seemed. I nodded toward the sleeping puppies. "They sure are cute."

"They sure are lucky you could talk to Oey."

Now I wasn't quite so relaxed. I didn't want to talk to him about it, not yet. How could I, until I figured things out better for myself? Besides, I wasn't ready to take the blame, to see his easy camaraderie turn to distrust like it did for everyone else in town.

He sensed my withdrawal and got up. "I'll change my clothes, wash up, and be right back so you can get some rest in your own bed. And a shower."

Which reminded me of my own disgusting condition. I jumped up. "Your poor couch."

He smiled and pushed me back down. "The couch is the least of my problems as far as you are concerned."

One of the dogs started snoring. Or was that me?

I woke up to hear a car door slam, then a screen door slam.

Melissa walked in and said, "You're late. I have an office full of patients and a hundred phone— Shit."

Matt was picking up soiled papers. "Yeah, Sick dogs do that."

She meant me.

I was sprawled on the sofa, a light blanket over me. Matt must have taken off my shoes, too. By the sunlight streaming in through the open door, and by Melissa's presence denoting office hours, I guess it was past nine AM. I'd slept for three whole hours. Not enough to face

Matt's skunk-haired niece. I ignored her and spoke to Matt. "Good morning. How are the dogs?"

"They are all going to make it. Their mental conditions and coordination are still uncertain. They're wobbly, but chowing down on the food, even Mollie. I can take them back to the hospital for the morning so no one has to stay here. The staff will spoil them rotten."

Not all the staff, by Melissa's grimace, which matched her black lipstick and nail polish. "So what should I tell the clients?"

"All of them have to be aware of the emergency last night. Tell them I'm sorry, and I'll get to them soon. If they cannot wait, reschedule for later, or tomorrow."

"That's Saturday. We only work half days."

Even Matt noticed the petulance in his niece's voice. He gave her a sharp look. "We take care of the patients, no matter when."

How awkward to witness a family argument. How lovely that Matt finally put the bitch in her place. I turned to the TV set, which must have been on all along, still showing the clips from the disaster. I'd slept through that? In Manhattan, traffic sounds and sirens were a lullaby to me. At my mother's, the crickets and tree toads kept me awake.

I'd seen most of the same pictures last night. "Any new news about the rescue?"

Melissa hung around, waiting to see if I left, I'd bet. She didn't answer, although she must have heard everything in the waiting room. If she cared. She had dark rings under her eyes so maybe she'd been up all night, too, volunteering. Yeah, and fish could fly.

Some of them could.

Matt had been watching since we got back here. "Amazingly enough, there's only one person unaccounted for, an elderly gentleman from England. Dozens more are in critical condition in various hospitals, but expected to survive. Out of almost six hundred persons on board, that's fantastic."

Except for the badly injured and the one still missing.

How long could an old man survive in the cold water? Not long. One death was one too many for my conscience, especially a psychic, as I suspected.

"A lot of the rest are on their way home this morning, courtesy of the cruise line that hired buses and limos to drive them. A few passengers are staying on in the motels to see if any of their luggage can be salvaged, again at the ship company's expense. The lingerers seem to be enjoying the celebrity, from all the interviews they're giving. A bunch decided to take their vacations in the Hamptons instead of hurrying home. The liner's largesse extends till Monday."

The TV showed an impromptu breakfast buffet for survivors and volunteers in the great hall at the Montauk Manor. The Montauk Bake Shoppe, the announcer reported, had provided the pastries.

Another shot had the Red Cross unloading enough food and supplies to feed six times the number of survivors. They weren't missing a chance for good publicity with the nation's spotlight on the miraculous recovery.

Matt had all the soiled newspapers stuffed in a black garbage bag; he had to wrestle Moses for possession of it. He laughed, which after last night sounded like heaven to me.

He pointed to the next graphic, a picture of the capsized *Nova Pride* from one of the motels along Montauk's beachfront. I hadn't realized the ship tipped over so close to shore. That explained the quick response, the lack of vast fatalities.

"They think they know why the ship didn't sink, permitting the rescue squads to get everyone out. It seems the huge wave had pulled sand and mud up from the bottom, at tremendous force, enough to form a shelf for the ship to rest on."

The commentator was explaining, for perhaps the tenth time, he had it down so pat, that the authorities feared the sand might shift with the next storm, so they had plans to right the *Nova Pride* as soon as possible. For now, he said, everyone is rejoicing. That new reef saved hundreds of lives.

People believed what they needed to believe. A reef forming in an hour? Holding up an umpteen-ton ocean liner? Or maybe they believed the cruise ship, already off course, just happened to land on a permanent underwater mountain no one knew about. In this era of topographical mapping from outer space? In one of the busiest fishing areas on the East Coast? They needed an explanation, so they invented one their minds could comprehend.

I drew a picture in my head, and thought hard about it, if anyone was listening. *Thank you, Oey, for getting M'ma's friends to build a platform.*

Matt turned off the TV and asked Melissa and me to help bring the dogs over to the clinic. He lifted Moses and I took Mollie, who still felt limp to me. And still felt heavy.

Melissa took one look at Maggie and backed away. "She's got shit all over her ass. And she must have stepped in it, too."

"Yeah, that's why I'm taking them over. They need baths and grooming. No dog likes to be soiled. I gave them all something to settle their stomachs from the trauma and the salt water, but the meds take time to kick in. I added some rice to their breakfast, too."

He put Moses down and wrapped Maggie in a blanket, then picked her up.

I'd put Mollie down while they quarreled. I hadn't noticed the mess, but now the smell got to me. I didn't bother with a blanket. My clothes already needed to be burned. "Could we get going? I think these things grow by the minute."

"I'm not carrying any sack of dog poop either. I answer phones and work the computer. That's it."

Poor Matt must have been up all night checking the pups, and now he had to hold office hours, with this gorgon of a geek. I volunteered again. "I can come back in a while if you need help with them."

Melissa sneered, but Matt said he'd call me if he ran into problems. Moses trotted right by his side, while he carried Mollie, whose tongue lolled out of her mouth as if she were too exhausted to keep it in. But none of the dogs shivered, and their temperatures were normal, he said. I thought about setting Maggie down before my out-of-shape arms and thighs gave out and I dropped her, but a kennel man hurried out the clinic's back door to help, and one of the vet techs took Mollie from Matt. Another young man went to the house to get the garbage bag into the hospital's dumpster.

He wouldn't need me. Which didn't make me as happy as it ought to.

Before he got busy in the clinic, I said I'd call our news in to the firehouse in Montauk. The volunteers deserved to hear that the dogs were recovering.

Melissa almost slammed the clinic's back door in my face. "Great, then we'll have reporters on the doorstep, as if we don't have a full waiting room already."

Matt shrugged. "She's right. Try to keep the dogs' whereabouts a secret for now, if you can."

"In Paumanok Harbor? You've got to be kidding."

He turned serious. He reached a hand to brush my cheek and looked at me with those soft brown eyes. "You folks keep a lot of secrets, Willy."

Yes, and mine were eating at my soul right now. I needed to talk to Oey. Or, sigh, my grandmother.

CHAPTER 18

THE FIRST THING I DID WHEN I GOT HOME was strip off my revolting clothes, right by the front door on the porch. No one could see, and the foul rags were not coming inside. Little Red took one sniff and lifted his leg on them.

"Nice," Susan said when I came all the way in, nearly naked, nearly frightened to death. The old truck wasn't in the driveway, and last I'd heard she was staying at the restaurant to keep cooking for the volunteers and the survivors. She tossed me the afghan from the couch and went back to filing her nails and watching the television, like just about everyone else in the region, I'd guess. She wore my old terry cloth robe, so maybe she just came home to shower and change. "It's a good thing that guy didn't come over."

I was too tired and too angst-ridden for another lecture about not bringing strange men home with her. I hated finding some bare-chested surfer dude raiding my refrigerator before I had a cup of coffee. "Yeah, real good. Thanks."

"He said he'd call first, but you never know."

I rested my head on the top of the couch. "Men are like that."

"He seemed serious about talking to you, though."

"If it's another reporter, tell him I've gone back to the city."

"No, this guy saw the poster about your mother's rescued greyhounds. He bought the old Mahoney place and wants a dog. He asked about you at the restaurant last night before all the chaos."

"Tell him she'll be home by Halloween." Wearing the afghan and nothing else, I watched another station, this one with breaking local news.

"The rejoicing in the Hamptons is short-lived," went the lead. I turned the volume louder to hear a bald man in a bow tie.

"In the midst of a miraculous rescue mission, unknown felons have taken advantage of the situation to escalate the recent crime spree."

Susan put down the nail file. "Damn, I guess I should have looked at my cell for messages." We both leaned forward, as if that made the story any more comprehensible. According to informed sources, which meant someone didn't want to give his or her name, almost every police officer in the Hamptons had been out directing traffic last night when they weren't helping pull people from the water. The main roads had to be kept clear for fast-moving emergency vehicles, so cops manned all the busy intersections to prevent more casualties. Some of them drove police cars to the hospital or the walk-in clinics when the ambulances were full.

So no one was watching Main Street. Except the wily robbers.

Tiffany's got hit in East Hampton. London Jewelers, too. Rose Jewelers in Southampton. That little place in Sag Harbor that fixed watches. A coin shop in Westhampton that advertised, "We buy gold."

Someone stole it. All of it. No one knew until morning that the alarms had been electronically bypassed, cameras disabled, automatic calls to the security companies interrupted, the storage vaults and safes silently detonated.

The FBI took over the investigation, now that large corporations like Tiffany and Company had been hit.

As if the thefts weren't scary enough, more money went missing from the government coffers. This time a million dollars of Southampton's bank account disappeared into cyberspace. Worse, nearly every employee of all the departments of that township had a hundred dollars deducted from their paychecks. A hundred dollars meant a lot to a part-time street sweeper or the divorced school crossing guard with four kids and no child support.

The town could repay the money . . . if the million dollars had been where it belonged. Now everyone would have to wait. Near riots started breaking out. Homeland Security had investigators in place. The new Federal cybercrime unit had investigators confiscating computers. The whole town was shut down.

"They call them black hat gangs," Susan told me. "Groups of topnotch hackers with no consciences who work together to steal as much money as they can. It's a game with them, at first, to see if they can break the codes. Then they get greedy. I heard they suspected Russ, because word is he's so good at programming. They found some kind of routing device from his computer at Town Hall to an unknown network. But he stayed at the command center all night with his laptop from home, which had no such gizmo."

"I bet he's mad as hell someone messed with his machinery."

"Outraged, more like. He thought he had the most firewalls and safeguards on the planet. Now he swears he'll find the crooks."

"They're going to let him help?" Like setting the fox to guard the henhouse.

"He swears to Chief Haversmith he had nothing to do with any crimes."

Which mightn't work for the FBI, the CIA, or Homeland Security, but if Russ passed the chief's test, he told the truth. If anyone could unravel the web back to whoever spun it, I'd put money on Russ, especially when his own honor was at stake.

"Do they think the street crimes are connected to the electronic ones?"

"They're not saying, but someone had to be good at shutting down the security systems."

"And no one saw anything?"

"They never do."

"Yeah, but enough people were coming and going for the rescue to notice people leaving jewelry stores with suitcases or sacks."

"You'd think so."

The next story on the news got weirder when some science expert got on to talk about a new species of dolphin discovered aiding in the disaster off Montauk. These larger, more intelligent animals seem to have been directing the more common species, identified by markings shown in photos from each instance, as the same pod that earlier tried to keep people out of the waters. Now the new ones had disappeared. Called back to secret laboratories? Retrieved by government covert ops? NOAA was sending marine biologists; PETA was sending protestors.

I was sending mental messages to whoever listened. *Go home!*

The camera went back to the newscaster in the bow tie. "And they say this is the off-season in the Hamptons. Well, folks, there's not a room to be had past the Shinnecock Canal."

I found the remote and turned the TV off. "At least the restaurant should do well."

Susan said she was too tired to cook. "I never want to look at a soup pot again."

"How about a peanut butter sandwich? I had scrambled eggs in another lifetime."

My brilliant chef cousin who could make flavors burst in your mouth until you smiled from the inside, laughed. "On Ritz crackers."

"Sounds good."

While we ate, I listened to phone messages. Uncle Henry at the police station wanted to see me. Oh, yeah, I'd be in a hurry to get there. Did the turkey answer the farmer's whistle the week before Thanksgiving? Ditto Grandma Eve, who already had the metaphorical hatchet in hand.

Friends from the city wanted to know if I saw anything. My editor wanted to make sure the new book would be done on time. My father sounded worried. My mother sounded pissed. That was about right, for them.

I couldn't face any of it. Maybe if I'd had enough sleep, or enough time. Or more information, not the kind that came from the TV either. I wanted to take the dogs for a walk on the beach, or take a nap. I wanted to go back and help Matt. I wanted to find Oey and figure out what was going on. As usual, no one gave a rat's ass over what I wanted.

First I put word of the Newfoundlands' recovery on the town's Facebook page. That would reach everyone in the Harbor and Montauk, too. I made sure to add that the pups were still too traumatized for public viewing, but they were out of danger, in a secure environment.

Then I called the hospital and got connected to Peg Winters' room.

She cried.

Shit. "Are you all right?"

She kept crying. "My babies."

"Listen, they're fine. I just saw them." I had no reason to tell her about the wobbles or the runs, nor could I lie. "They're not perfect yet, but Matt says they are good. They all ate breakfast."

Peg cried some more.

A nurse got on the line. "It's the painkillers. Some people react like that, especially after a trauma. Mrs. Winters will be fine in a couple of hours when the last of the heavy stuff wears off. You can pick her up then."

Me? Well, better driving to Southampton than into the abattoir of the council meeting Uncle Henry said they'd call this morning. I showered, twice, walked the dogs, and still had time to check in with my father. A worried parent had to be easier than an angry one.

"Stu, skunk, and a broken nose, right?"

"I never said your nose got broken. I never even said that he'd hit you, just that he wanted to. Now that you know, you can be more careful."

Okay, I'd stay out of bars and Paumanok Harbor

where everyone saw me as Calamity Jane. "Nothing about fish? Dolphins?"

"No, baby girl, they won't harm you. A cat might."

"A cat?" They kept a couple at the farm, half-feral rescues, to keep the rodent population under control. "One of Grandma Eve's mousers?"

"A mouser! That's it! With green eyes. It can give a nasty scratch and carry all kinds of germs and diseases. Don't get hurt, Willy. I love you."

"You, too, Dad. Don't play tennis in the sun."

Traffic hit a dead stop at the light on Montauk Highway near Wainscott, so I called my mother. I got her voice mail, hallelujah.

"Hi, Mom. Everything is getting back to normal out here, even the traffic jams. Not that I'm calling from the car or anything. I might have someone interested in a greyhound. I'll get his number, so you can check him out when you get back. We're really busy here, as you can imagine. Those Newfies are adorable and Matt says they should be okay. The rest of us, too. Talk to you soon."

Another long delay at Watermill. Another duty call.

"Hi, Grandma. I am fine, yes, Susan is too. Listen, I don't think the oiaca will be around today."

"Because it had a long night?"

"We all did."

"Well, the tourists are flocking east to Montauk, looking for dolphins and taking pictures of the boat on its side. We should have a quiet time of it. Quiet enough to hear your story."

She didn't mean the one I was writing, either.

"Sorry, I'm losing the connection."

Chapter 19

M RS. PEG WINTERS, MY NEW BEST FRIEND,
cried when I picked her up. She was so grateful the
dogs were safe, she was alive, she had a place to stay and
someone to drive her while her arm was in a cast and a
sling, that she gave me a hug. In one swoop I had the
breath knocked out of me with the heavy cast and my
turquoise silk shirt spotted with her tears. I hadn't brought
all that many clothes with me out to the Harbor this trip
because I was counting on being back in the city in days.
And half of what I had brought was in the garbage. So I
wore my favorite blouse, the one that made my eyes look
bluer. The fact that I would see Matt when I dropped Peg
off at his house did not have anything to do with my decision. He'd be too busy to notice me, anyway.

Peg wore a T-shirt with an MFD logo, donated by the
ambulance crew, baggy surgical scrubs provided by the
nurses, and a man's flannel shirt over her shoulders, because of the sling, from the hospital's lost and found department. She cried about that, too. She managed to
look both attractive and feminine in her hand-me-downs,
way younger than her forty-something years with her
auburn hair pulled back in a ponytail. If her green eyes
weren't so red from crying and her nose so red from wiping from the crying, she'd be really pretty. I wondered
how someone who appeared as delicate as Peg could
handle a full-grown Newfoundland. Sure they'd look
good trotting beside her in a show ring, but what about

on the road, if they saw a squirrel? Those puppies already weighed more than I felt comfortable managing. Of course I was used to a six-pound Pomeranian, and no one carried a Newfie around like an accessory.

I told Peg how good I thought she looked, considering what she'd been through. She started weeping again.

"All my clothes, I bought new ones for the cruise, like a trousseau for the first vacation I've had since the divorce, and now they're gone."

"We can stop in Bridgehampton on the way home. There's a shopping center with a lot of the chain stores you'll recognize. You'll want to get things like a hairbrush and underwear and deodorant, too. There's a drugstore."

"But I have no money!" she sobbed. "No wallet, no checks, no credit cards."

"I'll put it on my card for now—" which caused more tears of gratitude and another painful hug, "—and I'll call Mr. Whitside at the bank in Paumanok Harbor. If you give him your social security number, he can have a new card waiting for you by the time we get there."

I sincerely hoped so, because she bought a complete fall wardrobe, mostly black that looked really good with her red-brown hair, plus shoes, cosmetics, watch, and cell phone, all on my credit card. I bought a new pair of jeans and two long-sleeved jerseys with cash. She changed in a ladies' room. I stayed in my turquoise silk shirt. The spots were almost dry by now.

All that shopping—and controlling my impulses—made me hungry. Since I decided Peg needed sustenance after her ordeal, and since the Carvel store was right across the street, I treated for that, too. Peg, who still looked dainty, petite and put-together now, with a filigree hair clip and neat trousers and a tailored blazer draped over her shoulders because of the sling, had a kiddie cup of no-fat frozen yogurt. I had a coffee royale ice cream cone. With sprinkles, so there. And I only got a couple of drips on my good shirt. So there. And there. And there.

We talked about her dogs and her business and the expenses of showing a dog through puppy classes to cham-

pion status, so a bitch's offspring and a dog's stud service
had more value. Thank goodness my mother wasn't in the
car with us. Her views on dog shows and breeders did not
mesh with Peg's—by about a football field.

Tears started to fill Peg's eyes again when she worried
the puppies might not be salable now, if they lived. She'd
have to return the deposits, pay the vet bills, feed the
growing pups, start training them herself while she
searched for good homes for them, with no income until
next spring, when she hoped to have two new litters to
sell. Only Mollie, she felt, had show potential that might
never be realized.

She loved her dogs, but they were still a business and
her livelihood. I couldn't imagine someone turning down
a puppy because it wasn't perfect to its breed standards.
But who was I to judge? I loved a three-legged critter
with missing teeth and an attitude problem.

I didn't want to get Peg's hopes up about Frankie yet.
The middle-aged Romeo might change his mind and decide the fancy sports car was a better chick magnet than
a drooling puppy. "Look on the bright side," I told her.
"You are all alive."

Damn, the woman could cry! "I thought those pills
would have worn off by now."

"Oh, I'm always like this when I'm upset. Or happy.
Or tired. I just cry a lot. My ex couldn't stand it, especially when we went to a sad movie. He walked out."

Of the movies or the marriage?

She stopped weeping in time to get her new credit
card at the bank and withdraw the limit, which she used
to repay me, thank goodness, or I'd be paying interest on
my next bill.

She didn't cry much when she saw two of her puppies
bound out of the back room at Matt's clinic to greet her.
Mollie came slower, but she did wag her tail. Matt's last
two customers applauded.

Of course Peg turned on the waterworks again when
she threw herself into Matt's arms in joyous gratitude for
saving them, for keeping them safe, for letting her stay at
his own house when she had nowhere else to go.

I almost mentioned she could go to any of the Montauk motels reserved by the *Nova Pride*'s owners for the stranded passengers, but I liked her and liked how she appreciated the generosity of his offer. What I didn't like was Peg in Matt's arms, his hand patting her back. "There, there. It'll be fine."

No, it wouldn't, because my father's latest gloomy premonition just came true. There it was, the green-eyed mouser. Only he meant the green-eyed monster that clawed at my heartstrings leaving raw, bloody furrows. Peg and Matt were about the same age, both divorced, both dedicated to dogs. And she didn't have Little Orphan Annie curly hair or a too-flat chest, an extra five pounds—okay, ten—or weird and dangerous friends from other worlds.

She was normal.

I felt like crying myself. Yeah, Dad, it hurt. A lot. One of these days I'd have to admit to myself how much Matt meant to me. I knew we were friends, knew he might wish for more, but I'd made my decision not to get involved with any man, especially not one who lived in outer Bumhampton. So where did this jealousy come from, this knife-edged wound?

I decided to play Scarlett and think about it tomorrow. Today? Today it hurt.

Melissa coughed, reminding Matt he still had those last two patients to see. As I walked Peg and the bouncing puppies out the door, Melissa sneered and recommended club soda for the stain on my blouse. I almost told her she could use my grandmother's vanishing cream on the dark circles under her eyes, but I didn't truly believe it worked . . . at vanishing people, that is.

Over at Matt's house, I played with the dogs while Peg made the calls to the prospective owners and, predictably, came away crying. They'd all heard about the shipwreck and they all demanded to know how long the dogs had been in the water, what kind of treatment they'd received, their current conditions. Peg was honest.

As a result, a fellow breeder no longer wanted Mollie, not if she was traumatized. Too much work.

Moses' buyers had planned to show him in the puppy classes. The shaved IV spots would take months to grow in and they could not count on his future looks or personality, etc., so they backed out. Too much wasted time.

Only Maggie's family still wanted her. They had three kids and lived in a lighthouse on the coast. If Maggie could play and swim, she'd still be the perfect pet. I wasn't sure about the swimming part, not after what they'd endured, but she played hard, knocking me over once and stealing one of Matt's shoes near the door.

Having to return the deposits for the other two meant having to absorb two-thirds of the cost of the cruise ship also. Matt walked in to see Peg sitting on the floor of his living room surrounded by three dogs almost as wet as they'd been last night, from her tears, and one chewed-up sneaker.

I could see his face go white in panic. "It's okay, she just cries a lot. You kind of get used to it. And I'm sorry about your sneaker. I thought Peg was watching while I used the john, but she was too busy crying. Why don't you call Frankie and see if we can fix some of her problems?"

Frankie and his Porsche arrived in minutes, as if he'd been waiting in Paumanok Harbor for the call. Mollie went right to him and licked his face when he bent down, bronzer and all. He promised her a fenced-in yard, a man-made, spring-fed pond, a regular swimming pool, too. And he thought she looked beautiful all bathed and groomed.

We left them in the living room to negotiate while Matt put some cheese and crackers on a plate. I helped by not throwing myself at him.

When we came back, Peg's green eyes glistened with tears, happy ones now. The only problem was convincing Frankie to leave Mollie here for a few more days to be sure she had no lasting ill effects.

"I guess I'll have to. Can't keep her at the Yacht Club anyway. And I need time to get rid of Tina and buy the Land Rover. I decided to keep the Porsche for when I go places without the dog." He bent over her and promised that wouldn't happen often. She licked his face again, sneaker smell and all. He laughed. "Two days, Doc?"

"If she's eating and playing." He looked pretty certain she would be.

There were hugs and handshakes all around, and a few tears. Mine, too.

Frankie had to go pry Tina out of his suite, after taking her to East Hampton to a fancy dinner. He hugged everyone again for good-bye. Peg sighed.

"He is just what Mollie needs, a strong, generous, affectionate man."

I wondered if she was speaking for Mollie or for herself.

She went on: "I couldn't have picked a better family for her. Now I can think about getting Maggie to Nova Scotia, on the cruise ship's dime. Frankie suggested I ask them for the use of their company jet. My dogs do *not* fly in any baggage compartment. I'll insist they pay your bill, too, Matt."

"It's all taken care of. Frankie is making a donation to our local charities."

She sighed again. "What a fine gentleman."

Frankie was a letch. He'd squeezed my ass. "Maybe you can visit him when you get back from delivering Maggie. To check on Mollie's condition, of course."

I swear she gave a Tina-like smile. "Of course."

Matt wanted to know her plans for Moses. Did she have a waiting list of prospective buyers?

"A long one, though none as suitable as those I'd chosen. But anyone paying his fee will want guarantees I cannot give now. He could be afraid of water, afraid of the dark, afraid of being left alone."

Now she was talking about me? Nah.

"I have a better idea." Peg pointed to the big puppy leaning against Matt's leg. "You take him."

"Me? I don't have that kind of money."

"I don't need it, not after Frankie offered twice Mollie's price. Moses adores you. He left my side the instant he heard your footsteps at the door. A Newfie is the most loyal, loving dog in the world. Once he gives his heart, it's for life. He might even go into a decline if I place him with anyone else. Look how his eyes follow your every move. He went right behind you into the kitchen, didn't he?"

Little Red did that, too, for the chance at crumbs. Lord knew my dog wasn't loyal or loving, only fair. He bit me as often as he did strangers.

Peg turned those green cat eyes on Matt. "And he gets along with everything, dogs, cats, children."

"And parrots," I put in.

"Well, I never tried my dogs with birds, but I suppose you treat birds here, too. You'll have to teach him not to chase them, of course, but he'll learn anything, to please you."

Matt shook his head. "I work too hard to keep a dog of my own. Too many long hours like yesterday and today." He looked at me for confirmation.

I didn't give it. "He can go to work with you. How many dogs of working people can do that? And you have a whole kennel staff happy to look after him when you can't." Everyone but Melissa, but I didn't say that. "And you know you already love him." His hand hadn't left the dog's silky head. I refused to be jealous of the dog, too. Men, women, children, and animals all adored Matt. At least I was in good company. "You want him."

"I want a lot of things. Frankie's Porsche, two weeks in the Bahamas . . ." The look he gave me said he wanted a lot more, from me.

In front of Peg? I blushed, damn it.

He smiled.

I ignored his knowing that I knew what he really wanted. And tamped down my answering want to lean against him like Moses. "Yeah, and I want a penthouse duplex on the East Side." There, I'd reminded him I was not settling in Paumanok Harbor like some robin that forgot to migrate. "But this one you can have, today."

His soft smile turned to a grin. Which meant, I supposed, that he supposed that he could have me another day.

I grinned back.

Peg wept.

CHAPTER 20

MATT ORDERED PIZZA AND WE ATE off paper plates. He let Peg pay for it, not because he was cheap or not macho, but because she needed to reclaim her pride and independence.

Her young dogs didn't beg or whine or go to the door in a subterfuge to get noticed. Little Red and I had come to terms about my meals: he got some. We'd have words when I got home. Which better be soon so Matt could get some rest.

Unless he and Peg stayed up getting better acquainted. Damn.

On the ride home I called the police station. I felt safe, now that Uncle Henry would be home. I told the operator no, this wasn't an emergency, and I would call him tomorrow. I hadn't returned his call earlier since I was in Southampton picking up one of the survivors and assisting her to get settled, since she had a broken arm.

"Yeah, Willow. I got all that. Bottom line, you didn't want to talk to the chief."

Ah, the joys of Paumanok Harbor.

That call made, confrontation postponed, I considered my own unsettled situation. I liked Matt, more every time I saw him. I know I was waffling again. I wanted him, I didn't want him. I'd given up men, but gave part of me to this one. So I decided Peg could have him.

Good sense told me to back away before I lost more. And I had good reasons:

A: jealousy. Matt was a chick magnet, and I hated how that caustic emotion made me feel.

B: distance. Paumanok Harbor wasn't as far from Manhattan as, say, London, where the man I almost married lived. But I didn't want to live out here. Matt wouldn't want to give up his practice to live there.

C: scruples. Because of that distance, we'd only have a brief affair, which might be nice, judging from the good night kiss when he walked me to my car. I always felt cheapened after a physical affair, though, not like Susan, who lived for the moment. If our emotions deepened past lust and infatuation, I'd be shattered afterward, when I left.

D: my status as Paumanok Harbor's resident tsetse fly of epidemic disasters. Matt might be the only person in the village who didn't hold me to blame, but he would. Or his practice and popularity could suffer.

E: as if there weren't enough barriers to a happy outcome of what started as a warm friendship, add in a hundred-and-fifty-pound blockade that I helped erect. Matt had Moses now, a big, galumphing puppy who'd grow that big, at least. Smuggle him into my no-dogs-allowed apartment? Have both of them share my bed? And what about Little Red? What if Moses wanted to play with Red like a squeaky toy? I couldn't do that to my own dog.

Add it all up, and I had reason enough not to let any tender new feelings grow into a major heartache.

But that brief kiss did feel good, tingly to my toes.

You'd think I'd drive the car off the road, the way I vacillated with my own life. It pissed me off, too, that there were always issues. Nothing straightforward, like the way I wrote my books. Kids didn't have patience for equivocation, if they knew what the word meant. Instant gratification, that's what they liked, all action without introspection.

Too bad I wasn't a kid.

Too bad there was a familiar car in front of my house. The big white Ford SUV had the village logo on the doors. And a bubble gum light on the roof. I guess Uncle Henry didn't get my message.

He hadn't waited until tomorrow to hold his own council, either. The heavyset man sat on the living room sofa in front of the TV, sandwiched between the two big dogs, while Little Red hid under a chair, one of my socks chewed to a wad of thread. Damn, I should have bought more of them, too, when I shopped with Peg.

Uncle Henry had a mug of coffee in hand and a plate of brownies on the table in front of him.

Thank you, Susan, for making him comfortable. As if I wanted the grizzled old truth-maven grilling me about things I didn't know or understand!

I kissed his cheek — I'd known him since I was born — and picked up Little Red and kissed his nose. He let me, after I showed him the piece of pizza crust I'd packed up for him when Matt wasn't looking. The big dogs got some, too.

Uncle Henry wasn't as easily mollified. "We need to talk, Willy."

No, we needed to move inland away from danger. I didn't say that aloud. Why cause panic? Since outright evasion hadn't worked, I tried going on the offensive. "I have nothing whatsoever to do with your crime spree. Or your electronic thefts."

"Both of them are out of our hands now. So many initial agencies are on it, they'll be tripping over each other by tomorrow."

"I can't believe they think Russ is involved. He spent the whole night organizing the search and rescue efforts from the command center, so everyone knew what everyone else was doing."

"That's why they suspect him. He's too damn good, with no explanations for how he does what he does. But it's not only our tech they're looking at. They're pretty sure the cybercrimes originated at Town Hall, whether by us or someone using our computers from a distance with spyware they've installed. They've interviewed the mayor, too, on record, on tape. Problem is, they ask him where he was on such and such a night of a robbery, and he says he can't remember."

"Mayor Applebaum can't remember a lot of things."

"Which is damned suspicious in any person of interest, especially the mayor of a whole village. Only the county cops can't remember asking the questions, so they keep repeating them." He sipped his coffee. "It'd be laughable if it didn't expose Paumanok Harbor to even more investigation. I'm out of the loop now, but I get the feeling they think a whole bunch of us locals banded together to steal a fortune. They've done background checks on everyone, even Lolly, who cleans at night."

"Isn't Lolly . . . ah . . . ?"

"Handicapped. Slow. She is, but she comes on time, does a good job of cleaning, and never breaks things like the last night janitor we had. The idea of Lolly running some way-technical computer scam is absurd. She can barely spell to leave a note when we need more soap or vacuum bags. They had the poor girl in tears."

"Shit."

"Yeah, but Russ is working on it on his own. He'll find whoever's been messing with our computers. I'm not really worried about that."

And he wouldn't have tracked me down to discuss town business. I tried another diversion. "So have they found the missing passenger yet?"

He shook his head. "No, but they've got an ID on him. A troubling one."

"I heard he was old. That can't help his chances in the water. It's been almost a full day."

"More troubling than that. His name was—is, until we get a body—James Everett Harmon, PhD from London, England."

"Uh-oh."

"Yup. A direct descendant of Harry Harmon, who was the illegitimate son of the Earl of Royce who founded what much later became the Royce-Harmon Institute for Psionic Research. That first Harmon married the daughter of a Gypsy fortune-teller and a horse trainer. Same genes as a lot of us, now."

I took a brownie. "That's why Royce and DUE have been so worried about finding him?"

"That and he was a beloved professor of creative writing."

I swallowed a bit of brownie wrong and had to go get myself a drink of water. I poured a cup of coffee, too, while I was in the kitchen. God knew I could use the caffeine. This was going to be a long night.

The chief didn't wait for me to ask questions when I got back and tucked my feet under me in the big easy chair. "There's more. They say Harmon imagined things, fantastical beasts and odd humans, and he wrote about them. Kind of like Lewis Carroll, who I always figured was on drugs. Maybe he was a relative, too, who knows? Anyway, Professor Harmon never published his stories; he just used them as examples of what the human mind can conjure, for his students. The problem was, he got the ideas when he went off in trances. Dangerous if he was driving, scary if he was giving a lecture. They checked for seizures and sleeping sickness and psychedelic drugs. Nothing. When he returned from wherever his mind took him, he came back enraptured, as if he'd seen the heavenly angels, and full of new stories. Some people thought he was crazy."

I didn't.

"Harmon saw things. I don't know if he spoke to them like you do. He never called them here, like you do."

"I do not call them!"

Uncle Henry finished his coffee and set it down, nearer me. I got the hint and got up again to refill his cup.

He blew on it to cool the coffee, then took a sip before talking. "Three passengers saw him at the railing, wearing his life jacket, yelling at the wall of water before it hit the ship. Foul worm, he called it, as if the thing were alive, not merely a storm-driven wave or waterspout."

"Wyrm with a 'y.' It's an ancient word for dragon, or sea serpent." I gave up. I went to get my sketch pad for the newest book, along with the printouts of the drawings I'd done on the computer.

Uncle Henry flipped through the drawings of the pet store owner who became a superpower. "Looks a lot like someone I know." He gave me a wink.

Then he got to pictures of Spenser Matthews' companion. He studied the bird with the fish tail, then the fish with feathers. "I take it this is the rare bird everyone was chasing?"

"Very rare."

"Talks, thinks, vanishes?"

"And helps rescue people and dogs. I think she came to warn us, the same as those dolphins."

While he studied the drawings, from when I tried different combinations of colors and sizes, I rushed to tell him there were no dolphins in my book, super powered or not. Not yet, anyway.

He flipped the page and inhaled sharply. N'fwend.

He saw how I'd drawn a huge, transparent sea serpent rising from the swirling water that gathered to make it bigger, eyes whirlpools, mouth a bottomless pit big enough to swallow a small boat. Or twenty elderly professors.

Uncle Henry took a silver flask out of his pocket and poured some of its contents into his coffee.

"Uncle Henry!"

"What? I am not on duty. And I can't have a cigar. You ever hear about driving a man to drink? Your foot's on the accelerator."

"I didn't call it!"

"No? Somehow the wave that's caused millions of dollars in damage and expenses, not to mention lives lost or people injured, suddenly appears when you write about it. What am I supposed to think?"

"Maybe the professor saw it in a trance!"

"And shouted at it so the thing could suck him in?"

"Why else was he on that cruise ship, anyway?"

"No one seems to know. He packed up one day, told people he was going sightseeing, and left. He's not senile or sick, so no one could stop him. Poor bastard."

"I bet he knew what he'd see. He must have spotted the horrible beast in one of his trances and came to verify its existence, to prove his own sanity or to confront it. You don't think they'll find him?"

The chief tapped my sketch. "Harmon's old, like you

said. How long could he live in the water, if he didn't get swallowed? This thing could have dropped his body anywhere along the Eastern Seaboard."

"So we'll never know?" If I were Peg, I'd be crying. The man was almost family. Almost like me.

He shrugged. "DUE wants us to keep looking. Harmon's that valuable. We've got patrols up and down the beaches, aerial spotters doing quadrants, and they'll get dogs and divers back on the ship as soon as they right it, in case those witnesses were mistaken out of their own panic."

No. N'fwend was evil. If he sensed an enemy, he destroyed it. I assumed he came to vanquish his old nemesis, M'ma, or M'ma's friends. Maybe the sea dragon felt the power in Paumanok Harbor, or the power in Professor Harmon, power that he could usurp, or slurp as the case might be. Wasn't that a tradition in wizard wars, winner take all, and the loser shrivels up? Paumanok Harbor stood as a locus of the secret gates between worlds. Most of its inhabitants held unimaginable talents. Did N'fwend want them? Us? Me?

"What does DUE say about those other passengers who saw Professor Harmon talking to the wave?"

"They say when Harmon was a young man, barely out of Royce University, he flew to Bermuda for one spring break without telling anyone. Once there, he hired a small vessel and sailed it right into the middle of the Bermuda Triangle, where so many ships had been lost."

"Wow, what a brave fool! He lived through it, obviously."

"And no more ships go down in the area, no more than other places in bad storms and such."

"You mean . . . ? He . . . ?"

Uncle Henry held out the flask. Alcohol wasn't my drug of choice. I ate another brownie.

"We need him. They're thinking maybe you can find him. You found the lost colt."

"He found me. And I am not getting in a boat and searching the Atlantic Ocean."

The chief poured the rest of the whiskey into his cup. "Maybe you can talk to the thing like he could."

Go face-to-face with a wave as tall as a skyscraper? *Talk* to a wall of water? Hell, I didn't even swim in the ocean. "No, you'd need a Translator for that. Ask them to send Agent Grant back. Or find someone who can communicate with the deceased, to channel whatever Professor Harmon knew. Hell, DUE must have a hundred psychics on their staff who can find the professor if he's alive and bring him back to life if he isn't." I wasn't sure about the revivification stuff, but anything had to be better than sending me out in a boat.

"They've been trying. Nothing." He held his mug up toward me before pouring its contents into his mouth. "You're our best bet. Heaven help us."

"Un-uh. You are not pinning this whole salvation thing on me. Besides, we have more help than you know. We have Oey, if she didn't take herself back home to where she got her orders. She came to help, to warn us. So did the dolphins. Not on their own, I believe, but on someone else's urging. Someone who can defeat this monster. So we are not alone in the battle. We've got some big guns on our side, too."

That cheered him up. "You think we're out of danger, then? That this water demon has had its fun and gone away?"

"Truly?"

"What else would a truth-seer want?"

"Then, no, I don't think it's finished. I don't know that it has anything to do with us, actually. It's like *Clash of the Titans*, with two powerful foes from the otherworld fighting for domination."

He sighed. "An epic battle, eh? You know who suffers most in those movies?"

"Yeah, the extras. The foot soldiers and spear carriers."

"And the innocent villagers the armies trample." He sighed again. "So what are you going to do about it?"

Good question. No answer. "Ask Oey?"

"The bird? It's a parrot, for crying out loud. How much help could the blasted thing be?"

"She saved the lost dogs. And got help to keep the boat from sinking entirely."

"And no one can see her but you?"

"Not the way she really is. No one except Matt."

"Ah."

I didn't like the sound of his "ah." "Did you hear he's got a dog of his own now? One of the Newfoundlands Oey helped save. And he's got Peg, the breeder, staying with him."

"Ah."

I didn't like the sound of that one, worse. "I'm okay with both."

Now he clutched his stomach and reached in his pocket for the antacid tablets.

"See? You should not drink."

"And you should not tell lies."

CHAPTER 21

B Y THE TIME THE CHIEF OF POLICE LEFT, I was too tired to shower, too depressed to get out of the chair. The council expected me to save the world. And all the brownies were gone.

Susan came home while I lay sprawled out, my jeans unsnapped at the waist, shoes on the table next to me so Little Red couldn't get to them. I didn't turn around when she called hello.

"You're early and the brownies were great. I hope you brought leftovers 'cause there's no food in the fridge and I'm sleeping here tonight because I'd never make it up the stairs."

"Yeah, everyone's too tired for anything after last night. We decided to close the kitchen early. The place was half empty anyway, with the whole town drained after the rescue and upset about the robberies and how the Harbor is getting the third degree. I've got half a vegetable quiche for lunch tomorrow."

"Super." I waved her in the direction of the kitchen to put the food away. "I'll see you then."

She laughed, then said, "Oh, and I brought Axel over."

"Axleover? Like a turnover for the car?"

She laughed again. "No, Axel Vanderman, the guy I told you about who wants a greyhound. Axel, this is Willow. Willy, meet Axel."

I looked behind her before I screamed, "You brought

a strange man home at ten o'clock at night without calling first?"

I buttoned my pants while I looked at him. He was in his fifties, I'd guess, trim, semi-casual in dress shirt and slacks, loafers, no socks. He had salt-and-pepper hair and sharp features, the best being unusual black-rimmed, silver-gray eyes.

He apologized. "I am sorry, I was so eager to make your acquaintance."

"I'm sorry, too, Willy," Susan said. "I needed a ride. Dad had to use the truck.

"And Axel is so persuasive."

And twice her age! Good grief.

"Well, you've come here for nothing, Mr., uh, Vanderman."

"Axel, please."

"Axel. The greyhounds are not here for you to meet."

He kept staring at me with those amazing silver eyes. I wished I'd changed my shirt, stains and spots, but the turquoise did make my own eyes look bigger and brighter. Maybe he wasn't so rude after all. I sat up straighter. As if that gave me half the cleavage Susan showed in her floaty v-neck blouse. "All I can do is take your name and number."

"Oh, I think you can do more."

I blinked, breaking eye contact. Was he suggesting what I thought? "Come again?"

He chuckled. "I mean you can get to know me, so you can give your mother a good character reference on me. I was hoping to meet her, the famous dog trainer. Not that you aren't famous in your own field, Willy. That's the name on your books, isn't it, Willy Tate? Although Willow is lovely, like you."

He was looking into my eyes again—not at my chest like a lot of men, and not at the spots. His unwavering expression was full of admiration.

"Oh, you've heard of my books?"

"The whole town speaks of you. I had to meet the noted local author."

Little Red growled, so I looked down to see what he was doing.

Axel cursed. Little Red kept trying to grab his sock, except Axel wasn't wearing any, so the bad-tempered terror nipped at his ankles. When Axel cursed again, I picked up the dog before Red drew blood or Axel retaliated. I tried to make nice by smiling. "You can tell I don't exactly have my mother's knack for teaching dogs their manners."

Axel didn't smile back, but he did keep looking at me. Admiring or not, that fixed gaze was unnerving. "Um, you're staring."

Susan giggled. "He does that. It makes you feel like you're the only woman in the universe, doesn't it?"

"Oh, but you are," he told us both. "You are unique, as each of us is. And you are delightful."

The words were nice; the stare started to give me the creeps. "Well, it's getting late. It's been a hard couple of days and nights around here."

He didn't move, so I glared at Susan to get rid of him. She brought him, didn't she? I hoped she didn't intend to keep him. Something about the man struck me wrong, and not just the fact that he was old enough to be Susan's father. Little Red hadn't stopped growling in my arms, and I felt goose bumps on the back of my neck. Most creepy of all, Axel never looked at Buddy or Dobbin. What kind of dog lover came into a house and didn't try to make friends with the resident canines?

"I'll be sure to tell my mother about you. Do you have a card?"

He reached into his pants pocket without taking his eyes off me.

Now I felt more than uncomfortable. Maybe threatened, but I wasn't any telepath, no doom-seer like Dad. And I never had much intuition, either, just a lot of fears. Axel didn't come near to causing the same dread as electric storms or snakes, but I didn't want him in my house. I got up and started toward the door. A person couldn't get more obvious than that without calling the cops.

He got to the door first and turned to face me. Up close, I felt small. Not petite like Peg, but overshadowed, even though Axel only stood maybe three or four inches taller than me. I had a good view of his Adam's apple, unappealing in a lot of men, more prominent in this one. When he swallowed, my mind imagined a python digesting a mouse. I shuddered and looked up, into those amazing eyes.

He stepped closer, so I could see the silver glitter in his near-reverent gaze, like a New Year's Eve party decoration, with champagne and silly hats and laughter.

"I'd like to see you again."

From snakes to celebrations in the blink of an eye? Literally? Weird. "That's very kind of you, but I am really busy these days."

"Oh, but I'd like to show you my house, so you can see what a good home I can provide for one of the unfortunate racetrack dogs. I understand all good adoption services do home inspections."

His lips smiled. His beautiful eyes did not. "Um, we're not anything that official. And I have nothing to do with the process. I won't even be here when my mother gets back. She has her own standards."

"You could come see my new home anyway. I've had the whole house refurbished. I'm quite proud of it."

I could have looked into those eyes for hours. I ached to try to draw them, to try for that intensity and shine. Maybe if I visited his home I could get to see them in daylight. They might make better eyes for my hero than Matt's warm but ordinary brown ones.

Matt.

"Um, no, thank you. I am sure your house is lovely, but I'm not much into home decor, and I really am busy these days before I return to Manhattan."

He took another step closer and tilted his head until his eyes were mere inches from mine.

"Tomorrow?"

I wanted to spend time tomorrow with Matt, who said he worked half days on Saturday. I stepped back, and shook my head, hard, to get that snake image out of my mind. "Sorry, I have plans." Matt might not know about them, but I did. I wanted to introduce Red to Moses. I rubbed the dog's ears, hoping to calm him.

"But I insist."

He insisted? Who the hell did he think he was to insist I do anything? I didn't want a scene at my front door, so I didn't kick him in the shin or sic Little Red on him. "I'll think about it if I'm free." I waved his card in the air. "I have your number."

Oh, boy, did I, mister.

I shut and locked the door behind him, feeling his parting glare like a snowball down my back.

Susan started up the stairs slowly, not bothering to hide her yawn.

"You didn't really want to bring him home, did you?"

"No, all I want is my bed. He's too old for me. I think it's you he's interested in anyway."

"So why didn't you tell him to call tomorrow or the next day?"

"It seemed important to him and I guess that look in his eyes persuaded me. You meet his gaze and forget what you were going to say." She yawned again. "I could drown in that stare of his."

"Maybe you did."

"You need some sleep, too, if you're still thinking of those poor people on the cruise ship."

"I'm not thinking of them and I'm not kidding. Don't look in his eyes anymore."

"Huh? What am I supposed to look at, his mouth? That's downright suggestive. His crotch? Worse."

"Just don't get lost in his gaze, is all. Something doesn't feel right about it."

"I got it, cuz. He's a man, so he's not to be trusted. I don't know what's with you, Willy. Why you turned so gun-shy around men that you find fault with every one you meet."

"I do not, am not. I trust Matt and I—"

TWEE! TWEE!

"Shit, there's that frigging bird again. I swear if it keeps me up all night one more time, I'm selling its location to the tabloids myself." She unlocked the front door, opened it, then opened her mouth to scream at Oey.

"Don't!"

"Huh? You want to listen to that screeching?"

"I'll take care of it. Just go to bed. I'll let the dogs out for their last walk. That's sure to scare it off."

I hoped not. I sent mental messages of welcome, comfort, come, need, parrotfish in the willow tree pictures.

"You came!" I closed the dogs in their pen and went to refill the kiddie pool.

Oey had her parrot's head cocked in the direction of the dogs. "Petth?"

"Yes, Dobbin, Buddy, and Little Red," who was barking. He hated being in the same enclosure with the big dogs, even though he spent all day in the same house. I couldn't tell what any of them saw. Red barked at anything, and one of the old dogs couldn't hear much. The other one couldn't see much.

"Man?"

"No, Dobbin is a girl dog. A bitch."

Oey swiveled her whole body toward the dirt road, where dust from the last car still floated in the slight breeze.

"Man."

"Oh, him. That was a guy who wants a greyhound. Another kind of dog, a pet. His name is Axel."

"Athole?"

"That, too. Forget about him. Have you seen another man, an older man who was on the boat?"

I didn't have a picture to project. The chief hadn't described the missing passenger, so all I had was a stock image of a professor with a beard and thick glasses. Oey sat on the edge of the plastic pool, the fish tail in the water, gurgling happily. Or speaking words I could not understand. I kept trying.

"His name is Harmon. James Everett Harmon. From England."

Oey splashed and spread her rainbow-colored wings to bathe.

"He stood on the railing when N'fwend came. He shouted at him. Is he still here?"

Oey shrieked, "N'fwend heaw?" then leaped out of the water into my arms. As a fish. Yeck.

He was heavy. Not as heavy as the Newfie pups, but slippery. I didn't want to grab the tail in case I pulled out feathers, but I didn't want to drop him either. Shaking, I put him back in the water as gently as I could. "No one is here except the two of us."

After a few minutes the parrot head peered over the pool's rim. "Not heaw?"

"No, no wave could come that high, this far from the bay. Could it?"

"Biiig wave. Thunami."

"It's tsu—Holy cow, its name is Stu! A tsunami, that's what my father tried to warn me about." I'd seen those pictures of devastation, where whole islands got washed away. Big cities got leveled; people got swept out before they could reach higher ground. "I thought earthquakes caused them, not water dragons."

Oey tried to speak, but the message had to be too complicated. Instead she sent a picture into my head of something enormous bursting from the bowels of the Earth, causing shifts in the fault lines, causing quakes, causing tsunamis. Evil rising, like M'ma said.

"Someone would have seen a monster coming out of the ground!"

"Thee Oey?"

No. Hell, we had to find the professor more than ever. "Pro-featherth?"

How could I know if he liked birds. "Close enough. Is he close? Can you ask the dolphins to look? If he is alive, he can help us."

Oey went back to grooming, preening each wing feather with her beak. I watched for a while, then asked, "What's it doing here anyway? Those rules meant everybody has to stay on their own side. I know you came to help, but the monster is breaking the law."

"Banithed."

"You banish a devil and it ends up here, right on my doorstep? That's not fair!"

I swear Oey shrugged before she disappeared into the night.

So who said life was fair?

Chapter 22

I HAD A PLAN. WHICH WAS A WHOLE LOT better than waking up Saturday morning feeling as alone and lost as I'd felt Friday night. Like wandering through a desert without a hat, as if a sunburn was the worst of my problems. Now if my plan had half a chance of working, I'd be thrilled.

Find the professor, get him to vanquish N'fwend with Oey's help, and discover Matt's intentions. Great plan.

I made a list during breakfast. Vegetable quiche was like a healthy omelet and toast, right?

I did a mental run-through of the Paumanok Harborites whose talents I knew, writing down those I needed to speak with. Like, Bill the telekinetic at the hardware store couldn't find things, he could just move them. The weather forecasters couldn't help either. I knew the morning temperature was brisk from walking the dogs, so I had on a zippered sweatshirt. I also knew I'd be taking it off as soon as the sun warmed up, or putting a rain jacket over it if the clouds stayed. None of that could locate the missing passenger. I had a bunch of names and talents to try, though, so I packed up a bottle of water, my sketch pads, a pocketful of dog biscuits, and Little Red.

I wanted to be done by noon when the vet's office closed. Mom had a drawer full of dog leashes, so I had an excuse to call on Peg. And Matt.

Great plan.

I started with Mrs. Desmond on Osprey Street.

"I'm looking for the lost passenger on the cruise ship. Can you help me?"

"I can try, dear." She put a small pot of water on to boil and took down a jar of alphabet noodles. "What's his name?"

"James Everett Harmon."

"Harmon, did you say?"

"Yes, from England. That's why it's so important."

The H floated to the top of the pot first. I held my breath. Then the J and the E popped up to the surface. Yes!

I thanked Mrs. Desmond. She gave me some corn muffins and wished me luck.

Next stop, the auto repair shop.

"How's your big toe feeling, Kelvin?"

"Just fine, Willy. This carburetor isn't. What do you want?"

"Professor Harmon is alive."

"Good for him. So can I get back to work?"

"How's your toe now?"

"Fine, no itching."

I kissed his cheek.

My plan was working!

I hurried to the big building off Main Street that housed the village offices and the police station. The place seemed more crowded than usual for after the summer season, although no one stood on line at the front desk. That area opened half a day on Saturday so weekenders and people with long-hour day jobs could get beach stickers and dump permits and pay their taxes.

Mrs. Ralston sat stiff-backed and purse-lipped behind her plastic partition, while a woman I did not know looked over her shoulder. I hadn't intended to speak with the village clerk since Mrs. Ralston's talent, besides being an excellent office manager, was knowing the sex of a pregnant woman's child. I didn't need to find out if Mrs. Kale's new grandchild was a boy or a girl. My mother also kept a closet full of baby blankets in yellow and turquoise and stuffed dogs for baby shower emergencies.

I waved on my way to the police department's wing. Mrs. Ralston did not smile. The woman beside her stared at me through narrowed eyes, as if I had a weapon under my sweatshirt jacket. All I had was Little Red. She sneered and pointed to the No Dogs Allowed sign, but I kept going. Except that stare gave me an idea. I backtracked and asked if Mrs. Ralston knew anything about an Axel Vanderman. He wasn't on my list or part of my plan, but it never hurt to have information.

Mrs. Ralston gave a dirty look to the woman watching her, as if daring her to make a comment, then turned to her computer. She read out his address, the old Mahoney place, which I already knew. He bought the place three months ago, paid his taxes on time, applied for a permit to put in a pool, and got a beach parking sticker so he could use all of the East Hampton Township beaches, but not the East Hampton Village ones, because we did not pay them taxes. The locals were bitter about that, because we paid a fortune to use their high school. But that's another story.

"No dump permit registered to him, so he must have garbage pickup."

The other woman tsked. "That's supposed to be private information."

Mrs. Ralston turned to her. "And you are supposed to be frisking female prisoners at the county jail, not interfering with village business. If Willy asks, she has a reason."

"I don't care who takes his trash. And I don't want to know how high his taxes are or how much he paid for the house. Although," I told the female sent to make sure Mrs. Ralston didn't steal any paper clips or whatever, "that information is in the public record."

Now Mrs. Ralston did smile at me for putting her hostile watchdog in her place. "What else do you want to know, Willy? I cannot recall his appearance, or hearing any gossip about him. Which would not be in the official records anyway, of course," she added, with a glare for the intruder in her carefully organized domain. "But I would tell you if I knew."

"I'm not sure what I'm looking for. He's spooky, is all. I met him last night and something about him felt wrong."

"Woo-ee, just what we need, another whackadoodle person in this town."

I didn't know if the female from the prison meant me or Axel. "I think he might be some kind of sexual predator."

That set the guard back. She sucked in her lips, as if daring Vanderman to show up and try to get hinky with her. Mrs. Ralston said she'd pass it on.

I said I'd mention him to the chief, and went down the corridor. With my dog.

I wasn't surprised to find the police station full of people, not with the crime spree going on. What did surprise me was all the different uniforms from the county and the state, plus plainclothes cops with bulges under their jackets and men in suits with earpieces. Like Mrs. Ralston and her warden, Paumanok Harbor was under suspicion, and under siege.

I walked past the strangers toward the chief's office. I saw Big Eddie, but he looked grim, so I didn't stop at his desk, not even to pet his K9 partner who snored beside it. Neither one of their noses could help me yet. Nor could Baitfish Barry, standing over by an open window, unless I wanted to catch a fish for dinner. After holding Oey in my arms? No, thank you.

Officer Eric Kenton, the one they called Keys, might come in handy if I discovered the professor held prisoner somewhere and we needed to break in. With a search warrant, of course, with respect to the Feds present.

Uncle Henry Haversmith's office door stood open, so I walked in. I expected more law enforcement types, not the long-married chief of police holding a weeping woman.

"Thank goodness you're here, Willy." He pushed the female in my direction.

What was I, comforter of criers? "I—"

"It's Lolly, and she's upset."

No kidding. So was Little Red. I put him down before he got squashed or so scared he peed. He immediately lifted his leg against one of the wooden chairs along the wall.

The nightshift cleaning woman wailed.

Hey, it didn't get on her, did it? "I'll clean it up, I promise." I led her over to a different chair and told the chief to get some water and tissues for Lolly, paper towels and spray disinfectant for the chair. She told him which closet to look in.

While Uncle Henry was out, Lolly told me her woes, between sobs. They suspected her, all those awful men.

"Of what, Lolly?"

"Of stealing the mayor's pass codes, putting some kind of bug in Russ' computer, having bank accounts somewheres else. I don't even have a savings account here in town where I live! My sister does my bills for me."

"How could they suspect you, Lolly?" Why would anyone consider that a woman who didn't graduate from high school could hack into so many sophisticated, up-to-the- minute protected systems. "You've always done a good job here."

She held up her hands, reddened, swollen joints and all. "My fingerprints're on all the machines. A course they are. I clean, don't I? That Russ always eats his breakfast at the computer, and the mayor? He forgets to wipe his hands after eating a donut and I don't know what else."

"I'm sure they know all that, Lolly. They're just desperate to find answers."

"And they'll blame it on me 'cause I don't have the answers or money for a lawyer or alibis. No one's here when I clean, so no one can swear I didn't do nothing wrong. I seen all the cop shows on TV, I know what they do. They'll send me to prison for life!"

She started bawling again. Luckily Uncle Henry returned by then.

"Chief, tell her no one is going to arrest her."

He stayed quiet while I wiped up after my dog. "Tell her."

"I can't swear to that, Willy. I can't lie, either. They'll never get the charges to stick, but they don't care about intimidating people or trampling innocents. I'm sorry to say some of them care more about closing a case than they do about finding the real perps."

"But you can tell them that Lolly—" No, he could not tell the FBI or the anti-terrorist people that he knew Lolly told the truth because his stomach didn't hurt. And because he was one of the Royce truth-seer descendants, the same as Kelvin. "Damn."

"Yeah." He sighed and sat back in his own chair. "Besides, she can't remember stuff. Like if anyone ever came in while she cleaned."

"I told them the one time—"

He sighed again. "I know, Lolly. A young woman had to use the restroom. You shouldn't have opened the door to her."

"But she needed it. Bad. And she left right after."

"But you don't know her name or what she looked like or if she stole a key or anything. That could be aiding and abetting."

"I never bet on nothing."

I wouldn't bet on Lolly staying out of jail either.

"Okay, Lolly," the chief told her. "You sit and get yourself together while I hear what Willy has to say."

"Did they find the professor?"

"No. I could have told you that over the phone. We're pretty busy here, you know."

"I do know, but I need a copy of his passport picture or driver's license. I have to see what he looks like."

"All my men—and those other bastards out there— have copies. Not that any of the outsiders are interested in finding an old man missing from a boat. No, they only want the missing money. That's what's wrong with the whole damned government. Money."

The chief went off on a rant about politicians and how they needed so much money to get reelected, they couldn't be trusted to put the public's interest ahead of

their own. Meanwhile, I studied the grainy enlarge-
ment he gave me. The professor did not have a beard,
at least not when he had the picture taken. He did
wear glasses, and had a round face with a fringe of hair,
straggly eyebrows, and a gap between his front teeth.
He looked like what you'd expect from the word avuncular.

I made sure Uncle Henry, who was big and beefy and
weathered, not at all avuncular, was sitting down near his
bottle of antacids, just in case. "He's alive."

That got no reaction but a raised eyebrow, and a head
nod toward Lolly, meaning he wanted to know how I
knew, but not now.

I didn't know, not for absolutely sure. Alphabet soup
and a mechanic's big toe gave me hope, but I had to be
positive. The chief's stomach was infallible. So I went further.

"He's not in the water." I figured he couldn't be alive
and still be in the ocean.

"Good. I'll tell London. Go on."

I watched his hands, to see if they tended toward the
bottle. Nope. "He's somewhere nearby."

"Great, Willy, that narrows it down, doesn't it? To
what, fifteen or twenty miles?"

That was better than what we had last night. I couldn't
think of any other questions to ask without jeopardizing
the chief's digestion and my welcome with wild guesses.
"I'll go see what else I can find out."

"Yeah, kid. Come back when you have an address.
Better yet, come back with the professor."

"Oh, one more thing. Do you know anything about
Axel Vanderman? He bought the old Mahoney place."

"I know him," Lolly said. "I clean his house on Tues-
days."

I turned to her. "Is he nice? Does he treat you well?
Did he ever make suggestive remarks?"

"He suggested I use bleach on the deck furniture.
Sure, and it's not him as has to breathe those fumes. But,
lordy, those eyes of his! I look at them and sometimes I
forget where I left the vacuum or the clothes in the dryer.

But he never minds if I don't finish up the place on time. He just pays me for another hour."

"Well, I think he's up to something. Don't let him stare at you, Lolly. And don't let him touch you."

"Won't have to worry about that, will I, when they arrest me. He'll hire someone else." She started crying again.

Uncle Henry had typed in Axel's name. "No record in the sex offender's list. The federal crime database takes longer. But I'll look into it. Did he try anything with you? Threaten you? Want me to have a talk with him?"

"Not yet. Maybe it's just my nerves on edge, with the disaster and all."

"Right. Like you never had a man look at you before."

"Not like this, trust me."

"Hell, Willy, I'm trusting you with the whole town's welfare. Now go find us Dr. Harmon. That's the PhD kind. And take your dog with you. You know why we posted that sign that's supposed to keep dogs out?"

I was afraid to ask.

"Because the last time you brought him here he pissed on the leg of the Suffolk County District Attorney, the SOB." He looked down. "Good dog."

CHAPTER 23

"**Y**OU'RE GLOWING, WILLY!" Vincent stopped sweeping the sidewalk in front of his barbershop to shield his eyes.

I stood taller. Yes, I had a right to glow. I was halfway to finding the professor, all on my own, without the fancy FBI or the arrogant agents from DUE. One of which, the one I had been almost engaged to, hadn't returned my urgent message that we needed a linguist, like immediately. One of which Grant was. After a lifetime of study, he could speak or interpret some of the half-vocal, half-telepathic, half-imaged language of Unity, where all the magic came from. I know that's three halves, but that's how complicated their speech is. The only other Translator I'd heard of was Grant's father, the Earl of Grantham, with whom I was not, of course, on familiar terms. Shit, I'd slept with Grant! The least he could do was send an email. So much for promises of forever. Then again, I hadn't made it to the meet-my-parents part.

But I glowed. "Thanks, Vin. I am having a good day. The sun is shining, Little Red hasn't bitten anyone, and Professor Harmon is alive!"

"Great, but it's not that kind of glow."

While I worried about being radioactive—I had X-rays at the dentist's last week—he looked both ways to see if anyone could overhear his whisper. "It's your aura. I've never seen it so strong. Your power is growing,

Willy, whatever it is you do." He furrowed his brow. "I sure hope that's a good thing. We don't need any more trouble."

"I hope so, too, Vincent, because it looks like we'll be needing all the help we can get. You haven't spotted any strangers with auras, have you? Sensed anyone lost? Given directions to an older gentleman with a British accent?"

No one like that had passed the barbershop that morning. But he'd keep an eye out. I showed him the professor's picture. Then, for the hell of it, I asked if Axel Vanderman had an aura.

"I've only seen the man from a distance. Someone pointed him out to me at the Breakaway one night. He sat too far away for me to tell, what with all the candles and half the customers and servers putting out haloes. He doesn't get his hair cut here. Most likely goes to some fancy-shmancy salon in the city."

"Well, if he walks past, let me know if you see anything. But mostly I'm searching for the last passenger on the cruise ship."

"I'll spread the word."

By phone, twitter, or telepathy, I didn't care. "We need him."

Next I had to track down Joe the plumber. I'd left a message on his business number, but I didn't have his cell. So I went into Janie's Hair Salon. They were keeping company, as people used to say. I'd pointed them in the right direction, toward each other, which gave me another glow, this one inside. Not that I approved of matchmaking, but this pair was a natural. Janie loved to take care of people. Joe was helpless after his truck went over a cliff during the nightmare catastrophe. Now that he'd recovered, she still liked to fuss over him and he liked to fix things. Right now he was upstairs, where Janie lived above the salon.

"So he finally moved in?"

"No, he's renovating the bathroom. It's handy having a man like that around."

One of the ladies under a dryer snickered. "I bet he's good at other things, too, from that grin on your face."

"Yeah," Janie said, "he's real good at changing tires. My ex would have told me to call AAA and wait three hours. And Joe can barbeque."

Wow, a houseman. I hoped there was more between them, but it was a start. "Can I go up?"

Janie thought about that a minute, wondering at my motives. I understood jealousy—not that I was interested in Joe except for his talent—so I quickly told her I needed help with a water problem. She pointed to the stairs to her private rooms.

Joe was laying tiles around a new double sink. Maybe he had moved in, after all, or was going to soon. The bathroom looked like something from a style magazine, so Janie better appreciate him as an artisan, not a butt-crack handyman. Although I did wish he'd pull up his jeans.

"This bathroom is gorgeous, so I hate to interrupt," I said, "but I need your skill."

"It's Saturday. I only do emergencies on the weekend and charge double. Put a bucket under it and I'll be there on Monday."

"It's not that kind of problem. I'm looking for Professor Harmon, the lost passenger, but I have no idea where to start. Can you help?"

"Can't find deaders, you know. The old guy's a goner for sure, from what I heard. If the wave didn't pull him under, the boat rolled right where he was standing."

"I know it doesn't look good, but I'm pretty sure he survived. Chief Haversmith and Kelvin both agreed when I said he's alive. And his initials floated at Mrs. Desmond's."

"Then I guess he's still breathing. Hand me that towel, will you?"

I passed him a filthy rag, then the picture of the professor.

Joe filled the sink and stared at the photograph. Then he stared into the water. His intense gaze reminded me of Axel, but I put the weirdo out of my mind to concentrate on the water. Maybe if I tried real hard, I'd see what Joe saw. I saw his reflection. Chances are Joe couldn't see Oey, so we were even.

"I've got something. Someone lying down, with his eyes shut. If I didn't know better, I'd say he's laid out for burial. Maybe he's sleeping."

"Or unconscious. But where is he?"

"Hush." He added some hot water and swirled it around with his right hand. "No sand, no waves, so he's not on the beach or in the water. That's good." Joe put his face inches from the sink. "Wait, I think I see the corner of a rug. Greenish. He's in a house, no ... Yes, he's in a bathtub! The yellow life jacket is under his head for a pillow."

"So someone rescued him and took him home, thank goodness." But why hadn't they called the authorities? For that matter, what kind of person makes a rescued house guest sleep in the bathtub, no matter how wet or bedraggled? "Where is he so I can go get him?"

Joe shrugged. "I never know unless the person is in front of a street sign or a store, or someplace I recognize."

Damn. "He's not moving?"

"Not so much as a twitch."

"Can you tell how far off he is?"

"I used to check on my wife in Mineola. That's how I caught her cheating. Visiting her mother, my ass. I've never been able to view someone much farther away. Not like Hobbit stuff where wizards can see across continents. Maybe their water has something in it that ours doesn't."

"Well, closer than Mineola is a help." And a whole lot of territory. How far could the wave have carried him? Or the dolphins towed him? Unless someone drove him in their car. "I need more to go on. What if you looked in the bathtub here? Could that help, you know, like sympathetic magic?"

"Can't hurt to try."

We waited for the tub to fill, then Joe leaned over the side, tightie-whities and all. "You're right, the picture's much clearer. Closer, too. Hey, I recognize those faucet handles, crystal with jade inserts. They're a special order from a company in Chicago. If they're here in the harbor, I might have put them in. Of course, I'm not the only plumber to work in Paumanok Harbor, or the only one to have that company's catalog."

"But they are rare enough to make it a good chance the professor is in one of your clients' houses?"

"I'd guess eighty percent."

"Great. Which client?"

Joe scratched his head. "I can't remember. I remember fixtures a lot better'n I remember names. I can check my records, but there's a shitload of order forms and job estimates, and this one had to be from years ago."

"Look again. Can you see the color of the tiles? Are there towels hanging nearby? What about a shower curtain?"

He almost fell into the tub, trying so hard. "I see white, like most bathrooms, except for that green rug. I might — Nope, it's gone."

"What's gone? What did you see?"

"Flowers, maybe, maybe not. Sorry, Willy. And sorry I can't remember about those faucets."

"But you saw Professor Harmon, and that's what's important. Do you have the catalog, or can you draw me a picture of the faucets I can show around? Someone else might recognize them."

They looked familiar to me, once I had the sketch in my hand. Maybe the power of suggestion had me wondering, or maybe I did catch a glimpse over Joe's shoulder without realizing it. Either way, neither Joe nor I had a name or location.

I went back to Vincent. "Do we have anyone who can bring memories back?"

"The cops have Sodium Pentothal. That can work sometimes. Other drugs they might have confiscated here or there."

"No cops, no drugs. I just need a memory unlocked, not someone babbling about all they know."

"Then you need a shrink."

Now I have been told I need to see a therapist more

than once. I went a few times, too. And yes, she wanted me to talk about my past and bring back memories I'd sooner forget. I stopped going. I got past a whole lot of insecurity and fear on my own. Now I glowed.

"I don't think I can get Joe the plumber to a shrink. He'd talk to Doc Lassiter, but that won't get him to re-member where he installed those faucets." Doc lived on Shelter Island, but he worked by touch, spreading men-tal wellness through his fingers. You couldn't shake hands with the man without feeling better about your-self and your world. I'd love to see his aura someday. "I just need one lousy plumbing memory jogged."

"I didn't mean Joe needs his head examined, except for doing all that work for a little sex, but you need the kind of psychiatrist that works with past lives, buried memories, that kind of thing."

Which I used to think was all a crock. Now I believed anything was possible.

Vincent went on: "Or maybe you could find a lounge act in Atlantic City or Las Vegas, you know, the magic show where they get people from the audience to do stupid things they don't remember afterward. It can work both ways."

"Hypnosis?" I rolled the word around in my head. Hip noses. Like someone wanting to hit my nose? Could that be what my father meant? Before I could call him or ask if anyone else knew a better way of finding the house with crystal-and-jade water faucets, Martha from the real estate office walked by.

Just the person I wanted to see! She'd been in half the houses in Paumanok Harbor at one time or another. Maybe she'd recognize the fixtures.

Martha wasn't half as happy to see me. We had Issues. She did, anyway: Grant. She handled the purchase of the Rosehill estate for a Royce outreach center, and latched onto the handsome, wealthy, charming British lord as soon as I broke my not-quite-an-engagement to him. Did I mention wealthy? With the dip in the real estate business, Grant must have looked like Prince Charming to her. That's how he looked to my mother, too. They were both disappointed. Martha went to England, maybe meeting the parents, maybe going over plans to refurbish the estate and outbuildings, maybe trying to wheedle an invite to stay on in Britain.

She'd come back alone, and blamed me. I never talked about her to Grant, I swear. In fact, I was glad they'd hooked up for a while, so I didn't have to feel bad about breaking up with him. He must have mourned my loss for a week and a half. Anyway, I knew his family wanted a Royce dynasty match for him. My genes might have done, since our talents, me as Visualizer, him as Translator, meshed nicely. All Martha could do was never get lost. She mightn't know what street she was on, but she always knew true north, without a compass. I got turned around every time I backed out of a strange driveway. She impressed the hell out of me. Maybe she impressed Grant's parents less.

I showed her the picture of the faucet handles.

She barely glanced at it. "Oh, you and your little projects."

Little? The rogue wave/sea monster was anywhere from five stories to ten, depending on which eyewitness account you heard. I was not about to discuss a kraken in the middle of Main Street. "It's an important clue to finding the missing passenger, Professor Harmon."

"Harmon?" She looked more closely. "You know, I do recall seeing something like this, but it was ages ago, when the House got sold."

"What house?"

She looked over her shoulder, then whispered, "You know, the House."

Shit. Maybe bullshit, too. Martha might send me out to Paumanok Harbor's haunted house for spite. No one lived there, no one went there, yet the taxes got paid, the mail disappeared from its door slot, and the grass got mowed. Oh, and the House yelled at anyone who tried to enter. Now the houses on either side of it stood empty. Who'd want to live next to a talking building?

"Are you sure about the faucets?"

She waved a well-manicured hand in my direction. "I see so many houses, you know."

I knew she wanted to be a countess one day. Good luck. And don't blame me. His lordship didn't return my calls either.

I went back to Janie's and found Joe upstairs.

"The House? Hell, no, I wouldn't step foot in the place."

Me neither.

I asked Mrs. Ralston at Town Hall to make copies of the faucets to hand around. Maybe a cop had been in the place a long time ago. It was a long shot, but worth a try.

The ogre at her side curled her lip. "Now you are wasting time and money and man hours looking for bathtub knobs? What kind of operation is this town running?"

Good question, lady. Wrong people to ask.

Chapter 24

"DO YOU KNOW ANY HYPNOTISTS?" I asked Susan when I went home to drop off Little Red. He'd had a good day, too. He'd peed on every street sign and hydrant in town, barked at every car that passed with a dog in it, and ate Mrs. Terwilliger's sandwich out of her tote bag when I went to the library to get books on hypnosis. And another one on mythological monsters that I didn't ask for.

"Grandma says it won't work."

Grandma Eve did not believe in modern medicine, the Internet, or the two-party system of government. "How can she know? I've heard it's a respected practice now. All these books say so."

Susan kept moving things around in the refrigerator, maybe looking for the quiche for lunch. "They tried it on me at the hospital during chemo. They said it could help me relax and not get so many side effects from the drugs. It didn't work. Grandma says it's because we have a barrier in our brains."

"We, as in the Garland family?"

"We, as in Paumanok Harbor talents. It won't work on Joe if you tell him in advance, or you if you realize someone is going to do it to you. She didn't know if any of us could be taken unawares. Said it had something to do with protection, so no one could invade our minds without permission or steal our powers."

That was good to know. I'd always worried that some

of our telepaths could read my thoughts. On the other hand, I kept looking at the picture of those faucets, sure I'd seen them somewhere. "Maybe you could ask your mother if anyone knows a hypnotist anyway. I'd cooperate, if that helped, and if someone I trusted were nearby to keep it honest." Asking anyone else, like Grant if he ever replied, meant sending a message to DUE to check the rosters, waiting for clearance to open private files, then waiting to see if the esper would come. That could take days, days we didn't have, not with a life at stake. Not with a vengeful sea serpent on the loose during hurricane season.

"I wish I could recall where I'd seen them. Maybe I flipped a page in a magazine once and I'm wasting my time."

"While you're at it, maybe you could recall what you did with my quiche."

"Will you come with me to a house on Shearwater? Martha thinks she saw a similar bathtub there."

"A house or the House?" She knew by looking at me. "Not on your life."

"Then I ate your quiche for breakfast."

"Both portions?"

I didn't have to answer. She took another look at my guilty face—or my jiggly ass—and asked, "What if I said I'd go with you?"

"I still ate it for breakfast, but I'd buy you lunch."

"Not worth it. You owe me lunch, anyway."

"You'll have to take a rain check. I need to get to Matt's by twelve."

"Why, he turns into a pumpkin at noon?"

"No, but his office closes then and he might go off with Peg and the dogs. I need to talk to him."

"Well, whatever you said to that bird worked. I slept better than I have in days. And Grandma says the birders aren't a problem anymore. They're all too afraid of getting robbed or having their identities stolen. Everyone else is out looking at the shipwreck and watching for new kinds of dolphins."

"I'll take the signs down, then, so we don't scare off any farm stand customers."

Before that, I made calls and left messages: Could my father have meant hypnosis? Did my mother have enough homes for the greyhounds, because the guy here wasn't suitable? And Grant again, a long-distance, long message about Martha and monsters and where the hell was he? Then I gathered some old leashes—my supposed reason for calling on Matt—and headed for the door, without Little Red.

"Sorry, pal, but I don't trust the big pups yet." Actually, I didn't trust Little Red not to pick a fight he couldn't win. The phone rang while I broke a wait-here dog biscuit in pieces for him.

Speak of the devil. Or the devilishly appealing. Matt called me. He needed me. He wanted my company. I put the leashes back in the drawer.

He sounded desperate. "She keeps crying. I told her to make herself at home, she cried. She came to the office, saw a sick cat, and cried. I said the dogs are doing fine, even Mollie, she cried. Frankie wants to show her his new Land Rover, she cried. I need to get out of here before I strangle her, or start crying myself. Let Frankie hand her tissues all afternoon."

I was laughing, and glowing.

"It's not funny. I'm running out of tissues. And bedding. More company arrives tomorrow, and I never bought any sheets or blankets for the second guest room. Will you help me?"

"Only if you'll come with me to a haunted house."

"Great. That's my kind of woman. No dinner, no movie. So far we've been to a swamp, a sea rescue, and now we're chasing sheets and specters. You're a cheap date, lady. I thought I'd have to bribe you with an ice cream cone at least."

"That, too." This was a date? To buy bedding for his company? "So who's coming?"

A marine biologist from Woods Hole Oceanographic Institute was on the way, an old friend from vet school. An expert in the field, she was coming about the new dolphins.

She? I should help pick out sheets for an old college

buddy who happens to be female? How about cheap ones that scratched and tore when you moved your toes? Or blankets that gave you rashes if you didn't wash the dye out first? Yup, ugly jealousy ripped through me again and I almost said I didn't want to go with him, anywhere. Maybe I understood my mother for the first time in my life. She always accused my father of being unfaithful, even when he swore he wasn't. They'd split up eventually, after screaming at each other for years, which might be why I ended up in a shrink's office. Did she love him so much she thought every other woman in the world wanted him? A pot-bellied executive? She definitely believed he wanted them.

Maybe I should back out now while I still had a chance, and a spark of sanity. However—I try not to use "however" in my books; too old-fashioned for my readers—however, he intended the marine mammal expert to sleep in her own bed, in a separate room. And I needed him to go to Shearwater Street with me. And I refused to become my mother.

"So are you free?" he asked.

Like a bird, albeit—another word I loved and kids would sneer at—a bird that didn't know whether it was coming or going. Like Oey. Glub.

I met Matt at his office to save time. The waiting room was empty except for Melissa, who was gathering her purse and keys and sunglasses. Today she wore gray, head to toe: gray tights under a short gray piece of fabric that hardly qualified as a skirt, and a loose gray cross-under-the-boobs blouse that looked like a shroud. Her black hair still had its limp white streaks except, today, silver showed at the tips and temples. She wore heavy black eyeliner, and had heavy dark circles under her eyes. Either she'd given up on the skunk look and decided to go trick or treating as a raccoon, or she hadn't slept in days.

"Are you all right?"

"What's it to you?"

Whoa, a rabid raccoon. I backed away. "Sorry, you just look tired."

She slammed a drawer shut. "It's this shit job. Dogs messing in the lobby, having to commute to Hampton Bays in the stupid traffic. Now this dork town is all filled with porpoises and stranded passengers. Who gives a rat's ass?"

"There's a lost professor, too. We're searching everywhere. Here, maybe if you look at this picture, you can recognize the faucets. You might have gone to a party there or something."

Melissa shoved past me without looking. "You can shove it up your—"

Matt came out from the back. "Hey, Sissy, no call to be so rude. Two of my clients grumbled about you this morning."

"Those jerkoffs can all go fu—"

I broke in before things got uglier. " 'Sissy'?"

Matt tried to put his arm around her. She cringed, but stayed beside him. I guess she needed the job, jerkoffs or not.

"Her baby brother couldn't say Melissa, so he called her sis, or sissy. It stuck."

"Like a piece of dog shit on your shoe. No one outside the family uses it, so don't get any ideas."

"I wouldn't think of it." You euthanized animals with rabies; you did not make pets out of them. "Melissa's too pretty. Sweet, like in mellifluous." And Sissy Kovick didn't sound half as hip as Melissa tried to be.

Matt squeezed her shoulder. "I told her lack of sleep is making her grouchy, but she's young. Kids party. We forget."

We forgot a lot, these days. Like I forgot to warn her about Axel Vanderman before she flounced out of the office.

Matt shut the door behind her and put the closed sign out. "Whew. I guess she's not happy here, so far away from her friends and all. She seemed content last month when she was dating some guy, excited even. He broke up with her last week. Poor kid."

"What kind of man wants to put up with that kind of— That is, did you meet the guy?"

"No, they always met near Hampton Bays. That's what she told me."

"Well, it's only for a few more months if she's going back to college in January. And maybe she'll get over him by then."

"I'll miss her."

Now that's kinship loyalty, missing the wormy apple on your family tree. "Um-hmm."

He knew I didn't see any big loss. "She's great at the patient records and payrolls and bank accounts. I'll have to hire both a receptionist and a part-time bookkeeper when she leaves."

"Yeah, but you'll keep all your clients, which is more than I can say if Melissa stays."

"She'll get over her disappointment long before then. You'll see a different kid when she does."

Sure, maybe she'll be human by then. "So which first, sheets or search for Professor Harmon?"

"You really think he's alive? And in Paumanok Harbor? It's a long way from Montauk, not even on the same body of water as where the boat rolled over."

"I know, but we've got to look."

"Then let's do that first so you can relax."

How could I relax if we didn't find the professor? We needed him. I tried to explain it to Matt while he drove, how the wave was no wave, how the dolphins weren't real, how Oey'd tried to warn us. How the sea god's enemy could wipe out Paumanok Harbor in one tsunami. How the local psychics showed me the professor lived.

"And Dr. Harmon fixed the Bermuda Triangle when he was still in college. I think it's the same monster wreaking havoc again."

We almost hit a tree. "Oh, boy. Listen, a couple of weeks ago I was perfectly normal. I thought the world was, too, following all the usual rules of physics and logic I'd believed my whole life. Then I met you and the universe turned upside down. I saw impossible things, felt totally new sensations, understood the native people weren't like you and me. Well, not like me."

"You're like them now."

"That's what you say."

"You saw the fishbird. They can't."

"Okay, reality broke its boundaries and we moved into the *Twilight Zone*. But this . . . ? This new scenario is really, really hard to take. Horrific beasts, epic battles, vanishing professors." He shook his head. "I can't wrap my brain around it."

And he hadn't met the House yet.

I could feel the atmosphere change as we drove along Shearwater Street. No kids played in the yards, no gardeners raked or weeded. The air felt different. Or maybe that was my skin crawling, trying to push the car in another direction.

Matt took my hand when we got out of the car and walked up the gravel path to the white colonial. I tried to stop it from shaking. My hand, not the all-too-solid building.

"Come on, it's only a house. If no one's home, we can look in the windows and shout for your missing person."

No one was ever home here. That was the problem.

Matt rang the doorbell, then banged the knocker for good measure. We heard them echo, but nothing else, so he rapped and rang again.

A minute later "Hit the Road, Jack!" boomed in our eardrums. The small wooden portico we stood under really was shaking now. "And do not come back anymore anymore anymore."

"Some juvenile delinquent's playing tricks with a karaoke machine," Matt said, when he caught up with me back at the car where I was tugging at the door handle of the locked SUV. "Nothing else."

"You're not scared?"

"I'm too dumb to be scared of a silly prank. Come on, let's try again."

This time when he pushed the doorbell he also shouted, "We just want to ask if a professor is here, a Dr. Harmon. We do not wish to bother you. We'll go as soon as you answer that one question. Otherwise we'll call the cops."

"Shame," sang out. "Shame on you." Now the door trembled. Not just my knees or the porch roof, but Matt's hand shook, too.

"That was no karaoke machine."

His face turned a shade paler. I'm sure mine had no color at all. How could it, when my heart stopped pumping blood at the first notes?

"Listen, Mr. House." Matt banged his fist on the door. "You can't scare us away like you do everyone else."

It can't? I was ready to run home if that's what it took to get out of here. If the House wanted the car, fine.

Matt jiggled the doorknob. I prayed it was locked. Matt stepped back. "I can't believe we're talking to a house, but you ask him, Willy. Explain who you are."

I cleared my throat but nothing came out. Matt squeezed my hand. "You can do it."

Easy for him to say. He had a backbone.

He squeezed my hand harder. I tried again. "I . . . I am Willow Tate. They call me the Visualizer, but I can't see you. That is, I don't want to see inside you. I just need to know the professor is safe. And talk to him about defeating an ancient adversary of his. We'll take him away if he's trespassing. Please?"

The old timbers sighed. And then they sang something about tally men and bananas and wanting to go home.

"Huh?" Matt and I looked at each other. Was the House calling us bananas? Now I got insulted. House was the crazy one, not us.

"Does that mean Dr. Harmon is here or not?"

The wall sang again. This time about having no bananas today.

"Do you know where he is?"

Now it was "Home on the Range."

I thought a second, now that we didn't seem to be in imminent danger. "Do you mean he is at the ranch where they want to bring horses back? Harborview? Or maybe Third House in Montauk, where they tried to start a buffalo herd?"

". . . thrill on Blueberry Hill."

I didn't know of any Blueberry Hill in Paumanok Harbor or Montauk, and these songs were older than I was. How long had the House been this way?

I stamped my foot on the landing by the front door. "Stop playing games with us! Either tell us or . . . or I'll call in the fireflies to set you on fire. If you know anything about me at all, you know I can do it!"

I couldn't, and the House knew I couldn't, which proved it knew more about Paumanok Harbor and the otherworld than it did about modern day music. It chuckled and rocked slightly on its foundation. Matt and I stepped off the front stoop. The House started to croon "The Rose."

I shouted over the sappy song. "Professor, if you are here, make a noise. Any noise except this bad Bette Midler imitation."

"I thought it was Streisand, myself." Matt started humming along. "Have you ever heard the George Jones version?"

"What are you, crazy? A frigging house is singing to us and you are doing a 'name that tune' thing?"

The House ignored us and kept on about love being a flower and you its only seed.

"Yeah, yeah, and in the spring—" Rose? Blueberry Hill? "He's at Rosehill! Because it's going to be part of Royce Institute, the professor's home. That's got to be it! And I stayed there for a week in the spring. That's where I must have seen the green bathroom fixtures."

Matt shook his head. "Can't be. They're working there. Someone would have noticed an elderly gentleman in a bathtub."

The House repeated the last verse about blooming in the sun's kiss.

"It's huge. Who knows where they're working. And Cousin Lily, she's the housekeeper, went to visit her daughter and the new baby while the renovation is going on."

"Okay, let's call the police and get them out there."

I wasn't ready to admit to anyone how the House sang clues. How embarrassing could that be, especially if

I guessed wrong? Besides, the police station was full of strangers who'd lock me up instead of looking. "I think we have to check it out ourselves."

He looked at his watch. "Okay, let's get going. I've still got company coming tomorrow and I promised you an ice cream."

The House sang, "I Never Promised You a Rose Garden."

I put my palm flat on the door and tried to picture gratitude, smiles, reunions, Professor Harmon with his arms out, hugging a house, hugging a rosebush, then a willow tree. "And if we find him, I'll buy you a radio, so you can listen to some new music."

Then, before we could turn toward the car, stuff started flying out of the extra-wide mail slot: calendars, cellophane packs of Christmas cards, return address labels, dream catchers and paper poppies, even a couple of shrink-wrapped fleece blankets. All the crap charities send people in hopes they'll feel guilty enough to make donations. Which the nonprofits use to send more garbage no one wants. I've never understood why they don't just feed the hungry, heal the sick, save the planet, etc., without filling the trash cans.

Matt stepped out of range. "Is it throwing the stuff at us?"

"I think it's giving us gifts." I shouted a thank you to the house and handed Matt two of the clear-covered blankets. One had dogs and cats on it. All I could see of the other was red, white, and blue. "Here, you can use these for the dogs in the kennel. Or on the bed in the guest room."

CHAPTER 25

THE CLOSER WE GOT TO ROSEHILL, the more confident I felt that we'd find the professor. I mean, the House could have tossed shingles at us. It could have sung "Gone," "Blowin' in the Wind," or a zillion other sad old songs. And I hadn't panicked. After the first couple of songs, anyway. "We did it!"

"You rock, kiddo." Matt leaned over at a stop sign and kissed me.

Which rocked my world. Wrong time, wrong place, but feeling all right.

Matt started singing "The Rose," so I chimed in.

"Okay, so you can't carry a tune. But you're damn near perfect anyway. What's the plan for getting into Rosehill? Or locating the professor if the place is so big? And what if the old man needs medical help?"

"You're a vet. You've got your bag."

"With no defibrillator, no blood pressure cuff, no oxygen mask."

My great plan began and ended with finding Dr. Harmon and letting him save the world. Hmm.

So I called the police station—not 911—on my cell and asked for Big Eddie. The officer who answered wanted to know my name and business.

"It's personal. He missed our date last night."

"Poor lie, Willy, even if my nose didn't twitch. Big Eddie hasn't had a date in three years."

Not only did I get another of Paumanok Harbor's

truth-seers, but I had to get a gossipy one with instant voice recognition, too. "Well, I still wish to speak to Big Eddie without all the out-of-town cops listening in."

"Roger that, the Feebies haven't done anything but complain about our coffee. Hey, Ed," he called out, "you have a personal call on the line. She sounds hot. Why don't you take it in the interview room so we don't have to see you call up your credit card number?"

When Big Eddie answered, I said, "This is an anonymous call in reference to the missing cruise ship passenger."

"Shit, Willy, you got me excited for nothing." I heard him close a door. "So what've you got?"

"I think he's at Rosehill. I need your nose to locate him there, Keys to get us in, and an EMT in case he's ill. Off the record."

"Got it. I should pull half the force out on an untraced phone call. Want to tell me how you found him when we've all been chasing shadows?"

"Nope. Just meet us there. And keep it quiet in case I'm wrong. An anonymous tip, all right?"

"Chief ain't going to like this, Willy. He'll be moaning and groaning if I tell him a lie. Then he'll take the stomach pills out of my pay."

"Okay, bring him, too. But no one else."

Funny, some of the worst moments of my life happened here at Rosehill, but I wasn't afraid to come back. I was drugged, dragged to a car, kidnapped, and almost killed by a Hollywood starlet and her maniac father, but the house didn't talk.

No one did, when I tried to use the call box at the mechanical security gate.

"They must not work on Saturdays."

I tried the combination in use when I stayed here. It still worked. The gate popped open for us to drive up the long entryway and park in front of the majestic old mansion. The place was going to make a great learning and research center, with new dormitories and cottages being built in the far wooded corners of the property. We could see the raw rafters and bare wood frames from here, but the workers mightn't have noticed an elderly gentleman at the big house.

Big Eddie and Keys arrived a few minutes later, with the police dog in the back of the unmarked squad car. Then Russ roared in on a motorcycle, though I hadn't asked for him. He stood ready to disable the security system, which I should have thought of, so I was glad he came. Next an ambulance drove through, sirens and lights off, thank goodness, or we'd have the whole town on the alert. The chief pulled up in his official vehicle, and Mrs. Ralston, my grandmother, and Judge Chemlecki got out. Then Lou from DUE sped up the long driveway in a Lexus.

I jabbed my finger in Big Eddie's chest. "Did you have to bring half the village council with you? This might be a wild goose chase."

"Your granny was with the chief when I went to tell him. You think I'm going to tell her she can't come? She called Lou, because this sounds like DUE business, and he's staying at her house. The chief thought we needed Russ, and he needs to get away from that computer for a little while. And Mrs. Ralston almost decked the prison guard detailed to watch her. We figured she ought to claim a headache and go home. His honor has a blank search warrant, just in case, and those are my cousins manning the ambulance. They'll keep it quiet unless we have to make a run to the hospital."

"How'd you get everyone together without tipping off the Feds and the state cops?"

"Lunch hour, a doctor appointment, the ambulance needed service, and the mayor called a press conference to discuss the recent events. The undercovers disappeared and the rest of the big shots focused on getting their faces on TV instead of noticing the rest of us gone missing."

I supposed we needed two experienced emergency personnel, one to administer aid and one to drive. And the computer wizard could keep the security company from calling out the rest of the police force. A search warrant was a good idea, in case the CIA sent someone after us. Mrs. Ralston I could understand, but my grandmother? Sure, her reputation alone got her through any door she wished, and to hell with alarms and police lines, but she shouldn't be climbing stairs and searching the attics.

"Of course I had to come," she told me, and everyone else. "I attended a lecture once by Dr. Harmon. He was impressive. Now he might be the single most important person in Paumanok Harbor."

"After your granddaughter," Lou added.

Grandma Eve snorted.

Damn, now everyone looked at me, waiting for me to pull the professor out of my pocket. Just what I never wanted, the weight of the world on my quivering, quaking shoulders. Matt put his arm around me. He understood.

I glared at Lou, who did not. The senior agent from the Department of Unexplained Events intimidated me at the best of times. Now, with a weapon in his hand—okay, it was a thermos of coffee—he was terrifying. I didn't know his talents, and didn't know why he expected so much of me. I used to call him Lou the Lout, when he played the lecher who lived under the building across the street from my apartment. How was I supposed to know he stared at me because he was my assigned bodyguard? He dressed like a bum. Then he changed into a polished chauffeur, a ratty farmhand, a debonair senior citizen. Now, damn it, he was shacking up with my grandmother! He resembled a drug lord today; clean-shaven, long hair pulled back with a thong, an Armani suit and Ferragamo loafers.

He returned my glare with a wave. "This better not be your imagination working overtime, Willow. It's too crucial to mess up."

As if I didn't know that. "All right, here's what we're looking for: a bathroom with green rugs and crystal faucet knobs with green inserts. The professor might not be there anymore, but that's where he used to be. Joe the plumber saw him."

Everyone nodded, knowing I didn't mean Joe'd come upon the lost survivor while changing a washer.

"We'll take the guesthouse," Lou said. "Where my guys stayed last time." He led my grandmother to the path that led past the tennis courts.

Mrs. Ralston and one of the EMTs set out for the apartment over the garage. That's where Grant was supposed to stay, pretending to be a writer or something needing privacy. He stayed with me instead. I did not mention that.

Big Eddie's other cousin stayed with the ambulance, on call. We all entered his private cell number on our phones.

Big Eddie and his K-9 partner, Ranger, started circling the main house, Ranger's head low to the ground, Big Eddie walking beside him.

"He's got nothing to sniff for," Matt said. "The dog needs a referent, a glove, a shoe, something the professor touched."

"Yeah, but Big Eddie doesn't. He'll sniff for salt water, damp clothes, maybe the soap they gave out on the cruise ship. He'll recognize that by now. And fear." I worried I'd distract him, with the nervous perspiration trickling down my back.

Keys went around and unlocked the back door after Russ disabled the security system. They both moved on to the outbuildings to give the others access.

Uncle Henry and the judge started with Rosehill's basement, the wine cellar, the utilities rooms, the extensive home gym that had a shower and a sauna. No bathtub.

Matt and I took the first floor. We could skip Cousin Lily's apartment toward the back. I'd stayed there, and the bathroom was all white, with thick white rugs and towels. Matt said he'd check in case Lily redecorated.

On my own, I moved from kitchen to library to sitting room to TV room to vast dining room, calling out to the missing man. I didn't get any answer, but I felt better about wandering through the vacant house. I lost count of how many bathrooms the place had, but none of them had green rugs.

Matt came back and we went to the second floor. The chief and the judge passed us on their way to the top floor and the attics.

I spotted the guest bathroom with the Jacuzzi I'd bathed in, and where I'd conked Grant over the head with a pitcher of silk flowers when I thought he was an intruder. The pitcher had not been replaced. The knobs on the faucets were white porcelain with flowers painted on them to match the shower curtain, the tiles and the missing vase.

The master suite had two tubs, a hot tub and another Jacuzzi, plus a shower big enough to wash an elephant. But no green rugs or crystal handles.

Nor did any of the five other bathrooms we found on the next floor up, or in the attic.

Uncle Henry was sweating from the heat in the attic. I guess the air conditioner didn't cool that high. On a clear, warm day like this, the sun beat down on the roof, making that top floor an oven. The judge had found a seat on a divan in a vast room that had once been a ballroom. It was destined to be a lecture hall soon. Matt came out of the attached restrooms, shaking his head.

The chief sank onto the divan next to the judge. "Okay, Willy. Tell me why we're here."

"The House sang."

He took out a handkerchief and mopped his forehead. "This house?"

"No, *the* House. On Shearwater Street."

"The House? It didn't just shout at you to go away?"

"No, it sang."

"Damn, it never sang to anyone else. You really are something."

"That's what I said." Matt pulled me close enough that I could lean against his solid chest. It felt good, despite his slightly damp shirt. He smelled good, too, in a working man, virile way.

Uncle Henry turned to him. "You heard the music, too?"

"And felt the house tremble and laugh."

"Maybe when this crisis is over, you two can convince

the blasted thing to pack up and move off. Till then, I guess we keep looking."

We all trooped outside, hoping Big Eddie or one of the others had found a clue. We hadn't heard any shouts from the garage or the guesthouse or the gardener's cottage in the woods. The ambulance siren hadn't signaled for us to come, and Big Eddie's cousin shook his head. No one had called in with good news.

Big Eddie hadn't found a trace of ocean or beach scent. "If he got here, he didn't walk."

"So what's left?" the judge wanted to know. He opened the passenger door of the chief's car and got in, leaning back against the seat. He wasn't used to climbing stairs and poking in hot attics.

I lived in a third-floor, walk-up apartment, but my throat felt as parched as my optimism. I wished I had that ice cream cone Matt promised, or a bottle of water. I wished I hadn't called out the troops. I leaned against the car and thought. Matt watched me. The chief called the police station to see if they had any more tips.

Big Eddie gave Ranger a drink from the aluminum water bottle he carried. I might have asked for a sip, but Ranger drank straight from the bottle.

"He sure could use a swim," Big Eddie said. "Me, too, while the good weather holds."

"Maybe the pool hasn't been drai— The pool house! We haven't checked there."

I started running toward the side of the house where the Olympic-sized pool had another fence of its own, this one not locked. I remembered that the pool chaises all had green cushions, so maybe the cabana had green in it, too.

"We'll stay here," Chief Haversmith and the judge decided, "and wait for the others to get back."

"Maybe I better go with you," the EMT said, catching up to Matt and me. "As long as the chief stays by the bus."

"Don't you need equipment?"

He tapped his head. "Got enough in here for now."

The pool was empty, the cushions all packed away.

The cabana didn't look occupied. No one answered when we all shouted, "Professor Harmon! Are you there?"

Big Eddie was on our heels, without the dog. "I got something!" He sniffed the air, the ground, the closed sliders to the small cottage. "Montauk mist."

The glass doors were locked, with curtains pulled across so we couldn't see in. The single window had its blinds pulled. Matt hammered on the glass while I yelled some more. The paramedic went around to see if there was another entrance, or a window we could open. "Nope. I'll call Keys."

"We don't have time. I know he's in there!" I looked around for a rock or a loose paving stone. Or a chaise lounge. Before I could drag one over, Big Eddie was there, with Ranger's water bottle and his gun.

"I sure hope the judge's warrant covers this, or we'll be facing a lawsuit."

"No, I know one of the head honchos at Royce. He owes me." A phone call, at least. "But don't use the gun. We don't know where the professor is."

Big Eddie told us all to stand back, then used the water bottle. Matt held me protected from flying glass by his body, the big lunk. All we had to do was move another few feet away. I stayed in his arms, though.

The broken glass made enough noise to wake the dead—but not the professor.

Big Eddie climbed through, hurried to open the sliders. We crowded in to the one room. The wicker furniture had been piled up, the pool cushions stacked head-high in one corner. The small refrigerator stood open, unplugged, empty. The wheeled bar cart held nothing but a bottle of bitters and one of grenadine.

No professor.

Matt pushed past me. "There has to be a bathroom here, and at least a shower. That's what the place is for."

The door was behind the pile of furniture. Big Eddie flared his nostrils and pumped his fist. "Go!"

I pushed the door open, and nearly fell to my knees. We were too late. Dr. Harmon lay in the bathtub, the way Joe the plumber had described: the life jacket behind his head, unmoving, pale, lifeless. Joe hadn't mentioned the stench.

Big Eddie rushed out of the bathroom to clear his head. The EMT felt for a pulse. I could have told him not to bother, but Matt started laughing, just as Professor Harmon let out a loud rumbling snore.

I looked closer. At five empty bottles in the tub with the professor, three full ones lined up along the floor.

I guess he found the bar cart.

CHAPTER 26

"HALLO, MISS TATE. I AM DELIGHTED to make your acquaintance at last."

Dr. Harmon was cleaned up, sobered up, and sitting up, in Grandma Eve's living room, with a blanket over his knees. She'd insisted he be taken to her house, rather than some hospital room, where he'd only be embarrassed by the attention and harassed by reporters. I wanted to bring him to my mother's house, but I got overruled.

"Who is going to help him shower? What are you going to feed him? Where are you going to find him clean clothes?" She had the ever resourceful Lou, and a pantry full of healing herbs and comfort food.

But I needed to speak with him, desperately.

"He'll be better able to hold a conversation in a few hours. Come for dinner. You too, Dr. Spenser."

"Call me Matt, Mrs. Garland. And thank you, but I cannot. I have company coming tomorrow, and I still have to find sheets for the guest room."

Before we left Rosehill, Grandma Eve sent me to Cousin Lily's walk-in linen closet to borrow whatever Matt needed so that we wouldn't have to go shopping and he could join us for dinner. "You can bring them back laundered. You won't find half the choices anywhere nearby."

So while the EMTs worked at ensuring the pickled professor hadn't suffered anything worse than a hangover before transporting him to my grandmother's, I raided Rosehill's stock of umpteen threads-per-square-inch sheets. Not that Matt's guest deserved them, but Rosehill wouldn't miss them for a week, and I wanted to save us a trip back to Bridgehampton. I needed a shower and a change of clothes; Matt needed to check on his patients and Peg.

"And Moses. I'll have even less time to myself after Peg leaves. I forgot how much effort company takes, and a dog. Me who should know better. Moses is a good dog, but he can't be left to himself all day and night. Right now he has his sisters and Peg and Frankie, but I should be home bonding with him."

"I'd say that dog is bonded to you like hot glue. But I know what you mean. I can't leave Little Red too long or he feels abandoned. The other two are content with their blankets and bones as long as they get their dinner on time and an airing in the dog run. Not Red."

So we waited for Lou and the paramedics to load Dr. Harmon into the Lexus with Grandma Eve for the ride to Garland Drive, with Chief Haversmith and his two cops to help get the passed-out professor into the house. I went with Matt back to the clinic, greeted all three bounding, bouncing, boisterous Newfies, a buoyant Frankie, and, naturally, a blubbering Peg.

She was leaving tomorrow with Maggie, on her way via the cruise ship's private jet to Nova Scotia, thanks to Frankie's threats and ultimatums. Frankie volunteered to drive her to Islip-McArthur Airport to meet the jet, on his way home to Westchester to show Mollie her new digs. And find the best vet in the county to keep her happy and healthy. Matt gave him some names.

They invited us to dinner with them, on this last night, and pretended regret when we refused. I kissed everyone good-bye, including the two traveling dogs, in case I didn't see them in the morning. I kissed Matt and Moses good-bye too. Got licked by the wrong one.

I'd think about that later, when I saw Matt at the farm for dinner.

I walked and fed the dogs, took a quick shower,

scrambled into a pretty floral top and floaty skirt—for the professor's sake, of course. With pebbles in my sandals and no time to blow-dry my hair smooth, I trotted up the dirt road. I wanted to get to the farm early, to speak with the professor. Matt deserved to hear his story, too, but I couldn't wait.

Dr. Harmon's color looked good, and his hand, though gnarled and veiny, felt strong when he held it out to take mine. Grandma Eve stayed in the kitchen, cooking something that smelled so delicious my stomach rumbled, reminding me I hadn't eaten anything since the breakfast quiche. Lou brought out a platter of cheese and crackers and grapes, with a pitcher of iced tea.

"Thank you, my good man," the professor said. "I do not know what I would have done without you." He fingered the white button-down shirt he wore—which was far too big on his narrow frame—and the dark striped silk tie. He had on the same gray slacks, all washed and pressed, that he'd had on earlier, and brand-new, woolylined moccasins that I remembered giving to my grandmother last Christmas. He was also freshly shaved, and the fringe of silver hair lay smooth against his scalp. Even his shaggy eyebrows were less unruly.

Grandma Eve was right, as usual. I couldn't have provided for our guest half so well. The best I could do was spread cheese on a cracker for him.

Lou nodded his head. "Seeing you well has been my pleasure, sir." I noticed he did not offer either of us wine before he left us alone. I thanked him, and meant it, both for taking care of the professor and for giving us some privacy.

"Seeing you up and about is my pleasure, also, sir. I am delighted to meet you, too. Do you feel well enough to talk?"

"Fine, fine, dear girl. Your grandmother's tea was just what I needed."

"But did she give you something to eat? You must have been starving."

"Oh, no. I had a pocket full of biscuits from the ship's dining room that I was saving for later. Then I found a tin of peanuts with the liquors. Quite salty, but I had enough liquid to quench my thirst." His blue eyes twinkled at remembering how he'd spent his time and stayed hydrated. "And your grandmother insists on bringing me delicacies every hour."

"Peanuts and some biscuits were all you had to eat since Thursday night?" Here I was, scarfing down grapes and cheese because I'd missed lunch. "Please, have another cracker."

I poured the iced tea. "If you don't mind my asking, why didn't you leave the cabana? There were people working on the grounds, and phones and food and beds at the big house."

"I am sorry, my dear, that you had to worry, but you see, I am not very brave."

"You? You faced the sea serpent!"

"Ah, that was necessity, to try to save the ship and its passengers. My destiny, I suppose. But later? On dry land? I had no idea what waited outside the glass doors. My glasses were lost, you see—the formidable Lou found these for me; things are a bit blurry, but I can see how lovely you are—and I had no idea where I was, or that another building was as near as you say. I thought I might be held prisoner, so I waited for my captors to come demand ransom or some such. Or for you."

"You knew I'd come."

That was not a question, no more than my knowing that locating Dr. Harmon was my responsibility. "I apologize for taking so long, but we did not discover you were missing until everyone else was accounted for."

"I understand, my dear. Do not apologize. At least you arrived before the alcohol ran out. I don't know what I would have done then. Dutch courage, you know."

"I still say you are the bravest man I know. Can you tell me what happened on the ship? You must be weary of retelling the story by now, but I'd really like to know."

He finished his cracker and shook his head no, no more. "Oh, I haven't told anyone. It's for your ears only, my dear. I've told your grandmother I cannot remember how I got to that cottage, which is mostly true. I think I must have fainted at one point from the shock of the events." He had the sweetest smile, and his eyes lit with merriment again. "Drowning can have that effect on a body, you know."

"Half the people in this village will know if you tell a lie."

"As would half those at Royce. But we never speak of what so few know for certain."

"Unity."

He sighed. "Unity, our parallel universe where magic reigns. Which does not appear to be as united and pacific as we supposed."

I contemplated another slice of cheese. "The gods are angry."

"So it seems. But, Miss Tate, I have read your books and know you understand."

"You have?" I felt honored, overwhelmed that such an eminent scholar read my books. "I cannot believe you even came upon them."

"Of course I did, as soon as his grace informed me of your abilities."

"His grace?"

"The Duke of Royce. There is one, you know. Half-brother kinship to my own family. Of course they have been elevated to a dukedom by now, thank goodness. Or else my line might be forced to hold the world together."

There was that smile again.

"He keeps his eye on all the comings and goings of both realms. We were both sorry about Thaddeus, Viscount Grantham, that is. We'd hoped to lure you to England as his bride." He waved his hand in the air. "I know, two old men should know better than to plot others' lives. What will be, will be. But to get back to your books, I found them delightful, exciting and mostly true to what I have seen."

"I didn't understand, at first. I thought I made everything up."

"Oh, you did. You never went to Unity, never had a conversation with one of its people, not when you wrote your early works. You had—and have—a vivid imagination that tapped into your burgeoning power, plus the atavistic memories we all carry in our subconscious of when the spheres shared a common world."

I brushed at my eyes, to get rid of the dampness. "You cannot know how much your words mean to me. I feared I was a mere stenographer, scribbling down what others dictated."

He patted my hand. "Never, my dear, you are an artist!"

Damn, I was turning into Peg. I used one of Grandma Eve's linen napkins to wipe away my tears of pride and happiness and relief. "You know, I have read your books, too."

"Mine? I have no books, my dear. I've never published my childish stories. Think how that would look to the academic world, a scholar penning silly fairy tales. They were merely teaching tools for my students, to open their minds to creativity and imagination. I never found one half as talented as you."

Which kind of talent did he mean? I wondered, but this conversation was not about me. "You did not publish them under your name, no. But, you see, we have an amazing librarian here. She kept giving me books about mythological realms. I glanced at one called *A Bestiary of Fabulous Beings*. By an Everett James, and could not put it down. You, sir, happen to be James Everett Harmon."

"Ah, vanity. All is vanity, no? I could not let my children molder away in some dank corner of the university library with the rest of my lecture notes."

"You should claim them! Let them thrill other readers the way they thrilled me last night. Your books are truly brilliant, sir, and special. I could almost see the creatures through your eyes."

"Ah, I have seen remarkable beings, haven't I? Such colors, such sounds, such grace of movement—with scores of new species. There is a world of wonder, my dear, that we are fortunate to see, you and I."

I didn't know how lucky we were to face sea monsters, but yes, I felt blessed. Sometimes. "Of course I cannot see as much as you. I cannot go *there*."

"But you can speak with those who come here."

"Only when they speak to me."

"I envy you."

I envied him. I think. I had another grape. Or five.

He went on: "I had to put the marvels onto paper. I simply had to."

"I understand how it is with the need to write, even if no one sees your work."

"Exactly. If I had your talent with a brush, I might have tried to paint what I carried in my mind, still hiding the connection to a fusty old retired dean, of course."

I didn't tell him I used markers and the computer. "Yes, it's hard to describe colors in words. Especially colors that change and vibrate and transmit feelings of joy and good will. I doubt any artist could capture all that."

"Perhaps we should collaborate some day."

"I would be honored, if we get through this situation."

"A bit of a pother, isn't it?"

"You tell me. I believe you have faced the serpent before."

"But it is stronger, angrier. I never could send it back whence it came."

"It's been banished here, so it cannot return to Unity."

"Ah, that makes sense. Yet it stayed quiescent for decades after I confronted it. Now?" He shrugged inside Lou's shirt. "I cannot communicate with the Others as you can."

"It's the pictures. I try to draw a picture in my mind, and they can see it sometimes. I cannot speak their language either."

"I doubt any of us can because it is so complicated and so much of it is telepathic. Although your young man tries."

"Grant is not my anything. He does not even return my calls."

"Oh, did you expect the telephone to work from the International space station? I doubt it works that way."

"He's in outer space?"

"Yes, but that is very hush-hush. We are trying to see if anyone—anything—has been tampering with the ozone levels. And the lines of power, although not even the Russians know that part of his mission."

Good grief, I'd be a space widow if we'd married. I'd live in a state of anxiety glued to the TV or waiting for the phone call from NASA. Or the mental message from who-knows-what kind of official. I could live with occasional jealousy. Not constant panic. "Does he ever miss an opportunity to put his life in danger?"

The professor laughed. "Not since I've known him, which is since he was first out of nappies. Not good husband material, eh?"

I shuddered at the thought.

"Ah, I wondered about the veterinarian."

"We're friends."

"And somewhat more, by your blushes. That's not what the busybodies at Royce had in mind for you."

"He can see what I see. What you can see."

"Dash it, I must have missed that memo. Excellent. I'll be delighted to meet another of us."

The way he spoke you'd think we were related, which appealed to me. Dr. Harmon was the grandfather I never had: wise, caring, encouraging. And accepting me for what I am. "There's nothing romantic between Matt and me. We've never had a real date."

He patted my hand. "What's meant to be, will be."

I wondered if he had a bit of Doc Lassiter's genes, too. His touch, his voice, his smile all contributed to a feeling of well-being and confidence. I could handle Matt's lady friends. I could handle a sea serpent.

No, I couldn't.

"What's meant was for you to survive to fight another day."

He spoke with deep regret: "Yes, I suppose so."

Before he could tell me about the assault on the *Nova Pride*, Grandma Eve brought in brewed tea and tiny croissants and small jars of her homemade jellies. "It's not quite a proper English tea, but dinner is still an hour away and you need to keep eating small meals to regain your strength."

When she left, he said, "Your grandmother is a fine woman, Miss Tate. You come from excellent stock."

"Please call me Willow, or Willy."

Now he was the one to brush away a tear. "I wish I had a granddaughter like you."

Why did everyone cry around me? I was embarrassed for both of us, so I held out the platter. "Please, have a roll. They are still warm and Grandma Eve's jams are the best you'll find."

He studied the handwritten labels on the jars. "Ah, rose hips. I haven't had that since I was a lad. I don't think I ever tasted beach plum jelly."

While we ate—I needed to keep up my strength, too, didn't I?—Dr. Harmon finally told his story.

He never knew why he went on the cruise ship, just that he had to go, kind of like my father's presentiments. When first the dolphins— "Pink ones, Willy, with kaleidoscope eyes!"—forced the boat off course, and then a sudden storm cropped up, he realized why he'd bought a ticket to a place he never intended to see. He tried to warn the captain, who laughed and told him to put on his life jacket if he was so worried. He urged everyone near him to don theirs, too, which might have helped saved some lives.

Then came the wave. People screamed, panicked, nearly trampled each other in their efforts to escape. The crew couldn't lower the life rafts fast enough. The professor could see the wave growing, could see the whirlpool eyes, the whitecap fangs, that abyss of its giant maw, but he could do nothing. Not until the thing got closer. Then he started to shout at it, some in words he'd heard in his trances, some in words Grant's father had taught him ages ago, some in words from ancient texts.

He spoke in syllables and breaths and clicks I could not possibly understand, then translated: "Get thee hence, foul wyrm! Begone, I say, by the pact between the worlds. Begone or lose thy powers."

This time the words did not work. Perhaps he'd forgotten a phrase or an intonation. Perhaps the monster had nowhere to go back to, if it were forbidden Unity. The serpent came on, the boat tipped, and the professor found himself flung through the air, smashed into the sea, carried deep under the waves. He knew he could not survive. No mortal man could.

Yet suddenly those dolphins were beside him, beneath him, carrying him toward the surface, blowing bubbles into his face so that he could breathe. And then a giant hand lifted him. The hand of God, he thought, but I believed it to be M'ma, the serpent's true foe.

"I must have cried out then, about wanting to go home to Royce. I wished to be buried there, amongst my ancestors. Instead I found myself in that cottage, alive, with the most amazing lantern beetles hovering nearby, warming me with tiny fires, drying my clothes, keeping the darkness at bay. Then I slept. I dreamt of dolphins and birds and fish, and birdfish or fishbirds. And a willow tree. I knew it must be you. I knew you would come."

He pushed the last croissant in my direction. Tears filled his eyes as he looked at me, sad, fearful, yet resigned. "I knew the fight was not over."

Chapter 27

WE LEFT THE PROFESSOR'S STORY full of dolphin life guards and freakish waves and some unknown Samaritan transporting him to Paumanok Harbor
because he must have mentioned Royce in his delirium.
Then he'd slept through any calls or searches, recovering
from an ordeal no octogenarian should survive. Now he
needed to be in seclusion to protect his fragile health.

Close enough.

All of it rang true, as far as it went. Even Uncle Henry
could digest Grandma Eve's amazing butternut squash
ravioli in contentment. Everyone knew there was more
to the story; most knew they'd never see what Dr. Harmon didn't want to talk about.

I whispered to Matt beside me at the table that I'd tell
him later, though I was still guessing about a lot: that
M'ma and his minions had come to the aid of the dear
old friend who visited Unity in a trance state. Or perhaps
they helped total strangers because they felt responsible
for inflicting the monster on us. Now I doubted M'ma
remained in our world; he would have vanquished the
serpent for us.

Whatever the reason, the results were incomprehensible to ordinary, normal people. Telling the average citizen
or the news-hungry reporters the truth would be like telling them the water molecules separated out breathable
oxygen, or the grains of sand decided to build themselves
a skateboard ramp, right under an ocean liner. Dolphins

were known to help people since the earliest times, so
people could accept that. Not even Matt's imminent expert could disprove their capabilities, because she'd never
get to see the so-called new breed, much less experiment
on them. So she'd leave.

Which thought was as sweet as the homemade peach
ice cream Grandma Eve served for dessert.

During the meal, no one dwelled on the danger we all
knew loomed on the horizon or in the ocean depths. We
spoke about the immediate future instead. My grandmother had already put a call in to her niece, Lily, Rosehill's housekeeper. Lily said she'd be thrilled to have a
gentleman at Rosehill to care for again—a real gentleman, not the Hollywood moguls and dot-com million-
aires who'd been renting the place. Besides, looking after
a retired scholar had to be easier than chasing after her
young granddaughter and infant grandson. She loved
her daughter's children, of course; she'd be in Paumanok
Harbor tomorrow, Sunday.

Lou had called England, and the grateful people at
the Royce Institute instantly named Dr. Harmon liaison
adviser at the new facility, with a lifetime residency if he
wished to stay, and a more generous pension. Both the
professor and Paumanok Harbor were that valuable to
them. Lou did say they were hoping Dr. Harmon would
agree to remain until the current crisis had been re-
solved.

Since the professor had absolutely no intention of
getting on a boat or a plane any time soon, and since he'd
received such a warm welcome, to say nothing of my
grandmother's cooking, Rosehill's wine cellar, and ideas
for our new collaboration, he allowed as how he'd be
pleased to stay, and to be of service to his new friends.

Lou raised his glass of wine in a toast, and we all
drank to Dr. Harmon's health and longevity. He turned
pink with pleasure.

The chief had called off the search, to the whole East
End's relief, and joy that the survival rate was one hundred percent. More, if you counted the five dogs. Less if
you counted the lost parrot no one claimed. The papers

and online news feeds and TV still carried pictures of the ship, with tugs and barges and floats all around it, waiting for the right tide. They mentioned that no one had seen any new dolphins or the rare bird, which was yesterday's news. Some senator's mistress turned out to be a transvestite, and another celebrity couple's marriage ended in a knockdown brawl on a red carpet, so the public's interest focused elsewhere. After all, the Hamptons had no celebrities to speak of in the off-season, so why bother?

Now the South Fork could get back to searching for a gang of bank robbers and a gang of cyber black hats—unless they were connected.

How could that be? We all wanted to know.

The chief shrugged. "Russ and the government techs are working one angle, the boots on the ground are working another. It just seems too big a coincidence that both are happening at once."

"But they haven't been active recently?"

"Not since the night of the shipwreck. Maybe the gang has moved on."

Before we could discuss the chief's theory and leads and Russ' determination to clear his name and the machines he oversaw, or I could remember to ask about Axel Vanderman or hypnotism, the professor started yawning, then half nodded off right at the table.

Matt and Lou assisted him up the stairs after we all wished him well again, and I promised to visit in the morning to plan a strategy.

Matt drove me the two minutes to my house, with the extra food Grandma Eve packed up for me. She'd sent some jam for his company, too, which meant she liked him, not that it mattered to me. I liked him.

He helped me carry my stuff in, so I asked if he wanted coffee. I knew he ought to go, get his house ready for company, make sure Peg had everything she needed, play with his new dog. He said yes, he'd like a cup, which said more about how much he liked me than about his taste in beverages.

He tried to make friends with Little Red while I started the coffeemaker. I doubt Red remembered Matt saving his life from a homicidal pyromaniac, but he sure as hell remembered who cut off his mangled leg and his testicles.

I threw Red a chew stick—and bigger ones for Buddy and Dobbin—and we watched Red growl his into submission. We simply sat, next to each other on the dog-hair-covered sofa, sipping our coffees, nibbling on the chocolate chip cookies from my secret stash. Kind of like watching a fire in the winter: peaceful, comfortable, no pressure.

Until Matt broke the silence. "Your grandmother is amazing. You are so lucky to have her."

I laughed. "You've never seen her in action. She's on her good behavior when Lou is around."

"No, she's kind and generous and smart, and loves you so much I feel warmed by her affection, just by sitting next to you."

I felt warm sitting next to him on the sofa. "You're letting your new imagination show you things that aren't there again."

He pulled on one of my curls. "It's there. I know this is a bad time, but sharing in the rescue, visiting the House, having dinner with your family, I want more."

"Grandma Eve sent some of those little croissants home with me. I'll pack a baggie for you."

"You know that's not what I mean. I want more of you, your attitude, your courage that you swear is cowardice, your adoration for your grandmother that you try to hide, your silly dog. But I can't compete with a dude who can buy you the moon and the stars."

"He's not on the moon. He's at the space station."

"You've got to be kidding."

"No, that's what Dr. Harmon said. Supposedly trying to get a better look at the holes in the ozone and disruptions in the power lines, but I think he's calling out to the otherworld to shut the gates between Unity and us. There's been too much activity."

Matt wrapped the curl around his finger. "Okay, so your former fiancé is an astronaut, besides being a titled lord and the best linguist on Earth. I'll never be half as exciting, or half as heroic as your firefighting friend. I can't compete with that world-famous entertainer with the million dollar horse, either. I can't even compete with Frankie, who goes out and buys his dog a Land Rover. I'm just a simple country vet, and that's all I'll ever be. Tell me I have a chance before I dig such a deep hole I'll never find my way out. You are not the kind of woman a man forgets once he fixes her in his head."

I couldn't say anything. Matt was my rock, my pillow. How much more did he want to be?

"Come on, Willy. Give me an answer. I can't go on not knowing if we have a future. I thought we did after the fireflies, but you ran off to the city. I thought we didn't when you never called, but here we are, sharing adventures and family meals and kisses. You can't keep blowing hot and cold like that. I've got to know."

I was cold thinking about him leaving. Hot where his hand rubbed the back of my neck. He was right. It was fish or cut bait, shit or get off the pot, do or die. Not that I'd die if Matt didn't want to be my friend anymore. Not that I'd wither away if I never got to taste him. I'd live. I just mightn't want to.

Not because we shared Oey and M'ma and the Others. Not because he'd gone to a haunted house with me. Not because my pulse speeded up whenever he smiled and his touch on my neck had me thinking of those soft, soft sheets at Rosehill.

Because he was Matt.

"You have a chance, but—"

He placed his fingers over my lips, then replaced them with his lips. "That's enough for now."

Not by half, it wasn't. One kiss made me want more. Oh, he meant the chance. "You always had a chance, just—"

"Good. I was jealous of the old man. He adores you."

He was jealous of the professor? How lovely! "I wasn't flirting with him, not like you and Peg and you and Tina and you and every other female in a hundred-mile radius. And you're the one having an old friend come to stay. My old friend is eighty something. You can't say the same."

"You're jealous!"

"Damn right."

"That means you care."

"Damn right, but—"

He still wouldn't let me finish a sentence. I guess he didn't want to hear all my reservations and rules.

He kissed me again, which shut me up, then he said, "I know, no promises. Caring is a good start. We'll take it slow."

We already took it slow. I'd been thinking about him, thinking about making love with him, since the first time I saw him, weeks ago. With the chaos that surrounded me, how could I plan for tomorrow, and how could I turn down a perfectly good plan for today? I was ready to move onto the next stage of our big chance, in my bedroom.

He wasn't finished working things out in his head, the rational, logical man that he was. "Just so you know, I am not here for a quickie."

"No quickies." Un-uh. If we were going to do this, we were going to do it right.

"Or a weekend affair. I've hardly dated since my divorce because I don't like casual hookups and relationships founded on nothing but mutual satisfaction."

"Me neither. They're usually unsatisfying, anyway."

"Good. So we're agreed this isn't about sex?"

Um. "You're not talking about a platonic relationship here, are you?"

He grinned. "You've got to be kidding. I'm trying to play it cool and act the gentleman, not pull your clothes off with my teeth and leave razor burn from your head to your toes. But, no, this isn't about sex. At least not just about sex."

"That's good." On both counts. He wanted me, which was the best aphrodisiac in the universe. But he wanted *me*, not just a warm body. A body growing warmer by the second.

"Then you won't run off again?"

I couldn't leave the professor alone until the sea serpent left. After that . . . ? "I'll be here awhile, it looks like. And I won't go back to Manhattan without telling you, okay?"

"I understand. One day at a time." He got up and took a box out of his jacket pocket. "Don't panic, I'm not asking for any promises. I made a hasty marriage the first time. I'm not stepping into that mantrap again until I'm certain it'll last." He tapped the box. "It's not like I'm offering you a ring or anything."

"So what's in the box?"

He opened it to show a small radio. "For the House, so it can learn new tunes. You promised an iPod, but we don't know if the place is wired for Wi-Fi, or if there's a computer to download. This has a battery and a cord."

Hell, we didn't know if whatever lived there had fingers or opposable thumbs, but it didn't matter. Matt had bought a haunted house a present! What a guy. I threw my arms around him and gave him a big kiss.

About ten minutes later he said, "So that's a yes? Without forever. Yet."

"It's a yes."

"So can we get to the sex part now?"

We ended up on the floor, naked. That is, we started on the couch, and our clothes ended up on the floor, on the furniture, on the ceiling fan. I think Little Red carried my sandal away to gnaw, but who cared?

The first time was a quickie after all.

I apologized.

He laughed, and I could feel it in his chest, under my cheek. "Hell, speedy, if you're that fast and easy, this is going to be even more fun than I imagined."

"You imagined making love with me?"

"Every night since I met you. No, before that, when I saw you at the rodeo. No, when I read your books. No, when your mother told me about you."

I didn't believe him. "That long, huh?"

"Maybe longer. You just might be the girl of my

dreams, the one I've been waiting for all my life. I knew I couldn't do anything about it while the Brit was here, or the cowboy, or the firefighter. You've been damned busy breaking hearts. Then you packed up and disappeared before I laid mine on the line."

"I was afraid."

"Of me?" He tipped my head up so he could look at me.

"Of falling for you. Feeling for you. We have so many logistic-type problems. Location, jobs, even the dogs. How could this work?"

"We'll figure it out. You'll see."

"But I changed your life without meaning to. I didn't want you changing mine."

Too late.

The verses of that song kept running through my head, the words about love, not that I used the l-word in reference to Matt and me. That was way too scary. The words about a hunger, though, an endless burning need. It seemed we'd never get enough of each other. Like we had to make up for the wasted time all in one night.

Now I lo—liked him more. Sex did that. Good sex did it faster, deeper. I couldn't figure how this could work, but I knew I'd regret not trying for the rest of my life. Give up a man who made love like you were his first love? Like you were a precious gift to be savored and cherished? Like he'd never grow tired of you and your perfect body—even when your body wasn't perfect to start with, and on a downhill slide? Matt made love like he lived his life, with unselfish dedication and purpose and great passion for what he believed in.

He believed we had something special. I believed in him.

We knocked the lamp off the end table, and our coffee mugs and everything else off the coffee table. Then the leg on the old couch gave out and we landed on the floor, laughing so hard we rolled into the bookcase, sending my mother's dog books and my mother's dogs in every direction. We scattered the scatter rugs and threw the throw pillows out of the way. Matt tipped over the magazine rack when he picked me up, and my foot hit the hall umbrella stand when he carried me upstairs. I forgot to tell him about the refrigerator door when he went down later to get us some cold water—not that water was going to lessen the heat—and so he didn't give the door the good shove it needed to latch tight.

I guess Buddy stuck his long nose in the fridge, then Dobbin helped empty the contents onto the floor for easier snacking. They dragged Grandma Eve's goodies into the living room, onto the broken couch and displaced pillows. Who needed chew toys when they had plastic containers and tinfoil-wrapped bundles?

We never heard the noise. Or when Little Red, pissed that he'd been locked out of the bedroom with a soft pillow to sleep on, shredded the feather pillow up and down the hallway and stairs.

The house must have looked like it had been ransacked by the Hamptons' Gang. At least that's what Susan screamed when she called 911.

We heard the screams and the cries of "Where's Willy? What have they done to my cousin?"

I flew down the stairs in time to have her call the police back and cancel the emergency.

Which would have been fine if I wasn't naked, and if the dishwasher at the Breakaway hadn't helped her carry in a new set of pots and pans.

Chapter 28

THE DISHWASHER, FOR CRYING OUT LOUD! Who was related to every chambermaid and gardener and house painter in the Hamptons. This wasn't as bad as when a snake slithered over my leg while I was messing around at a swimming pool with a blond life guard when I was a teenager. I ran screaming through a cocktail party at Bayview Ranch that time, bare-assed. Maybe that's when my father decided to move to Florida permanently.

Susan sat on the floor, howling until tears of laughter ran down her cheeks. I couldn't flee up the stairs because Matt was there, wearing a pillowcase and some feathers and a big goofy grin. I couldn't get to the kitchen because I'd have to step on the mess the dogs left. And the floor did not open up and swallow me. Who says God answers prayers?

"You didn't see any of this," Matt told Julio, righting the umbrella stand with the hand that didn't hold the pillowcase.

"You the mayor? The one who makes you forget?"

"No, I'm the vet who'll neuter you like I do all the male dogs in town if you mention one word."

Julio looked at Little Red, then at Buddy. "One word about what?"

Right.

Susan finally tiptoed through the debris to get a big black garbage bag. For me, not the garbage. I'd have to put down the pillow I'd grabbed from the floor and Little Red, who wasn't an effective fig leaf anyway. I glared at Matt until he found the dogs' blanket behind the dead sofa and wrapped it around me. Then I snagged his pillowcase when I ran past, for laughing at me.

Susan whistled, Julio dropped the pots and fled. "I didn't see none of that, either." And Matt lifted the golden retriever.

He called up the stairs: "You want me to stay and help clean up or you want me to go away so you can hide under your bed for the next thirty days?"

"I want you to put me out of my misery like you'd do for a sick cat. Or get out your tranquilizer gun and shoot my cousin."

"Maybe you should lock the door," she yelled up.

"What good would that do? You have a key." By now I'd found sweatpants and a T-shirt. I went back to help Matt find his clothes. Red must have hidden one of his socks because we never saw it.

Matt and Susan were filling the black bag, righting the furniture, and grinning like idiots, which did not improve my temper.

"C'mon, speedy, what's the big deal?" Matt asked while he held up the sofa so Susan could stack dog-training books under the broken leg. "I've seen you naked, Susan doesn't care, and you made Julio's day. You've got nothing to be ashamed about anyway, not with that gorgeous body."

I felt better, until Susan dropped a book. "Speedy?"

"Get out! Get out, both of you! I never want to see either of you again as long as I live."

"I'll call tomorrow after my company comes. I don't know Gina's schedule, but maybe we can all get dinner. What's the special for Sunday night at the Breakaway, Susan?"

"Shortbread, two-minute eggs, instant pudding."

"Which is all you'll have time to make," I said, "'cause you'll be too busy packing. And we didn't need more pots."

"Sure, paper plates in the microwave and tinfoil in the

toaster oven work for you. Some of us are kitchen artists. We need better tools to create better dishes for the fall menu."

"Well, if you're aiming high, I bet Julia Child would have seen about getting the refrigerator door fixed."

"Well, if you hadn't brought us another catastrophe, maybe Ike, the repairman, wouldn't have been too busy driving the ambulance."

So that's who came to help Professor Harmon. Instead of fixing my fridge. I put the throw pillows back on the sofa. "For your information, I did not bring the wave down on that boat. Professor Harmon says so."

"Professor Harmon also goes off in trances."

I spent the rest of the night cleaning up, by myself. I found my missing sunglasses, a five dollar bill, and Matt's sock, though how it got in the fireplace I'll never know. I threw it in the trash bag. Laugh at me, will you?

I had to laugh, too. That's how mature I am these days, more than fifteen years after that first flashing. I didn't even blush. Maybe I did, but I was too mad and mortified to notice.

I smiled every time I remembered the look on Susan's face when she realized she'd laughed so hard she'd wet herself. That was one person who wouldn't be spreading news of my latest embarrassment. Not when I could post sketches of her in a puddle on my website. Matt wouldn't say anything. He was too much of a gentleman. And he wanted to be invited back to my house and my bed. Besides, I had the sketch in my head of him trying to hold a big shaggy dog and his dignity.

Then there was Julio, most likely regaling all his friends with the story right now. I laughed at Matt's threats—they wouldn't fool a child—and got a head start on the town's merriment at my expense.

At least the professor wasn't chuckling when I went over to my grandmother's for Sunday brunch. We had nothing edible left after the dogs' party at my house; ketchup and mayo and an old tin of sardines didn't count. Susan was still sleeping, or still avoiding me. Grandma Eve had cut-up fruit and waffles. My kitchen couldn't match that, not even on a good day.

I thought Lou looked amused while he read the *Times*, which I never found the least humorous. Maybe he got lucky last night, too. With my grandmother. I lost my appetite.

I had a lot of errands to do this morning. Matt had to wait for his new company, and see off his old company and her dogs, so I asked Dr. Harmon if he wished to come along, to see some of the town where he'd be living.

Lou decided he'd drive. He didn't ask if I wanted him along or if I'd mind being seen in his *look at me, I'm rich* car. He'd set himself up as bodyguard to both the professor and me and seemed relieved to have us together. I wondered if he truly thought we were in danger, and if he'd call in backup if we separated. And if I'd know it. DUE kept its cards close to its chest, and Lou didn't share much.

The professor didn't see much. So much for showing him the town. Our first business had to be finding an optometrist who could fit him for proper spectacles, as the old man called them. One in East Hampton agreed to open specially on a Sunday afternoon, for a survivor. And for the couple hundred dollar incentive Lou offered. We decided to take care of my errand in the Harbor before the glasses place opened.

I directed Lou to Shearwater Street. "You can both stay in the car."

Dr. Harmon wanted to come. Lou said he'd make some phone calls while he waited. Hah! The big guy from the scary agency didn't want anything to do with the House. Neither did I, but a promise was a promise.

I had the radio in one hand, the professor's hand in my other to guide him up the walk until he got new glasses. Neither of us believed that.

The junk mail was gone.

"It throws things," I warned the professor. He peered around, ready to run. I clasped his elbow. The man truly was as chickenshit as me. As I, I corrected, since he used to teach writing.

I started talking before we got to the front door. "Hello. It is I, Willow Tate. And Dr. James Everett Harmon, from the Royce Institute. You helped us find him, and we wanted to thank you."

The House rumbled. I couldn't tell if it were going to shoot shingles at us, or if it meant hello. We stepped back, in case. When nothing else happened, I went up to the door. "I brought a gift to show our appreciation."

I fit the little radio through the mail slot, hoping there was a doormat beneath it, or a pile of catalogs to break its fall. I didn't hear a crash, and nothing came flying back at us. "It's got batteries and an electric plug, for whichever works best for you. I can stop back to check if you need new batteries."

I'd send Matt.

"And it gets a lot of stations. I tested it near my house. Classical, rap, country, stations that play show tunes and ones that play old rock and roll songs. There are political talk shows, too." Sometimes those opinionated bigots made me so mad I could spit. Heaven knew how the House would react. "Maybe you should stick to the music."

The cement stoop beneath our feet felt warmer, but the House did not talk to me. I felt silly, wondering if the professor thought I'd made the whole thing up.

"We'll be going now. I know how you like your privacy." I slipped one of my mother's cards through the slot. I'd written my cell number on the back. "But you can call me if you need anything."

"Or me," Dr. Harmon added, speaking up now that we'd survived intact. "Although I am presently without a telephone. Heaven knows how long I would have waited for the dear girl if you hadn't directed her."

We started to leave, relieved but disappointed, too. Then the house sang to us about a bad moon rising.

"What is that?"

"Creedence Clearwater Revival. I think the House is warning us of trouble ahead."

"Thank you, sir or madam. Can you be more specific?"

Nothing.

"Well, if you do think of anything, please call. I fear we shall need all the help we can get."

"All you need is love."

"Very true. Thank you. I'll keep that in mind."

We hurried to the car and Lou. Neither of us mentioned what the House said. Why bother? Everyone knew doom lurked on the horizon.

Next, our visitor needed clothes, not Lou's hand-me-ups.

Ralph Lauren had a store in East Hampton. In fact he had Polo this and Ralph Kids that and even his daughter had the candy shop near the movies. Dr. Harmon loved the flannel shirts, the corduroy pants with lots of pockets, and the exotic jelly beans. He insisted on ties to go with the shirts and Starbucks coffee to go with the jelly beans. The five hundred dollars the cruise company gave to each survivor did not go far. Lou used his credit card.

I checked out the bookstore on Main Street. No romance novels, no chick lit. None of the professor's books. And none of mine. When I asked why, the clerk talked at his computer, not to my face. "Temporarily out of stock, is all."

Yeah, they were out last time I checked, too, the snobby bastards. I didn't buy anything. They were always yipping about people supporting the local stores. What about them supporting their local authors? When the professor said he liked mysteries, I told him he'd love Mrs. Terwilliger at the library. For free.

We had lunch at a mostly vegetarian place on Newtown Lane that was mobbed, despite the exorbitant prices. For some reason the wait staff wore their pajamas. And they thought Paumanok Harbor was weird?

I thought I spotted someone who looked like Axel Vanderman, but he left the restaurant in a hurry. On purpose?

My phone rang before I could mention it to Lou. I checked the caller ID.

"House?" Dr. Harmon asked.

"Nope, it's just my father. I'll call him back when you're at the optometrist."

"What if he's got a warning for you?" Lou asked this time.

If he knew about my father's auguries, he knew time didn't matter much. Still, I stayed on at the restaurant, to the snarky waitress' disapproval, with another cup of coffee and my phone.

"Hi, Dad. What's up?"

"I wanted to warn you about Desi, sweetheart. It's real dangerous."

First Stu, then my nose and skunks, now Desi? "Come on, Dad, you've got to be more specific. I know a dream is just a dream, but you've got to stop scaring me with stuff I can't figure out. I don't know anyone named Desi, and I've got a real mess on my hands here without adding him to my list of worries."

"Yeah, I heard about yesterday."

Uh-oh. "What did you hear? And do you know a guy named Julio?"

"Julio? No, I don't think so. But I heard the House sang to you and you found Harmon."

The House wasn't all that sang, but I felt better. A person does not want her father metaphorically waiting at the doorstep for her to come home after a date, no matter her age.

"The House is okay. What about Desi?"

"Don't you listen to the radio, baby girl?"

"No, I gave one to the House, though."

"Well, put on the TV or something. Desi's no dream of mine. It's a hurricane that might barrel up the East Coast, the worst in decades, they say. They're starting to evacuate the Keys, and the thing is days away."

"Desi is a hurricane?"

"That's what I'm trying to warn you about. It's as big as the one that wiped out Paumanok Harbor and Montauk in thirty-eight."

Just what we needed, a hurricane to add its strength to the water dragon. I'd take one of my father's predications any day.

Lou knew all about the storm. We had three or four days, he figured, before they had a projected track with any high degree of probability. He also checked: the Paumanok Harbor meteorologists couldn't do much to change the odds. They couldn't budge a storm of that size. A category one or two, maybe. Category four? If it came, we'd get it.

"Maybe it will go out to sea." The professor held out hope.

"Maybe. If it's left on its own." I felt the hope slip away from all three of us, and we had not mentioned the sea serpent out loud. Add the two together, you got category kiss your ass good-bye.

CHAPTER 29

DR. HARMON'S GLASSES WOULDN'T BE ready for three days, but the optometrist, for another ransom amount, provided better stand-ins. So we moved on to the shopping center in Bridgehampton where I'd taken Peg. I kept an eye out for Vanderman, with no luck. While the men shopped for underwear and other essentials like shoes and belts and a warmer jacket for nighttime and a raincoat and boots for Desi, I shopped at Victoria's Secret, for Matt. My plain white cotton bikinis and oversized T-shirts were not appropriate attire for a woman having mind-numbing sex, which I fully intended to repeat. Or for tweaking a certain veterinarian's interest, which I also intended to repeat as soon as he was free of the dolphin expert and before Desi.

I tried to think of Matt and sex instead of the hurricane. It didn't work. Even the anorexic saleswomen talked about where they'd go to ride out the storm.

Hurricanes said a lot more about people's personalities than any Rorschach test. Some fools welcomed them as a great adventure, holding hurricane parties and printing "I survived" whatever its name was. Surfers came from miles away to ride the waves, until the towns shut the beaches as too dangerous. Newscasters would be coming back to the east end of Long Island to whip up the frenzy and the angst about storm surges and beach erosion and loss of business. Other people took the danger more seriously, more personally. They boarded up their windows at the first hint of eighty mph winds. They hauled their boats out of the water and bought gas for their generators and their cars. They had dry ice, emergency bags packed and waiting near the door, crank-handle radios, rolls of duct tape, and enough cash on hand to tempt the Hamptons Gang.

Then there were cowards like me, who basically fled before the storm got as far north as Cape Hatteras. Hurricanes were terrifying, unpredictable, and came with thunder and lightning. Why wait to panic when you could do it today? Delaying until the Weather Service made its final prediction meant the roads would be clogged, the buses and trains filled. Power lines would be down, trees on roofs or in the roads, roofs on lawns, boats on lawns, lawn furniture on roofs. No, better to get out now.

I'd head for Manhattan and my cozy apartment. A couple of windows on high-rises blew out in bad winds, maybe the lights flickered. So what? New York City did not come to a hysterical standstill in a storm. People used to everyday anxiety generally handled crises fine. No panic until the bars closed.

The problem was, how could I leave? My head said start packing. My heart said hold on. Those ties to Paumanok Harbor I'd spent years unraveling had me by the throat.

Little Red went where I went. But what about the big dogs, and Mom's house? Could I walk away?

Hell, yes. Uncle Roger knew what to do way better than I did. Susan was used to caring for Buddy and Dobbin. The house had survived since before I was born.

As for the professor, Lou would take good care of him. And of Grandma Eve, too. They could all go to higher ground, perhaps Rosehill. The village itself? If all the weather wizards in Paumanok Harbor couldn't keep it safe from a hurricane, my presence meant diddly-squat.

It might mean something to Matt. I did not know if he'd prefer red or black lace, nightie or camisole and thong. I did know he would never leave the Harbor. He'd feel he had to be on hand to rescue animals, with memories of those dreadful New Orleans images in everyone's heads when people had to choose between their own lives and their pets'. He'd want to believe I'd be at his side, helping, instead of tucked up safe a hundred miles away. And I cared what he believed. Except when he believed I was brave and brilliant and loyal and steadfast.

I might as well try to hold back the hurricane as try to be the woman he wanted. This could be a one-night stand after all when I told him I'd be leaving in the morning. I promised to tell him if I left, but maybe I'd wait till tomorrow to tell him I was going. Give the new lingerie— I bought both the red and the black—an outing, and give myself one more night to remember. A two-night stand sounded better.

It sounded like another heartbreak for me. Which is why I never wanted to get involved with Matt and Oey and the village and the kraken altogether. Dumb, dumb, dumb.

And dumb to think I could walk away from the sea dragon of my book. I didn't have a chance in hell of affecting Desi. Professor Harmon might have a hair-thin chance of sending N'fwend back to hell or the center of the Earth, with my help.

Without us, and the Others we could try to call on for assistance, everyone I loved here could be washed out to sea.

The radios on in the stores spoke of storm surges. Twelve feet high, twenty feet high. They never said how far inland that surge could travel, at that height. Paumanok Harbor's main street should not be in danger, a couple of miles from the bay, but the docks, the harbor, all the low houses with water views would be gone. And we'd be cut off from civilization if the roads flooded. The single highway to Montauk had washed away in the past, leaving it an island. Paumanok Harbor could be just as isolated, alone with a ravening water monster supercharged and intensified by the hurricane, determined to wipe out its enemy and steal the power. Or use the swallowed-up talent to get back to Unity, to wreak havoc and revenge there.

So I bought batteries for flashlights and radios, bottled water, candles, and chocolate bars. I figured I was as ready as I could be without Prozac for any eventuality, except the long lines of people buying batteries and water and candles and peanut butter and crackers. Uh-oh. I forgot the hurricane staple that never went bad, never needed cooking or refrigeration. I got out of line to add them to my cart. And bought more dog food. And cookies.

I wanted to hurry home so I could eat the ice cream in the freezer before it melted when the power went out.

Lou laughed and said we had days left to prepare, and did I have boards to nail over the windows. I tried to call my mother to find out. Then I had to worry she was in the Keys, helping with the evacuation there. I left a message that tried not to sound like my father with his doom-sayer worries.

Dr. Harmon wanted to see Rosehill through his new glasses, to see if there truly was room for him, without inconveniencing anyone. We all smiled. You could house Hannibal's army in the place, and still have room for their elephants.

Cousin Lily welcomed Dr. Harmon like her favorite uncle, and offered to give us a tour. The professor did not wish to put her to more trouble. He said he'd be comfortable in the pool house where we'd found him. An electric heater, some blankets for the open-out couch and he'd be fine. The half-size refrigerator and the electric hot plate were all he needed. Perhaps he'd get himself a dog to keep him company on strolls about the lovely grounds. My mother had greyhounds, did she not?

Everyone vetoed that, the pool house, not the greyhounds, although Lily didn't seem all too pleased about the dogs. The pool house had too much glass, was too unprotected, too far from Lily's kitchen, too noisy when the pool was open.

The guesthouse also got voted down. That was being converted to administration offices and small classrooms, weeks from completion, and out of sight from the main building. Lou insisted the professor be close to help, in case of an emergency. No one wanted to say that our new friend had too many candles on his cake to live alone, but we all understood Lou's concern.

The apartment over the garage was also rejected, already being divided into separate suites for resident staff.

Plans were to make the two main floors in the mansion itself into lecture halls, study centers and conference rooms, with the third floor bedrooms divided smaller and reserved for junior instructors and visiting lecturers.

No way could our gentleman live there. I'd already worried how I could get Dr. Harmon up the three flights to my NY apartment. But up Rosehill's grand arching staircase several times a day? There had to be an alternative. I knew Cousin Lily's apartment behind the kitchen had no extra bedroom, but surely in this vast complex there was a private spot, safe and secure, for their esteemed, elderly resident consultant?

Cousin Lily grinned and told us to follow her. Lou helped the professor up the stairs and I followed, wary of his eyesight and stamina. We all moved down the hall to the master suite.

The professor took one look inside the door and went no further. "But they must have designated this for someone really important, like the Duke of Royce when he comes."

"He can stay in a hotel," Cousin Lily said. "I am not keeping this whole apartment clean and aired for someone who might never appear."

I'd been in the rooms, searching for the green bathroom, but Lou and Dr. Harmon went slowly from the vast bedroom to the vaster sitting room with a corner dining area and a tiny kitchen nook, to the dressing room and the walk-in closet and the bathroom with a tub big enough for an orgy. Lily was already planning on having her helpers turn the dressing room into a spare bedroom for company, and moving the furniture to make half the sitting room into an office more conducive to meetings.

"But . . . but I am used to a bed-sitter flat at Royce. I'd get lost here with all this space."

"Nonsense, you'll fill it with books and students and new friends."

"But the stairs . . ."

Lily smiled again and took us back to the hall to another door I never noticed. "There's an elevator left from when the estate had scores of servants to serve the family. They used the elevator to bring food from the kitchen, so it arrived hot, or drinks cold. That elevator is how we're getting approval from the building department for being handicapped accessible. And it's been inspected and maintained, so you do not have to worry about the mechanics of the thing."

"A lift of my own? I cannot—"

"Professor, come look at this," Lou called out from the sitting room. He'd pulled floor-length curtains back from the windows and stepped out onto a wide balcony, complete with hot tub, that looked out over the lawns and gardens the estate encompassed, to the wooded areas left undeveloped. Over the trees glistened a postcard view of the water. "I bet you can see Connecticut on a clear day."

Dr. Harmon seemed more interested in the manicured grounds and the woods. "Oh, my, how positively beautiful. I've always wished for a rose garden. Can you imagine a greyhound or two running through the trees?"

I pictured Oey flitting through the branches, ducking into the hot tub. "I have a feeling you'll have lots of company. And remember, you'll have a whole batch of Royce personnel here soon, perhaps friends from your teaching days."

"No, they are all gone. The new ones are dunderheads." Then he must have realized how alone he'd be up here in his private turret. "You'll come visit, won't you?"

"Of course. And Grandma Eve will, too. The whole family will come."

"I like the sound of that. Yes, at my age, a family."

I warned him that I might go back to the city, but I'd always come visit. From the look on his face I realized I'd disappointed someone else. "I intend to come out most weekends," I blurted from the back of my mind, where I'd been trying to figure how to make a relationship with Matt work. I'd come out here, and Matt could come in to visit me on alternate weekends when he had no sick boarders. Maybe he'd take an occasional Monday off so we could do Broadway, the museums, even the dog show, walks in Central Park.

With Moses. In my apartment. Red would get trampled, eaten, or have conniptions. So would the management. I'd get thrown out. Damn.

Dr. Harmon was having second thoughts, too. "I never—"

"You will," I answered for him. "You deserve it for your years of service and after almost drowning. And if we manage to defeat the dragon, you'll have earned it ten times over."

He stood taller. "We shall, my dear. We shall."

Chapter 30

I WENT HOME AND WATCHED SEVEN stations hype Desi into the storm of the century, any century. I got so nervous I ate half my hurricane supplies.

My mother called. Uncle Roger knew where the storm shutters got stored; she was not in Desi's way but in Arkansas, shutting down another puppy mill; the greyhounds had all been adopted; don't I dare mess up her good relationship with the vet; and why were people calling me speedy? If I got too many tickets in her car, they'd impound it.

"Gotta go, Mom, getting ready for the storm, you know."

Matt called. He invited me and my grandmother and Lou and Dr. Harmon out to dinner with his guest Gina and her partner.

"Research partner or life partner?" I opted for the life partner.

"Both, it seems."

Good. "And they're both staying at your house? Without telling you there'd be two of them? You okay with that."

"Sure. She's nice."

"Of course she is. She's your friend."

"No, I mean her partner, Vicki."

"Oh. You okay with that?"

"Hey, who am I to cast stones? My lady friend talks to

creatures that don't exist. Vicki and Gina try to save the dolphins. You try to save the world. No big difference, right?"

That's why I lo—liked Matt so much. He could laugh at the small stuff and take the big stuff in stride. "Are you worried about the hurricane?"

"I'd be a fool not to. I've got a guy coming to cut down some big old trees too near the clinic. And we're almost at capacity for boarding animals people can't take with them to the hotels or relatives inland where they're going to stay. My head kennel guy lives in a trailer park that's bound to be evacuated, so he's planning on bringing his wife and kids to stay at the clinic to keep the dogs calm. I trust him implicitly, so I can be with you, wherever you want me."

Yup, he's a keeper. "What about your company?"

"Gina and Vicki will be leaving before the storm gets close. They've got some injured dolphins at Woods Hole they need to secure before Desi gets there. Right now they're out in a spotter plane off Montauk looking for those new dolphins."

The whale-watching boats used planes. So did so-called sport fishermen, though how sporting was it to have someone in the sky direct you to exactly where a swordfish or marlin or shark was sunbathing?

"They're not going to find them, are they?" he asked.

"Nope."

"That's what I thought. Anyway, I want to take the two of them and the rest of you to dinner tonight before they leave."

"Sounds good to me." Matt and dinner out and his old friend was gay. Woo-hoo.

Grandma Eve called. She'd spoken with Matt, what a fine young man he was, but she and Lou weren't going with us to the Breakaway. They were headed to Shelter Island to have dinner with Doc Lassiter, to try to convince him to leave his home before he was trapped there when the ferries stopped running.

"You think he'll be safer in Paumanok Harbor?"

"I think he'll be among friends. And we might need him here."

A shrink whose touch could calm an entire village? Grandma Eve's tea leaves must be showing that bad moon rising, too. Dr. Harmon, she told me, did not want to ride the ferries to Shelter Island, not even with one of her composers or a bottle of blackberry brandy, so he'd be delighted to dine with Matt and me. I needed to pick him up at six-thirty.

Chief Haversmith called. He was at the police station, even though it was Sunday. Had I seen any more of that suspicious character, Axel Vanderman? Uncle Henry finally had an hour to look into my warning, between meetings of the emergency preparedness task force.

I hadn't thought about Axel in days, it seemed, and never saw him after that once. I told the chief I'd check with Susan at the restaurant later, to see if he'd showed up there again.

My father called. Look out for the backside, he told me. I put down the chocolate chip cookie. Nope, he wanted to remind me that hurricanes spiral. If the front side doesn't get you, the back side can be worse. "Don't go out when you think it's done. That's just the center passing over. It's the eye you have to watch out for. I saw it in the shower."

"You saw the eye of the storm?"

"No, just an eye, full of evil and malice. Be careful, baby girl. And don't worry about me if the phone lines go dead. I'll be in the clubhouse. We're going to have a marathon Scrabble tournament."

"Anything more about the skunk?"

"Funny you should ask. You know how sometimes you think you see something out of the corner of your eye? A shadow or a flicker? That's what I saw last night, a skunk, real quick. Only you weren't in danger, so I forgot about it until now. The skunk was in a trap, not you. Now that I think about it, though, it would be just like you, baby girl, to try to save the critter. Just like your mother would, ignoring the danger. Don't do it."

"I won't, Dad." I couldn't if I wanted to. There weren't any skunks in Paumanok Harbor. And if there were, and it was caught, I'd send Matt to get it out. Wild animals were his department, weren't they?

Someone else called, without caller ID. Not even a "number unavailable" message. I seldom answered those, usually telemarketers or charities. This time I picked up. "Hello?"

No one was there.

"Hello," I said, louder.

"It is a hard rain that is going to fall."

"Who is this?" It sure as hell wasn't Bob Dylan. He didn't have my number.

The caller repeated "hard" three or four times.

I knew. "Thank you. You be careful, too."

Before dinner, I tried to work on my book a little. The sketches of the sea monster were scarier than I'd intended, now that I knew it existed. The eyes, especially, all whirlpools and flickering lightning, could give a kid nightmares. Hey, I was a good illustrator, maybe too good for the YA readers. I thought about changing the eyes, but they fit the character. Now that the chief had spoken about Axel, those swirling eyes brought him back to mind. They fit him, too, how his glittery stare fixed on me, as if they wanted to suck me into his realm, or suck away my will, vampirelike, sea serpentlike. I felt the hairs on my neck raise, just thinking about him and N'fwend in the same picture, as if they were two embodiments of the same evil, one mortal, one made of water and magic.

No way could the two be related, except in my imagination. I'd check with Uncle Henry about Vanderman in the morning.

Instead of frivolous nightwear that was bound to come off almost instantly, I should have invested in a new outfit for dinner. Matt's company was dressed to kill—Gina's shoes alone cost more than everything in my closet combined—and the women were mad enough to do it, too.

First, they couldn't find the new dolphins. Second, the people in charge of righting the cruise ship had decided they couldn't wait for the proper winds and equipment and full moon tides, not with the massive storm predicted to arrive during that same full moon. Which was the worst possible scenario for the shorefront.

The tugs and barges and mini-subs had to get to safe harbor themselves, not to mention all the personnel in the storm's possible path. So what the idiots, Vicki's word, not mine, were going to do was blow up the reef the ship rested on, then hope the *Nova Pride* was still seaworthy enough to float.

I said that sounded like a good idea, if they could do it right, like how lumberjacks knew where to make the cuts so the tree fell exactly where they wanted it.

"But what about the dolphins?" Gina demanded, as if I'd suggested using them to carry the dynamite. "Do you know what a depth charge can do to a dolphin's sonar? What the percussion can do, the water displacement, the disturbed sediments? The jerks could be murdering a completely new species, purported to be the most intelligent sea mammal yet, before we've done any research on them."

To me, if the dolphins survived the kraken, a few small explosions in a newly made underwater mountain wouldn't faze them one bit. If they were still around. Then again, if they were what we all—we being Paumanok Harbor's insider espers—believed they were, nothing could hurt them.

Vicki and Gina were so aggravated and agitated, not even Susan's incredible feel-good food could appease them. Of course Vicki'd ordered shrimp, Gina'd ordered salmon. The only two things on the menu that couldn't be fresh because they weren't caught in local waters. The other food was amazing, as always. Matt kept smiling and Dr. Harmon kept looking skyward, as if thanking heaven for dropping him and manna in this wondrous place.

Gina banged her fork on the table. "Those fools will never get it right. The ship will sink, creating a worse disaster for sea life."

What choice did the Coast Guard or the Army Corps of Engineers or whoever made the decisions have? If they didn't try, the storm was sure to dislodge the *Nova Pride*, sinking it or sending it crashing into shore, perhaps doing immense damage there, too. If it floated at all, the ship could end up a hazard in the shipping lanes.

Vicki told us about what happened a few years ago when an enormous dead right whale came ashore in California. It stank. It attracted vultures and rats and stupid tourists who wanted to climb on top of the rotting carcass for photographs. They couldn't tow it out to sea and they couldn't bury it. So they decided to blow it up into small pieces that could be bulldozed away.

People came from all over the state, filling the parking lots and the adjoining roadways and beaches. And what did those morons do?

They miscalculated, that's what. So tiny bits of decomposing flesh rained down on the people, the cars, the beaches.

Matt and I and Dr. Harmon were laughing so loud that Susan's uncle Bernie, owner of the Breakaway, came to see if we were all right. So we told him, and he clapped his hands and brought us another bottle of wine before rushing off to retell the story.

"It's not funny!" Vicki insisted, showing she had great taste in shoes, but no sense of humor.

I got the feeling she and Gina were like my mother, so driven by their beliefs, their causes, their righteous indignation on behalf of helpless creatures that they'd developed tunnel vision. Her dogs were all that mattered to Mom. The dolphins, and each other, filled Vicki and Gina's world. At least they shared their dedication.

The new bottle of wine didn't placate them either. They guzzled it down like lemonade.

The professor sipped, but matched them glass for

glass, not that I was counting how many he'd had. He'd lived this long without destroying his liver, so tippling tonight made no difference. And I was driving anyway. Soon, I hoped. I wanted to spend time with Matt, who did not drink either. We had to make plans. For the storm, naturally. I still had to decide on the black or the red negligee. Not for the storm.

The women weren't finished with their rants. They cleaned their plates without once complimenting the food and kept bitching about the imbeciles in command and the hurricane keeping them from locating the missing dolphins.

"You must have seen our subjects," Gina demanded in strident tones of the professor. "What were they like?"

"He was underwater at the time," I snapped. "Without his glasses. Half dead." And he was an esteemed scholar, not a suspect undergoing the third degree.

The wine kept Dr. Harmon his usual pleasant self, so he answered politely. "You cannot trust anything I might recall from that night. I believe I saw my first sweetheart in the waves. She married my cousin and moved to Scotland. She died almost twenty years ago."

They weren't interested. I, of course, wanted to know what she died of, if he ever spoke to his cousin, and if he still missed her.

Gina interrupted my questions. "And you, Willow. Did you see anything odd?"

"Me? I was onshore with Matt, waiting for a call about the dogs, long after most of the survivors had been brought in."

"Crap, you're as useless as everyone else we spoke to. All we get is rumors and hearsay, or eyewitness accounts from people suffering hypothermia or the rapture of the deep. No damned evidence."

Vicki patted Gina's hand. "There will be other new species for you to name. I'm certain of it."

They drank to that, and drank to Matt, who was paying for the outrageous bar tab, too. Then they kept drinking to nothing at all.

I suggested we leave while they could still stand, inviting everyone back to my house for dessert and coffee. Good thing I hadn't eaten all the ice cream.

The marine biologists didn't accept my invitation. They claimed phone calls to make, protests to lodge, guidelines to give to the ship captains and the underwater demolitions crews. In their condition? I didn't care if they called the President.

I wanted to get Matt alone. Too bad I'd promised the professor a chance to meet Oey. And the wine hadn't made him the least bit sleepy, damn it.

Matt yawned, though. Maybe another all-nighter wasn't such a good idea, but with the storm coming, the water worm coming, who know when we'd be . . . together again.

The dinner bill was high enough to buy a flat screen TV to watch the weather maps get bigger and scarier. Uncle Bernie ripped it up. "You look after my girls. That's enough."

I didn't know if Uncle Bernie meant his two Jack Russells or me and Susan. She was his real niece, on her father's side, and no relation to me at all. I smiled anyway.

"And thanks for the great story. They're taking bets on which way the *Nova Pride* will go, straight down or up in pieces. Oh, and Susan packed up some cream puffs for you to take home, speedy."

I tried to laugh. "We've taken to jogging on the beach. Last one home has to buy dessert."

Uncle Bernie's right falsehood-detecting leg started twitching and tapping against the wooden floor. He hurried back to the kitchens.

"An old war wound," I told the curious diners at the next table. Since I was on a roll, I told Vicki and Gina what a pleasure it was to meet them, and I'd be sure to let them know if I spotted any peculiar creatures.

We could hear Uncle Bernie's foot tapping from all the way across the restaurant.

Chapter 31

BEFORE WE LEFT THE RESTAURANT, I remembered to ask Susan if Axel Vanderman had been back. I stepped into the kitchen and tapped her on the shoulder.

"No, thank heaven. After what you said, he felt really skeevy to me. I told the other girls around town. Fran dated him once, but she couldn't remember why they didn't hit it off."

"Weird. The chief is looking into it." And then I did an evil thing that felt really, really good. I picked up a cream puff from the dessert tray and crammed it into Susan's mouth. "Now maybe you'll learn to keep your lips closed, puddles."

Matt waited in the parking lot after helping Dr. Harmon to my car and his two guests to his. None of them were steady on their legs. We ducked behind a parked van for a quick kiss. Mine tasted of whipped cream, from licking my fingers. He groaned.

"I'll be over at your house as soon as I get them settled. Is it okay if I bring Moses, though? Vicki isn't crazy about dogs, and he'll be lonely without his sisters."

"Sure. We have to introduce the dogs sooner or later." Then we'd both know the relationship couldn't last. Like if you hated your boyfriend's mother, or his kids from a first marriage. "We can let Moses play in the dog run if it looks like Little Red is in danger."

"Hell, I'm worried more about Moses. I've seen the Red Baron in action, remember?"

He could make jokes, but the six-pound Pomeranian didn't have a chance in any confrontation, especially if he started it.

I promised to save Matt a cream puff . . . if he wasn't too long. Not that I truly thought he'd get up a three-some with Vicki and Gina, but I was my mother's distrustful daughter, my father's constant worrier.

The professor liked my house. "This is more what I had pictured for my retirement, old dogs and comfortable, old furniture, not the elegance of Rosehill. I do not see how I can be at ease in such opulence."

"You'll get used to it," I said while I set out paper plates for the cream puffs. Everything else was in the dishwasher or the sink. "Imagine dining on delicious food off fine china, with someone to clean up after you." My idea of heaven.

"Ah, but with no one with whom to share a cup of tea, no matter how lovely the table setting. Perhaps I should return to my roots after all. When we are done here, of course."

"Give it a chance before making up your mind."

"Is that what you are doing with Matthew?"

"Oh, listen, I think I heard a *twee* off in the distance."

I made him comfortable on the porch with a snifter of cognac from Mom's liquor cabinet and a blanket. The September nights got chilly, especially if a wind picked up.

We sat listening for a few moments without hearing the distinctive bird call, or Matt's SUV.

I started to fret, but the professor seemed to be enjoying the quiet interlude. "This is lovely," he said. "It has not rained in three whole days, quite different from London's environs. And I can hear the insects, instead of noisy university students and nattering instructors."

"Do you miss your friends, is that why you are thinking of returning?"

He sighed. "I have outlived most. Others of my contemporaries left to live with sons and daughters, which they swore never to do. I expect the children did not want them, either."

"Then why . . . ?"

"I told you, I am not particularly brave. The unfamiliar appears daunting at times."

I understood that very well. "Yet you took a cruise to Nova Scotia on your own."

"And see what happened." He sighed again. "I suppose Rosehill will suit me well enough, in time. As long as you and your grandmother and Matthew keep your promises to visit."

"We will, I swear."

"And I'll still be useful, talking to new talents, helping to assess strengths and weaknesses."

"You'll be wonderful. I wish I'd had someone like you to guide me. But we had no one like you here in the Harbor and I refused to go to London. I think I was like you are now, leery of the unknown." Maybe things would have been different if I'd known Dr. Harmon a decade ago. Or not.

My cell phone rang. I supposed it was Matt, calling to give some lame excuse why he couldn't come after all. I'd pretend, but I wouldn't believe him. I could feel my insides already curling up like a withered leaf. I tried to cheer myself: one more cream puff for me.

I didn't believe that would help either.

The caller ID didn't work again. "Hello."

This time it was "Lying Eyes."

"Hey, have you been speaking to my father?"

I heard a chuckle before the music went on, or maybe that sound came from creaking boards.

"Yeah, that's what I figured, too. The police are checking."

And I'd ask Russ if it was possible for the phone to ring without the caller's number showing on past incomings.

I filled the pool with fresh water and called "twee" while I mentally pictured the parrotfish, a willow tree, welcome, friend, talk, beautiful bird, shining fish.

I think it was the beautiful part that drew the vain creature, or maybe she was lonely. "Oey, there you are! And looking very handsome."

She preened, fluffed out her feathers, and rubbed her head on my shoulder. I tried to avoid letting the fish tail touch my arm. Then I pointed out the professor on the porch. "You helped save Dr. Harmon. Thank you, noble friend. Will you talk to him?"

She cocked her head. "Thaved?"

"Twice, I believe." The professor had come down from the porch and now stood near me, but not too close. His eyes were wide behind his glasses, the familiar sense of Oey-awe written on his face. "I believe I saw it over seventy years ago. I was a sickly child, always ill with fevers and such. One time they thought I'd die, I drifted into a coma for so long. But a parrot came to visit me, a beautiful talking bird who made me laugh. I thought my parents had bought it to try to keep me from fading away. It worked. The parrot gave me great hope and incentive to fight the disease. When I returned to consciousness, the bird was gone. I remember crying, but no one knew anything about any parrot."

"Are you sure?"

"It had pink feet and a lisp."

"What about its tail?"

"Long and beautiful, with all the colors of the sea and sky, like this chap's."

"She's a girl, mostly. And I think you need to take a better look at the tail, now that you are not an ailing child."

Oey had flown to a hydrangea bush nearby, her head cocked in that curious way she had. "Immie?"

"That's right, Jimmie. And you are Oliver, are you not? That is what I called you, at any rate."

"Oey."

The professor laughed. "That's right. You could not say Ollie. Ah, what a good friend you have been."

"Thaved."

"Indeed. I am grateful that you did, and delighted to see you again."

Oey bobbed her head, then flew to the side of the pool.

Jimmie—I could see him as a frail child—still hadn't noticed the fish tail. He was busy inviting Oey to visit him at Rosehill, where the bird could have a whole suite to perch in, no matter what Miss Lily had to say, and a balcony porch for coming and going, whenever his dear friend got tired of being out in the wild, or got cold or hungry. Or lonely.

Then Oey dove into the pool.

"Um. Ah. Oh." The professor took his glasses off and wiped them. He put them back on. "Quite. Which explains a great deal, does it not? Well, there is a hot tub outdoors and a huge bathing tub inside."

Oey splashed and gurgled.

"And I would enjoy the company. Miss Tate has a life of her own, although I intend to tempt her to visit as often as she might."

Oey leaped out of the pool, shook himself, and then perched on Dr. Harmon's shoulder. "Immie," she cooed. "Petth."

So he petted her feathered head. I didn't think that's what she meant, but I changed the subject. "Oey, do you know anything about Desi?"

"Dethwy."

"No, Desi, the hurricane."

"Dethwy."

Jimmie thought she wanted to tell us the storm was deathly. Which every newscaster had already told us.

"Can we stop it?"

"Thtop the wind? The wain?" The whole parrot body swayed side to side, no.

"What about N'fwend? Can we stop him?"

She looked at the professor with those rainbow eyes. "Thaved."

"Yes, you did," I agreed. "So that he can help? He's the one who can stop N'fwend?"

Oey didn't get to answer because Matt drove up then, with Moses. Little Red, who I'd barricaded behind a baby gate on the porch, set up a frantic burglar alarm. Oey squawked and disappeared. I wished I could, too.

Moses came galumphing up the path like a hungry baby elephant, while my tiny handicapped mouse kept throwing himself against the gate, ready to do battle for his territory. Mom might know how to do this. I sure didn't.

Matt suggested we put Moses in the big dog run, and let them sniff each other through the wire fence. Moses pranced and play-bowed and wagged his whole rear end. Red tried to bite him through the mesh, when he wasn't barking himself hoarse.

The professor laughed, but then he coughed. Matt's cell rang. He stepped away to answer it, while I scooped up Little Red before he had a heart attack, and found Dr. Harmon's brandy for him.

When Matt came back, he looked grim.

"An emergency?"

"Yeah, the geniuses at my house flushed something down the toilet—" obviously an item of feminine hygiene from his self-conscious omission, "—and now the whole system is backing up. I didn't realize I had to put up a sign, or explain we have cesspools instead of sewers. I have to go. I'll drop Dr. Harmon off at the farmhouse first. Can I leave Moses here in the pen so he doesn't drool all over the professor?"

"Think nothing of that, my boy. Your lad is a wonderful, happy dog. I'd be pleased to sit with him. And have you both visit me at Rosehill next week when my rooms should be ready. I'm hoping to have a pet of my own, but Moses is welcome when you need a babysitter."

We both appreciated the offer, me thinking of Matt coming to visit me in Manhattan, sans black behemoth. But Matt wanted to leave him here for now, so he'd get used to Little Red.

As if Little Red would ever get used to Moses. But I agreed, since it meant Matt had to come back.

Moses whimpered some when the men left, until I brought the big dogs out. They didn't look so big anymore, next to him, but he went submissive and licked them and followed them around without once trying to jump on them or wrestle with them. He really was a nice dog. Little Red wasn't. He vibrated in my arms he was so angry.

Then I had an idea. I whistled for Oey and sent out an illustrated mental plea for help: dogs, willow tree between them, being battered from both sides, fear, desperation, wanting peace. "Oey, I need you. The petth need you."

"Immie?"

"Immie is not your pet! Sure you look out for him and worry about him and want him to be happy. Um, maybe he is your pet. But that's what friends do, too. Right now I have a problem with these pets, Matt's and mine. Moses is one of the dogs you saved, remember?"

"Matt petth?"

"No, Matt is a friend. A good friend. Moses is his pet. I want Little Red and Moses to be friends. Can you help?"

She swiveled her head. "Twain?"

"Train? I don't care about sit—" Moses sat. Oh, boy. "But I don't want him to think Little Red is a toy."

"Teath."

"No teeth. No biting!"

Oey clacked her beak. Yeah, I was frustrated, too. My whole relationship with Matt, if there was to be one, depended on harmony between the dogs. "Oh, you can teach them to get along?"

"Thaved. Thpoke."

Of course, Oey'd brought the Newfie pups to safety. "So can you talk to them, tell them to get along?"

Those shiny eyes focused on Moses, then Little Red, who was yipping, growling, straining to get out of my arms to do battle.

Oey swiveled her head back to me. "All ballth, no brainth."

A lot of males were like that. "He's fixed."

"Din't wouk."

Neutering was not a concept to explain now, or how Red's personality resulted from grievous suffering. "He can be charming. I love him, despite his bad temper. What about Moses?"

"Thaved. Thpoke."

"Yes, I know. Can you explain about my dog? Teach Moses to be patient and kind and forgiving. And careful."

Oey did not make a sound, but Moses came to the gate and lay down, his big head between his front paws, his eyes staring at Red. I opened the gate and put the Pom down, ready to jump between them. Red instantly tried to get his jaw around a foot or a tail. Moses rolled to his side and licked Little Red's face. He wagged his tail, careful not to knock the little guy off his three legs.

Little Red gave up. Just like that. He sat, stared, then lay down nearby. Moses sighed. Red sighed. I sighed.

"Wow, what did you say?"

"With gweat powew comth gweat rethponth—"

I couldn't wait for her to get it out. "Does Moses have great power?"

"Big."

"As big as Jimmie?"

"Thaved."

"Yes, you are a hero. Did you give them powers, the way I seem to have shared mine with Matt?"

She preened her feathers. "Petth."

"No, friends. People cannot be pets."

"Old pet fwend."

"Yes, you saved Jimmie years ago. Oh. Yes, he is old, now." The thought made me sad. Oey, too, from the soft keening sound in her throat. "We do not live forever. But you will be good company for him, won't you?"

She bobbed her head.

"Does that mean you'll help us fight N'fwend?"

She disappeared, which I could never get used to. But Matt came back before I could call her to return.

He looked at the dogs, fast asleep, tails touching. "See? I told you they'd work it out."

I didn't trust him. Little Red, not Moses, not Matt. I'd already trusted Matt to see me naked, with the lights on. I trusted him not to fly off to the moon or Mt. Everest.

Hell, I trusted him to be at my side if we had to face the kraken. Unless he and the professor and Oey could go by themselves, which I would not mind at all.

And Moses really was a nice dog, already socialized and calm enough for a show ring.

Little Red? I hid my shoes whenever I had to leave him. I kept Band-Aids and Bacitracin in my pocket for when he drew blood. I always had an extra shirt handy for when he nervously peed on me. Trust him not to aggravate the manners off Moses? Not a chance. So we put the baby gate between Moses in the living room and Little Red with us and the cream puffs in the kitchen. Moses could have knocked it over with one paw, but he knew not to.

Matt and I had a lot to discuss, but we put it off in favor of flaky pastry pockets filled with rich whipped cream, topped with chocolate syrup, and drizzled with raspberry sauce. For this I might be tempted to stay longer in Paumanok Harbor.

I looked at the last one on the plate, the one I'd forgotten to pack up for the professor to take home. "Want to split it?"

Matt had a better idea what to do with that whipped cream and chocolate syrup and raspberry sauce. For that I might be tempted to stay in Paumanok Harbor forever.

I never got to choose between the red or the black lingerie.

And yes, I was quick again, but only the first time. Blame the chocolate sauce, and Matt.

Much later, after a hot shower and a check on the dogs and another long, slow, lovemaking that left us hot, sweaty, and sticky again, without the chocolate, I lay sprawled on top of Matt, skin to skin, heart to heart. Neither of us had the energy or the desire to move.

Matt played with my hair that I hadn't bothered to brush smooth after the shower. He wound a curl around his finger.

"Don't, you'll make corkscrews."

"I love your hair. I could touch it all day and never get tired of seeing it wrap around my fingers, see the colors change, sometimes dark gold, sometimes bright as sunshine."

Man, this was so much better than a cream puff. I sighed in utter limp contentment. Except for where I rubbed my thigh against his, just to make him take a deep breath.

"Insatiable wench," he said with a smile.

"No, gloriously satiated. For now."

"Thank goodness. You know, I've been thinking about your hair, your smile, your blue eyes—and your exquisite body—all day when I should be thinking of getting ready for the storm and whatever else it'll bring."

I rolled off him. We really had to talk. "Me, too. I've been thinking about you so hard I forgot to be afraid of what's coming."

"Do you think the storm will bring another tsunami with fangs?"

"I never saw it, but if that's what made the rogue wave, then yes, it'll be back. In the eye of the hurricane, I believe."

"And what do you believe will happen, to us, afterward?"

I knelt over him, because he smelled of sex and my soap and man and I didn't want to think about the future. "We can talk about it later, if we survive."

"If we survive the lovemaking or the dragon slaying?"

Chapter 32

M ATT LEFT WITH MOSES BEFORE I found enough energy to open an eyelid. Damn, I'd wanted to make him breakfast. Pour out the orange juice and cereal, anyway. We had to make plans. Not for the rest of our lives, not for next month, but for now.

According to the news, which had hurricane coverage and nothing else, the killer storm had unexpectedly picked up speed after making its murderous path through the Caribbean and the Keys. This was good for the southern seacoast, because it meant less time being buffeted by the ferocious winds, less time for inches of rain to flood rivers and roads.

The increased forward velocity was bad for the central and northern shores. That meant Desi could get here sooner than expected, sooner than the preparations got completed or evacuations got started. Sooner than I could make sense of the glimmer of an idea in my sleep-fogged brain.

The latest path had Desi brushing the length of the entire eastern seaboard, picking up wind and water and strength from the warm open ocean before making land-fall—at the tip of Long Island where it jutted out into the Atlantic. Us.

I knew why Desi aimed straight for Paumanok Harbor, why it kept gathering energy. I knew what rested in the center of the storm, steering, chivvying, pulling, plotting its revenge. I drew a quick sketch of the whirlpool-eyed monster towering over the roiling ocean, slavering with the expectation of gobbling up Paumanok Harbor and all its power, opening the gates between worlds, using Desi's strength to destroy its enemy. And us.

Yup, nightmare time.

And what had I done? I'd spent the night in the arms of Matt and Eros—no, not a threesome; they were one and the same—without making a single plan. I *knew* getting involved with Matt was a bad idea. I just never guessed how catastrophic it could be for the rest of my world.

The last bit on the news was about the cruise ship—smack dab in the way of the hurricane. The Coast Guard estimated they could not tow the ocean liner far enough into the ocean to get it out of the storm's wide path in time to save it, if they righted it. It couldn't fit through the jetties to Montauk Harbor, and taking it north, around Montauk Point, wasn't an option, either. Montauk's protected Fort Pond Bay was already filled with tankers, barges, and big commercial fishing boats. Besides, the '38 hurricane wiped out that side of the island, too. So they were still going to detonate the reef the *Nova Pride* sat on, but let the ship sink where it was, safe on the ocean floor, to be raised up when the storm had passed.

"No!" I shouted at the TV. "We need the ship!" I got dressed in a frenzy, fed the dogs, walked the dogs, asked how soon the professor could be ready, made an appointment to talk to the chief at the police station and called my father to see if he had any warnings.

"You know that skunk?"

"Yeah?" I didn't want to hear about some stinky animal. I wanted someone to tell me my idea stank. It was too dangerous, too impossible, too far beyond my capabilities to manage. I hated the idea, but didn't have a scrap of another. No matter, no one would listen to me anyway.

Instead my father said, "Well, it's got a lollipop in the cage with it. Now they're both sticky and dirty and you're still trying to get them out. Don't, baby girl. Stay away from them!"

As if I didn't have enough to do. "Okay, Dad. But what about the storm? Or a sea monster that wants to eat up Paumanok Harbor?"

"You been reading your own books again? That place has survived a lot worse."

And would survive this, if my father's dream visions held true. He didn't seem as worried about Desi as he did yesterday, so I must not be in mortal danger, only a panic. Which didn't comfort me. What about Dr. Harmon and Matt and Oey? And Grandma Eve and the rest of the townspeople? The physical village might make it, but what happens to the people who live here and depend on it for their livelihoods? Visions of New Orleans, Haiti, and Japan kept swimming in my head, trying to drown my dreadful plan.

I needed more help. How I wished I could drag Matt away from his animal hospital to hold me, to tell me there was another way, to take the burden on his broad shoulders. I couldn't do it. This was my war, not his. I'd leave him the skunk.

When I went to pick up the professor, I tracked down Lou who was helping Uncle Roger board up windows and take down hanging baskets and hammocks.

I demanded he find a way for me to talk to Grant. "I don't care if he is on a secret mission to Mars. Use codes, use some dead foreign language no one but Grant and twenty other scholars know. Hell, use telepathy. I need to talk to him. Today! And get a way to record what he says. We'll need that, too. And do not let them sink the ship! Call Royce if you have to!"

"I can talk to his grace," the professor offered. "He has a lot of influence everywhere."

"Get him to work with his weather people, too. Everywhere."

Lou listened to me and my half-assed, horrible plan. Then he took some special phone device from his inside pocket, put it in his ear, and said, "Get me the White House."

I kissed him. That's how hysterical I was. Doc Lassiter touched my shoulder and said I could do it; I could pull this off. I kissed him, too. He and Professor Harmon knew each other ages ago, so after they shook hands, Jimmie said he felt a lot better about staying on, about taking on the Wyrm again.

We all agreed to meet up at the police station in an hour.

I charged my cell phone in the car as Dr. Harmon and I drove. It didn't ring when we entered Shearwater Street, but "Collapse" by Rise Against suddenly blared from the House. Not a good sign.

I pulled into the driveway and got out of the car. "Can you help us?"

Silence met me. I guess not. "Can we help you get ready?"

Something flew out of the mail slot, another shrink-wrapped free promotional item from some charity or sales gimmick. This one was a glass bead on a leather cord. A common Turkish bead, I thought, with a turquoise center.

"It's to ward off the evil eye," the professor told me. "Put it on."

"These things work?"

"Who knows? They can't hurt."

So I called up Margaret at the wool shop and asked if she had any, and could she string all of them into necklaces for as many espers as she could equip. It wasn't much, but it was something.

In town, we stopped at Joanne's deli for breakfast. I never did have my juice and cereal. I got coffee and a muffin instead. Dr. Harmon got tea, with milk, without asking.

Mrs. Terwilliger was unlocking the front door of the library when we went past and beckoned us in. She had books for the professor.

"But I did not ask for any. I do not have a library card."

"Of course you do." She handed him one already filled out.

He got a book on parrots, one on the history of Paumanok Harbor, and the LMP, Literary Market Place of publishers and agents. "For the book the two of you are going to write."

She also handed him a volume of poetry, with a bookmark in John Masefield's page. With trembling hands holding the book, and a tremor in his voice, the professor read: " 'I must go down to the sea again, to the lonely sea and the sky.' "

My hands shook, too. "But you won't be lonely. You won't be alone. And there's no other choice. I'll be with you"—if it killed me— "and Matt will be, too." I knew that, in my heart. Whatever Doc Lassiter did with a touch, the simple thought of Matt, his smile, his voice— and his touch— did it better.

Mrs. Terwilliger handed me the biography of Alfred Mesmer, the first famous hypnotist, from where we got the word mesmerizing. I tried to hand the book back. "I don't have time right now to deal with Axel Vanderman and his wicked schemes."

"Make time," she said, shutting the door behind us and putting up a "Closed for the hurricane" sign on the library door.

Half the stores on Main Street were locked and shuttered. The Community Center's glass doors and walls had boards nailed over them. So did the church's stained glass windows.

We passed few pedestrians, only a couple of people leaving the hardware store with the last batteries and gas cans, or the grocery, whose shelves were nearly empty.

I got a text message from Aunt Jasmine at the school. They were closing early, and for the rest of the week, so the school could be used as an emergency shelter and families could head west, but Margaret called and yes, the art department had some of those Turkish beads. Should she get the kids to string them?

Yes, I typed back. And get one on every kid's neck. And every teacher's.

The fire department had all the equipment out on the lot, being checked and serviced and supplied with extra everything. Paumanok Harbor would be as ready as it could get.

The village hall didn't have the mobs of reporters from last week. They were all out at Montauk, taping the sinking of the ship and the beach, to use in before-and-after shots.

Mrs. Ralston had six phone lines going at once. She could have used that prison guard, she told us, useless as the dimwit was, but the woman had gone to guard prisoners filling sandbags. Sure, like the Dutch boy's finger in the dike.

The police station wing wasn't as crowded either. The state troopers and county cops had been reassigned to evacuation routes, while the Feds scurried home after their motels got shut down by Town of East Hampton orders. The Homeland Security people left too, deciding they had more to worry about than the cyber thefts. What was a little embezzlement compared to a category five catastrophe? Even our local police were out on the ocean beach, waiting for the *Nova Pride* to go down and making sure no jackass surfer or dipshit reporter went down with it.

"It cannot sink!" I shouted at Uncle Henry. "We need it!" The chief shook his head when the professor and I explained our plan, rough as it was. "We need more help."

"Can't put that many people in harm's way. And I don't know if our weather guys can pull this off, either, even if you get DUE and Royce working on it."

I knew he wouldn't listen. Then I showed him my sketch of N'fwend.

He got on the phone.

Lou and Doc Lassiter and my grandmother showed up. Big Eddie carried in more seats.

Lou said we had the ship, but we'd look like fools if we couldn't make my plan work. So would the President, which was never a good policy. Grandma Eve promised her friends. Doc Lassiter signed on, too. Now my hellish plan could destroy more lives, besides a whole commander-in-chief's reputation.

Chief Haversmith tried to make a list of who we could count on, where to meet, when to call, but he couldn't find paper or pencil, only crumpled papers on his desk and overflowing his wastebasket, along with squashed cardboard coffee cups and deli wrappers.

"Sorry for the mess. Lolly never came to clean this weekend, and we all worked overtime." He called to the outer office for someone to bring pads and pens. While we waited, he asked how come his switchboard operator said Miss Speedy Tate was on the line when I called this morning.

"Oh, that? Matt and I had a contest to see who finished the *Times* puzzle first. In ink. I won. It became a joke around town."

The chief clutched his stomach. "You trying to kill me?"

"Just getting you to mind your own business."

Before Grandma Eve could ask why she hadn't heard the joke, Lou handed the chief a bottle of antacid tablets that had fallen to the floor and Russ came in with a box full of yellow pads and pens, and his laptop computer. He didn't look good, all rumpled and unshaven, as if he hadn't slept since the auditors accused him of stealing the town's money.

"I got those tracers you asked for on Axel Vanderman. No priors, no listings on sex offender lists. It's all pretty standard except for one thing: He didn't exist five years ago."

"Come again?"

"There are no records anywhere. No tax forms, no bank statements, no loan applications. Not even a credit card."

The chief grunted. "I'm not surprised."

I was. It sounded to me like Vanderman was in some kind of witness protection program, given a new identity and a new location. I watched the cop shows on TV, too. I just couldn't see him cooperating with the Feds.

Chief Haversmith swallowed the tablet but didn't lose the pained expression on his face. "He didn't. The government knows nothing about him. He saw to that. I had Russ run the files, but I also had Lou check with DUE about finding a hypnotist for you. Top priority, bypass privacy rules, etc. They sent me reports of a master mesmerist, a wild, unrecorded talent, years ago. They heard the bastard was using his talent to take over people's minds and bodies and bank accounts. He used his eyes."

Russ used his computer to get Vanderman's current driver's license up on a screen behind the chief. Yes, those were the eyes I'd seen, only they weren't as threatening in a static flat picture. I passed around a drawing I had made of him, with as much intensity and menace as I could get in a sketch. Lou let out a loud breath. The chief held that picture next to the one I'd showed him of N'fwend.

"Holy hell."

It was Lou who continued: "DUE scooped him up before he got himself arrested, or killed by one of his victims. They tried to teach him values and the proper use of power. When that didn't work, they threatened to divest him."

"Divest? You mean you can take away someone's talent?"

Lou wouldn't look at me. "For the greater good."

Uh-oh. What if they decided to wipe my mind? I'd never write another book. "And that person was Axel Vanderman?"

"Vance Axelrod."

Russ put another driver's license up on the screen, this one from the UK, a much younger man, with a different hair style, a longer nose, but with those same piercing eyes.

"Shit."

"Yeah. He got away. And he's so good, he can cover his trail anytime he wants by hypnotizing anyone he wants—as long as he stays clear of another psychic."

Uncle Henry nodded. "We think that's how no one saw anything at the robberies. All the scumbag needed to do was get them to look at him, which they'd naturally be doing if had a gun and a ski mask. He got them to forget, kind of like the mayor's talent, but for his own gain."

"But what about shutting down the security systems and bypassing the codes? You can't hypnotize a machine."

"And computer hacking wasn't in his profile, but he must have learned, to create the false identities and wipe out the old ones."

"No, he only had to find someone good at it, and make them do it." Russ added that he'd found an Ajax Vance and an Alastair VanDyke who fit the descriptions, both with arrests for financial misconduct, changing wills, absconding with dead people's money, bilking single women out of their life savings, but no convictions. The computers were still looking for more.

Meanwhile, the professor was standing close to the screen, studying the magnified driver's licenses. "According to the early one's birth date," he said, "Vanderman, or Axelrod, was born nine months to the day after I confronted the Wyrm off Bermuda. Which means he would have been conceived that very night. I would not be surprised if his parents honeymooned there."

Lou started pushing buttons on his Blackberry.

Grandma Eve shook her head. "They cannot be related. That is simply impossible. An evil water spirit and an evil man?"

"Both with maelstrom eyes, both with no conscience. One conceived while the other lost its power," the professor mused. "When dealing with magic, anything is possible."

Anything but understanding it.

Chapter 33

"SO WHERE IS HE NOW? Why haven't you picked him up?"

"I went by his house on the way here, just to talk," the chief said. "No one answered the bell, and I had no warrant to break in. Half the townspeople left before they get flooded out or stranded here, so that's no surprise. We have an alert on his car, but with so much going on, it's not high on anyone's list. I've got a call into the Suffolk DA for the warrant, but it'll be a tough sell. The judge is at his sister's in Ronkonkoma. We've got nothing to charge Vanderman with, nothing to tie him to the robberies. We don't even have his fingerprints on file to prove he's this Axelrod guy."

"Lolly cleans his house," I reminded him. "She must have a key, and she could get one of his drinking glasses, with prints on it."

"Which would be inadmissible evidence and screw up any chance for a conviction. Not that I haven't considered it, but Lolly's gone missing, too."

We all thought about that. How there was more than one robber, how a master hypnotist could get a person to do anything he wanted, especially a susceptible woman like Lolly.

"I say we go get him." Lou patted his inside jacket pocket, maybe where he carried his Divesters-R-Us device. Okay, so I'd seen all the *Men in Black* movies a hundred times. I'd watch them again, for the pug.

The chief shook his head, in regret. "It's got to be by the book. Otherwise the robbery cases stay open and we stay under the Feebies' thumb."

"What about Lolly? She could press charges."

"If we knew where she was. Her aunt has no idea, and she didn't call in sick. It's too soon to file a missing person's report, with Lolly an adult, and not with the whole east end population on the move anyway because of the storm."

Mrs. Ralston brought in a tray of coffee. The chief poured something from his silver flask into his cup and the professor's. Everyone else declined.

After we filled the village administrator in on the latest news, Mrs. Ralston tried to find some hope. "Perhaps Mr. Vanderman took Lolly with him to a safer location. Her aunt's house is quite near the water."

"And she didn't tell her aunt where she was going? Didn't call in to take time off from work so we could get a replacement? That's not like Lolly."

Mrs. Ralston held her coffee mug out for additional fortification. "No, it isn't."

"Wait a minute," I said into the gloom. "My father had a vision about a lollipop. In a cage. Could he mean Lolly? The lollipop was in with a skunk."

Russ almost spilled his coffee on his laptop. "Did you say skunk?"

I shrugged. "That's what my father says he saw. He wanted me to stay away from them. But you know my dad and his—"

"I've been tracking the black hat infiltrators, trying to find where the embezzled money went, where the commands came from. Twice I've come upon the letters, SKK. That could be the skunk!"

I wasn't sure. My father could barely send an email. How could he know someone's screen name?

Then Matt rushed in, crowding the little room worse. Before I could ask why he'd left the vet's office on such a busy day, why he looked so disheveled and pale, he went past me to demand the chief send out a missing person's report. "My niece has disappeared. She didn't

show up for work and when I called her house, her room-
mates said they hadn't seen her since Saturday morning.
She doesn't answer her cell. That's Melissa Kovick." He
slapped a picture of her on the chief's desk. "She's only
twenty years old."

I put my hand in his. "Maybe she got back together
with that boyfriend and they forgot about the time, cel-
ebrating."

"She wouldn't do that, not when she knows we have
all those boarders coming, all needing Bordetella shots
against kennel cough. No one else in the place knows
how to run the computers to check for vaccinations and
enter contact information, much less back it up in case
we lose power. Sissy wouldn't do that to me."

Russ made the connection first. "Sissy Kovick? As in
Skk? Does she know Axel Vanderman?"

"I don't know."

I didn't either, but I knew she put a white stripe
through her black hair. "There has to be a connection."

"To what?" Matt wanted to know, ready to fly out the
door to find his sister's kid.

The chief explained how Lolly was missing, too, how
she cleaned Vanderman's house, how we all suspected
him of hypnotizing people into taking part in his crimi-
nal activities."

Matt shook his head. "Not Sis. She's no crook."

"Not intentionally," I assured him. "But think about
how she's been so tired and temperamental lately. Maybe
she had guilt feelings."

"Damn it, she's a kid who had her heart broken.
They're always emotional. That doesn't make her a
thief."

"But dressing like a skunk? Russ can check your computers to see what screen names she uses."

He put as much distance between us as he could in
the crowded room. "You never liked her. Now you're
trying to pin some frigging felonious conspiracy on
her?"

Doc Lassiter tried to lay his hand on Matt's shoulder,
but Matt shrugged him off. He turned to leave. "I'll go

find her myself, if you inbred, arrogant bastards won't help."

I got in his way and gave him a shove, which naturally didn't budge his solid body. "Hey, buddy, you're one of us now, even if you don't have it in your genes. And I never liked your niece because she's a bitch who treats your clients like dog poop. And that's the truth. Look at the chief if you don't believe me. He's not groaning, is he?"

Uncle Henry waved his hand at Matt. "Sounds true to me."

"She was rude when I met her a month ago, before I ever laid eyes on you. But she *is* a computer geek. She *was* dating a man she never introduced to you. She *does* try to look like Pepe le Pew these days, and her initials *are* SKK. If she's been under someone's thumb, made to do things she wouldn't, it's not her fault. No one is blaming her. We just need to find her so she can help us get to Vanderman. We need him to find Lolly before she's lost in a hurricane somewhere."

Russ offered him a seat. The chief offered him some whiskey. Doc offered a hand. He took mine, instead. "Melissa couldn't rob a bank."

"Neither could poor Lolly. But your niece could hack into the computers, if Vanderman forced her to."

"So where do we look?"

"We call the plumber."

"No, I got the toilet unclogged with a plunger and—"

His phone rang at the same time my cell did. So did the chief's. We all picked up, hoping for good news. Instead, we heard music.

"What the hell is this?" Uncle Henry shouted into his receiver. "You are interfering with police business."

"Don't hang up!" I yelled. The chief switched his phone to speaker so we all heard the sound.

Russ recognized it first. "It's 'Eye of the Tiger.' You know, from the martial arts movie."

"Okay, thanks," I said into my phone. "We're on it. You okay?"

When the phone clicked off, I set it down.

The chief slammed his back on his desk. "Who the hell was that?"

"The House. It's been calling me. I think it wants us to watch out for the eye of the storm. That's where the worst trouble will be." I touched the picture of the water demon. "My father says so, too. Except . . . maybe everyone is telling us we *need* that evil eye, that hypnotist, to defeat this other monster."

The chief drank straight from his flask.

They brought Joe the plumber in a squad car, sirens squealing. Janie came after, in her own car.

"No one needs their hair cut for a hurricane, and I love to see Joe in action. When he bends over a toilet . . ."

More than we needed to know. We needed water, though, so we all trooped into the ladies' room, explaining the situation as we went.

"We're looking for girls, ain't we?"

And the men's room was not a sight fit for feminine eyes, according to Big Eddie, not with Lolly being AWOL for a couple of nights.

Joe filled the sink after Janie wiped it down with paper towels. He stared into the water, then at the picture of Melissa that Matt handed him. He knew Lolly, he said, so did not need her photo ID from her employment record. He bent over to get closer to the water and stared some more. I tried not to stare at Janie, who was staring at his ass. Everyone wanted a turn to look in the sink, but no one saw anything until Joe stuck his finger in the water and swirled it around.

"Got them, both of them together," he called in triumph.

I stood ready with my sketch pad in case he could describe their surroundings.

"And I think I found your tiger, too. There's tiger stripes on the upholstery where they're sitting, tiger stripes on some pillows. I think that's a bronze tiger head on the wall."

The House was right!

"Yeah, but where are they? And are they alive? Are they tied up?"

Joe swirled the water some more. "They looked asleep, kind of rumpled, but I can't tell more. It's gone."

He described what he'd seen and I quickly drew it, adding colors with marking pens.

None of us recognized the scene, except maybe from pictures of Graceland's jungle room.

The professor closed his eyes, searching his memory. "I think . . . Yes, I am fairly certain that's the decor of the lounge where I had a few drinks."

"Where was it, this lounge?"

"Why, on the ship, of course. Some woman sang there."

"Tina?" Matt and I asked at the same time.

"I never got her name. Lovely to look at, dreadful voice. Wouldn't smile for an old man like me."

"That's Tina. So the girls are on the *Nova Pride*?"

Good grief, what if it sank after all?

We flew out of the bathroom and put on a TV in the outer office. The ship was upright now, and men in wet suits and life jackets were tossing lines back and forth, to tugs and every other kind of boat they could commandeer. We could see pumps shooting water out of doors and windows and hatches, but saw no one signal for a life raft or a helicopter rescue.

The announcer speculated that the authorities—or the cruise line's insurers—must have declared the *Nova Pride* seaworthy enough to be towed toward Montauk Point and the Sound, instead of being scuttled where it lay.

That's what they told the news people, anyway. The ship was actually going to turn the corner at Montauk Point and keep coming to us.

We all wondered how the hell Vanderman got the girls on board.

Hypnotism, that was how. The Coast Guard wouldn't suspect boarders in uniform, divers who looked official, or an inspector with trunks of equipment that needed to be carried onto the ship. Not if Vanderman worked his juju on them. They'd carry the girls themselves if he told them to, then forget about it afterward. They'd forget a tiger lounge existed, too, so no one would look.

Now everyone here got on phones and computers.

Neither the chief nor Lou could get a helicopter to the ship in time, not one manned by espers, anyway, who couldn't be influenced by Axel's eyes. They'd need to be combat trained in case Vanderman was armed. Lord knew he was dangerous.

DUE had a whole squad of para paratroopers— scattered around the country. They'd be no help.

We knew where the girls were—the professor gave a good description of the ship's layout—but had no idea if the hypnotist was with them. Joe tried to find him in the men's room, but couldn't get a clear picture, the sink was so filthy. We still did not know if Lolly and Melissa were hostages or partners in crime.

We all agreed the girls weren't getting off, or Vanderman if he was on board. No life boats or rafts remained on the ship, and it was way too far to swim. I thought he planned on riding out the storm on the boat once it was righted, then letting his watery alter ego take him anywhere he wanted to go, after destroying Paumanok Harbor, with enough money in hidden accounts to live like a king for the rest of his misbegotten life.

Working together, Lou and the police prepared a boarding party of psychics for tomorrow, when the ship should reach Paumanok Harbor at its slow, careful speed of tow, mere hours before the first edges of Desi arrived. They'd be espers; they'd be cops or Lou's people; they'd be ready with blindfolds. And stun guns.

Till then, orders went out to keep cameras on the ship from every angle, to check the IDs of everyone in sight, to make sure that no one got off the cruise ship until it anchored, not even a rat.

Especially not a rat.

We went over the plan again, as much as we could without knowing what part the two women played in the drama. I thought Matt would have paddled a canoe out to the ship if he could. He wanted Joe to try again, or Lou to find an esper who could reach Melissa telepathically, or the Air Force to fly planes with heat detectors over the ship to locate Vanderman, then shoot him. Something, anything, rather than nothing. Doc Lassiter finally convinced him the girls would be safest right where they were, out of any crossfire or desperate moves by the mesmerist if he knew he was cornered.

I told him to go back to his office, to call Melissa's mother, his sister. I'd come soon to help with his waiting room, if he wanted. He did, and apologized for being brusque with me. I understood. I was so nervous I swore I'd strangle the next person to call me speedy.

The next person to call was Grant, from freaking outer space! Lou got the transmission to go through Russ' computer, and projected on the screen in Uncle Henry's office. So much for a private call.

He looked good, despite the grainy picture, in a NASA T-shirt and shorts, floating in the capsule. He also looked worried.

"We can see the storm from here, Willow. It's huge and moving fast, headed straight for you."

"I know. We're trying to get ready, but that's not why I had to talk to you."

"You're not pregnant, are you?"

"Grant, people are listening." No, they were snickering. "I am not pregnant. I need you to give me a word, a phrase."

He ran one hand through his hair. "There's no phrase that can stop a hurricane."

"That's not the problem. Well, it's only half the problem. It's what's in the eye, directing it, that needs a linguist."

"Sweetheart, nothing directs a hurricane but the prevailing winds and the water temperatures."

"I need a phrase, damn it." I didn't want to spell it out for him, not knowing who listened at his end, or in between. "I have to hear the words your father gave to Professor Harmon years ago, you know, when he visited Bermuda. The professor cannot recall it exactly and your father is in the hospital having both hips replaced. He says you'd know it because your memory never lets anything slip away."

Either he was too stunned to answer or there was a delay in the transmission. "Shite, Willy, Bermuda, too?"

"Bermuda, too. The recent earthquakes and volcanoes and tsunamis, also. It's back and bigger."

He cursed, in several undecipherable languages. "You know the words don't mean anything without the images, the emotions, the whole gestalt. They're a signpost, nothing more."

"Don't spout Wittgenstein at me, damn it, just give me the freaking phrase."

"Okay. Have you got a recorder?"

I signaled to Russ, who nodded. "Right here."

He said something that sounded like a cat coughing up a hairball, with violins and castanets, on a jetway during takeoff. I made him repeat it. "Okay, got it. Now tell me what it means."

"We cannot be certain, but something like 'return to your roots, where you belong, whence you came.' "

Without mentioning Unity, I told him they wouldn't take it back. They'd sent it to the Earth's core.

I heard the professor behind me: "The phrase could mean back to its inception, perhaps to an egg."

A worm egg in the center of our world, where it could not escape for centuries, at least. "Excellent. That's exactly what we need!"

If we got close enough to lay the curse on the fiend.

"Be careful, Willy. I am sorry I can't be with you."

"Yeah. Me, too."

"But not very sorry?"

"I've got a lot of help this time, the professor, his pet, some of the villagers. And I'm hoping for some of the Others." He'd understand the unspoken capital letter.

"And the veterinarian I hear you touched with power?"

"Matt. Yes, he will be with me. He's strong and a lot braver than I am."

"I'm glad, Willy."

"But not too glad?"

He laughed. "Unless you are ready to reconsider . . ."

"A man who takes a quick jaunt into orbit the way

some people go to Atlantic City on a whim? No, thanks.
But I am happy that you got to experience space travel,
for your sake. You must be in heaven."

"Dashed close to it. Too bad all the excitement is in
Paumanok Harbor."

"I'll trade you."

He laughed again, a sound I once thought I'd never
have enough of. "You don't like flying."

"I am terrified of it. And boats and electric storms and
snakes and having someone steal my mind. They're all
looming."

"You'll do fine, Willy. You always do."

No, I always cried and quivered and ate too much.

We said good-bye.

I went looking for chocolate cake.

CHAPTER 34

GRANDMA EVE HAD CHOCOLATE MOUSSE cake. I left her the professor and took the cake. And the whipped cream. Would I ever see whipped cream again without thinking of Matt? That was better than thinking of tomorrow, or those poor women today.

I saved him a piece. Okay, a small piece. But I felt better after eating the cake and if he cared for me as much as he said he did, he'd want me to have it. So I ate his piece, too.

Five pounds heavier and three "oh, dears" guiltier, I gave Little Red a good-bye cookie, and went to help Matt in his office. I needed to keep my mind off the storm and my ridiculous plan that didn't have a chance in hell of succeeding, but a hellishly good one of getting me and the professor and who knew how many others killed. Like Matt, whose cake I'd eaten, among my other faults, like getting him involved in the first place.

I should have saved some of the cake for my last meal.

The vet clinic had havoc of its own: appointments backed up because Matt was gone for an hour; the vet assistants and kennel staff trying to work the computer instead of holding animals for Matt to work on; the waiting room full of nervous dogs, yowling cats, and panicked, impatient owners. Everyone wanted to get on with their emergency plans before the storm. Even placid Moses seemed distressed at being ignored.

I don't know who was happier to see me, Matt or his

dog. Maybe the rest of his staff because I took over consoling the puppy and managed the front desk. I was damn good at it, too.

Sure Melissa had set up the computer system to be navigable by an orangutan and the directions for credit card transactions were almost as simple. Maybe she could do it better, faster, more efficiently, but I helped reassure the worried people their pets were in good hands. Hypnotized or not, she never cared enough.

Moses leaned against me behind the counter, drooling on my shoes, which was better than Little Red peeing on them, so I cuddled him and talked to him between patients, and we both felt better.

Especially when I found the portable TV on a shelf in the hall so I could stay in touch.

The Weather Channel's hurricane expert reported a sudden change in Desi: a shift farther out into the Atlantic, away from shore. Somehow the Gulf Stream, with its warm waters, had taken a favorable easterly bend. Desi tried to follow.

I sent a silent thank you to the wind and water wizards at DUE.

A hurricane lost some of its strength over cooler water, which was why hurricane season didn't usually last far into the fall. Something about hot air rising. Desi got downgraded to a category four, still wildly dangerous, but not absolutely guaranteed to destroy everything in its path. Cape Hatteras, sticking out from the mainland the way it did, escaped a devastating blow. Now all the attention and red flags got pinned on eastern Long Island, still in the killer storm's trajectory. Desi hadn't lost its size or its forward motion, only a few mph's in the wind speeds. In fact, to the forecaster's admitted surprise, all indications had the storm traveling north at a greater velocity than he'd seen in a lifetime of hurricane watching. Its first bands might reach the Island's South Fork as early as late tomorrow, far ahead of earlier predictions. Which, of course, sent everyone in the waiting room into a frenzy, with fights breaking out and messes on the floor. And the dogs didn't behave well, either.

I handled it.

What I couldn't handle was not knowing if Paumanok Harbor's own meteorologists were watching the radar screens, too. Someone had to tell them to hurry. Heaven knew what the shorter time frame could do to our schedules. They had to work harder, faster, better. The ship had to get to us. The girls had to be rescued. Our equipment had to be loaded. Vanderman had to be neutralized. And those were only a few of the pre-storm plans.

I thought about Vanderman, and Lou, who was still the scariest man I knew. Capable and efficient, yes. Cold-blooded and ruthless? Maybe. Was neutralized a more polite way of saying eliminated? Assassinated? Killed? And what about that chilling mention of divestment? Did they dissect a bad dude's brain and leave him dribbling and diapered?

If Vanderman had a part in bringing N'fwend to the Hamptons, if he used Lolly and Melissa against their will, I'd cheer Lou on. Mind control had to be one of the most dreadful crimes against humanity. But making Lou judge and jury? And executor? Were DUE's actions okay if they used it to protect the rest of us? I'd ask Matt what he thought, later. For now he thought I was an angel and a goddess, and if I ever got tired of writing stories or ran out of ideas, he'd hire me in a minute.

When the waiting room emptied and his staff could take over the phones and the files, I went home, after a detour to Shearwater Street.

The House stayed quiet, there amid its deserted neighbors. I said thank you anyway. And then I asked it for more help. "If you have any influence, tell them we could use some assistance."

"All you need is love."

Sure, tell that to Vanderman and the water dragon.

Oey was waiting for me at my house. She seemed anxious, agitated, hopping from branch to porch railing, into the tub, swimming in circles, blowing bubbles.

"It's coming, isn't it?" I knew better than to mention N'fwend's name, which usually had Oey disappearing.

The bubbles turned blood red.

"We are going to need your friends, the new dolphins."

The parrot head popped out of the pool. "Thmart."

"Yes, they are." But were they smart enough to know we'd need their help, or smart enough to stay far, far away? "Will they come?"

"Thoon."

"Good. They won't be hurt by the riptides and storm surges, will they?"

Oey clacked her beak. I knew by now that meant I was dumb as a dodo. Which were dumb enough to let their whole species get wiped out. "Okay, the dolphins can disappear. We can't. So we might need the big guy."

"Rulth."

M'ma rules his kingdom, or he won't break the rules? He did, for his own safety and for the sake of his symbiotes, or to warn us. All I could think of was that phrase about needing to break some eggs to make an omelet. Oey might get offended by the words "eggs" and "omelet" in the same sentence. "It is his enemy, too."

Oey did not comment.

"Do you know anything about the two women on the ship? Are they alive?"

"Theen. Not thpeak."

"They're dead?" How could I tell poor Matt?

Oey shook her head, sending drops of water down my shirt. "All boobth, no brainth."

"Oh, they couldn't talk to you? Or thought you were too stupid to talk to them? They are ordinary people; it's not their fault. Melissa is supposed to be very smart. Lolly tries."

"Cwies."

"Has he hurt them? Are they frightened? Hungry?"

"Bwought foodth. One thcweamed. One cwied."

"That was kind of you for trying. What did you bring?"

"Eelth."

"Uh, live eels?"

Those strong beaks clacked together again. What other kind was there?

Suddenly all that chocolate cake did not sit so well on my stomach.

Matt came over, with Moses, who greeted me as if I hadn't seen him an hour ago. Little Red did not mind, except he raised his leg on Matt's foot.

Matt was too tired to complain. He looked exhausted, worried, anxious. Matt? The rock whose sanity I depended on?

"What's wrong?" Other than that a hurricane is coming with its killer coxswain, two girls are on a sinking ship, along with the village finances, and no one knew the whereabouts of a malicious mesmerist.

Matt folded me in his arms. "I'm scared."

I held as tight as I could. "You? You're not afraid of anything! You like my grandmother and offered to take Lou fishing. You tell my mother some dogs are not worth saving. How could you be afraid of a hurricane?"

"It's not the storm."

"What, then? Trying to stop the sea serpent? Having all of Paumanok Harbor think you're insane because they can't see it? Going on a ship that's already proved unsteady?"

"No, those are your worries. I'm afraid of losing my niece, having to tell my sister I brought her baby here to Paumanok Harbor only to have her enslaved, corrupted, kidnapped by a madman."

Melissa as a baby was a new concept, but I guess everyone was a cute little cherub, once. I rubbed the back of his neck, feeling the tight muscles there. So Matt was human. I liked him better for it.

"We won't lose her. We know where she is. We'll get her. The plan is already working. Feel how cold the night is?" I felt chilled, but maybe more for his fears than the temperature.

"It's September. The nights always get cool."

"Not this cool. It's our weather wizards, working overtime."

"They can't freeze the harbor in one day."

"Of course not, but they can chill it. So can those

rocket launchers Lou called in." DUE couldn't get planes close enough to seed the storm—Desi was too big, too dangerous—but they could fire ionizers, or whatever it was the science guys did, to turn the hurricane's rain into frozen sleet. Both Desi and N'Fwend's strength had to be sapped in the cold. "Remember, the damned thing used to hang out in Bermuda, then at the molten center of the Earth. It's bound to be weaker in the cold."

"You can't know for sure."

I wasn't used to Matt having doubts. I was the one who waffled, who second-guessed and self-doubted. "You have a better idea?"

"Yeah, let me keep holding you."

Yup, a much better idea. I could forget about tomorrow in his arms, forget about everything except Matt and his needs, my need for him to stay strong and confident. We comforted each other, took strength from each other. Loved each other, with our clothes on, too, to prove this wasn't merely a physical attraction.

"God, how I needed you. I couldn't get out of the clinic fast enough to come to you."

"And I couldn't wait for you to get here. Can you stay the night? The dogs seem fine together, and everyone has your cell number."

We settled on the couch, surrounded by the dogs, just holding each other, breathing each other's scents. We were both so tired we'd fall into exhausted naps only to wake up minutes or hours later, remembering the horrors, and drawing closer again.

"I couldn't get through this without you, Willow," he said, pressing his lips to my forehead.

"Me neither. I couldn't think about facing tomorrow if you weren't at my side."

"I think—no, I know—I want to be there, here, wherever you are, tomorrow and the day after, too. Maybe forever."

"Forever?" I heard the mouse squeak in the cat's paws. That is, in my voice. "It's too soon to talk about forever. The ship only went down less than a week ago."

"It feels like a lifetime ago. A lifetime wasted because you weren't in it."

How could anyone resist a guy like that? I could. I had to. His words felt too sincere, his arms felt too good. But Matt was tired and worried, and it was too soon, with too much else to think about.

Tomorrow comes before forever.

CHAPTER 35

MATT DID NOT STAY THE NIGHT. Maybe he really had to check on the dogs in the kennel despite half his staff staying there ahead of the storm. Maybe he had to reassure his sister. Maybe he just didn't like my answer, which wasn't an answer.

If ever there was a time for one of those soul-scraping, heart-dredging, where-are-we-going relationship conversations, this was not it.

And we both needed a good night's sleep, so I didn't argue or complain or whine.

I didn't get any sleep. My mother's house had never felt so empty, my bed so cold. I turned up the heat, dragged Little Red under the covers with me, put on socks, and still felt the chill. The weather dudes were doing good. I wasn't. I argued with myself, complained to Little Red, and whined.

Matt looked as bad as I did when we met at Rick's marina in the morning, after leaving all the dogs at the vet clinic. Grandma Eve handed us apples and muffins from a sack she'd brought. No eye of newt, anyway. I couldn't eat.

Matt took my hand. Then I got hungry.

Half the town had come to the shipyard to watch a fleet of tugboats nudge the *Nova Pride* close to shore the next morning. The tugs fled for safer waters—maybe up Three Mile Harbor's long creek, or inland near Louse

Point. They had time, although the hurricane's rain and winds were already picking up.

Heavy ferro-cement barges replaced the tugboats. They brought winches and weights and anchors and espers. Our people stood watch from every side of the cruise ship, to make sure Vanderman did not get past. The anchors were going to make sure the liner didn't come crashing into the beach or onto the piers, where Rick was still hauling boats out of the water as fast as he and his crews could. I didn't think those high cradles the yachts and fishing boats sat on looked any safer than the docks, but what did I know?

I knew I was freezing, exposed to the frigid wind and stinging rain, despite all the foul-weather gear I could layer on. The waves were high enough to wash over the lowest wharves, so Matt suggested we move back to the clam bar area, where a lot of the Harborites waited.

We watched the men on the barges work, and watched the water get choppier. And colder.

"That's good, right?" Aunt Jasmine asked me.

Good for us, not so good for the guys working on the barges, or the dolphins I could see leaping around the *Nova Pride*. Big, beautiful creatures, with extra fins and pinkish skins, seemed to be watching the ship as carefully as we were.

"What do you see?" I whispered to Matt.

"No species I ever heard of. Too bad Vicki and Gina couldn't see them."

No one saw them as odd but us. Maybe the professor could have, but the police chief declared the weather too treacherous to chance losing our primary resource before the moment of truth. Close to sunset was the latest projection, almost eight hours away. Dr. Harmon had a warm, dry place in Rick's second-story office over the ships' store. I guess I was dispensable. Lou sent Grandma Eve and Doc Lassiter up the stairs, along with Lolly's aunt and Melissa's parents, who'd arrived in town earlier.

When the crew chief declared the *Nova Pride* secured, the carefully selected boarding parties approached from three directions, in Zodiac inflatable rafts and rescue boats.

Someone on shore had the operation frequency on responder, so we could hear their loudspeakers calling Vanderman, urging him to surrender. "You have nowhere to go. Release the hostages. Get out of the storm."

We did not hear any response. Soon men in wet suits—what about Kevlar vests? Could they float?— swarmed over the sides of the ship on rope ladders, then more ran up the ship's gangway that got let down to one of the barges.

They couldn't find Vanderman or the girls. The jungle lounge was empty except for some dead eels. Static jammed the radio as commands for a search operation went out. We couldn't hear anything but the wind and the waves breaking nearby.

"I'm going."

"NO!" I screamed at Matt. "Those men are trained and armed and have diagrams of the boat."

"I have a niece."

And a responsibility to be at my side at sunset, I wanted to yell, but I couldn't. "If you are going, so am I."

"That's crazy."

"Yeah, get used to it."

He browbeat Elgin, the harbormaster and head of the weather crew, to take us out to the barge. Someone shoved a life jacket over my head and buckled it, then we ran between waves to the end of the wet dock, down a ladder, onto the madly rocking boat, then over to the barge, jumping across—over open water!—then up the gangway to the *Nova Pride*. None of those horrors mattered; I had my eyes closed the whole time. I think I lost the apple and muffin somewhere—I could hear Elgin cursing—but I never let go of Matt's hand.

At the top of the gangway, Matt pulled his hand away—I could see the marks where my fingernails had sunk into his skin—and told me to stay. Moses might have obeyed the command. I went after Matt.

A diver handed me a flashlight. The ship had no power, but the girl in a wet suit and scuba gear said techs were working on it. All available generators ran the pumps and the spotlights on deck for the workers, and for spotting Vanderman.

Uncle Henry held command in what would have been the front desk in a hotel. Maybe the reception area when passengers first boarded the ship. The chief had cut-away schematics of the ship spread out under portable lights, three different phones in front of him, with one Bluetooth in his ear and an unlit cigar clamped in his teeth.

"I swear, Willow Tate, I'm going to arrest you for hampering justice. Unless you find those women."

We passed psychics everywhere, trying to locate the girls by casting mental nets. Joe the plumber stared into a bucket of rainwater. Margaret handed people woven finding bracelets. Other men and women had heat-seeking detectors. Big Eddie had his useless K-9 dog, Ranger, and his own nose, but there were too many bodies, too much water damage and mildew. Did Matt know what perfume Melissa wore?

He had no idea.

"No matter, the whole place still reeks of fear."

That was me.

I stepped into the first empty space I could find, a small office behind the concierge's desk, dragging Matt with me by flashlight. "We don't know where to begin. We need help. You tweet."

He knew I didn't mean on his cell. He chirped, while I sent mental calls to the parrotfish. *Oey, help!* I pictured a willow tree, cold, wind-tossed, alone. Then a lollipop and a skunk, shivering, crying. *Lost, need, fear, hope, brave Oey, beautiful Oey. Find.*

"Twee." *Love, friend. Find, Oey, find. Help.*

Big Eddie came back to our office, to rest Ranger, he said. To clear his sensors, more likely. He cursed about the neoprene wet suits, the spoiled food, the dead eels, my shampoo. Everything stank of stagnant water. "Even the parrot smells like a fish."

"The parrot!"

"Yeah. It must be the one they lost in the big wave.

Somehow the stupid thing found its way back to the boat, instead of heading for land."

"You should be so stupid!" I snapped at poor Big Eddie. Then I apologized and asked where he'd last seen the parrot.

He pointed and Matt shouted, "Follow the bird!"

We raced down dark corridors and stairwells with no windows, no lights, no sounds. I thought I felt the ship rocking. Maybe groaning. "What's that?"

"Don't think about it." Matt had my hand again, and we paused every few yards to listen for Oey.

We called. She answered! "Twee!"

Then we heard Lou swearing as he ran to catch up to us, a miner's light on his head, a weapon in his hand, three of his agents behind him. We waited for him, catching our breaths.

"Damn you, woman, you have no business here. Vanderman's got to be desperate by now, and we aren't a hundred percent convinced the two women are all that innocent. You could be walking into a trap or a shootout, not to mention how precarious this damaged ship is."

I wished he hadn't mentioned the boat's condition. I thought I felt movement under my feet, which didn't help settle my stomach or my nerves. Why had I thought I needed to be on board anyway? Melissa was Matt's relative. Hell, I didn't even like her.

Lou wasn't done ranting. "I'd use the stun gun on you right now if I didn't have to explain it to your grandmother." He looked at Matt. "And I trusted you to look after her."

That helped put some starch back in my spine. "Hey, I don't need a babysitter." Good thing the chief wasn't around to hear the lie. Or maybe the truth. I needed a keeper, not a babysitter. Then I heard Oey call again, and I remembered why I had to be here, why Melissa and Lolly needed me. "Hush up and listen."

"Twee."

"Yes, we're coming." I tried to show her what I was seeing so she'd know we were close. Then I heard the squawk out loud and the surprise in my head: *Twee! He theeth.*

Thit. "Vanderman has more talents," I told the others. No one asked how I knew.

We were so far down into the ship's belly by now that the rows of close-together doors we passed must be crew quarters. They were small, windowless, narrow, and drab, with bunk beds stacked on both long walls. A few personal possessions remained, photos, slippers, magazines, all tumbled about when the ship heeled over. Everything felt damp, although this side of the ship had stayed above water. I did not want to think about leaks.

Lou pointed to the varied marks on every door. They'd all been searched many times looking for survivors, but not yet today, looking for Vanderman and his captives. Like Matt, I wanted to believe Melissa and Lolly were victims, not co-conspirators. Besides, Oey'd sent pictures of them in distress.

Lou's agents and the three local cops in their wake opened every door, weapons drawn. They weren't taking chances, no matter what I believed. I heard them giving our location back to the chief as we moved.

Listening to Oey's calls, not Lou's curses as they searched room after room, Matt and I went ahead to a different corridor. The doors here had fewer marks on them, as if the inspectors and searchers hadn't noticed this section—or had been hypnotized to ignore it.

One cabin was locked. I knew Keys was with Lou's group, so I called for him to come open the door. They all came, plus some others who'd heard us, or heard the bird.

At first the compartment appeared smaller then the others, shallower, with a single narrow bed and an Indian blanket as a wall covering. Then Matt pushed past Keys and shoved aside the blanket to reveal the rest of the cabin, and broken walls leading to the partitioned rooms on either side. One room held sacks on top of sacks, all filled with money and jewels and electronics. The other room contained two women, bound together and tethered to a table bolted to the floor. It also contained Vanderman, with a gun aimed at Melissa.

Matt roared and would have charged, but Vanderman moved the gun barrel to aim at him, then at me.

Me? I lost my footing when Lou came up behind me, shoving others aside to get in. I stumbled, skidding closer to Vanderman than I ever wanted to be. I didn't have Big Eddie's nose, but I could tell Axcl had been drinking, and not bathing.

He grabbed my arm, then pressed the gun into my scalp. Shit, Dad warned me not to try to rescue the lollipop and the skunk. Now I needed rescuing. Matt watched, helplessly.

"Put down your weapons," Vanderman ordered, staring into Matt's eyes, then Lou's and the cops', with his swirling, whirling bottomless gaze. No one obeyed. No one was susceptible. "Fuck."

"You're cornered, man. Drop the gun."

Vanderman laughed, without humor. "You won't shoot. Not to chance putting a hole in the hull, or into her."

"Me?"

"You're the one with the power. The one I need. These"—he waved the gun toward Melissa and Lolly; I could sense Matt's fury—"served their purpose. Now it's a witch I need." The gun came back against my temple, which didn't hurt half as badly as being called a witch. "So you tell the others to leave and I'll let your girl-friends go. Maybe the boyfriend, too, though I hear he's got some of your talent."

I couldn't see a happy ending here. All I could do was try to stall the inevitable. "How can you make threats when you are surrounded, on a ship in the water?"

"Because I have friends, too. Coming soon." He looked toward the door at the agents and the cops. They'd all stopped, paralyzed into inaction not by ensorcellment, but by danger to civilians. "I'll say it for the last time. Put your weapons down or I shoot. I shoot the Tate woman, and without her you'll all be left at my mercy."

They believed him. "It's true," the chief huffed from

the back of the crowd. "Even if we kill Vanderman, we still have to face whatever waits in the eye of the hurricane, without Willy." Two cops nodded. "It's true. We need her. But so does Vanderman. Alive."

Vanderman lost his composure, or his sanity. "I need her! I need her power."

"It won't work, Axel," I tried to reason with him. "You can't hypnotize me."

"But I can kill you and the vet and win it that way!"

Lou snarled out, "You'll be dead before she hits the ground, you asshole!"

Vanderman looked confused. He tried to see beyond Matt to find out how many threatened him, but Oey got in the way. "My petth!" The huge parrot flew straight for Vanderman, smacking his head with that powerful fish tail.

A gun went off. Vanderman's? I thought so. Had he hit me? I was too numb to be sure, but I didn't think so. Oey? No. The parrot had blinked out of sight, which confounded Vanderman enough that he took his eyes off me and Matt for an instant, long enough for Matt to tackle him and wrest the gun away. Lou and his agents rushed in, weapons waiting for a safe shot.

"Don't shoot him! You might hit Matt! We need him." And I needed Matt. "And don't wipe Vanderman's talent away, either."

Lou hit Vanderman with the stun gun before I finished telling him what not to do.

That worked. So did the plastic ties they bound him with, the gag in his mouth and the blindfold over his eyes, just in case.

Matt ran for Melissa. The chief gathered up Lolly as soon as the ropes around their wrists and ankles were cut. Both women were filthy, wet, cold, sobbing. But they were alive. Melissa was so distraught she thanked me.

And Matt— Well, he shoved her into Big Eddie's arms and came for me. Big Eddie pushed her in Russ' direction. "You're the computer geek, you take her."

Matt came to me, to hold me, to kiss me, to check every inch of me for wounds. Me, instead of Melissa.

I could breathe again.

"Do not ever, ever do that again," he said between kisses.

I was busy making certain Vanderman hadn't hurt him, either. "I'll try not to."

I'd try with every ounce of my being to keep Matt from danger. What kind of life could I have if he wasn't in it?

CHAPTER 36

"SO TELL ME WHY WE NEED VANDERMAN?"
the chief asked.

We were all in the enclosed forward observation
lounge of the cruise ship, we being most of the psychic
half of Paumanok Harbor, Lou and his DUE crew, and
Vanderman, tied to a chair. We couldn't observe much,
with the dark gray rain coming in sheets against the
super-strength glass window. Someone had rigged lights.
The amount of bodies in the room raised the temperature, and all the restaurants and delis in the village had
provided sandwiches and coffee.

I still wasn't comfortable. They all looked at me. The
senior council, that was. The others huddled together in
groups, listening to radios, glued to their iPads and tiny
TV screens. Matt wasn't back yet from checking on Melissa and the veterinary hospital, out in flooded roads,
washed-away shoulders, downed trees and wires. How
could I be comfortable?

At least I knew Melissa and Lolly were safe and out of
danger—from their imprisonment and from prosecution.
They were in good condition, physically. Vanderman had
scavenged supplies from the ship: blankets, flashlights,
and candles. Mentally, they were wrecks.

Once they'd been checked by the EMTs and calmed
by Doc Lassiter's touch and Grandma Eve's tea, they'd
been interviewed by Chief Haversmith, several other

truth-seers, the village attorney, and Judge Chemlecki, who'd just arrived.

Neither woman had known what they were doing. Everyone agreed they spoke the truth about that.

Lolly knew she worked extra hours at Vanderman's house, but the place never got clean. He gave her extra money to run errands for him, but she could never remember where she'd gone or what she'd done. No fresh dry cleaning, no new groceries appeared. When she asked Vanderman, he told her to take the money and mind her own business, so she did because she needed the job.

Melissa thought he loved her. Sure he was old enough to be her father, but he was smart, almost as good at a computer as she was. They had games to see who could break what codes sooner, just for fun, he said. And she helped him move some money through cyberspace, but all his own money, he swore. He told her some catastrophic financial upheaval was coming and he wanted funds out of the country, totally legal, he insisted. He'd take her with him when he left, he promised. So she found ways.

She couldn't remember exactly what they did together for all the hours missing from her nights. She had no record of dinners out, movies they'd seen, concerts they'd attended, other couples they'd met. Yet her gas tank was always empty. Most troubling of all, she could not remember having sex with her exciting, older, sophisticated, wealthy lover.

Eventually, she confronted him with her complaints and concerns. But Lolly was there, cleaning, and he would not talk. He just looked at her with those eyes that kept her fascinated, that said how much he adored her, that she was the only woman in his life. She and Lolly. Infuriated, she looked at the other, older, frumpy, stupid woman and saw what she'd missed, that they were being used and manipulated and God knew what else. "Look away!" she screamed at Lolly, too late.

Vanderman had them bound and immobilized, no

matter how hard they tried to keep their eyes closed,
their minds free of his tainted touch. He didn't care, Melissa told the listeners. He said he'd be leaving, but they
were too dangerous to his plans to let free, no matter
how they promised to keep quiet. No matter if he left
suggestions in their minds, someone could unlock those
spells. Melissa, especially, knew his intentions. She just
didn't know that she knew.

They had no memory of getting aboard the cruise
ship, only periods when he was gone, when they realized
he was going to leave them to die in that tiger-striped
lounge, or the tiny cabin. They pretended to be sleeping
or in shock when he came back, hoping for a rescue.

Melissa promised to help Russ recover the missing
money, even if she had to be hypnotized to remember
Vanderman's account numbers and passwords. She never
meant to break the laws.

"That's the truth," the chief said, happily chewing his
pastrami sandwich. Rick Stamfield nodded. So did Kelvin from the garage. No one itched, twitched, or belched.
It was true.

There'd be no charges, just a lot of community computer service for Melissa and counseling for Lolly. And
they'd get Melissa out of town, back to college, with only
a small portion of her memory permanently wiped out,
thanks to Mayor Applebaum's talent.

That left Vanderman, and what to do with him.

They couldn't hand him over to the FBI or the state
cops. He'd be in the wind before they could blink. The
same with putting him in a cell somewhere with ordinary
guards, ordinary criminals.

One of Lou's men was all for killing him right then,
tossing him overboard and claiming the storm took him.
Someone else thought they ought to blind him so he
couldn't use his warped talent again. Lou fingered the
small device he carried in his inside pocket. But even
without his power to mesmerize, Vanderman still threatened Paumanok Harbor and its paranormals. He knew
too much. And he'd caused too much damage.

"But we cannot become what he is!" I shouted. "We

cannot use our powers for our own ends, even if our motives are purer. What about his rights? What about the law? You haven't even read him the Miranda card or offered him a lawyer. That makes us criminals, too!"

"We haven't arrested him yet," the judge declared, "so there's no need to extend him his civil liberties. And this might be a case of terrorism, where other standards apply."

I'd heard that before, and liked it less every time. Everyone knew he was guilty. Everyone knew he was evil. Only I thought we had a use for him, intact and willing.

I explained as best I could. How I thought the sea serpent had come to Paumanok Harbor to avenge its imprisonment and banishment. Now I believed it had come here because of Vanderman, its kindred spirit. He'd known the thing was coming, and he went on his crime spree to prepare for his future after Paumanok Harbor got destroyed. He came here, to the boat, so N'fwend could find him, could carry him away to start taking over the rest of world.

Without him, we had no hope of slaying the beast, or sending it back to its prison in the center of Earth. No evil eye beads, no magic words from Grant and DUE, no pictures I'd drawn showing the dragon reduced to a tiny egg, could get rid of the monster. Not without holding its soul mate hostage long enough to get its attention.

"So we dangle Vanderman out in the storm to let the wave serpent see him." Lou never took his eyes off the prisoner. "Who's to say the monster doesn't steal Vanderman's power and overtake our efforts? Or we subdue the kraken, but it transfers its powers into him, like when he was conceived."

I didn't have all the answers. I just knew we needed Vanderman if we were going to succeed. If not, we'd all be swept under the sea serpent's tsunami of hate and greed and genocide. "We'll have help," I told Lou and the others. The dolphins circled the ship. Oey called from somewhere nearby. As the dark day grew blacker still, I thought I saw flashes of light, like fireflies in the lightning. "We are not in this alone."

Someone cautiously mentioned that the last time the rogue wave appeared the professor and his fancy curse could not subdue it.

I held the old man's trembling hand. "That is true, but remember he vanquished it decades ago. This time he does not have to recall the exact words. We have them on tape. And Dr. Harmon will not be facing the demon on his own." I felt his hand squeeze mine. It almost killed me to say it, but I did. "I'll be there."

"And I." Matt came in then and stood behind my chair.

"No, you cannot confront N'fwend. You are not . . . not one of us."

I never saw him so angry, so hurt at the same time. I looked at my hand in the professor's while he cursed. "Bullshit. You made me one of you."

"But we don't know what effect the serpent will have on you. You could fall under its spell."

"More bullshit. I faced Vanderman, didn't I? I looked straight into the bastard's eyes to gauge his moves, and didn't get sucked into his vortex. And you need me. How many others here can see the serpent in the water? You don't know. But how many can see the parrot?"

Hands raised, and a few voices muttered they'd seen the big bird.

"Yeah, but how many of you saw its fish tail? How many of you counted the extra fins on the big dolphins or realized the creatures are pink? Who saw your dead whale fly away in flames last month?"

"The bird has a fish tail?"

"Pink?"

"Flames?"

"That's right. It's you and me and the professor, Willow Tate. That's your A Team. Everyone else is the backup squad, the home team advantage, the cheerleaders and the loyal fans. So what kind of crap are you pulling?"

The professor squeezed my hand again. "She's trying to protect you, lad, that's all."

Matt looked at the chief, then at Rick and Kelvin. They all nodded. So did I. It was true. I'd have nightmares forever seeing Vanderman's gun pointed at Matt. Put him in the path of a killer wave? Not if I could help it. "I can't bear the idea of you in so much danger. And . . . and the animals need you."

"But I need *you,* Willy. If you face the monster, I go with you. Danger, disaster, disease, whatever. We're a pair. Got that?"

His cheering squad clapped. I thought I heard Grandma Eve say, "And about time, too."

Uncle Henry wanted to know if that was a proposal they all heard. "Sure sounded like 'till death do us part' to me."

Matt dragged me away from the others and kissed me, long and hard and full of promise. "When I propose, it'll be in private, and I'll have a ring, and go down on one knee if you want. I'll promise your father I am solvent, and promise your mother to give her grandchildren or die trying. And I'll slay as many dragons as you need, by your side."

He brushed a tear from my cheek. "After we take care of this one."

How romantic was that? I gulped and said okay. How lame was that?

Matt smiled and led me back to the council, whose members pretended the whole scene never happened.

"So let's hear the plan again," the chief demanded.

That was easy. We stand on the deck of a sinking ship in the middle of a hurricane and tell some dire monster to go away, in a language we don't understand. We all try to project my cartoon of the loathsome beast shrinking to the size of a pea, wave our beads, and don't look in its eyes. Oh, yeah, with an eighty-year-old gentleman scholar leading the chant and a mastermind mesmerist as hostage.

"Works for me."

"And me."

And everyone in the big room, except Vanderman. Lou's agents pulled him forward and took the gag out of his mouth. He spit on the floor. "Why the hell should I help you?"

Everyone looked to me. I looked at Matt. Together we faced the skeezy scumbag. "Because that man over there, the one who looks like a hit man for Al Capone? That's what he is. What he does. He cleans up scum like you to make the world a safer place for psychics like us, who make the world a better place for everyone else. And the council here? They don't believe the constitution applies to them. You used your talent for really, really selfish reasons. So you're going to lose that power, one way or another. If you help us, you might save your life."

Matt took over. "If you don't cooperate, we can just tie you out on the prow of the ship, like a goat to bait a man-eating tiger. Your friend capsizes the ship, you go down first. If you're already dead, maybe we can add your power to ours to subdue the kraken. It won't matter to us."

"It will come for you." I was certain of that; my father's omen of a danger named Stu held proof enough for me. "It'll come for your power. For your conjoined, twisted minds. Your job is to keep it still and close so we can lay the geas on it."

Professor Harmon adjusted his glasses. "I do not know that we truly need the dastard's cooperation. It might be enough for the great wyrm to sense him near and hesitate in its path of destruction. I calculate we require five minutes to cast our own counter magic. And if that doesn't work, we can always throw the bloody sodding blighter to the sharks. Or to our friend Lou."

CHAPTER 37

FIRST WE HAD TO WAIT OUT THE HURRI-cane.

Holy shit, I was on a damaged boat in a freaking hurricane!

Before I could work up a full-scale panic attack—or beg to be taken back to shore—more people came into the lounge area. They all wanted to shake the professor's hand, and mine, and Matt's, to wish us luck, to tell us how confident they were we'd succeed, to promise their wholehearted and superpower-minded support.

All through the battering storm people stepped forward. They wore yellow slickers, orange life vests, and determined looks. They were here to save their homes, their friends, their unique talents. And they all counted on me to lead them.

On us. The professor held my hand. I knew we were both terrified, but we never let the people, our friends, see our fear. Matt didn't leave my side, which helped a lot.

I showed them the screen Russ had rigged to project my drawing, of the sea monster dwindling to almost nothing, to a tiny egg. I handed out crayon-colored origami evil eye beads from the school kids when we ran out of glass ones. I ate some dry crackers, which was all anyone let me have, knowing my weakness in waves and water.

Someone put on music to drown out the sound of the

storm and the ship's moans. I felt vibrations under my feet, and a few times had to grab onto Matt to keep my balance, but the ship held. The anchors held. Or the dolphins held the whole thing together. And then, hours later, it was over.

The wind died to a breeze, the rain stopped, and off to the west we could see a tinge of red where the sun sank into the horizon. Red sky at night, sailor's delight. Whoopee.

"It's time."

This was the center of the storm, the moment of truth, maybe the end of the world.

A handful of us led the way out onto the open deck of the ship. As we walked, people behind us cheered.

"We're with you, Matt."

"You can do it, Professor."

"Good job so far, Willy. Now get rid of the thing."

Grandma Eve kissed my cheek and told me to be careful. "I love you." I imagined I heard my mother's voice echoing hers, and my father's, and Susan's, and hundreds more. I stood tall and took my white-knuckled place at the railing, between Matt and Dr. Harmon.

We watched the water race from the shore, like someone pulling a blanket off a bed. The ship settled lower, with a grinding noise as the hull touched bottom, but it stayed upright. Lower and lower the tide roared out, leaving every boat still in the harbor sitting in sand or mud, exposing fish and rocks and ribs of sunken wrecks.

The bay's water had to be going somewhere. We all knew it. We all held our breaths. And then, off in the distance, N'fwend rose.

I heard the gasps behind me, felt the fear as people saw a wave like no other wave in their experience. It rose and rose from the sucked-out sea, into a skyscraper, into a mountain, into a tornado that reached from the bottom of the bay to the first night stars. It roared, it screamed, it bore down on us.

People started crying. They saw the wave, the surge, the tsunami. The professor and I saw the dripping fangs, the maelstrom eyes, the pulsing venom, the thunderous hatred. We both shook in reaction. Vanderman saw it all, too, once Lou pulled the blindfold off.

"You cannot stop it."

"We have to."

Vanderman would have leaped over the side of the ship if he weren't handcuffed between Lou and one of his men.

Matt saw the monster, too. He saw it, knew it, felt the terror of it, and stood firm. "Come on, you bastard, we're ready for you. Show us what you've got."

My rock, my oak tree, my lover—taunting a dragon? "What, are you insane?"

"Get used to it." Then he kissed me for luck.

All you need is love.

"NOW!" I shouted. And I started picturing the monster's demise in my head, while I heard Grant's voice streaming undecipherable sounds over and over again through the loudspeakers. I sensed people behind me telegraphing hate and anger and fury and begones, and my sketch of a shrinking wave.

Still it came on.

"More! Louder! Think harder! Hold hands to connect our powers!"

The loathing behind me was so strong I might have fallen but for Matt's hands around my waist. Grant's voice thundered. My sketch floated in the ether. "Be gone, be gone."

The monster kept coming, not one drop of water smaller. Its swirling eyes seemed fixed on Vanderman, so Lou and his agent pushed the bastard forward. They had to hold him up, because his knees wouldn't. "Look at it," Lou ordered, "hypnotize it and tell it to go away."

"It—it doesn't listen. Its power is far stronger than mine."

But it did still for a moment. Enough time for the professor to stand on a rung of the railing, then lift his hands out like Moses parting the Red Sea. Matt and I rushed to his sides, to hold him steady while he matched Grant's words exactly, and with my mental images and the villagers' emotions to go with the ages-old curse.

"Get thee hence, foul wyrm. Go back to thy beginnings and thy prison. I thus command thee."

And N'fwend howled so loudly glass broke behind us.
Then the wave started to diminish, from hundred-mile-
an-hour tornado winds to a tropical storm, to a rain
spout, a sea puss, a spray that might have been a whale
spouting. Then it was gone and the seawater rushed
back, so the *Nova Pride* floated again. We could see the
dolphins righting tipped boats in the harbor, see them
leaping and playing and whistling with joy.

There was jubilation on board, too, except for Vanderman. Lou and his agent were struggling, trying to
hold onto something as slippery as mercury, as thin as
smoke. It oozed out of their handcuffs, growing smaller
and thinner, until it splatted on the deck between their
feet. Lou drew out his device—which turned out to be
a flashlight he focused on the circle of slime that remained.

"The bastard's getting away."

The professor bent down to look. "No, he's gone back
to his beginnings, a zygote. A fertilized egg."

We all looked on in horror, wondering what to do
with him. It.

"Who'd want to give birth to that?" I heard. "Could it
survive in a test tube?"

I could see Lou ready to raise his foot, to stomp on it.
Oey got there first. Those strong beaks opened up, a pink
tongue came out and scooped up the remains of Axel
Vanderman. Then a rainbow-hued fish dove off the
cruise ship.

All you need is love.

And a friend in high places. I held up my hands the
way the professor had, feeling overdramatic and foolish,
but I called on the sea god M'ma to seal the monster's
tomb in the center of the Earth for all time. And to seal
the gates, to follow the rules, to take his friends home
where they belonged.

The professor cleared his throat and flapped his arms
like wings.

"Oh, except we'd like Oey to stay if you do not need

her, him. We're very fond of the bird, you know. And it loves us. Oey thinks we're all petth."

We heard a sizzle, smelled a burst of ozone, felt another tremor in the boat, then heard laughter rumbling across the sky instead of thunder. The lights of a million tiny flying suns shone instead of lightning, and the night, the water, the wind went still. We all stood outside, waiting for the back end of the storm.

It never came. The newscasters on radios and TV and the Internet reported the storm dropping off the Doppler radar like a plane that crashed.

Back inside the ship's lounge there were cheers and tears of relief, excitement like New Year's Eve, with everyone kissing and hugging and crying. They broke out the ship's champagne and it turned into a World Series locker room celebration, with more champagne on everyone than in them. No one cared, especially not me and Matt, who found that back office and locked the door.

We had our own private celebration, telling each other how brilliant we were, how brave, how absolutely bonkers. And how we won! What a great team we made. What great love we made.

Most of the villagers had left when we returned to the lounge, leaving only the senior council to debate what to tell the world.

"Tell them we survived. That's all they need to know."

My mother called the next day. After congratulations and pauses to wait for an engagement announcement that I did not make, she mentioned she'd been offered a contract to host a TV talk show on animal behavior, to be filmed in NYC. She needed the apartment back.

"It'll be great fun. We'll share the cooking and cleaning, and you can write while I'm at the station. We can travel out to the Harbor on weekends, just like we used to. We'll talk about it when I get home for All Hallow's Eve."

Fun? Living with my mother? I'd move in with Matt first. Not that he'd invited me. Yet. He would.

"Um, I might be staying out here, working on my next book."

"Something new?"

"Yes. I'm going to collaborate with Professor Harmon on a picture book, but I'm also thinking of writing for the adult market this time, no drawings. It might be one of those generational things about mothers and their daughters."

I'd call it *Sand Witches in the Hamptons*.